Also by D. E. White

Remember Me

The Forgotten Child

D. E. WHITE

ONE PLACE. MANY STORIES

HQ
An imprint of HarperCollins*Publishers* Ltd
1 London Bridge Street
London SE1 9GF

This paperback edition 2019

First published in Great Britain by
HQ, an imprint of HarperCollins*Publishers* Ltd 2019

Printed and bound by CPI Group (UK),
Ltd, Croydon, CR0 4YY

For my single mum friends – you are awesome!

Chapter 1

'Milo, can you turn your game down, just for a bit please?'

'Can't hear you, Mum. What?'

Holly took a deep breath, swallowing the tears, trying not to glance at the text message on her phone. She, of all people, should have known better, but the words seemed to burn into her brain, '*Milo*, please turn it down.' Better, that sounded calmer, she thought, and he was still so engrossed he would hopefully miss the fact she was upset. His life had been torn apart enough recently.

In the mirror she could see his little face, his mop of blonde hair, freckles dusting his nose, and the smear of mud across his forehead. The electronic bleeping toned down a notch and she took another long, shaky breath. He glanced up quickly, and grinned at her reflection, before returning to his dragons.

The traffic was horrendous, and at five o'clock on a filthy wet February night, the darkness had already closed in. In an effort to distract herself Holly moved her phone further into her bag, so she couldn't see the screen, and turned the radio on. Beyoncé filled the car with 'If I were a Boy', and she almost smiled, trying to relax the coils of tension that seemed to be wound like snakes around her torso, squeezing her stomach painfully. It was

1

a favourite song, and Holly determinedly sang along under her breath. She had this under control.

The car in front braked again, and the long line of red lights strung out into the night like a strand of Christmas decorations. The pain of last Christmas would stay with her forever. Even now she could still hear her own voice, telling him exactly what she thought of men who played away . . . For months she had ignored that nagging feeling that something wasn't quite right, the fact that he kept jumping on his phone, shouting at her for silly little things around the house.

Finally she had actually answered his mobile when Beth called. He had been in the shower, thinking she was downstairs getting Milo's tea, and had left his phone on the pillow. The other girl had put the phone down as soon as Holly identified herself, but she took the opportunity to scroll through his pictures. It was enough.

Tom had been outraged when she chucked him out of the house, telling her she was crazy and deluded, even suggesting she needed help. Fucking bastard. She would need to fight Tom to have Milo stay with her. So be it, he was the shit who had been unfaithful, although his family later implied if Holly had been a better wife, he wouldn't have needed to sleep with someone else. Fuck them all.

The next turning was normally a longer way home, and the roads were narrow, winding through steep woodland towards the coastal town, but anything was better than this motorway hell. She indicated, and neatly extracted herself from the queues. Holly was a good driver, a safe driver, but tonight she was exhausted. Work had been tough recently. It always was, but in the winter months, getting out of bed at 4 a.m. for an early shift, or returning home at 7 a.m. after a night shift, took dedication. It also took epic childcare organisation when you were a single mum.

Leaving the other cars behind she swung left at the roundabout, avoiding a daredevil motorcyclist, who was taking the bend at high speed, and turned down Mill Road. A couple of other cars and a van were on the roundabout, and maybe a couple more queued behind her. The usual evening traffic. Mill Road would take her all the way to Panfield, and from there to Westbourne and home.

Holly's shoulders sagged a little as she relaxed, watching her headlights slash a path through the darkness. It was going to be all right. She glanced in the mirror again, but this time took in her pale, exhausted reflection. Her green eyes were edged with shadows and her long black hair hung heavy around her face.

'Mum, I'm hungry!'

'Look in the blue bag. There was a bar, and some crisps, if you haven't eaten them already . . . We're nearly home.'

'I ate them,' Milo informed her. 'I shared them with Becky. Can we stop at McDonald's?'

'No. We aren't going that way. Look, sweetie, can you just cope until we get home? There's a stew I put in before we left. It's your favourite,' she said encouragingly. There was another car taking the bend behind her, its headlights in her mirror making her blink. She didn't really like driving in the dark anymore. Maybe she was getting old.

'Did you put my hoodie in the boot?'

'Yes. It was all muddy. Why?'

'I left some sweets in the pocket. Coach said we were so good he gave us all some Haribo, and I forgot to eat mine. Can I climb over and get them out?'

'No. Sorry, darling, but can you just last out?'

'No. I'm starving. I scored four tries today.'

'I know, and I'm super proud of you . . .' The car behind was far too close, right on her tail. She accelerated a bit, but the road glistened wet and dangerous, and she knew there were a few hairpin bends coming up. Her jumper clung to her back, her T-shirt wet with sweat now, the sour, icy sweat of fear. She muttered, cursing the driver.

'What arsehole needs to get back, Mum?'

'Sorry, bad word. The person behind us is a bit close, that's all.'

3

'I'm still hungry.'

Hidden in her bag, Holly's phone beeped with another text. Her hands were shaking again, clenched on the wheel, panic rising in her chest. Why couldn't he just fucking leave her alone? He had what he wanted . . . But he didn't have everything he wanted.

The other car was so close now, its lights were almost blinding her. She moved her rear-view mirror to one side, taking the reflection away from her eyes. Was the driver flashing his lights?

No other traffic, the rain was hammering down now, and the shadowy forms of tree trunks like cage bars on the high banks either side of the road. It wasn't like she was going exceptionally slowly . . . Forcing herself to stay calm, she navigated the two sharp bends, before she noticed movement in the back. Milo's legs were waving in the air as he nosedived into the boot, clearly in search of food.

'Milo! Get back to the seat and strap yourself in,' she yelled.

'I'm just getting . . .'

'No! *Sit down.*'

She risked another glance. He was climbing back now, bag of sweets firmly clasped in one hand. She should pull over . . . But the other driver was still so close. She even thought he was flashing his lights again – once, twice. Did he want her to pull over? Was there something wrong with the car, or was this just a ploy to get her to stop? On this lonely road in the darkness, there was no fucking way she was stopping unless she had to. Maybe she should call the police. A wave of fear ripped through her body, made her gasp, but again she forced herself to calm down. She was just tired, stressed out. It was only some fuckwit who wanted to get home quicker. There was no way of overtaking in this tiny lane. He could just wait. It was bound to be a man . . .

Milo landed back in his seat with a thump. 'My seatbelt's all twisted.'

'Well, untwist it.' She shot out from the tree cover and accel-erated along a straighter bit of road. There was a long drop on one side now, which eased the claustrophobic feeling, but the car behind stayed on her tail. The lights seemed to flash again, making her blink. They were going around corners at speed, and the headlights of both vehicles were slashing through the shadows, bouncing off the blackness. She slowed a fraction to take in another hairpin bend. At any moment he was going to touch her bumper. But she didn't have her hands-free kit with her, and she wasn't going to stop and get carjacked or worse.

Carefully now, considering the options, she reached over and eased her phone out of her bag, placing it between her knees. What if this was more than some idiot trying to race home? What if the driver behind succumbed to some kind of road rage and actually tried to bump her car?

Holly risked another quick glance at Milo and slowed. To her relief, the other car drew back a little, but she kept the phone where it was. As she wondered if she was actually freaked enough to call the police, it beeped again and the screen flashed up another message:

You aren't fit to be a mother, bitch.

The abusive tone was exactly the same. Why would he send her something like that? Holly shivered, swinging round the next corner, wincing as the driver behind kept pace, his headlights almost blinding her. Her windscreen wipers whined as she turned them up to max, trying to clear the torrent of rain. Desperate now, her shaking fingers were fumbling with her phone, trying to press the buttons.

Lights blinded her in an eerie white flash as another vehicle approached at high speed, from the opposite direction. She thought it was a van, and the driver was making no effort to pull over to his side of the road, but continued to aim straight at Holly. She hit her horn, hard, driving as close to the side of the road as she dared. The wheels crunched on grit and she felt the pull of mud on the tyres, as they swung off course. She yanked the wheel, her phone tumbling into the footwell as she straightened the car. Missing her by a hairsbreadth the other vehicle stormed past, away and up the hill, red brake lights flashing before it vanished. Holly slowed again, shaking.

The car behind hit her with a bang. The force of impact jolted her violently forward, before flinging her back against the headrest.

'Milo? Are you okay?' They were still moving, slowly but she didn't dare stop. Her neck was twanging with pain.

'Mum, what's happened? Did we crash? *Mum*!' His voice was sharp with fear.

Holly's heart was racing, her breath coming in short, sharp gasps, and her head was pounding. What the fuck was going on tonight? She glanced back at her son, opened her mouth to say everything was fine, and at the same time tried to kick her mobile away from the accelerator pedal where it had fallen.

Milo screamed out a warning, high-pitched and terrified, 'Mum, *stop*! There's a deer!'

A dark shadow plunged across the road, its eyes briefly illuminated by her headlights, before Holly hit the brakes as hard as she could. The car swung from side to side, before it aquaplaned across the road, and for the second time, she felt the impact of the car behind. She was yelling for Milo, hands locked on the wheel, still fighting with the vehicle, as they slid off the road, and the car began to tumble down the long slope to the woods below.

It was a kaleidoscope of pain and blurred shadows. She screamed at Milo to get down, and ducked her own head, closing her eyes. There was a sharp pain, and then a bang in front of her, and after that nothing but darkness.

***

Holly opened her eyes. The steady drum of rain on the windscreen, the stench of wet earth and trees, the stillness and the cold, took a moment to sink in. She had no idea how long she had been unconscious. Her face was sticky and wet. She licked her lips, blinking. Blood. She could taste blood, sour and metallic. The rain was pouring through the shattered windscreen. Oh dear God, she had crashed the car. She had been trying to get her phone . . . Guilt mingled sourly with the pain, and Holly retched. The blackness spun, sending her back into her nightmare. Milo, where was Milo?

The nausea woke her properly, and she wriggled, aware of sharp stabbing pains in her neck, her back, and her chest, but ignoring them. '*Milo!*'

There was no sound from the back of the car, and she couldn't turn any further. Panic flooded her body, hot and vicious. It gave her the strength to wrench herself free from the space between her seat and the detonated airbag. She was half kneeling now, one leg on the passenger seat, pushing away a mess of sports bags and camping gear that had been thrown from the boot. Tears and rain were washing the blood from her face, and she was shaking with the shock and cold.

The car was battered, but at least the right way up. At some point she remembered it rolling over, surely . . . But apart from the bonnet and windscreen, it seemed fairly intact. Some freak of engineering meant the headlights were still on, their twin beams sending dancing white paths of light into the woods. But the darkness and the shadows gathered all around the light, overwhelming it, jostling and claustrophobic.

Both windows on the right-hand side, Milo's side, were smashed. His seatbelt was hanging free. She could see his hand, still and pale, stretched out across the seat, but she still couldn't get far enough to see more. Her hands were shaking, but she continued to rip away the debris. As she struggled, one foot caught the driver's door, hard, and it opened with a bang. Abandoning any thought of wriggling through the narrow space between the seats, she squeezed frantically past the airbag, out into the woods.

The rear door was stuck fast and she hauled at it with all her strength. It wouldn't budge. Holly screamed, and the rain-savaged woods echoed with her son's name. She kicked viciously and uselessly at the metal like an animal caught in a trap. The smell of rotten wetness, tainted with fuel fumes brought her back. She needed to keep it together. Christ knew where her phone was. The pain in her leg and chest was excruciating, but she carried on yanking the door. Inch by inch, resisting her sweaty, bloody fingers, it finally opened, slowly and with a protesting whine of metal. There were the stabbing pains in her neck and back again, but she ignored them, panting through the pain.

'*Milo!*' She was in the car now, scrabbling for his hand. 'Milo, are you okay? Can you hear me?' Of course he couldn't or he would have answered, but the sound of her own voice was a small comfort in this nightmare.

Holly wriggled further across the back seats, clinging to the headrests, fumbling in the shadows. There was a torch in the towrope bag in the boot but who knew where that had ended up. Milo was half sitting, half lying on his side. There was a cut on his head, and a small stream of blood was snail-trailing down his cheek onto the seat. His small chest was rising and falling in a reassuring manner, but his skin was cold under her frantic fingertips. Where was her bloody phone?

But as Holly shoved her way further in, moving another bag out the way, she saw Milo was no longer alone in the back. Another boy, also apparently unconscious, but with no visible injuries, was sitting in the other seat. His head was lolled sideways, his face a pale blur against the shattered window.

'*What the fuck?*' Holly realised she had spoken aloud again, her words thrown into the sullen, spattering rain, echoing up to the silent trees. A ghost, it had to be a ghost, this child who had materialised inside her car. Either that or she was actually unconscious and dreaming the whole thing.

She reached a shaking hand across the car and touched the other boy. As her fingers met his cheek she had to force herself

8

not to recoil. His skin was cold and clammy, and she thought she could see a head wound, but, as with her own child, she could see the steady rise and fall of his chest. Holly let out a long breath and inched back towards Milo, squeezing his limp hand, reassuring herself. A high-pitched whimpering made her jump, until she realised it was herself making animal sounds of fear. Where the fuck had he come from?

Squinting towards the road, she could just about make out the path of destruction the car had made as it left the road and hurtled into its final resting place against this cluster of giant trunks. There was no sign of the other vehicle that had rear-ended them, and no clue as to how her other passenger had arrived in her vehicle.

Realising she was wasting time staring blankly at the two children, Holly yanked herself back to reality and started yelling for help. Her cries echoed through the trees, seemingly futile in the vastness of the wood. Perhaps she should try to climb back up to the road, flag down the next car. But she seriously doubted she could make it, with the injuries that shot pain along her limbs and stabbed inside her head. Anyway, she couldn't leave the children. Not one, but two children . . . She shouted again.

What if the other driver had meant to run her off the road? He could have stopped his car further along, and could be climbing down to . . . To what? She squinted into the shadows, icy fingers caressing her spine. Had he already been down and left another child in her car? There didn't seem to be any other explanation, because she had sure as hell only had one passenger when she left the road.

A sound made her gasp, and it took a moment for Holly to realise it was her phone ringing. She blinked round, puzzled, finally locating the illuminated screen a few feet away half buried in the leafy forest floor. Relief flooded her body and tears coursed down her cheeks, stinging her cut face. Holly wiped them away and took a deep breath, glancing back quickly at the boys.

She staggered towards her phone, checked as an electric flash of pain reminded her she was injured, and went down on her knees to crawl instead. Every movement made her wince now, as the adrenalin wore off, and by the time her trembling hand touched the plastic casing of her phone, tears were streaking her cheeks again. The missed call was from an unknown number, and they hadn't left a voicemail. It seemed to take ages to tap out the three digits she wanted, and all the time she stayed half sitting, half lying against a wet tree trunk, her eyes on the two children who sat so still and pale in the back seat of her car.

Finally, as she was starting to worry about the lack of phone signal, she got through to the operator, and waited again, patiently, answering the necessary questions as best she could.

In a surprisingly short time blue lights and sirens pierced the blackness. The rain was clearing, or at least she was sheltered, so deep in the woods. Holly was back at the car. With difficulty, gasping in pain at every movement, she had dragged an old picnic blanket out of the chaos, and tucked it carefully around the boys.

Checking their breathing, she wiped away the blood from Milo's head with a folded T-shirt from his bag, careful not to move either child. The jelly sweets were strewn carelessly across the seat, and Holly bit her lip at the sight of them. Please, God, let Milo be okay . . .

The rear passenger seats were reasonably dry, roof still intact, but the front of the car was trashed. She couldn't stop herself from gently touching the other boy's cheek again, almost to reassure herself that he was actually real. This time she smoothed his hair back as she had Milo's, and a rush of emotion hit. This poor child had been abandoned in her car. He wasn't a ghost or a dream, but a real boy who someone had dumped in a crashed car. Perhaps whoever did it had thought she was dead, had hoped they would all die . . .

His hair was dark brown, and now she was closer she could see it was indeed streaked with blood from his head injury. There was something about the shape of his face that prodded her memory. Had she seen him before? He was about Milo's age, perhaps a little older. At school, perhaps?

Shouts from the road cut into her thoughts, and soon a reassuring number of people were climbing carefully down to her car. She shouted back, in answer to their quick questions, and waited as they manoeuvred carefully through the undergrowth.

Holly stayed where she was, wincing at the clinical harshness of the floodlights, trying to ignore the pain that burned through her body. In one hand she held her son's cold, white fingers, but her eyes still dwelt protectively on the other child as well.

Her phone, thrust deep into the pocket of her bloodied top, buzzed with a message, and automatically she drew it out with her free hand. The tone was vitriolic and the number familiar.

'*Fucking bitch.*'

Chapter 2

Holly kissed Milo's head, resting her lips on his now warm forehead for a long moment. He was still unconscious but the doctor told her the scans were clear. They just had to wait for him to wake up. His left leg was broken in two places, and the head wound required five stitches. It would leave a scar, which she knew he would be perversely pleased with. Her darling boy. Nothing else and nobody else mattered.

But even so, after checking her son was still sleeping, she wheeled herself away to ICU. The other boy was lying still and silent too. He was in a worse condition, with more severe head injuries and some swelling to the brain. She watched him through the narrow window, her brow furrowing, pressing her fingers to the glass.

Had she seen him at rugby? Or was he the kid who had a laugh with Milo in the queue at Tesco? Had she seen him at the pool? If he opened his eyes, if she could see his expression, it might fix that nagging feeling that she *did* recognise him. The big white clock on the wall ticked towards nine o clock. She had been up for almost twenty-four hours and her brain simply wasn't working anymore.

The child's long lashes and the slightly hollow cheeks gave

him an air of vulnerability. She had supposed, and the doctors confirmed, he was around eleven or twelve years old, but skinny, with his bony hands lying neatly outside the white sheet. Almost too skinny for a boy his age, she thought. His dark brown hair lay tousled and greasy on the pillow around his face. There was a bruise on his cheek, and she knew he had stitches in the back of his head.

'Who are you?' she whispered. 'Where did you come from?' The dreamlike feeling of unreality had extended when Holly had been told that no missing children fitting this boy's description had been reported in the area. He was a still a ghost child, or a phantom. Her heart wrenched to think that somewhere surely his parents were searching for him . . . Or was it more painful to think that they were not, that her first guess had been correct and somebody meant them to die?

Someone had dumped him in her car like an unwanted stray. It couldn't have been premeditated, because who could have predicted the crash? Even if either of the reckless drivers from last night had intended her to drive off the road, how could they have counted on her swerving for the deer or known she'd be knocked unconscious whilst they popped another child in her car? None of it made any sense. Perhaps she was going mad. She tried to remember if she had seen anything out of the ordinary yesterday. But she was sure it had been no different to any other Sunday, right up until they drove down Mill Road.

Troubled, Holly took herself back to her son and with some difficulty transferred herself from the wheelchair to the armchair next to his bed. Her leg was bruised, with a possible torn ligament, and the wheelchair they had insisted on was only until a scan hopefully gave her the all clear. But the headache was back and she couldn't sleep. Too many questions whirled in her brain, too many worries danced behind her eyes. She pushed back her long hair away from her face, tied it into a knot, and rubbed her sore eyes.

Holly's phone vibrated and she snuck a guilty look at the other patients, before glancing at the illuminated screen. Messages from her friends and Aunt Lydia, but none from her ex-husband. None from her dad either, but that was hardly a shock. Lydia said she'd been round and told him what had happened. Holly knew her aunt had been hoping for a reconciliation between father and daughter for years. Donnie Hughes was slowly drinking himself to death, and hadn't featured in her life since she'd walked out of the Seaview Estate as an emotion-driven teenager. She smoothed a thumb across the screen, thinking about her dad.

He'd tried to stop her leaving, even though he had seen what the trial did to her, seen how much she needed to escape the twisted memories and leave everything behind. Her exhausted mind drifted back to her teenage years.

'You can't just fucking walk away! You're my daughter, and you're the only one left who can take care of the business.' Donnie had been waiting for her after the trial. It had always been *'Donnie'*. Never *'Dad'*. His voice was a pitch lower than it had been in her childhood, and he broke off to cough violently, peering down at her from under a greasy fringe. His face was ruddy, and his eyes bloodshot and hung with violet bags.

She'd gone into her room and grabbed her bags, already neatly packed and awaiting her final exit. But Holly was still shaking, still high on fear and grief, her mind replaying the judge's words and her answers over and over, like a crazy recording she could never erase.

'What made you think she was dead?'

'When did you last see your brother?'

Holly had made it back down the stairs to find her dad leaning firmly against the front door, his mouth set in a scowl.

'Get out of the way, Donnie. You didn't even bother to come to the trial, and you don't actually give a shit about anything except your business.' She reached the door and extended her hand towards the handle. 'I've got news for you. Your business is finished. The Nicholls have won, and all you've done is fuck

14

everything up – Mum, me, Jay. You're a sad, deluded old man.'

He didn't move, didn't speak. The towering giant of her child-hood reduced to this shuffling, glowering creature. But as she moved forward, his hand wrapped around her wrist, sweaty fingers pinching the skin.

Holly pulled away, but he held on, yanking her closer. She turned her face away from the stench of his foul breath. 'You don't know shit, girl. You could have been something, taken us back to where we were, and yeah, even taken on the Nicholls brothers. I know what goes on with Nicholls Transport, and the human cargo that gets stashed in the back, the girls they bring down here to work in their brothels. It's sick, and now you're running away from all of us. Well, don't ever fucking come back, you useless bitch!' He spat right in her face.

She'd stood frozen in horror, just for a second, before she wiped the glob of spittle away, warm and wet on her cheek. 'I won't be coming back,' she told her father.

As he raised a hand to hit her, she snapped her wrist away, and sidestepped, already up on the balls of her feet. Years of training had made her moves instinctive. His hand whipped past and he made another futile grab at her shoulder, tearing her shirt.

Holly moved her body, jabbing with an elbow, bringing herself nearer the door, throwing the man aside with effortless ease. The horror of her dad's words, his attack, would sink in later. She was trying to leave it all behind, but Holly was a trained fighter, and she accepted that probably wasn't ever going to change.

Donnie collapsed, panting against the peeling wall of the hallway, yelled a few breathless obscenities after her, and she cut him off by kicking the door shut.

The heat of late afternoon had blasted through her jeans and T-shirt, and she could feel sweat beading on her face, but she'd kept on walking.

***

15

A nurse rattled past with the drugs trolley, jolting Holly out of the past. She glanced quickly at Milo, reassuring herself before purposely keeping her thoughts in the present. Hell, it wasn't like there was a lack of drama here either. And a whole load of swirling fears.

Whoever the other boy was, she had still been looking at her phone moments before the crash, and driving at the same time. The guilt and anger at her own stupidity in allowing herself to be distracted by her phone made her breath short now. She was always so careful! The vicious texts danced through her brain. They had only started a couple of weeks ago, and at first she had refused to believe that Tom would be so vindictive. But now, each time they arrived, she tried to make herself pick up the phone and confront him, and each time, so far, she had funked it. She could hardly tell the police her own ex-husband was bullying her by text. It sounded so stupid, and she didn't trust the police anyway. Well, with her upbringing, why would she?

She woke to footsteps and the curtains around Milo's bed being drawn apart. Holly blinked hard, pushing herself upright in the chair, trying to drag herself back to consciousness.

'Mrs Kendal, I'm DI Harper, and this is DC Marriot. If you feel up to it, we just need to ask you a few questions.' His voice was low, rumbling, and deceptively gentle.

She got a sick feeling deep in her gut at the sound of his name, at the sight of his long face, with its sharp cheekbones and prominent beak of a nose. This couldn't be happening. How was he still on the scene? Surely he should have retired, leaving everyone in peace by now? The long, thin nose had a dent and was twisted out of shape.

'And you fuck off, you bloody nosy copper! My wife has been murdered and all you can do is accuse me. Go and find out who did it, because if I get there first, I'll string them up from that tower block . . .'

'We are trying, Donnie, we just need to ask a few more questions. Perhaps you should come back down to the station with us?'

The sickening crunch as her dad broke the police officer's nose had almost been drowned by his exclamation of pain. It was fair enough, Holly had thought at the time. Bloody Harper had been sniffing around for years, chipping away at her dad's business interests. Luckily it was only the Nicholls' dealers that got banged up, and they deserved it.

Holly studied the familiar police officer now, this tall, gaunt man, with white tufted hair and hollows under his eyes. Fuck. Of all the people to turn up. Detective Inspector Harper. He'd clearly landed a promotion since they last met. He stood a little apart from a serious-looking blonde woman, whose thin lips were currently pursed with apparent disapproval as she glanced down at her phone.

Feeling Holly's gaze, she looked up and smiled. It was a cool, professional smile and it didn't reach her glacial blue eyes. The DI was talking again. 'We understand your son is doing well? A broken leg and some concussion, I think the doctor said.'

Holly pulled the regulation blue and white hospital gown tighter around her body, and blinked sleep from her eyes, wishing Lydia would hurry up and get here with her clothes. Her aunt had come straight to the hospital last night when Holly called, but went home around eleven when she had been reassured that her niece and Milo were not in any life-threatening condition.

'He's still unconscious, but the doctors say he's going to be fine. I guess he'll be furious about having his leg in a cast though . . .' Why was she babbling like she was guilty of something? Best get it out in the open. She had told the uniformed PC last night, but she needed to explain, to make them understand that it was wasn't her fault. 'There was a car behind that was far too close, and then another car came the other way and nearly hit us. I had to go on the verge and . . .'

'It's okay, Mrs Kendal, we've read your statement,' DC Marriot told her, cutting her off mid-sentence. 'We can talk about that later. For now, we just have a few more questions.'

Holly nodded, uneasily, her eyes still on the man. They didn't care. They wanted to know about the other boy. Well, that was okay, because so did she.

DI Harper nodded. He stood next to the window, arms folded. Did he recognise her as she did him? Of course, she was Holly Kendal now instead of Holly Hughes, but surely he must know. And wasn't it odd that a DI would come for a chat with a car crash victim? But it was a car crash with a twist, and she figured he knew all right, and he was as curious as hell.

His grey eyes were faded now, sunk deeper under bushy grey brows, but he still had that aura of energy, alertness, and that distinctive voice. Her mum had always said he was clever for a copper. She had instructed both her children to keep away from the police who came snooping around their family home. But that was in the past, and with a dad like Holly's it was no wonder her mum had been cautious. She could never have known that this 'clever' copper would be the one who investigated her own death. Investigated, but never bloody found out who did it. Holly switched her thoughts quickly back to the present. It was like being dragged through a mud bath, the past swilling over her, sticking in patches, reminding her she might have walked away but she could never completely escape.

'Did you find out anything about the other boy?' Holly asked tentatively now. She passed her tongue nervously over sore lips.

It was the woman who answered. Her voice was sharp and what Holly's Aunt Lydia would certainly call a bit posh. 'No. As I'm sure you've been told he is still in a critical condition.'

Holly was still struggling to get her head around the accident, let alone the fact she had, somewhere between leaving the road and waking up in the woods, acquired another child. Someone had *given* her a child. Now this man, with his cool grey eyes and air of officialdom, was back in her life, and suddenly, as other memories stirred it was all she could do to prevent herself from bursting into tears. The DI still hadn't met her eyes. 'What about the driver who was behind me, or the idiot in the van who drove right at us?' she asked quickly.

DI Harper exchanged a quick look with his colleague. 'Obviously there are no cameras after the Mill Road turn-off, and several vehicles followed you off at Junction 10, but we have no way of telling if any of them took the first exit, as you did. There is also the possibility that the driver behind you joined Mill Road later on, from either Hill Lane or Silver Lane. I do appreciate it must have been hard, but the vague description you gave us of both vehicles doesn't give us much to go on.'

'It was dark, and pouring with rain, and I was afraid I was about to be carjacked. You try memorising details in that situation,' she shot back at him, a flare of confidence returning. The other police officer raised her eyebrows at this show of anger, but said nothing.

'I'm not trying to insult your intelligence, I'm just telling you we are examining every possibility,' he said. There was a flash of something that might have been amusement in his grey eyes, before his expression returned its usual sombre mask.

He was still fucking annoying, Holly thought, remembering suddenly that he inserted the word 'possibility' into just about every sentence. Nothing was ever 'confirmed', or 'definite', with him.

'Moving on, you already mentioned when you were interviewed last night that you have no idea how this other boy came to be in your car. We have checked he doesn't match the description of any missing children in the local area, but we are circulating his details further afield. Obviously a missing child generates an extensive search operation and we are working in close contact with our neighbouring forces.' DC Marriot was scrolling through her iPad. 'We did receive another call to the ambulance service at 17.22. It was a male caller who said he had just driven past a crashed car. He gave your location, but said he didn't know how many people were involved. He then rang off. The phone number was untraceable.'

'You think that was the driver behind me?' Holly said, confusion making her brain heavy, her thoughts sluggish.

DI Harper frowned. 'At this stage we aren't sure. Your call came in at 17.31. It is a possibility that the initial caller wasn't involved at all. Do you recall anything unusual about the afternoon? Anyone who might have been at your son's rugby game who wasn't usually there? Or perhaps someone who might have spoken to you when you stopped for petrol?'

'No! Do you think I haven't been going over and over this all night? I have no idea how that child came to be in my car and, to be honest, it hasn't been the best of nights. I'm sure you can understand that.' She was glaring at the DI now, willing him to react, but he kept his eyes averted.

'Try to think. I appreciate how distressing this must have been for you,' DC Marriot said, her voice soothing. She had a slightly pointed face, and small pointed ears, like a pixie. Her make-up was immaculate.

Holly scowled, but allowed her mind to run back over the events of yesterday. 'Milo always has rugby practice on a Sunday in the winter. Unless they have an away match, it's always at Prince Edward's park from two till four. It ran on a bit yesterday because one of the coaches was late, and then I had a coffee afterwards whilst Milo played in the clubhouse with his friends.'

'So you left rugby at four-thirty, you said?'

'Yes . . . I think so, because I remember hoping I wouldn't catch the rush-hour traffic, and then realising it was Sunday so I didn't have to panic.' She managed a weak smile. 'We stopped for petrol at the next service station. I know the route well, and I often stop there for fuel and groceries.'

'Did you speak to anyone in the services, notice anyone paying you particular attention?' DC Marriot pressed her.

She shook her head. 'No. It was just normal, quite busy but normal.'

'Now just to recap – you didn't stop at all when you left the motorway? You didn't pick up any hitchhikers or see anyone on the side of the road?'

Holly shot him a look of disbelief. 'Don't you think I would have mentioned that? Of course I didn't see anyone else! Everything seemed to happen at once – the deer and Milo shouting, and the headlights of the car behind . . . I was just so scared.' Her hands were shaking again as her mind replayed the moment they had left the tarmac, tumbling down the hill.

They watched her some more, clearly waiting, but Holly had no more to say. Actually, she felt a twist of nausea rising in her stomach. It was just too weird. She felt a sudden urge to go back to ICU and reassure herself the boy was still there, still alive . . . Who the hell was the tailgating driver, and more to the point who was the child who had been left, unconscious and injured?

DI Harper gave a barely imperceptible sigh. 'We spoke to your husband . . .'

'Ex-husband,' Holly corrected wearily.

'Sorry, ex-husband. Obviously he is away at the moment, but there is a possibility he might be able to help with our inquiries. He may recognise the child, perhaps.'

Holly looked up, nausea fading away, as anger returned. 'Tom hasn't got a clue who Milo sees, or who I see. He's the last person who would be any help. When I phoned him about the accident he just assumed it was my fault, and as soon as he heard Milo was given the all clear, he said he would carry on with his lecture tour. He'll pitch up in a couple of days, I expect.'

They both looked hard at her, and Holly squirmed. Too much information, but she was so fatigued that her mouth was running away with her. DC Marriot spoke again. 'Mrs Kendal, can you think of anyone at all who you might have spoken to recently, who may have been connected with this child?'

'*No!*' She was surprised how insistent they were being. 'I've been back to look at the poor boy and I keep trying and trying to think if I recognise him, but I don't. I'm not saying I haven't ever seen him before, but he's just another kid. He *might* have been at rugby that afternoon, or karate last week, or even in the queue in Tesco last month, but I can't say for sure!' She was getting agitated, raising her voice, breathing heavily, and they were watching her warily.

'Thank you, Mrs Kendal.' The woman police officer nodded politely now, but her eyes remained on Holly's face. She placed her iPad carefully on the table next to Holly. 'Can I show you something? This is CCTV footage from the BP station where you stopped on your way home.'

Bewildered, Holly leaned over, focusing on the grainy picture. She saw herself and Milo in the long queue, waiting to pay, then a man approaching the empty till at the bakery. He glanced over at her, and she frowned. Something about the tilt of his head, his profile, was familiar. In the footage she was fumbling with her credit card. She remembered the contactless hadn't worked so the transaction had to go through again.

The place was busy, but amongst the crowd, the camera picked out Holly and Milo leaving, with the man fairly close behind.

'And then this is the CCTV next to the toilets,' DI Harper said, scrolling across the screen.

The man was standing, smoking, half facing the wall, apparently waiting in the queue for the toilets. Holly's heart thumped painfully hard against her ribs, and her head was spinning.

'Do you recognise him?' DC Marriot asked.

Holly swallowed hard, her heart beating uncomfortably hard as a shot of adrenalin coursed around her body. It had been years, but of course she knew who he was. He was part of the past, the same past that had killed her brother, her mother, and had been bathed in bloodshed because of who she was. Her voice cracked with emotion. 'That's Devril Mancini.'

Chapter 3

'We believe so,' DC Marriot said. Her voice was cool and slightly mechanical in its reassurance, as she noted Holly's reaction.

DI Harper was watching her closely now. 'Have you had any contact with Devril since the trial?' There it was. Bang, the past hitting them full on with him staring right at her.

Holly found her hands were shaking like she was back in the courtroom, waiting for the assembled crowd to hear her crimes. 'No.'

'Really? Not in eleven years?' He was clearly sceptical. But then he would be. Harper had stalked their family her whole life.

Holly tried to speak, but her throat was tight and raw, and her eyes stung with tears. She cleared her throat, annoyed at betraying so much emotion. 'None. You know exactly what happened and why I wouldn't ever want to go back. I moved on, went to university, got married and had a kid. There would never be a reason to go back. But just for the record, do you really think Devril would have tried to run me off the road?'

'We're not saying that all. I'm just pointing out that he was at the garage at the same time you and Milo stopped for petrol on your way home. And as far as I know, he's been away from the area a long time. It seems a strange coincidence for him to show up again now after all these years. I only recognised him because of our connection.' He was admitting it now at least. 'I do appreciate that this is difficult, Holly, but you must see that we have to consider all the possibilities.' The earnest look of concern, that almost paternal voice and the gentle mannerisms could fool anyone without half a brain into thinking he actually cared. 'You know Niko Balinta was released last month?'

Another ghost emerging from her nightmares. 'I do know. So what?' It came out defensive and snappy. She cleared her throat again, picking up the glass of water from the bedside cabinet. Her mouth stung as she sipped. The tiny glass cuts she had acquired in the accident stretched from her lower lip to her forehead. God, she had been so lucky. She glanced at Milo, sleeping soundly. They both had.

DI Harper nodded slowly, and then echoed her words. 'So what, indeed. Anyway, our primary concern at this moment in time is to find out who the boy is, and why he was in your car, but apart from that . . . well, I'm keeping an open mind.'

She scowled at him now. 'You haven't mentioned Jayden.'

A quick, bright look from under the bushy brows. 'Do I need to mention your brother? As you say, it would be raking over old and painful ground. You know how sorry I am about the whole affair. I tried so hard to help him.'

'Fine, but you brought it up. You mentioned Devril and Niko, so clearly you think the boy in my car and the crash are somehow connected to the past. To my past. What is it?'

'We are following up all the lines of inquiry. As DI Harper says, there is only a possibility that there might be a connection. It may well be, and this does happen as I'm sure you are aware, that we get some more witnesses come forward. Meanwhile, we will be doing everything we can to find out what happened last night,' DS Marriot said smoothly. She smiled at Holly.

'Yeah, I'm sure loads of people will come forward if there's any connection to our family. You know what Seaview Estate's

24

like, don't you?' Holly said incredulously. 'Us, the Balintas and the Mancinis owned it and everyone on it.' Then she jabbed a finger in DI Harper's direction. 'He knows what happened when the Nicholls came in and took a slice of the action a few years before Mum died. Nobody talked to the police. Ever. Since my dad scaled down and Mason Balinta's been sick, the Nicholls have properly taken over. The Mancinis are turncoats and they ride with anyone who's onto a winner – they don't give a shit which family that is. It'll make it weird now Niko's out though. They say *his* dad hasn't got long.' At their look she shrugged. 'My best friend and my aunt still live on the estate, so I know what's going on. But I'm not a part of it anymore, and I'm not the same person either. My life has changed, and I have a kid to protect. He knows nothing about any of this, and now isn't the right time to tell him. When he's older, maybe . . .'

DI Harper was watching her intently now. 'At this stage we are just making inquiries. DC Marriot will be taking the lead on this case, so be sure to contact her if you remember anything else and apologies if I have upset you. You should get some rest now. But of course, if Devril Mancini should be in contact . . .'

DI Harper pulled out his phone, moving quickly, almost as if he was running away from her. The curtains swished closed behind him. DC Marriot lingered for a moment and passed Holly a business card. 'If you do think of anything else, Mrs Kendal, you can call me at any time. We'll be in touch if there is any more news.' She was still an ice queen with perfect eyeliner, but suddenly there was a small, genuine smile touching her lips.

'Thanks.' Holly took the card and put it on the cabinet next to Milo's bed. The woman hurried to catch up with her superior, and Holly listened to the tap of their shoes as they made their way along the line of beds to the door. Deep in thought now, seeking reassurance, she slid a hand onto the bed and found her son's, linking their fingers as she had done when he was a baby.

Suddenly her composure shattered, and for the first time since the accident she gave way to proper tears, laying her face on the pillow next to Milo's to muffle her sobs. Devril Mancini? Bloody hell. It was a long time since he'd left the Seaview. She'd kept tabs on him via social media, telling herself she was just safeguarding her secrets, but she never imagined she'd actually meet him again. Too much history, and too many nightmares lay between them.

Holly hunched further into her chair, wrapping her arms around her body, frowning into space. Memories of Dev, an aching in her heart, were clouded by the fact that he knew what really happened back then, the night of the murder. He was the one person who could make her life worse than it already was. And now he was back.

***

'Mum?'

She was drifting, drained and uncomfortable in the chair next to his bed, when her son's voice brought her back to what mattered.

'Mum, are you okay?' His face was still pale, and his green eyes were bewildered, but he was sitting up, wincing at the pain.

'Milo, you need to lie down, love, and I'll get a nurse,' Holly said quickly, happy tears hot behind her own eyes. Relief made her dizzy for a second. He was all right; he was actually going to be okay . . . Nothing else mattered.

'Why? Don't go . . .'

Holly pressed the call button and one of the nurses came over to take Milo's observations. He scribbled a few notes on the clipboard and then smiled at both of them. 'Looks fine to me. We'll need to keep the both of you in for a while, but his obs are normal. Any pain, mate?'

Milo nodded. 'Only my leg.'

'Okay, I'll get you something for that,' the nurse said. He grinned suddenly. 'They said you play rugby. I do too. I'm Matt and if you need anything at all, Milo, you just call for me, okay?'

Milo nodded. 'Okay.' All his usual bounce and self-confidence was stripped away. He looked younger, more vulnerable, and Holly leant over to hug him gently, stroking his hair back from his forehead. He was so pale his freckles were like a spattering of blood across his upturned nose, and his lips were red and sore.

'The doctor will be around soon, but in the meantime he can have sips of water if he wants them,' Matt said.

Holly thanked him. The child in the next bed was suddenly violently sick and Matt hurried away. She looked down at her son, one arm still around him, and he wriggled over and snuggled into the crook of her arm, head on her shoulder, and their fingers entwined.

'Mum, I'm really sorry.' His voice was faint.

'What do you mean?'

'I'm sorry you crashed the car. It was my fault, wasn't it? You looked round at me before the deer jumped out because I called you. If you hadn't looked round we might have still . . .' Tears trickled down his cheeks.

'Sweetie, you didn't cause the car crash,' Holly said hastily. 'Of course you didn't. It was a combination of things and bad luck.' She glanced at him, afraid of traumatising him further.

'There was the car behind, wasn't there?' Milo said thoughtfully. 'He crashed into us when we swerved to avoid that van, and again before we went down the bank.'

'Yes.'

'There was a man too. He was in the woods after we crashed. I think he brought the other boy.' His voice was dreamy now, and he snuggled further into her.

'What? A man? Who was he?' She'd just assumed Milo had been out cold like she'd been. 'Had you seen him before?' She couldn't stop the surprise in her voice, and hastily softened her questions, soothing him. Her mind was buzzing. 'Milo? Was it someone you had seen before, sweetie?'

The boy paused, his head still on her shoulder, his forehead crinkling as he considered. 'No, I've never seen him before. I couldn't see much in the car because it was all shadows. I tried to call out for you but you didn't answer. I was scared and I tried to move but I couldn't. It felt like I was half sleeping but then he was there and the other boy was next to me. The man smiled at me, and he touched both our faces like this . . .' Milo reached up and stroked Holly's cheek with gentle fingers.

'He . . . *touched* you? Did he say anything?' She forced herself not to sound too horrified, to keep the conversation going, but her stomach lurched. A man had been there whilst she was unconscious. He had delivered a child to her car. He'd touched Milo's face. It made no sense at all.

'No, but he went all round the car and looked at you in the front. He touched your neck.' He vaguely tapped the area below his jawline.

Jesus. Who was this lunatic? Someone had checked whether she had a pulse, was dead and then they'd vanished? She needed to call DC Marriot, but not in front of her boy. He seemed to be coming out of this okay, and it wouldn't be fair to scare him further. But as soon as she could . . .

After Milo had eaten some toast, Holly scrolled through various social media sites and finally pulled up a fairly recent picture of Devril Mancini, snagged from his Instagram page. She had kept an eye on all of them over them over the years, despite cutting herself off from the past. He'd been a personal trainer when they were younger, but now his profiles just said 'Freelance writer', which was pretty vague. She found Niko's Twitter feed. Brand new and with just a few followers. His Instagram feed seemed to consist mostly of jars of sweets. Which was weird. Had Niko bought the corner shop? Squinting more closely she saw that there were emojis of snowflakes and pills, subtly advertising to those who knew exactly what was on offer. No, not candy, but drugs. Fresh out of jail and already Niko was back in business.

There had been news articles occasionally, examining the case, and the papers had dredged everything up when he was released. Hesitantly, she showed photos of both men to her son.

She zoomed in on a shot of Niko. He hadn't changed much – older of course, dark eyes wary and his smile just short of real. 'Milo, is this the man who was in the car?' She was holding her breath, almost willing him to say yes, to solve one piece of the puzzle at least.

He leant over, peered at her phone, and shook his head.

'Or this one?'

Her son squinted at Devril's picture for longer, frowning, toast crumbs decorating the side of his mouth. 'I don't think so. It was dark and I had that floaty feeling but I don't think it was this man. He had a baseball cap pulled down over his eyes. It was a red one like Dad has . . .'

'You mean a GAP one?'

'Yeah, and the man had a ring on his hand. I felt it when he touched me.' Milo yawned and, still leaning against her shoulder, drifted back to sleep.

Waiting until he was snoring, Holly moved his head gently back onto the pillow and extricated herself from his clutching fingers. She picked up the card from the cabinet and wheeled herself down to the main entrance towards the coffee machine. Even hospital coffee was better than nothing and she needed to wake up. She was missing something here. Every movement hurt her body and tiredness fogged her brain. She took out her phone, then hesitated.

No way she wanted to speak to the police again so soon, but this mattered. If only to show that she had been telling the truth about not knowing who the child was or how he got there. Although she had to admit it was a bit extreme to think both police officers had doubts about her sanity, hell, she did too at this moment in time.

'DC Marriot.'

'It's Holly Kendal. Milo just woke up and he says that he saw a man in my car after the crash. He thinks he brought the other boy.'

'My God. Did he recognise him?' Her voice was sharp, excited.

'He says not but I think he'd be able to give you a description.' No need to say she had already shown him a picture of Devril Mancini, or they'd be bound to wonder about the connection again. She could still hear her dad yelling at her brother to never trust the fucking police, and after years of that the mistrust was stuck in her brain.

'Good. Look, I'm tied up at the moment but I'll send a colleague back down to the hospital to chat with Milo, if that's all right? Does he remember anything else?'

'I don't think so. He hasn't said.'

'That's fine.'

Holly rang off and sat just inside the doors, watching the busy car park. Ambulances were lined up outside the side entrance, queuing to deliver their patients, and a steady stream of walking wounded tottered into A&E. Every time the doors opened, a blast of icy air hit her face, reminding her it was still winter.

But the sky outside was a perfect pale washed blue, and the morning sunlight cast a feeble brightness across flickering shadows on the tarmac. A grimy concrete pot of spring flowers stood next to the overflowing rubbish bin. Their green shoots and yellow petals were struggling through the sour earth dotted with cigarette ends, but by some miracle they were still growing.

Chapter 4

Dear Mum,

There is so much shit I need to tell you, but it's hard to put it into words. My fingers are shaking because it's really cold in the flat, but I can see you watching me from the wall and that helps a bit.

I've got all your photos up, Mum, and I've got this cool list that Dad gave me that has all your favourite things. He doesn't just write you letters, he talks to you all the time. Are you really there? Perhaps it isn't him who's gone mad; perhaps it's just that the others can't see you.

Anyway, I wanted to let you know we're never going to forget you and we've got a plan that will make you happy. Dad says if we do little things in your memory then it will help until we carry out the plan.

I'm not sure if it does help, because he sometimes cries, or shouts your name and punches the wall. The neighbours yell and bang on their side when he does that. Not on your wall, of course. Yours is beautiful. We painted the whole side of the room yellow like sunshine, and we pinned up loads of pictures, a copy of the list, and some of your clothes. It's really special and every night we light a candle and Dad says we have to spend a while just thinking about you.

I kind of like this time of night, because it's quiet, and I can feel you close when we are near the wall. The smell of beer makes me feel a bit sick, but at least Dad is sleeping too. Sometimes he chokes and throws up, but after the first time, I know what to do. I just clean up and I make sure when he passes out his head is turned to one side because Layla at school said she does that for her mum too.

Are you really there, Mum? I kind of need to know, but if you can't tell me don't worry, I understand. I know you're looking out for me. Can you keep an eye on Dad too? Just when he goes a bit crazy. I'm worried that he might do something stupid and they'll take him away. Don't tell him I said so.

I love you, Mum

x

Chapter 5

'She's dead!'

'Listen to me. Put both hands on the centre of her chest, one on top of the other. Are you doing that?'

'Yes.'

'Now push down hard and fast. Don't be afraid to push too hard. You can help her . . .'

'I'm doing it! I'm fucking doing it, okay?'

'Great. Well done. Keep going. One, two, three, four . . . I'll stay with you until the ambulance arrives. Is the door unlocked?'

'Yeah.'

'Keep going. One, two, three, four . . .'

'I can't . . .'

'It's okay. Keep going, sweetheart, you are doing so well. The ambulance is nearly with you.'

'I can hear sirens.'

'Keep going.'

'Oh, the police are here!'

'It's okay, just keep going until the ambulance crew take over.'

'They're here!'

'Okay, you can hang up on me now. Well done, Holly.'

Holly drifted back to consciousness, fighting her way through the ragged remains of nightmares. Her own brother's girlfriend and she hadn't saved her . . . It was like a knife, jabbing quickly, mercilessly under her ribs.

Her eyes darted around the room as she took deep breaths, feeling her pulse slowing down to normal. At least they were home now, and she was in her own bed, in her own house. She hadn't had that dream for ages, and the memories were unwelcome, dripping through into real life, into her perfect real life that she had so carefully constructed. Except it wasn't so perfect anymore. Tom had turned into a cheating bastard, and she was left struggling to pay the bills on her own. Not to mention his charming text messages. Since the accident she'd had only one more, but she was now seriously considering telling DC Marriot about them.

She struggled out of bed, feeling the twinge in her leg, adjusting her weight to compensate. But she was okay. If she kept telling herself that, she might even start to believe it. After all, the hospital had given them the all clear and discharged them both; medically they must be all right. Milo was calling from his room now, something about a dragon egg hatching into a wolf. She could do this. 'Coming! Can you reach your crutches okay?'

'Yeah, I just want to show you this really cool evolving dragon egg!'

Holly pulled a thick fleece on over her pyjamas and staggered towards his room, pushing away the dregs of the nightmare, focusing on what was important. But she couldn't help thinking about the other boy. The silent, pale child still lying in his hospital bed, who had nobody to shout for, nobody to claim him. The rush of protective emotion she had experienced after she found him in her car was still there.

Her aunt was already busy crashing around the kitchen downstairs, making one of her famous fry-ups. Holly, who preferred to get at least two cups of coffee down before she even thought about food, felt her stomach heave slightly at the smell of bacon.

But Milo was soon sliding down the stairs on his bum, dragging his crutches behind him, apparently desperate for food. 'Lydia, can you leave my eggs all runny please and can I have a sausage too?'

***

'Lydia, I'm fine. I can do it.' They were sitting in the living room, which after Lydia's assault with the Hoover and dusters was unusually clean and tidy. Milo was drawing at the kitchen table.

'Holly, you most certainly are not fine. You told the police someone almost ran you off the road, and now they seem to think all kinds of things about how this other boy got in the car. Before you say a word, you know I believe you. As if you wouldn't say if you knew who he was! That DI Harper sticking his beak in around here again isn't going to help anyone, is it? Now what's all this about you thinking you're going back to work on Monday? You're barely back on your feet!'

Holly took a deep breath and let it out slowly. 'Don't be so dramatic. I have to go back to work because I need the money. You know I always work overtime shifts to cover the extra on the mortgage, now Tom's gone.'

'You should move house, get somewhere smaller instead of killing yourself working all hours. Come back to the Seaview, love,' her aunt told her. Then her expression softened. 'Of course, I'll have Milo when you're working as usual, but give yourself a break, love. The two of you have only been out of hospital for a few days.'

'Thanks, Lydia.' Holly smiled at her, silently adding that whilst she was still sane and breathing there was no way on earth she was going back to live on the Seaview. The mirror opposite the sofa reflected them, so similar both physically and mentally. With the pale winter sunlight shining through the window, casting a gentle glow across her face, Lydia looked so much like Holly's mum.

Lydia was the older sister, pushing sixty-eight now, but the black curls were glossy and as usual she was heavily made up, with red lipstick and lashings of dark eyeliner. Lydia's husband had died four years ago, and she had dealt with the grief as only she could – by joining a swanky health club and spending lots of money on clothes.

Lydia had no kids so she had always had a lot of time for Holly and her brother. She could have moved off the estate years ago, but she said she was happy in her flat. Her husband, Mick, had invested in property and a bar in Spain, and Lydia said as soon as Holly was settled she'd go and live in the sunshine.

The older woman got up and moved over to the window. 'At least you haven't had any reporters hanging around in the last few days. Whilst you were in hospital they were parked out front for a bit, even knocking on the door when I was over stocking the fridge, and I told you I went over and had a word . . . I get that it's a good story but they've got no right to turn up on your doorstep. That poor boy . . . I just keep thinking why the hell haven't his parents reported him missing? It really gets me to think maybe he doesn't have anyone, any family to worry about him . . .'

The phantom child in Holly's car was a great story, but so far both police and journalists had drawn a blank. A police appeal had been on the national news, giving sparse details and focusing on the fact that somewhere, someone must know a child was missing. Her name hadn't been mentioned but from her previous experience she knew journalists had ways and means of tracking people down. Although DC Marriot had told her the boy seemed to be improving and the most recent scans were encouraging, nobody could really be certain he was okay, until he regained consciousness.

She would go back and visit him this week. Perhaps subconsciously he would know that somebody was looking out for him. In a weird way he had been given to her, and she felt responsible until another superseded her claim.

'*Do* they know who the other boy is yet?' Milo asked suddenly, abandoning his drawing and hopping into the living room. 'I mean, what if they already know who he is but they aren't telling us?' He was fiddling with the TV remote, half his attention on the task in hand, half focused on this intriguing subject. He'd brought it up numerous times every day since they'd been out of hospital. After a couple of days of being pale and withdrawn, he had gradually recovered his bounce and confidence. But the questions were the same: Was the boy conscious yet? Why was he in the car? Who put him there? Lately he had started on this conspiracy theory, and become convinced the police knew the boy's identity.

DC Marriot's colleague, DS Steph Harlow had carefully questioned Milo, but he said he remembered nothing after the deer leaping across the road, until he woke up in hospital. When Holly reminded him what he had said about the man leaving the other boy in the car, his chin set stubbornly and he shook his head. The nurse told her later that the memories could come back, but it was also possible that now Milo was fully awake, he was simply blocking out the whole traumatic event, and even if he did remember, he didn't want to share it.

The doorbell rang and Holly made a move to get up, even as her aunt went to the door, her high-heeled fluffy mules tapping on the wooden floor. She could hear the initial stilted conversation, and frowned. Great, Tom was the last person she wanted to see. It was a shame he couldn't have stayed abroad. He had returned from his overseas lecture tour two days after the accident, but had made sure his visits to Milo in hospital didn't coincide with Holly's. Then, reassured by the medical staff that Milo was on the mend, he had resumed his tour, and departed for a further three days in Berlin.

'Dad!' Recognising the voice, Milo scrambled for his crutches and hopped proficiently out of the room.

'Hallo, mate, how are you doing?'

'Yeah, I'm okay. Mum's doing well too, says her leg is nearly better but mine is actually *broken.*'

'I know. I wanted to come back sooner, but I needed stay for this work conference . . . Still, it's all done now. Want to see what I bought you?'

'Yes! Am I coming to stay with you when Mum goes back to work?'

'Come inside properly then, and I'll show you your present.' Tom had been walking down the hall as he greeted his son but now they both appeared in the doorway. Tom was carrying a large square box, wrapped in shiny green paper.

Holly nodded politely at her ex-husband, but couldn't bring herself to speak. The sight of yet another expensive present for Milo made her wince. She supposed he was doing it to make up for the divorce, but it made things awkward, and highlighted the fact she couldn't afford to buy her son expensive presents. Her aunt scowled at Tom, muttered something about a cup of tea and vanished into the kitchen.

'So, Holly, how are you feeling?' He was clearly forcing himself to be civil, and without waiting for an answer he carefully pulled Milo close to his side, dropping a kiss on his blonde head. 'Thank God Milo is okay.'

She managed to respond to this. 'Yes, he's fine now. He's going back to school on Monday. Milo, can you go and help Lydia while I chat to your dad? He can come and play football with you in the garden in a minute, okay? And then you can open your present too.' Holly smiled. 'I did say he shouldn't be playing football, but he's determined to be goalie at the very least.'

For a split second they shared a look over Milo's head. A tiny golden moment that reminded Holly of when Milo was first born, and they used to stand next to his crib, watching him sleep, totally in awe of this tiny human being they had created. But then it was over, Tom's expression changing to one of disdain as he spotted her roster on the coffee table.

'Are you really going back to work?'

'Of course.' She smiled thinly. 'I need to earn money somehow, remember?' She turned back to Milo. 'Go on, sweetie, go outside for a bit while I speak to your dad.'

He frowned, looked from one to the other and then reluctantly hopped towards the kitchen.

Holly looked at Tom. His brown hair was just slightly too long, his navy tweed jacket worn over a crisp blue-striped shirt that emphasised his dark blue eyes. He had picked up a faint tan, despite the fact that he always complained he never saw the outside world when he was on a lecture tour. He smelt of his usual expensive aftershave. Once, the combination had turned her on, but now she wanted to throw up. It was such a cliché to have fallen for her university lecturer. Even more of a cliché to have imagined she could ride off into the sunset with him.

She had a sudden flash of memory – Jayden sitting on her bed, seizing her book, chucking it out the open window, and telling her fairy tales were total bollocks. As an elder brother he had clearly felt it was up to him to lay down the law. He must have been about eight when he said that, but she had already grown taller than him. Little git.

'Are you really managing with the mortgage repayments? I would have thought you should be thinking about downsizing,' he said, sitting casually on the sofa. Tom's upper-class voice was light, almost disinterested, but she was sure there was a bit of sarcasm in there.

Memories stung. She had been in love with him, she was sure of it. Now he had moved on. Another young woman, another home, soon probably another kid on the way. Lydia was one of only two people who had ever expressed doubt over Holly's choice of husband. He had fooled most of them with his charm and good looks. 'We're fine, thank you for asking. I've been doing overtime.'

'Still working in the call centre? You should have finished your degree, Holly.' His smug, self-satisfied face was highlighted by the crisp winter light as he stood, poised in front of the big bay windows like an actor on stage.

The unfairness of this statement made her catch her breath. 'Whatever you want to think. I'm sure we don't need to meet up to go over the childcare arrangements for the next month, so why don't we just do this by email in future. It'll save us both the hassle,' Holly told him. She hated herself for still searching his face some kind of affection, anything but this cold, amused sarcasm. Why did he hate her so much? She should mention the texts, she really should.

'I'm sure that will be fine. Beth is so good at working out my diary, and now we have the spare room organised Milo can come and stay for the weekends.' His eyes were challenging her to comment.

'I'm sure he'd like that. While he isn't in the room, Tom, I would like to speak to you about something.'

His expression was wary, and he leaned back a little, away from her.

'I can't pretend that everything is okay, and that I'm not still unbelievably hurt by what you did, but you made your choice.'

'You threw me out remember, Holly. It wasn't my choice at all. You've changed since you've been working. Why you couldn't just get a job that fitted around school hours instead of shift work, I don't know.'

It was an old argument, and she wasn't going to get sucked in. 'You tell yourself whatever you want, Tom. We can be civil for Milo's sake, and we can make sure he is still loved and cared for.' She took a deep breath, and met his eyes. 'But you need to stop asking for him to come and live with you. He is getting so confused. You also need to stop sending me shitty text messages. Why are you so mad at me, when it's you who cheated on us?'

'I knew you wouldn't be able to stay civil for long . . . Thank you, Lydia.' He smiled at her as she dumped two mugs of tea on the table.

Lydia scowled back at him, deliberately ignoring his words. 'I'll go into the garden with Milo for bit,' she said, addressing

40

her words exclusively to Holly. Her dark eyes, almost hidden by the weight of her false lashes, were flashing with indignation, but she silently swapped her mules for shiny red stilettos and tottered out of the room.

'Thanks.' Holly waited until the back door banged, and then she turned back to Tom. 'It isn't me who isn't being civilised about this.'

'I don't know what text messages you are referring too, but I don't think any of mine can be classed as shitty,' he told her.

Holly reached over to the table and pulled her phone towards her, her injured ribs tweaking as she did so. She scrolled down and pushed the device towards Tom.

He picked her phone up delicately, as though it was something insanitary. His expression was blank, as he read down the list of vitriol, but when he came to the end his brows drew sharply together, slightly thin mouth pursed. 'I don't know what game you are playing, Holly, but I didn't send these.'

She rolled her eyes. 'They've come from your phone.'

'I can see that, but I didn't send them. This one . . . last week – you don't surely imagine I would say that about you?' Tom's eyes were dead, blank, and his mouth was set in a thin line, daring her to contradict him. 'Are you going completely mad?'

Chapter 6

Actually, Holly did doubt her sanity at this moment in time, but Tom's denials seemed genuine for once. Then again, he had always been good at playing the helpless academic fumbling through life, destined for greatness. He was an excellent speaker and an expert manipulator.

'Who else has access to your phone?'

He shook his head. 'Nice one, Holly, but Beth would never do anything so petty.'

'And I would? How could I possibly send texts to myself from *your* phone? I didn't even finish my first year at uni, remember, Tom.' She couldn't help but let the bitterness seep out and instantly regretted it as he pounced.

He stood up, shaking his head, buttoning his jacket. 'You've lost the plot, Holly. I don't know what's going on but I'm having serious doubts about your state of mind at the moment. First the accident, now these odd accusations. Perhaps you need to see someone? I only came to check Milo was okay after the accident, so I'll go and see him for a bit. You're right, we can email about childcare arrangements.' His square chin was set, like Milo's when he was being stubborn about something. His eyes were contemptuous. 'I'm sure you'll see, in time, why Milo would be better off with me. You'll never keep up with the repayments and pay the bills on your wages. I'll wait and see how long it takes you to dig yourself into a hole, Holly, and then I'll take my son to live with me, where he belongs. You can't offer him anything.'

'I'm his *mum*.' Furious that her voice came out as a hissing whisper, Holly fought back tears.

He was already halfway out the door. 'So? As I said, you nearly killed him in a car crash, and you work all hours so he hardly sees you. Perhaps it isn't just work, maybe you go out with other men too, leaving your son alone in the house. That doesn't sound like a good mother to me.'

'What the fuck? I would never do that. You're the one who was unfaithful, and you're also the reason I have to work over-time.' Her throat was choked with tears now, and the fire of fury was burning in her chest. Trapped, he had her trapped. Well, it wouldn't work. No matter how hard she had to work, or what she had to do, he was never going to have Milo full time. Hopefully Beth would get pregnant soon, and a new baby would take his attention. Holly heard voices in the garden, Milo laughing, the sound of a ball bouncing off the wooden fence.

Tom looked hard at her. 'I don't know what you do when I'm not around, but your past isn't exactly copybook is it?'

'Neither is yours,' she shot back, and then took a step back as his face changed into a mask of icy fury. The switch between his everyday persona and what she thought of as his 'other face' was terrifying. It didn't happen often, but she'd seen plenty of glimpses of the real Tom in the nine years they had been married.

'We agreed that would never be mentioned, didn't we? Trading secrets, I believe it's called. The deal still stands, but I was actually talking about your brother, and your family *history*. That's hardly something you have successfully been able to hide, is it? I really believed you when you said you could change, Holly, and I feel like *you've* cheated on me. You are not the woman you promised you could be.' He held up his hand, palm facing her, as though to stem any retaliation, and his face relaxed. Tom was on familiar ground now, lecturing delinquent students, shaking his head at bad behaviour. 'No, don't say anything, because you'll regret it. Now, I'm going to spend a little time with my son, and then I'll see myself out.'

Lydia passed Tom in the doorway, and whilst still ignoring him, took one look at her niece's tear-stained face and pulled her into a hug. 'What's he said now?'

From the back door, Tom made an impatient noise, and slammed his way outside.

Holly blew her nose. 'Still the same thing. He wants Milo, and he thinks he can get him by proving I'm an unfit mum. He says I'm not the same person he married, but I never lied to him about the family, and I was never ashamed of where I came from. I chose to get out because I wanted to, not because of some stupid snobbery. It's him who doesn't understand. He never did . . .'

'I know, love, and you did the right thing. Your mum wouldn't have wanted you to stay on Seaview, or have anything to do with the business. But Tom was always wrong for you. You should have stayed with the Mancini boy, although I know your dad would have liked to have seen you with a Nicholls. He used to say that with Joey having kids all over the place he was sure you'd find one you liked.' She laughed, harsh and without amusement. 'We all make mistakes, darling, believe me, I know.'

The thought of her mum gave Holly a little snag of pain deep in her heart. In her mind, the hit-and-run driver who had killed her mum was all tied up with Larissa's murder and Jayden's death. Violence was a way of life on the Seaview, and she didn't want that for her son, but Tom had always been wrong about the majority of normal families who lived there.

There was fierce loyalty in the tight-knit community. That was the part she missed. As kids they had roamed all over the estate, accepting the contents of the pockets of drug dealers as easily as they did the bustling older people who fussed over them. The fact that one group offered coloured pills that sent you high, and the other group sugary snacks that made you hyper, was never a problem.

'When I first got together with Tom I thought he was amazing, and now I can only remember his snide comments about kids from the estates.' Holly paused. 'He was surprised I did well enough at school to get into uni. In fact, he reckoned all of us lot – Jay, Devril, Niko and me – were thick just because of where we grew up.'

He aunt watched her with narrowed eyes. 'Holly, love, you have to let it go. I know you were trying to change, to be someone else to escape what happened, but you don't have to change. And you don't need some bloke to chip away at your self-confidence either. We know who we are and where we came from, and there's no shame in that. As for intelligence, I hate to say it but it takes a bit of brain to run a business like your dad did, and Jay was a little genius when it came to computers, wasn't he?'

Holly smiled suddenly, recalling her big brother locked away in one of the derelict flats, hacking into various bank accounts, removing a little here and there and running his own version of his dad's business. 'Yeah, it's just a shame he didn't stop at the tech and stay off the drugs.'

Lydia picked up the empty mugs. 'Tell you what though, Tom was right about one thing. Niko is fucking thick as two short ones!'

Holly grinned back, strength returning. 'Anyway, loads of kids have parents who work shifts. Tom has no idea. He always had this feudal idea of me staying at home and pretending everything was perfect. That's partly why I went to work with Cath, to piss him off. And to top it all off, he says he didn't send those texts, and tried to make out I was going mad.' She followed Lydia into the kitchen. 'I promise to shut up about him in a minute, but how does he always manage to make everything my fault?'

Lydia dumped the mugs next to the sink and started rearranging the cutlery in Holly's dishwasher. Straightening, she glanced through the kitchen window. Watching the boy hop round the garden, her own eyes were bright. 'Think about Milo, love. He's your kid and you should be proud. Tom doesn't have a clue what goes on in real life. He never did.' She turned to face Holly again, hands on hips. 'He likes the cheer squads, the admiration that goes with his job. Obviously he's clever, so he gets it at work, but he needs that at home too. That's why he married you so young, and probably why, now you've grown up, he's gone off with this other girl. How old is Beth?'

'Nineteen.'

'And he's thirty-eight? Well, there you go.'

'I suppose. There's no way he's going to win though. I'm keeping the house, and I'm keeping my son, even if it kills me. You know, he hardly mentioned the crash, the other boy, or the fact that there was someone following me. If there was one person I would suspect of trying to run me off the road, it would be him.'

Her aunt looked her sharply, one hand resting on the granite worktop, the other picking anxiously at a loose thread on her shirt. 'Really? But he was in Portugal and this other boy . . .'

'Oh, I know it wasn't him. Milo would have recognised him when he saw him in the car anyway, and what would he be doing with a spare child? The point is, when I was scared, driving through the dark, thinking I was about to be carjacked or something, I thought it would be him. He really hates me. Whatever he says about the texts, it must be him or Beth. Nobody else would have access to his phone. He used to have a fit if I even answered it for him when we were together.'

Her aunt nodded slowly, biting her lip. 'I did wonder . . . Don't take this the wrong way, love, but all that old trouble with Jayden . . . Niko's out now, and you told me the police saw Devril Mancini at the petrol station. Could this be something to do with your brother?'

Holly blinked, shocked. 'Jesus, Lydia, of course not. That was all finished with ages ago, and I've not had anything to do with that lot for years. And Jayden's . . . Well, he's dead isn't he?'

Lydia looked away, cheeks flaming. 'Yes, of course. I'm just saying, that's all. Let's not talk about it anymore. I just wanted

46

to say . . . But you're right, it will bring back bad memories.' She dashed a hand across her eyes and started rummaging in the cupboard. 'How about cottage pie for dinner, love?'

Holly watched her for a moment, but let it go. Clearly her aunt had more to say on the subject, but she knew from experience not to push it. Why would anyone go after her anyway? The answer sprang up in an instant, and the thought made her gut clench with fear. Because what happened was her fault.

The door banged as Tom marched in from the garden and made his way out of the house. He called a cheerful goodbye to his son, but ignored the two women.

Milo bounced back into the kitchen, swinging along on his crutches, showing Lydia the ripped-open box of Ninjago Lego that was his latest present. With a sudden stab of emotion Holly thought of the other child again, the one who was never far from her thoughts. What kind of a life did he have? Did he play with Lego like Milo, or have furious games with dragons?

Preoccupied, Holly watched her ex-husband stride out into the road, getting carefully into his new Jaguar F-Type. He adjusted the driving mirror, taking his time, smoothing back his hair, clicking his seatbelt into place. The car was just another status symbol, another example of the toys that his reputation had brought him. Lydia was right, he loved the adoration from his students, the praise from academic journals, the spotless and much-talked-about career. She thought of what Tom had said about trading secrets. Well, yes they had, but how long would the trust hold, how long would it be until one of them had nothing to lose by telling the truth?

Shoving the emotions away, Holly picked up her phone. 'Lydia, I'm just going to ring the hospital and see if there's any news on that other boy.'

Lydia appeared in the kitchen doorway, tea towel in her damp hands, her dark eyes bright with interest. 'That's a good idea, love. I hate to think of a kid all alone, and you said he doesn't seem to have any family. Whoever left him was wicked, plain evil.'

Chapter 7

DC Marriot called just after Holly dropped Milo at school. 'Mrs Kendal? It's DC Karen Marriot. Are you at home?'

'What? Sorry, the signal is really bad.' That and the noise of a hundred screaming kids hurtling around a playground. A dozen footballs bounced off the chain-link fence next to her. Holly moved away, dodging through the crowd to a space near the bus stop. 'I'll be home in about fifteen minutes.'

'I can meet you there. I'd rather speak to you face to face about this.'

Her voice was sharp, almost excited. Holly shivered despite her coat and scarf. It had to be something about the boy. Who he was, obviously, and it was clearly interesting or the DC wouldn't be dragging herself out to her house. Perhaps he had woken up. Which would be weird, as when she'd spoken to the nurse last night they said there'd been no change, but he was 'comfortable'. Holly walked faster, almost jogging, until the nagging pain in her injured leg forced her to slow down.

DI Harper hadn't been in touch after that odd conversation at the hospital. It was almost like he was keeping away on purpose, but she supposed he must have other cases he was working on. He had said his colleague was taking the lead on this one, and with so much drama in her personal life she'd been grateful the police had left her alone. Until now.

Arriving home breathless, and worried, she barely had time to tidy the junk in the lounge, and chuck the breakfast dishes into the sink, when the doorbell rang.

DC Marriot was accompanied by her colleague, DS Steph Harlow, and although both women were polite and almost friendly, Holly felt a flicker of nerves.

'Do you want tea?'

DC Harlow smiled reassuringly. She was a pretty, round-faced woman with grey hair tied up in a messy ponytail. 'I'll have one please. Two sugars would be great.'

'No thanks.' DC Marriot was immaculate as usual, her blonde hair gleaming and pinned up in a chignon, her charcoal grey suit jacket and trousers perfectly pressed. But her cool expression betrayed a flash of excitement. 'I'll come straight to the point. The swab we took from the child in hospital shows that there is a genetic link between you. These results only give varying degrees of probability, but in this case there is a *high* degree of probability that you are related to this boy.'

'Fuck me.' It wasn't possible. Holly swallowed hard and switched the kettle off before it had finished boiling. Realising what she had done, she turned it back on and faced the two women, fists clenched. Her stomach was churning, and she found she was breathing fast. 'How could I be *related* to him? I don't have any other kids!' Her mind was spinning and the shock turned her voice into a squeak. So many possibilities hurtling through her brain. Had her parents had another child? A half-brother or sister who in turn had given birth to a boy?

'We obviously know about your brother,' DS Harlow said gently.

'What? But Jayden's *dead*. Oh shit, how old do you think the kid is?' Without waiting for an answer, words tumbling from her mouth, Holly continued, 'Oh my God, what's my aunt going to say? You're saying this is *Jayden's* kid, aren't you?' Quickly she did the maths. What had the doctor said? That he thought the boy was about twelve. That would make him Larissa's child. Her other child. Not the lifeless baby girl the paramedics had found in the flat. *Another* child. But there had been no trace of another kid in the flat . . . There hadn't!

Holly pulled some mugs from the cupboard, hands shaking. One of the handles slid from her grasp and shattered on the tiled floor. 'Shit!' She burst into tears, blood oozing from a cut thumb.

DS Harlow got up, and took the remaining mugs from Holly, gently disentangling her fingers. 'Go and sit down. I'll make the tea. Sorry, Holly, but this is why we wanted to break the news in person. I understand it must be a shock.'

Wiping her eyes, Holly slumped opposite DC Marriot, but she couldn't bring herself to look at her, instead staring at the wooden table. She grabbed a tissue and wrapped it around her injured digit. 'Have you spoken to Lydia? To my dad?' Fucking hell, Donnie would go mental when he found out. Depending on whether he was having a day off the booze, or if he was busy drinking himself insensible. Mind you, he'd taken zero interest in Milo.

Whatever Donnie had been up to in previous years, he no longer played an active part in anything unless it came out of a bottle. It was hard to believe he used to be the kingpin of all the local crime families. In the years before her mum died, Donnie had dipped a toe in most illegal activities you could name: drugs, of course; trafficking; robberies. There had once been a lot of money to burn but now it was gone.

She and Jayden had grown up knowing that other people were scared of their parents. They'd been raised with the Balintas, the Mancinis and later the Nicholls' kids. And that had turned out so well. Holly dropped her head in her hands for a moment, lost in the past. A past she had turned her back on. For a while she had been successful, but now it seemed that everything was slowly unravelling. At the back of her brain the words beat a drum tattoo: 'Another child, another child.' If the police were right, she had a nephew. Milo had a cousin.

She raised her head and looked up at DC Marriot. 'Sorry. Just a bit of a shock. Oh thanks. Um . . . Are you sure about this? I mean, is it possible there's some mistake? My brother is dead. He . . . We had a memorial and everything.' She trailed off. The other woman put a mug of tea in front of her. Holly, seeking mundane comfort, wrapped her hands around the hot mug, inhaling the steam.

DC Marriot was watching her, blue eyes intense, and when she spoke, she seemed to be choosing her words carefully. 'We'll talk to your dad next, and then your aunt. Holly, I'm sorry to have to ask this, but is there any possibility that your brother is still alive?'

Holly blinked hard, seeing his face, seeing Larissa's face. The room seemed to spin, and her hands grasping the mug seemed her only link to reality. Christ, no wonder the child had seemed to have an edge of familiarity. There had been that niggling thought that she did know him, but she hadn't been able to place him. Despite the fact Jayden had been blonde, and even though this kid had been asleep when she saw him, now she knew she realised he was the image of his dad.

They had always been a funny pair, her and her brother – striking, with their totally different looks. She was so dark, with her skin and hair colour a legacy from her mother, and he was so blonde and green-eyed. Donnie had been blonde of course, and when Jayden had been her dad's golden boy, doing as he was told, it had all seemed perfect. Donnie had a son to take over the business, and that was all he cared about. But father and son had been estranged for years by the time Jayden died. Donnie hadn't even bothered to come to the candlelit memorial Lydia had arranged when, seven years after they last saw him, Jayden Hughes was officially declared dead.

The police officers waited patiently, as she got a hold of

herself, pushing through memories. '*You* lot told me he was dead! I saw what they did to Larissa and the baby, so I had no reason to assume otherwise. You said Jay's *blood* was in the room, and his footprints, and then when that dealer said he'd helped get rid of his body . . .' Holly was getting agitated again now, fighting her emotions, trying to stay in control. For the first time in ages, despite the recent dramas, she felt like she needed to fight. The sweet release of tension, the sweat and the pain in her muscles, and the high of victory that beat anything drugs could offer.

DS Harlow passed her a box of tissues, and she grabbed one, wiping away the tears in annoyance. She wasn't generally a crier, but the last few months she seemed to have spent her whole time bursting into tears.

'It's okay to be upset and you don't have to hide it. I'd be in total shock if it was me. This was eleven years ago, wasn't it? Can you talk us through the last time you saw your brother?' DS Harlow said gently. She was taking notes on a pad, chewing the end of her pen, whilst her colleague tapped away on her iPad.

'You must have it all on file. You know all about it, and bloody DI Harper was there!' It came out defensively, but DC Marriot just nodded. 'Holly, I'm not going to lie to you, this is an oddball case. That's why we are trying to get as much background as possible. Naturally DI Harper has provided us with the previous case files, and we know all the officers involved believed Jayden to be dead, even before he was legally declared so. There was never any mention of another child, though. We just think it might help to go over the details from your point of view again, which may in turn tell us why the boy is here.'

'It won't help me,' Holly muttered, scrubbing at her flushed and wet cheeks with another tissue. What the hell was going on?

DC Marriot propped her chin on one hand, studying her iPad, eyes flicking from Holly to her screen. 'There are other options, of course . . .'

'Let's go with the theory that this is Jayden's son, to start off with,' DS Harlow said, with a quick glance at her colleague.

Holly took a deep breath and waited another long moment. She found she was flexing her fingers, feeling a tremor that rippled along her biceps, instinctively clenching her fists. 'I saw Jayden the week before Larissa was killed. He'd cleared off eighteen months previous and we thought that he'd moved right out the area. But he was waiting outside the gym late one night. I'd been teaching a class, and suddenly there he was, just the same as ever, asking for money. He asked for ten thousand pounds to pay off the dealer he owed. He knew I didn't have that kind of money, but he said he was desperate. We'd been there before. I'd lent him money, my mum lent him money before she died, my aunt, everyone . . . I was . . . shocked to see him. Angry too. I thought he'd gone for good, and maybe finally sorted himself out.'

'And your dad? Did he lend him money?'

'No. He did to start with, when he thought Jay was going to be useful in the business. You know, dealing and that, but when Mum died he told Jay to fuck off, quit using the merchandise and sort his life out, so instead Jay worked mainly either dealing for the Balintas or helping out Gareth Nicholls on deliveries. You know, Nicholls Transport?'

'We know it,' DC Marriot said dryly, exchanging a quick, loaded glance with her colleague.

'Joey and Gareth were pretty young when they first came down to the Seaview, and my dad always said they wanted to be the top dogs. They pretended to be happy with a three-way territory split with my dad, and Mason Balinta, but I know they started paying Alexi Mancini to do them favours, give them contacts, right after they arrived,' Holly found she was rambling now, with Dev's cheeky grin all mixed up with the horrors of the trial. But there were happy memories further back. All of them as kids, her and her best mate Cath beating the boys at basketball, and her discovery that she was good at boxing. Bloody good. She was soon competing for the local club, progressing to the NABC Boxing Championships, and it had escalated from there: the agent, the professional photos . . . It was a long time ago now.

'Anyway, I haven't seen my dad properly for years, and he's only met Milo once. This is ancient history and it doesn't change the fact that my brother was officially declared dead. When he died, I didn't know he had one baby, let alone another child. If he survived though, and had a child to take care of, he would have contacted me, or Lydia.' Or would he? Perhaps he knew what she had done, the betrayal of trust, of family ties and everything she had grown up with.

'Go on. Humour me, Holly. The DI wants to help, and he knows we're talking to you about this. He'd be here himself if he didn't have another case running alongside this one.' DC Marriot paused almost imperceptibly. 'If there is a chance your brother is alive and back in the area, added to the fact that Niko and Devril are back in Westbourne, it would be a strange coincidence. As you say, the older generation of your families were once in business together, weren't they?'

Holly ignored her question. What was going on? It would do no good to be chippy and defensive with the police though, not with something this important. She didn't trust them, and years of prejudice didn't vanish overnight. She forced her mind back eleven years, picturing her blonde, skinny brother, with his pointed chin, and hazel-flecked green eyes. His breath had been like white smoke in the wintry darkness outside the gym. She had still been in her kit, sweaty hair pulled back, hoodie thrown over her Lycra top. Her brother's appearance, his pleading for money, had made her furious. 'I told Jayden to fuck off. It was his usual form to beg for money. He would always say he was in danger, and as soon as he was bailed out, he'd get back into debt.'

'He was an addict?'

'For a while, yes, but he refused any help. Once, we got him into the rehab place in Panfield, but he walked out after a couple of days.' Holly was drifting through her thoughts. They stabbed sharply, needles in her heart, and the helpless frustration she had felt then was bubbling back up in her belly. 'Like I said, when he vanished the first time, it was almost a relief. We were worried, of course, that he might have got into worse trouble, or wound up dead. But we knew Mason and his heavies hadn't found him, because we had the whole Balinta family on our backs wanting money to settle debts Jayden had run up when he was meant to be dealing for them. Lydia didn't tell me at the time, but Jayden sent her an occasional text to say he was safe. And my dad, well, he gave out that he didn't give a shit but I reckon he was glad Jayden had gone, so he didn't embarrass him anymore. It was tough for us all after Mum died. I was thirteen when she was killed, and Jay was fifteen. It was the worst thing ever, and Jayden never got over it. I thought he'd OD or something, it was that bad for a while. He couldn't think of anything except his next hit.'

'And Jayden had been in a relationship with Cathryn Davies?' DS Harlow queried.

'Yeah. He had the twins with Cath: Ronnie and Sean. I'd hoped being a dad would have straightened Jayden out. But they were too young, and they were never going to last as a couple, even though Cath was sure they could make a go of it. She was in bits when he started ghosting her, and then when he just left without another word it nearly destroyed her. That was another reason I was glad when Jayden didn't come back. He trashed everything, caused all this shit, left debts and stressed everyone. It was better that he wasn't around.'

'According to your original statement, this time when you refused to give him the cash, he then stole money from your aunt.'

Holly nodded. 'After he met me and I said no, he tried Lydia. He went round to visit her, and managed to get on and off the Seaview without anyone spotting him. Bloody luck of the devil he always had, my dad said. Anyway, Lydia said she could only give him part of the money, but he took her card and emptied her bank account.'

'And when did you next hear from him?' DS Harlow took a sip of tea, making quick notes on a pad whilst Holly talked.

'A week later. He rang me and said he was really sorry he took Lydia's money, but he still needed an extra twelve hundred to clear the debt. Lydia always forgave him, but she told me this time he had taken everything from her savings account. She'd worked her backside off for a lifetime and he had stolen it all. And then he had the nerve to ask me for more money.' Holly knew what was coming and she needed to be careful. The anger was still threading through her voice, even after all these years and everything that had happened since.

'You were a boxer, weren't you? DI Harper said you were really good.'

Holly glanced up from her tea, surprised. She supposed it just reinforced her impression that DI Harper had always been obsessed with her family. 'Yeah, I loved it. I was modelling quite a lot by then too, because I'd won a lot of competitions. The last one was at the National Championships.' She smiled, oddly nostalgic, wistful even. 'My life was crazy good, and I had an agent and everything. She got me a sports magazine cover and it just went from there.'

'It must have been tough to give all that up,' DC Marriot said gently.

'Yeah. When I look back, I think it started to go wrong again when Jay came back. You know, I felt like here was my brother, dragging me down again. That sounds really bad, doesn't it? He was . . . he was crying down the phone. Anyway, he told me to take the extra money in cash to an address . . .' She paused, keeping her face a careful mask of concentration, as if she was just trying to remember what had happened. 'Jayden told me to meet him at the address at eleven that night with the extra money. He said it had to be cash because it needed to be untraceable.'

'Why did you agree to give him the money when you knew he had just stolen from your aunt?' DS Harlow's voice was colourless, but her chin was still proper on her elbow, eyes raking Holly's face.

Holly met her gaze. 'He promised that if I gave him the money he would just go this time, really go right away. I asked where he'd been, what the hell he'd been doing and all that, but he just ignored the questions and went on about how this was going to save his life. He *never* at any point mentioned a girlfriend or any kids.' She felt it was important to hammer this home.

'But why did you believe him this time? You've just told me he was a habitual offender, and a liar.' DC Marriot was flicking through notes on her screen. 'Was there a particular reason, something he said that made you believe he had changed?' She pushed back a stray wisp of hair. As she leant forward Holly could smell her perfume. It was unexpected, light and floral and didn't seem to suit her icy persona.

'I don't *know*. I suppose I didn't really believe him, but I had sorted my own life and just wanted him to go away again. I just assumed he was back on drugs. When we were talking, I even had ideas about making him take me to his dealer and giving them the money myself, sorting it all out . . . How stupid is that? I was furious, and . . . I don't know what I was thinking. Probably the same as all the other times – but also what if this time it was true and he really *was* in danger?' She said this carefully, remembering almost too late she needed to be cautious, not honest. It hadn't been that at all. She had been so angry, so furious with him for invading their lives again, for taking Lydia's money that pity had been the last thing on her mind.

'You never thought of calling the police?' DS Harlow asked doubtfully. She was tapping the pen against her teeth, eyes narrowing as they rested on Holly's face. Her round cheeks were stained red in the warm kitchen, and time and lifestyle had scored harsh lines around her eyes and mouth.

'Of course not. Look, DS Harlow . . .'

'Make it Steph,' the other woman said helpfully. She made a few more quiet notes, watching the other two women.

DC Marriot continued, 'We know how the estate worked, and how it works now, and yes we're on first-name terms with most of the Nicholls family. Not to mention Mason Balinta.'

Holly flashed her a sharp glance, but she smiled. 'I'm being honest with you. We know we aren't welcome on Seaview and never have been, but that doesn't mean we have to let people like the Nicholls family run wild. Returning to that night – you eventually went to meet Jayden to give him the money?'

'Yes. I was half an hour early. The bus stop was right next to the estate he was living on. It was so close, only in Panfield, that I felt like he had been laughing at us all along. Christ, we'd all looked for him, and he'd been holed up in that rabbit warren only a stone's throw from us. I found the right block of flats, and went up to the eighth floor. The door to 101 was open, just a bit . . .'

She was lost in the past, walking through that door into the hell that lay beyond. Her heart sped up, and she clung to the side of the chair, hearing her own voice from miles away . . .

She was used to replaying these memories. But this time there was a difference. She couldn't stop thinking about the boy. Why had nobody picked up that there had been another kid? There had only been one cot in the flat, surely.

'Jayden?' She stepped nervously through the door, glancing from left to right, phone out in one hand, the cash safely stashed in her pocket. She'd been freaked walking around here with a wad of banknotes, but she'd made it.

The sour smell hit the back of her throat, and she fumbled for a light switch in the narrow hallway, hand shaking. The flat was tiny, just a big room with a kitchen area at one end. Two mattresses were laid next to each other on the threadbare carpet, and sprawled across both, on her front, arms outstretched, was a woman.

The blood was soaking into the carpet, splashed across the wall in a horror-film arc, and smeared on the side of the kitchen units.

The place was torn apart, with paper, magazines, clothes and toys strewn around the body.

'Jayden?' It was a whisper. There were two doorways leading off the main room, and Holly instinctively stepped back towards the front door, looking over her shoulder, terrified that the attacker was still here, waiting, watching her. But her voice echoed around the flat, and after a while she plucked up the courage to walk towards the second doorway. A tiny bathroom, and beyond, a small bedroom with peeling wallpaper. In the corner stood a cot piled high with blankets. Jayden had a baby? A girlfriend?

The place was empty now. Whoever had done this had gone, and she could hardly leave without doing anything. Shoving away the thought of an intruder jumping her from behind, she knelt next to the woman. Her first thought was that she was dead, but her skin was warm. She had no obvious wounds, which was puzzling given the amount of blood in the flat. Her dark hair spread across the floor and her head, turned sideways, showed her eyes were shut. Around her neck, also caught in the material, she wore a gold-coloured necklace, letters twisted around a chain, which formed the name Larissa.

There was no sign of breathing, and in the silence of the flat Holly could hear nothing but her own gasping breath, feel nothing but terror in her own drumming heartbeat. She fumbled to press the right buttons on her phone.

Chapter 8

'Do you want a glass of water?'

She could hear someone running a tap, an arm around her shoulders, but she was still miles away, years away, crouched alone in the flat with a dead woman. It wasn't until the emergency services arrived that the other body had been discovered. A three-month-old baby girl had been suffocated where she lay, and hidden under the pile of blankets. At last she sat up, blinking away tears. 'Sorry. I tried not to think about it and I've managed to shut it all away. But now . . .'

'It's all right, you're doing well. I'm sorry to have to ask and upset you, but this could be really important.' DC Marriot leant across the kitchen table again. 'Can you manage to finish for us, do you think?'

Holly took a gulp of water and nodded. The shame flooded her, as she had known it would. But she had admitted all this in court, there was no point in denying it now. 'The ambulance call handler told me to start CPR, and I . . . I told her I was doing compressions, but I wasn't. I just froze, and I couldn't bring myself to press down on her chest. I just stared at her all that time . . .'

'I read the coroner's report, Holly, and you must know what it said. Larissa died of strangulation. Going by the estimated time of death, by the time you arrived there was probably nothing anyone could have done. She was dead already,' DS Harlow told her.

'I know . . .' But there might have been a chance, a chance she could have saved her, and nothing anybody said – then or now – could convince her otherwise. Holly bit her lip, and continued slowly, 'I was terrified they would find Jayden outside somewhere, dead too, but later the police said he was a suspect. There was so much blood, I was sure it had to be at least partly his. There was never anything mentioned about another child, though. There wasn't!'

'No, we reviewed the files, and it appears that Larissa was never officially registered at any doctor's surgery or hospital, and her child, or children, weren't either. In fact, legally her baby didn't exist. I've double-checked, and it looks like – if I had to hypothesise – perhaps if they had another child, they slept on the sofa-bed? It does seem odd that there was no evidence at all of a boy.'

'They would have been so near in age that perhaps any baby clothes, supplies and toys would have been assumed to be the dead girl's.' DS Harlow shrugged. 'If this boy was living there with his parents and sister there was nothing obvious to suggest his existence. In fact, the few possessions they owned were already packed up, as though a move was imminent.'

The other woman nodded. 'It was assumed that once he had the money, your brother and his family were going to run. But after Larissa's murder, Jayden never got back in contact at all? Not even to collect the money you were bringing him?' DC Marriot was tapping the table idly with one hand now. Her fingernails were short and colourless.

'No. The money he took from Lydia wasn't in the flat, and his bank account hadn't been used for months.' Holly looked directly at both police officers. Her voice flat, she said, 'The investigation was pure hell for my family, with police interviews and then dealers from the Seaview being arrested. The other families blamed us for bringing police onto the estate; my dad had a fight with DI Harper . . .'

There was a glimmer of amusement, quickly hidden, in DC Marriot's glacial eyes, and even Holly, torn between emotions and fighting hysteria, felt her lips quirk.

Steph continued, 'But the evidence showed the blood in the flat belonged to Alexi and Roman Balinta, the men who eventually confessed to killing Larissa and her baby girl. There was no sign that Jayden had harmed either his baby or his girlfriend. Yet both men denied seeing your brother. It was Larissa who attacked both men with a knife, obviously defending her children.'

Holly nodded, fiddling with her phone. 'Yes. I still remember how in court they said Larissa fought back.' Her voice shook precariously but she carried on, 'But Jayden was gone again, and then just before Christmas, the police came round to say that some random dealer, a real small-time player, had confessed to helping get rid of Jayden's body. He said he dumped it off Rydden Bay soon after Larissa was murdered, and that he did it on Roman's instructions.'

Holly choked a bit. 'As you know, his body has never been found, and Roman wouldn't say anything at all about the dealer's claim. As far as I remember he just kept saying no comment. I suppose I almost hoped Jay was dead by then. The waiting for the court case and seeing Lydia and my dad struggling to get by . . . It was all in the papers about Jayden's past, and our family got dragged through the dirt. They made it sound like we were pure evil. It was a really shit time, but we just about got through it.'

'Larissa was one of the girls trafficked by Joey and Gareth Nicholls, wasn't she? I saw on the files that Gareth was charged with several offences, but he only served three years because of a technicality. There's been nothing on him since.'

Again, that change of tone when the Nicholls brothers were mentioned. Nicholls Transport were still doing their thing, all these years later, and the police still couldn't touch them. 'Yes. It came out that Larissa originally thought she was engaged to some bloke up in Yorkshire – that's where she came from – but she was only fourteen, and he turned out to be part of a scheme to round up girls arranged by Joey. Larissa's mum was a junkie and Larissa had been skipping school, hanging around the town. I suppose she was an easy target, and when you lot looked for her, she'd just vanished. She apparently told her mum she was moving away with her fiancé.'

'They call it the "lover boy" sting, or the "Romeo game",' Steph volunteered. 'These men find vulnerable girls, sadly often those who have fallen through cracks in the care system, and present themselves as romantic interests. Once the girl is hooked, they slowly draw her away from any friends or family, and then when she runs off to "get married" it comes out that girl is a frequent runaway, skips school, maybe has a history of petty crime already . . . In reality of course she is then sucked into a system of abuse and is exceptionally difficult, if not impossible, to trace. We do our best, and naturally missing children are a priority, but I've worked on cases where a teenager has been missing for weeks before anyone starts to take notice.'

'I never could understand why Jayden didn't mention Larissa and the baby when he asked for money,' Holly said. 'We never even found out how they originally met, but I suppose it might have been when he was dealing. The boys used to deliver to the clients at these special houses, and then eye up the girls who were working there. But if Jay had fallen for Larissa so much that they'd not just had a baby, but had two children, why didn't he tell me?'

'Your brother knew you were friends with Cathryn Davies, so perhaps he thought you might be angry he had left her, and his other children, for Larissa,' DC Marriot suggested. In her mind's eye Holly could see the boy, Jayden's boy, lying helpless and unconscious under his white shroud of hospital sheets. *Another child.*

'Yeah, maybe. Roman and Alexi were high, weren't they, when they went to collect Jay's debt? Mason was always bigging up his sons, even Niko, the baby of the family, saying they were going to inherit the business, going to be millionaires . . . But they were always losers, and violent with it. They didn't have to kill Larissa, or her baby.' Holly felt empty now, hollow and sick. She still had nightmares about the baby, even though she hadn't discovered the tiny body.

'Supposing the boy in hospital is Jayden's . . . He would have been around a year old when his mother was murdered, so perhaps your brother took him to safety? We aren't saying your brother is definitely alive, but I would say it's a possibility. The other possibility, of course, is that Jayden did escape that night, with his other child, but was later murdered, and the child has been raised by someone else.'

'If he is alive . . . Fuck, I can't even think . . .' Holly shook her head, scraping back her hair with all ten fingertips. 'I just can't imagine it, but my dad is going to go mental when you tell him it's a *possibility*.'

The two women stood up to go, and DC Marriot turned back at the front door. 'Holly, be careful, won't you? This isn't just about the boy, and his possible identity. We also have to consider who left him in your car.'

Holly sighed. 'I'm hardly going to forget, am I? But yeah, thanks, I'll take care.'

***

Holly watched the two policewomen get into their car and head off to her dad's flat. He still lived next to the betting shop, but one of her cousins ran the bookies business now. Most of the time her dad was too pissed to remember his own name, so good luck them getting anything coherent out of him. They'd probably get the wheels nicked off their car too, just for going onto the Seaview.

What a mess. Her head was buzzing, and she wandered around the house picking things up and putting them down. Jayden's son? If he was alive why had he never been in touch? Larissa had had another child – given the timeframe, it fitted. Either that or they were wrong about the age of the boy in hospital and Jayden had survived, and got over Larissa pretty quick. Perhaps they were right with the second theory. Maybe her brother had given his baby son to someone he trusted to look after him, but then got himself in trouble with the wrong people. Again.

Chapter 9

Holly reached for her phone. 'Cathryn?'

Her best friend answered on the second ring, her voice quick and sharp. 'Where the *hell* have you been, girly? I've left four messages on your voicemail since you came out of hospital, and I've only had *one* text and *one* phone call. What's going on, Holly? I've been so bloody worried about you.'

'Sorry. It's been weird. Look, can I come over?'

'Of course. I'm just putting Angel down for a nap. I'll open a bottle.'

'It's twelve o'clock,' Holly said, her heart lightening, despite herself.

Cath was always there for her, always ready to help despite being a single mum with five kids. She was the type of girl who only ever wanted to have fun, and had slowly morphed into the type of woman who inspires awe in her friends by juggling kids and work on her own, whilst being blatantly honest about how tough it could be. Her huge clan of aunts, uncles and cousins all helped out with the childcare, but the kids' dads had all buggered off. The fact that two of the dads were Niko and Jayden hadn't altered the friendship. Holly's best friend, Lydia often said with a smile, was a force of nature.

'Whatever, I've had a bitch of a week, babes. We'll walk to school to get the brats later, then I can take the twins in the buggy and they won't screech so much.'

Holly grabbed her coat, pulling the fake fur hood snugly around her face, and set off for the Seaview. Her road of respectable Victorian semis ran down to the railway bridge. After that the houses became blocks of flats, with smaller buildings squeezed together, dwarfed by the grim tower blocks.

The light drizzle was whipped across Holly's face by an icy lash of wind. She crossed the road, head down, and took the footpath that led to Cathryn's house. High wooden fences either side killed the wind, but the path was dank, and gloomy, the mud strewn with cigarette butts, rubbish and empty bottles.

Stepping over an odd assortment of rotting furniture, which included a sofa and the remains of a double bed, Holly allowed her mind to drift again. Every step was familiar from here onwards. She and Jayden had played football in that road, had smoked in that playground, spinning slowly on the creaking swings, feet scuffing the gravel. Niko had tried his luck with Cathryn behind those green-encrusted concrete garages. Roman, Alexi and Devril had played basketball next to that tower block, and Cath's mum owned the chippie in the next road. She would give the kids greasy paper bags of salty chips drenched in vinegar and only charge them half the usual price. The usual mix of emotions when she came back to the Seaview made her stomach roll uneasily. There was sadness, nostalgia, a touch of fear that she didn't quite belong anywhere now.

A car screeched past, jammed with teenagers, the radio blaring, and there was a gang of five kids playing football on the scrubby grass that bordered the Seaview, on the edge of Beach Road. Their yells echoed across the wasteland, bouncing off the concrete walls of the tower blocks.

Cathryn's house, part of a block of grimy terrace houses, was strewn with the chaos of five children, and Holly, as usual, felt instantly at home. The rooms smelt of polish, perfume and babies, and there were piles of clean washing on the table, contrasting with the piles of dirty washing on the kitchen floor. Make-up covered the tiny worktop, and Cathryn's uniform was hung up to dry over the sink.

Relaxing, she sank down with a sandwich and a glass on the crumb-encrusted sofa, narrowly avoiding a dozen plastic Lego bricks.

'Right, babes, what the fuck is going on?' Cathryn sat opposite her, baby monitor wedged between two cushions, wine bottle on the table between them. Her long platinum-blonde hair was tied up in a knot, her pretty face was bare of make-up, and she wore her usual ripped skinny jeans and cropped pink velour hoodie top, which showed off her flat, improbably tanned stomach.

Holly took a deep breath. 'The police came over to mine after I dropped Milo at school this morning. They said they got the DNA results back from the lab, and the boy in hospital is related to me. Cath, they reckon he's Jayden's kid.'

Cath stared with her mouth open, baby blue eyes wide and shocked. 'But Jay's dead, so how . . .' She stopped talking, leant over, and sloshed white wine into both their glasses. 'The fucking bastard. Do you really think he's just been living somewhere else all this time?'

'I don't know. They don't know either. Going by the age of the boy they reckon he's Larissa's kid, unless Jayden had someone else on the go. Suppose Jayden is alive, I don't understand why that dealer would have lied and said he helped get rid of the body?'

'Dunno, but if I find out he's still alive . . .' Cath took a long, shuddering breath, 'Why would he not contact us? Me and the kids, Lydia, your dad and you? Even just to say he was on the run or whatever? I've had to tell Sean and Ronnie that their dad's dead and now what do I do?'

'Nothing,' Holly told her quickly. 'We can't do anything because we don't know if he *is* alive.'

'You said before that the police went on about Niko and Devril?' Cath was frowning. She lifted her glass to her mouth but put it down again without drinking, and sloshed wine all over her fingers. 'I can't believe this.'

'Yeah, me either. Do you think there's something going on? Niko's out, Devril is hanging around again, and then Jayden shows up with his kid?'

'I really don't know, but if they're planning some kind of business takeover they can forget it. The Nicholls have everything sewn up round here, and nobody asks any questions. Rohan, you know he's one of Joey's sons, and he is *fit*, well he came over a few months ago asking about Niko. I think they were checking him out, because it was before he got released.'

'Why would they do that?'

'To see if he was worth talking to? I dunno. I told you, Niko had always said he had some money stashed. When we were together he used to go on about it and how we could move house and all that. Am I a mug or what?'

'You're not, even if I really can't see how you could have sex with Niko, let alone have a kid with him,' Holly told her. 'Not that I can talk, but your taste in men is terrible!'

Cath flicked her a V-sign, and continued, 'And the Mancinis are doing a lot of the driving and a lot of the dealing now, so they're well happy being part of the Nicholls' operation. Mason's about to croak, your dad won't give a shit who's doing what . . . I dunno. My family just do their thing no matter who's in charge, whether it's legal or not, as long as they get paid.' She thought for a moment. 'Except my mum, but she's got the chippie, hasn't she? Anyway, Dev would never hurt you, Holly, whatever's going on. Did you know he's a journo now though? Freelance and does a bit for all the red tops. Lots of dramz and uncovering juicy stories.'

'No! Since when? I knew he was a writer but I never thought of journalist.' A journalist – Devril had chosen a profession that they had all hated ever since Larissa's death. It was almost as bad as joining the police. Holly bit her lip, swallowing hard. Her experience of journalists, from Jay's trial to the present interest surrounding Jay's son, wasn't good. They were tricky bastards, and they wrote whatever they wanted, no matter what you said. 'You never said!'

'You never asked. Actually it was only the day before you had the car accident that I found out, so there hasn't exactly been a good moment to tell you. I heard a bit of gossip, and I'm a nosy cow, aren't I? Hell, you know what this place is like, but I googled him and for once the old bags are right. The word is he's come back to get a story on Niko's release, but I'm sure that's a load of crap. Niko's hardly the most interesting crim, is he? But Jayden, fuck me, my mind is totally blown . . .' Cath shook her head, blue eyes suspiciously bright as she chattered away. 'We need to change the subject for a bit, so I can get my head around this. Talk to me, Holly. How's Tom behaving? Any more bitchy texts? I bet he's absolutely loving all this drama. It proves he was right all along about your dodgy past.'

Holly was still thinking about Devril's career change. It wasn't mentioned on his social media pages. She had supposed he must be a copywriter or something. It had never crossed her mind he would be a reporter. *Had* he been following her? What story could he hope to get out of her? 'Tom's still an arsehole. He also thinks the accident proves I'm an unfit mother and he accused me of sleeping around. Actually, since I asked him about the texts they've stopped coming. He told me I was going crazy and I must have sent them to myself.'

Cath rolled her eyes, seizing her sandwich and taking a huge bite, as Holly continued, 'He popped round with another massive gift for Milo, and pissed off back to his fancy lecture tour. Total bastard. What about Liam?' Cath's most recent ex had left her with another child and more heartbreak.

Her friend swallowed hard and ran a long bubble-gum-pink nail across her lips before she answered. 'Total bastard. Hasn't paid

69

any child support for the last three months now, and he's shacked up with some other girl in Panfield. It's like history repeating itself. They can all fuck off, the whole lot of them!' Suddenly she was crying and laughing at the same time, tears streaming down her cheeks, and spluttering crumbs and spit. 'Oh fuck, Holly, what are we going to do? I'm not sure I can handle this. Jay's been dead for a long time now, and I'm not sure I want to deal with all that stuff again. And what are you going to do about his kid? I really, really want to feel like I've moved on, but we never can, can we, if this is true?'

Holly moved across to sit next to her best friend and wrapped her arms around her skinny body. 'I know, I don't think I can take any more either, not with the divorce and everything. Hey, did you get a new necklace? That's cute.'

Cath rested her head on her friend's shoulder, her voice muffled as she spoke into Holly's navy jumper. 'Got it on sale. We should be glad if Jay's not dead. If only he could see us now, he'd be gutted we're not dancing on the table and opening another bottle of Prosecco.'

'Depends why he's back. Depends why they're all back, doesn't it really?' Holly murmured, half to herself. They clung together for a moment, before the baby monitor flickered and emitted a high-pitched wail.

When the babies were settled comfortably on Holly and Cath's laps with their bottles, Cath continued, 'Remember when you and Dev used to go to the gym together? Niko never believed you were actually training, until you started competing.'

Holly smiled, shifting the baby to her other arm, revelling in the warm scents of baby skin and hair. It was a sharp reminder of the child Larissa had lost. She would have held her like this, comforted her when she cried . . . and the boy too. 'Niko was too lazy to imagine anyone going to the gym to work out. He just used to pose with weights at Shoey's because he couldn't actually lift them.'

Cath giggled. 'Looked all right though. And he had a good body considering he didn't do anything.'

Holly scrunched up her nose. It was weird, having a perfectly normal conversation, whilst there were all these electric undercurrents floating beneath their banal words. She and Dev had been part of the gang, but as the kids started to pair off in their teens, it was always Cath and Jay, and her and Dev.

It was funny she and Cath had stayed friends. Tom hated Cath, and the feeling was mutual. When Holly got pregnant, her best friend had sat her down and told her exactly what she thought of Tom, and suggested Holly move in with Lydia and raise Milo on her own.

Cath was watching her, straightening her baby's clothes with gentle fingers. 'You two always wanted to get out of the Seaview, didn't you?'

'I suppose.'

'You did. Dev would always talk about getting away from his uncle and setting up on his own, and you were super clever at school. You wanted to be a vet once, do you remember?'

'Yeah,' Holly sighed. After she walked out the evening after the trial, she'd gone to stay with a friend in town. She had been a savvy teen, and it hadn't taken long to sort out accommodation, to set herself up away from her past. The fact that she'd got good grades seemed to be a sign, and she drifted along, reinventing herself. At nineteen, studying English Literature had seemed like a good idea, but then so did dating Tom, her tutor. 'I think I thought I'd go into teaching after my degree.'

'You would've hated it,' Cath told her.

'How do you know?'

'Same way I knew we should work together.' Her best friend grinned. She glanced at the clock, 'Look, Holly, I know you're freaked by this whole Jayden thing, hell I am too, but I think you need to be careful. Someone put Jay's kid in your car for a reason. You need to watch out, okay?'

The fun faded from the room.

Cath started to put the twins into their pushchair, pushing her hair off her face, and straightening to face Holly. 'People are saying there's going to be some kind of trouble between the Balintas and the Nicholls now Niko's out. Something's going to go down, hon, and we are stuck right in the middle of that lot. Besides, why else would Jayden come home after all these years?'

'You really think he's alive?' Holly still couldn't quite make the leap from lighting candles at her brother's memorial, to him returning to Westbourne.

'Honestly? I was so shocked when you told me I couldn't even think straight, but now . . . I think I do, yeah.'

72

Chapter 10

Dear Mum,

I'm having a shit day and I wish you were here so bad that I can almost taste it. Sometimes I kneel in front of your wall and screw my eyes tight shut. Dad says if I stay like that and count to one hundred you might reach out to me. If he's had a bad day he makes us both kneel and times us. We have to sit still for an hour and he gets mad if I move and says I'm ruining it.

I don't really know what he means. He says he can feel you though. If I'm honest, I can't feel you at the moment.

We've moved around a lot since you died, and of course I don't remember a lot of the places we've been, but we've been in this flat for six months now. It's another different school and they take the piss all the time and say I'm weird because my accent is different to theirs. Whatever. I'm not like Alice Cauldon who says she wants to be a pole dancer and lets the boys look at her pink bra, and I'm not smelly like Ben Alder or stupid like Alex Smith. I'm just me. But they don't like that, Mum. Sometimes I don't think Dad likes me either, even though I've taught myself to cook and work the washing machine. When he gets hammered, I try and make sure he passes out on the sofa or in his bed.

I look in the mirror and try to figure out why I'm different and

73

why my life is different. But I just see a normal kid with messy hair and a few freckles. A kid who's got his mum's black eyes, and his dad's pointed chin. He's not fat or thin. He's not small or tall. He's just normal on the outside. But they still don't like me. It's Kyle Wilson who's the worst. Today he said I was a loser and a freak because I don't have a mum. How does he know that? It worried me a bit because part of the plan is that people don't know much about us, about where we come from or where we are going.

Today when I went back to the shooting range with Dad, I imagined Kyle's face on the target, with his big white teeth and square face, and I got my highest score ever. Dad was really happy because he says it all counts towards the plan. Every single thing we do is training. When Dad's not been drinking he can be fun.

But it hurts when people say stuff. Dad says to man up and to be strong or we'll never be able to make you proud. But it's hard at the moment and I feel like crying. It hurts inside and I can feel the pain tingling in my fingers. I'm cold too. The flat has mould growing up the walls and the heaters only run if you shove coins in them. If I don't remember to ask Dad for coins before he starts on the cans then it stays cold.

Don't worry, Mum, I won't cry, because boys don't cry. I know he's a liar though because I've seen him crying for you. I won't tell him because it might make him crazy and he's been kind of okay for a few weeks now. Thanks for making him okay for a bit, and if you could keep him away from the beer that would be great.

I love you, Mum x

Chapter 11

After she had dropped Milo at school the next day, Holly dealt with the usual housework and washing, ironing her uniform ready for work. It was weird to be doing mundane things when her life seemed to have gone mental. Part of her wanted to rush back down to the hospital and check on Jayden's son, but his condition hadn't changed. And what if whoever dumped him in the car was watching the hospital? Were they waiting for her next move? The protective feelings she had tried to push away since she found him huddled in her car were obviously stronger since the revelation that they were related, but fear of the whole situation was underlying her stray maternal instincts, plus she had Milo to look out for.

Cath's warning rang in her ears, and she almost felt she had to look over her shoulder the whole time in case she was being followed. Gut instinct still told her that her brother was dead, but if Jay had left his son with someone else, and that person had brought him back to Westbourne . . . what next?

Holly shoved another load of washing into the machine and yanked her thoughts away from the puzzle. At least Milo was loving being back at school, and his whole class seemed to have signed his cast. Tom seemed to be complying with her suggestion of email communication and hadn't sent any more text messages. Maybe it would all be okay.

Her phone rang as she finally sat slouched with her cup of coffee at the kitchen table, enjoying the weak sunlight that flooded the kitchen. DC Marriot was not an especially welcome caller.

'Holly? I just wondered if you had seen the news?'

'No. Sorry, what?' Her heart was pounding, and she was clutching her cup so hard her knuckles were white.

'There was a fight at Yorke Prison early this morning, and two prisoners were stabbed to death.' Her voice was cool as ever, but clearly there was more. 'The two prisoners who died were Alexi and Roman Balinta.'

'Fuck me. I mean . . . How could that even happen?' Hot coffee splashed over her fingers and she swore again.

'We're trying to find out. Are you at home?'

'Yeah.'

'I probably should come round if you don't mind. I have something to show you.'

Oh double shit, this didn't sound good. Holly made another coffee whilst she waited. She didn't need more caffeine; her nerves were jangling as it was and she had the beginnings of a thumping headache. Alexi and Roman were *dead*? Well, she couldn't pretend she felt sad that someone had killed the murdering bastards, but how could that happen while they were in prison? And both of them together? She thought she could guess what DC Marriot was going to say, and it would be along the *'why the hell is all this happening now?'* line.

Holly stood watching the street until the car arrived. She tried to figure out how she felt, and what the fuck was going on. She checked her Twitter feed and found a news item on what was described as a double stabbing. The brothers were thought to have become involved in an argument over drugs. Thoughts jarred in her brain, and the rumble and crash of the bins being emptied

76

outside made her jump. *Why would someone bring Jay's son back into the middle of this?*

DC Marriot was immaculate in navy pinstripe and a long dark coat. She marched up to the front door, accompanied by a uniformed officer.

The DC got straight down to business. 'We're still working on the details, and obviously the prison service are being fully cooperative, but basically Alexi got into an argument with another prisoner as he was coming back to his cell from the library.' The DC was uptight today, her petite pixie-like face alert, and her eyes bright as she reeled off the facts.

'The library?' Holly queried. She didn't remember Alexi reading anything more that the back of a ciggie packet.

'Yes. The argument happened to take place at a time when his brother, Roman, was coming in from the yard. He saw Alexi being attacked, went to help, and the prisoner responsible stabbed them both.' The uniformed officer looked up from his notes. His expression was sombre.

'Bloody hell. How did that even happen? I mean, where were the guards or whatever?' Holly glanced at the uniformed officer, but he was sitting quietly now, still taking notes on the conversation. 'Actually, I do remember when one of Cath's cousins was in prison they sent him stuff by drone. But it wasn't knives, it was just pills and a phone.'

DC Marriot sighed. 'It is possible to get a knife in, or make one, and yes, drones are commonly used. The prison officers do a great job, but they can't cover everything. They are convinced, as are we, that this wasn't a random attack. It was carefully planned to take out both men.'

'What about the prisoner who killed them?' For a tiny, crazy moment Holly almost expected her to say Jayden had turned up inside the prison and done it himself to get revenge for Larissa and the baby. This was nightmare stuff. He couldn't be alive . . .

'He was a long-term resident, as they all were in that block, and he was recently diagnosed with cancer. Unfortunately the cancer is untreatable and he has just months to live. He doesn't seem to have had a particular reason to take out the Balinta brothers, but we're working on that. According to him, Alexi was disrespecting him, they had a row, and he pulled the knife to defend himself. Naturally we are looking at Larissa's case amongst the other offences that all three men were originally charged with.'

Holly found she couldn't speak. It was too freaky for words. Could the Nicholls somehow be responsible? Cath mentioned they were asking about Niko. Perhaps they had threatened him, blackmailed him with a hit on his brothers? She shared her thoughts with the two officers, and they nodded, clearly accepting the possibility.

'But look at this. A piece of paper was found in the pocket of Alexi's trousers.' DC Marriot pushed her phone over to Holly.

Holly stared at the photograph on the screen. A piece of lined paper, slightly bloodstained, maybe torn from a notebook:

'FOR LARISSA'

'So, what, someone – this prisoner who killed them I guess – put this in his pocket? Someone took out Larissa's killers for revenge, or at least wanted it to look that way?'

'Possibly.'

Holly was thinking hard. Alexi had always been a bully, and from the age of ten he'd beaten up all the little kids on the Seaview. Roman was slower to be drawn into a fight, slightly less evil-tempered than his brother, but willing to do anything Alexi said. They had loads of enemies, from every stage of their lives. Even before they killed Larissa and her baby daughter, there would have been a list of people willing to take them out of play. Plus, of course, with them gone, the Balinta family was reduced to just Niko and his dad . . . .

'It is a possibility that this is not related to anything that has been happening recently, but I don't believe in coincidence.' DC Marriot was sipping her takeaway coffee now, eyes narrowed, clearly thinking hard, echoing Holly's thoughts. 'We are still very interested in the current dynamics on the Seaview, especially how this will affect certain business deals. But I can't ignore the fact that all the key players have links to Larissa. Added to this fact, we have the obvious extra information that Devril Mancini has been seen in Westbourne, Niko Balinta is out of prison, and your brother . . .'

'You really think my brother is alive and has come back with Niko and Devril?' Holly considered this, heart pounding, and swallowed hard, trying to force herself out of the nightmare.

The DC shrugged. 'Again, we honestly don't know at the moment. It could be that the perpetrator is leading us towards that conclusion, but the reality is something totally different. Obviously, we will be talking to Niko, and trying to track down Devril Mancini, to see if either of them knows anything. Some of my colleagues are with Mason Balinta.'

'They drew the short straw then? Sorry, this isn't funny. I just can't believe it. Are you going to question my aunt again? She's going crazy wondering if we buried Jayden, metaphorically of course, or if he's suddenly going to ring the doorbell one night.'

'At this stage, we're just trying to establish if there *is* a link between the incidents. If you can think of anything that might help us, or Niko or Devril, make contact, just ring me.'

'Yeah, I will.' But she couldn't even begin to think where Devril might be hiding. Both Westbourne and Panfield had miles of estates, stretching from the coast to Highton Downs. The thought of Dev getting in touch set her nerves buzzing again. Niko would be back at his dad's and she couldn't imagine why he would ring her. But both men brought unwelcome memories. Had she totally wasted her time trying to turn herself into someone else? Someone normal . . . Tom's voice came back to her, raised in anger during one of their many arguments. *'You can't do it, can you? Can't really leave it behind. In your heart you're still one of them, and I don't want that in a wife!'*

79

'Holly?' The DC's sharp voice broke into her thoughts. 'You might as well call me Karen, and screw the formalities. I know you don't trust us, and I get why, but we need to work together.' She smiled properly. 'This is turning into a bitch of a case and the DCI is going to want daily updates. Not to mention DI Harper keeping a close eye on things.'

Yeah, she could imagine the nosy bastard was thrilled at getting a final chance to turn over the Seaview estate before he retired. Holly found herself smiling back, warily, years of ingrained prejudice still preventing her from responding to the overture of friendliness, but she liked the energy this woman emitted. She had felt the same when Steph reached out, but she had to admit these two had been level with her from day one. 'You mean the DCI is jumping on your arse wanting answers?'

'Pretty much. He's not the only one. The prison is involved now, not to mention increased media interest. I'll be honest, at the moment we've got very little to go on. We are hoping that Jayden's son, if he really *is* Jayden's son, regains consciousness and can shed some light on where he's been for the past eleven years.'

'You know DI Harper dealt with my mum's case too . . .' Holly said it slowly, watching the other woman. 'You could say he's always been in the family – even before my mum died, he was crawling over my dad's business, so I can see why he might be sticking his beak in now.'

'Your mum was killed in a hit and run on Beach Road, wasn't she?'

'Yeah. I was thirteen, and one night she just didn't come home.' Holly bit her lip. 'Everything fell apart after that, you know.'

'I'm sorry.'

'S'okay. It was a long time ago. DI Harper arrested my dad, but he never had enough to charge him with.' Holly decided not to mention that for a while she had been pretty sure her dad had killed her mum, only letting go of the idea when an unshakable alibi came to light. 'Obviously he wasn't a DI then. I think he was working on some drugs case, and he seemed to be really keen to nail my dad for everything going. Bastard. Nobody was ever charged in the end, so he failed. Whoever killed my mum got away with it. Yeah, I'm dead happy for DI Harper not to be around too much.'

Karen's phone rang and she snatched it up, one eye still on Holly. She snapped out yes and no and killed the call. 'Got to get back to the prison. I can't promise to tell you everything that's going on, but I will try and level with you, okay?'

'Why? If we're being honest . . . you don't have to tell me all this.'

'You're right, I don't and I'm sharing a whole lot more than I normally would, because I have a gut feeling you might be key to whatever is about to go down. I also think you need to be careful, Holly, and ring me anytime if you are at all worried about anything.' Her blue eyes were back to glacial and Holly shivered.

As she watched her cross the road with the other officer, and drive away, Holly thought about her mum. The pain was still there. You never forgot, of course, and at times she missed her terribly, but life went on and you went with it, carrying fresh scars from each new battle. For a while, as a teenager with access to pretty much any illegal substance she wanted to sample, she had been tempted, as Jay had, to blot out her grief with chemicals, or as her dad had done, with alcohol.

But instead she had turned to boxing, which had worked pretty well until Larissa's murder turned her life upside down once again. Then when Jay went, she'd been almost glad her mum hadn't been there to see it, hadn't had to search for her son and then declare him dead. But as she got her life on track, and especially when she was pregnant, when Milo was a baby, she would catch herself thinking how many things she wanted to ask her mum, and how much she would have loved being a gran.

Her phone buzzed with another message, and she saw she had three missed calls, one from Lydia, the others from Cath. What could she say? Apart from, *'Oh shit, the police think Jayden's alive and has somehow got Alexi and Roman murdered.'* It was the stuff of fantasy, or nightmares, and she wasn't sure she could handle either.

Holly glanced in the mirror, and with an effort squared her shoulders and pulled her dark hair into a high ponytail. She raised her arms up for a stretch before stopping abruptly . . . It was a shock to realise she could slip back into her old routine, the old Holly, so easily. This was her pre-fight prep, when she mentally prepared herself for a boxing competition. She used to do it on a weekly basis. Somewhere deep inside, the fire was still there, and from the sound of the way things were going she was going to have to use it.

The past was dragging her back.

'If you want to find him, we can try. I'll go with whatever you decide.' He paused and glanced sideways at her averted face. *'Aren't you glad he's gone though? It solves a lot of problems.'*

'Yeah, sort of but only if he's going to get clean. You don't think he still owes Niko money, do you?'

Devril pulled her back down on the sofa. *'Niko says he does. He reckons that Jay coughed up for the last lot, then bought a load of gear on credit. He told the boys he wanted a new start so he could be anywhere. Niko's still pissed though. He needs Jayden, now he's got nobody to work the North Street area. He'll fucking kill him if he finds him, for bailing on the business and stealing the cash. Apparently Jayden took all the client contact numbers with him, and just walked.'*

Holly turned, her face close to his. His arm was around her shoulders. *'If he's really gone I'm glad. I was just worried that . . . you know that Niko had done something to him. It's got worse now the Nicholls are hanging around, causing trouble. There was that fight in the park last week and one of the boys got stabbed. This is serious; they aren't kids with a bit of blow anymore. This is real money and hard stuff.'*

82

'I know.' He kissed her. 'That's why I'm getting out too.'

She propped herself on her elbow. 'Where are you going?'

'Not far to start with, but I'm done with the Balintas and I want my own life. I've signed up for a PT course at college. Hell, I've got a great body and I reckon I can get people fit if I want.'

'Modest, too, aren't you?'

'Always.'

'That's great, Dev, I'm so proud of you.'

'Yeah, and you with your modelling and boxing. One day I'll get one of those posh-boy apartments across the river.'

Dreams, stupid castles in the air, and young love. For a few months it actually did go all right. Devril studied and Holly competed, and they went out to all the hot places, with all the right people.

The Balinta family had spent the time consolidating their stranglehold over the surrounding towns, ruling the estate with fear and addiction. Their fragile alliance with the Nicholls led to fights with the other local pimps, and another stabbing made the local news. It led to various arrests. But there was no news about Jayden. He had vanished and Holly and Lydia hoped he really had started again.

Holly had begun to think about taking time out to travel with Devril, maybe apply for university. All her plans pissed off her dad. Donnie, with one child left to take over the business, wanted Holly to work with him. Things had to be kept in the family, he had insisted. The Nicholls' haulage business, now nicely established in the area and spreading tendrils along the South coast and up towards London, was instrumental in trafficking vulnerable kids and drugs across the county lines, and they were making a fortune. Even though he was drinking more, and working less, Donnie couldn't bear to see his slice of the action get eaten up.

But Jayden going had released Holly somehow, and she'd allowed herself to dream, to fall more in love with Devril, plan for a life doing anything other than working for her dad. Cath, a

83

teenage mum with twins to look after, was bitter about Jayden's departure and it was a sore subject. Jayden and Cath had always been linked, on and off, ever since school and most people assumed when she got pregnant he would stick by her. But he hadn't. The first chance he got, he'd run.

In her heart Holly had felt it might be better this way. Cath was her best friend, but she and Jayden had been toxic together – dabbling in various drugs, joyriding, even a bit of arson down in the derelict warehouses further along the coast. Holly could remember flicking the TV on and watching the flames on the screen towering above the sea. Her brother and his girlfriend, curled up on the sofa, had been busy texting and putting pictures on social media. When she'd asked what they were doing, Cath proudly told her that they were responsible for the fire, adding it was the best high she had ever got when the flames took hold.

'Holly, it was fucking amazing! The noise and the smell . . .' She took a drag of her cigarette. 'It was so hot I could feel the burn on my face from up on the hill.'

Holly looked at them blankly. 'Why did you do that?'

Jayden rolled his eyes. 'Because it was fun, and because we can. Just because you don't ever to do anything wild, doesn't mean we can't break out a bit.'

Cath pretended to be engrossed in her phone. Jayden would often slate his sister, but although she didn't ever join in, Cath rarely told him to shut up.

And it was all fine, until the day Jayden called Holly, desperate and afraid. And she had failed him. The one time it was true, all she had felt was anger, anger that it would all begin again, anger that her brother could be weak enough to fall back into the junkie trap.

Chapter 12

Holly zipped a hoodie over her uniform, yelled to Lydia that there was pizza for Milo's dinner, and walked out the door, praying she wasn't running too late. If she missed this bus, it was a twenty-minute wait for the next. Walking faster, despite the niggling pain in her leg, she sighed in frustration. Normally she would have been running.

Her phone rang, and she fished it quickly out of her bag. Tom's number flashed up on the screen. It had been such a relief not to have to speak to him since his visit. Emailing over childcare had quickly become a far more efficient and less stressful way of communication.

'Hallo, Holly. I'll make this quick, but Beth insisted I should tell you before you heard any gossip.'

Holly waited in silence, heart thudding, her boots sloshing through puddles on the pavement.

'Holly? Are you still there? I said Beth wanted me to let you know she is pregnant.'

Without hesitation Holly pressed a button to end the call. Her road, with its steady stream of traffic, the red-brick houses, the scrubby hedges, all seemed miles away. She took a hold of herself. So Beth was pregnant. So what? It could be good news.

Tom might lose interest in Milo. She told herself she didn't care, but it was another kick in the gut.

The pale February sunshine had dragged the weeds from their winter slumbers, and green shoots decorated the grass around the bus shelter. Only a couple of minutes to spare, but she'd made it. She was working a two till midnight shift, and thanked God for the coffee and Haribos that weighed her bag down. Friday night shifts were always busy.

After a couple of days' respite, her ex-husband had sent a random text last night. It was nasty, vitriolic and totally unnecessary. Holly scrolled through until found it, and replied carefully:

Please stop sending me messages.

That would do. She had asked him to stop, and much as she wanted to add her own brand of vitriol, if she was taking this further she needed to keep control, be blameless. When would Beth find out what an arsehole Tom really was? Pregnant. Jesus, poor girl, being stuck with that control freak. No doubt in a few years' time he would get bored with her, or she might dare to voice some opinions, or get a job he didn't like, and she would be dumped as well.

Holly still hadn't got around to getting another car. The insurance company hadn't worked everything through yet, though they had promised a rental car whilst the claim was dealt with. In the meantime, the bus was fine. Although her injuries were healing fast, her leg was still slightly sore, and she wasn't sure if she could even drive again yet.

A couple of men walked past, then an old lady with an Alsatian. She pretended to be engrossed in something on her phone, but she was checking them all out. Maybe Alexi and Roman had pissed someone else off, well, of course they had, but enough to kill them and blame it on Larissa's murder?

Holly sent a quick guilty text to her dad, saying she hoped he was okay, but not mentioning Jayden. She wondered if he had even answered the door to the police. Probably not. Lydia had been in a right state about Jayden's son though, and she was heading up to the hospital tomorrow to see the child. The more recent news of the Balinta double murder hadn't bothered her half as much, except where it might concern Jayden. Holly had tried to talk her out of going to the hospital, still worried that someone was targeting her and the family, but Lydia was having none of it. Family was the only thing that mattered to her and she'd always taken it badly that they'd been unable to help Jayden.

The night of the crash, her fear and confusion at the two jostling drivers, had become blurred in the last week. She had dismissed the idea that either car had been intentionally trying to push her off the road, but unable to get the boy out of her mind, she fitted in a quick trip to the hospital yesterday afternoon, before the school run. The boy was still lying stiffly between his white sheets but this time she had been allowed in, talked softly to him, about Milo, about Jay as a child, about pretty much anything that came into her head.

When she left, she had dropped a quick kiss on his pale cheek and smoothed his brown hair from his closed eyes. Did the child know what she had done the night Larissa was murdered? That it was her fault? The hot rush of guilt, that had been buried for so long, shot right back up into her stomach, nausea making her swallow hard as she left his room, walking swiftly out of the hospital.

It wasn't just that the whole thing was her fault, it was that when it came down to the wire she had failed Larissa in every sense. Whilst she'd been on the phone to the ambulance, she had been doing nothing but stare at the dead girl, and her bloody hands. It didn't matter that Larissa had been past help. Holly had stood up in court and explained she had put her hands on the chest and been unable to do anything more. And she'd failed the baby, too. Failed to find it nestled in the cot, lifeless. Everyone had heard how she fucked up. Thank God they never knew the rest.

As the years had gone by, with Devril off the scene and Jayden dead, she had felt safer about her secret. Even confessing to Tom, just before they were married, had seemed like the right thing to do. He had said all the right things, but stashed away her memories to use against her. What would the police say if they knew the truth? Lydia and her dad would never speak to her again if they found out.

Shoving her problems away, she tried to switch gears into work mode. This wasn't the kind of job where you could drift along with half your mind elsewhere. It required attention to detail and no mistakes. It was one of the reasons she enjoyed it.

As she walked through the doors to the tall, concrete and glass building, she sent Lydia a quick text, saying she would call Milo later to say goodnight. It was a ritual, and something that made her feel less guilty about leaving her son for the night. Not that he cared; in fact, he was always happy to spend time with Lydia, who enjoyed spoiling him rotten.

'Hi, Holly, how are you feeling?' Kevin, the security guard on reception beeped her into the main building.

'Almost better, thanks, Kev. How's the baby?' She managed a grin and checked her watch. Ten minutes to go. Might as well be early for once.

'Settling a bit more now, ta. We're getting some sleep at last. I heard about your car crash. Did they find out who that other boy was?'

Holly shook her head, not wanting to share, not sure if she was even allowed to. 'Not yet.'

'Man, that is weird.'

'Yeah. See you later, Kev.'

Kevin had worked on security for years now, and was always happy to chat. He was like family to pretty much every employee and Holly had never heard a bitchy comment pass his lips. His wife was dead lucky, and now they had a baby.

Her team leader was busy with paperwork, but he waved and smiled. The huge room was warm and bright, huge picture windows along four sides of the room showed the rain-soaked car park and the cranes on the building site next door.

Holly snagged an empty workstation, and various friends waved and smiled. The big screen on the wall at one end of the room showed the number of calls waiting. As usual it was flickering on red. Although it would be a tough shift, Holly felt herself relax a little. She was good at her job, and she loved it most of the time.

There was time to grab a coffee, take the piss out of Ben from Dispatch, and catch up with her colleague Ruby's colourful love life before she plugged her headset in, and logged onto the computer. She checked her work emails, deleting most of the boring admin stuff, and pulled up her maps.

'Hi, babes, you all right?' Cath was sitting on her other side, and she ended her call and began typing notes.

'Yeah fine. Is Colleen babysitting?' Colleen was one of Cath's elder sisters.

'She's got all the kids tonight, but you know what she's like, she loves it,' Cath said. She spun her chair round and lowered her voice. 'You look like someone just slapped you in the face. What's up? Is it Jayden or something to do with the Balintas? I heard Mason has gone mental and he wants blood from whoever killed his sons, pints of it. And Niko went straight over to the Nicholls' yard and got into a fight with Rohan and Dixie. He swears it was them that ordered the hit on his brothers. He wants to see someone suffer.'

'Yeah, you said, but this isn't to do with that shit.' Holly leant back in her chair, spinning slightly to her right, whispering as Ruby took a call on her other side. 'Beth's pregnant.'

'No fucking way! That was quick. Or is that why Tom moved on so quickly?'

'The thought had crossed my mind.' Holly's name popped up on the big screen, four from the top, and she took a big slug of coffee. She wondered vaguely about reverting to her maiden name, and decided she probably would. Holly Hughes sounded better than Holly Kendal, and she didn't want to keep anything of Tom's, didn't want anything that tied them together. Tom had always been so patronising about her 'call centre' job, taking it as personal insult that she chose to work, rather than studying for 'something better' – as he put it. He really was a total bastard. It was just a shame it had taken her so long to see it.

Her phone pinged and she hit the button, fingers poised over the keyboard. 'Ambulance service, is the patient breathing?'

As the shift went on, she dealt with the calls methodically, topping up her coffee periodically. The night shift came on at six-thirty and included six new recruits. There were four women and two men, and they were all looking pretty terrified. Welcoming any extra distraction, Holly offered to mentor to one, and was given a pale, nervous girl called Sara. Holly grinned as Ruby promptly introduced herself to the best-looking of the two blokes, practically dragging him over to her computer.

It was a tough job, and staff turnover was high. Most people didn't last more than a couple of months, and many were lost during the training, simply because they either didn't pass the exams, or the combination of harrowing calls and shifts didn't work for them. Holly had quit her degree soon after she and Tom got married. She had been trying to mould herself into the perfect housewife and mum, and couldn't see any point in finishing a degree when she had no idea what job she was going to get at the end.

Later, when the fighting started, working with Cath at the ambulance service seemed a perfect way to atone for her past failure, and also appealed to the adrenalin junkie in her heart, which she had never quite managed to suppress.

'Have you got kids?' A couple of hours later, nearing the end of her shift, Holly had persuaded Sara to relax a little in between calls.

'No. My boyfriend's all broody because his cousin's just had twins, but I want to wait a bit.' Her voice was very quiet and she was hunched over the keyboard, one thin, pale hand clutching her headset as she watched her name climbing to the top of the board. Her red curls were held back with a pink plastic clip, and she looked about ten.

'You'll be fine. Everyone starts off like this, but you'll be writing your Christmas cards between calls by the end of the year,' Holly told her, smiling encouragingly.

'I can't imagine it,' Sara said softly, twisting the headset wire between her fingers. 'Can I stay with you for the mentoring shifts?'

'Sure, if I'm on. You got your roster yet?'

'Here.'

Cath chucked a handful of jelly sweets across the desk, and Holly took two and passed them along the row. 'You'll probably put on a stone in this job, because we eat to keep awake.'

Sara looked at Cath, who was a size six, and Holly grinned. 'Except her – she just burns it all off talking too much.'

Cath, stuck on a call, poked her tongue out at her friend, but continued speaking soothingly into her headset. 'Can you see the baby's head yet?'

***

At half past midnight Holly passed out of the warmth and lights, into the ice and the darkness. As Friday nights went it hadn't been too bad, and hopefully that fifty-seven-year-old male with the cardiac arrest would survive. She would check tomorrow. Although she tried to leave work at work, sometimes the calls invaded her nightmares and it was hard not to become personally involved. Two HGVs passed her on her way to the bus stop, but apart from that it was almost peaceful in what she liked to think of as 'dead hour'. The streets were devoid of people, and her breath was white in the clear night air. Above the grime of the city the sky was painted with stars. Normally she quite liked being up when everyone else was asleep, but tonight there was just too much going on in her tired brain.

Thank Christ it wasn't pissing down with rain. She slipped into the bus shelter, finding a space on the end of the wooden seat. The homeless, the alkies and the druggies made space for her. The stench of piss and sweat filled the little structure. After five minutes Holly needed some air and she staggered to her feet again. A man in a ragged jumper and two threadbare coats scowled at her as she disturbed his nest.

'Sorry.'

'No worries, love, mind how you go.' He grinned at her before resettling carefully into his layers of blankets and cardboard.

The bus was on time, and the lower deck was empty apart from a couple in the back seat. The boy and girl were glued together, her sitting on his lap, legs apart. Holly wondered if they were actually having sex.

She checked her phone. A voicemail from Tom saying that he knew she had left Milo alone in the house last night and she would be hearing from his solicitor regarding *his* son. What the hell was that all about? And where did he get ideas like that anyway? He knew Lydia always stayed over if Holly was working nights. It didn't make sense. And if Beth was pregnant, why did Tom still want Milo? Milo was hers.

Just as she erased the voicemail with a shaky finger, her screen flashed with another text:

Bitch. I know what you are really like, and soon everyone else will too.

Chapter 13

This was getting ridiculous, not just hurtful and insulting. But if she reported her ex-husband for sending threatening texts, it would surely just make things even harder for her. Milo was upset enough – unable to see why his parents couldn't live together, didn't love each other anymore.

She studied the times and dates. With the exception of the ones before the car crash, the texts all came in late at night, between eleven and one. So did Beth wait until he was asleep and then use his phone to send the texts?

She frowned. But what about the times when Tom was away? He was hardly going to leave his phone at home, and he'd been away at the time of the car crash. The business with the boy and Jayden had distracted her from pursuing this, but she needed to get it sorted. Perhaps she could ask Beth about the texts? Holly supposed now that his girlfriend was pregnant he would be extra careful not to upset her, but the memory of his icy anger made her reluctant to mess with his new girlfriend.

A man got on at the next stop, his hood pulled down over his face. He wore black jeans and a red Converse top, and walked with an athletic swing. Holly noticed him, waited for him to go past, and then gasped as he slid in beside her.

The man slid the hood off his face, rubbing his hand over damp black hair. She caught a glimpse of artwork on his right hand, and bit her lip, heart pounding.

'Hallo, Holly. It's been a long time.'

His light grey eyes, bright and unexpected against his dark skin, glittered with amusement but his expression held genuine affection. She shivered, instinctively pressing back against the cold sticky windowpane. 'What do you want, Devril?'

He stretched out a hand and unzipped her hoodie, quick and agile as a cat. She slapped his hand away, and he laughed. 'Just wanted to see the uniform, darling. You know I've always fancied women in uniform. Imagine you ending up working for the ambulance.'

'Whatever.' She tried to ignore the history that pulsed between them, the dark threads that tied them together. Would he bring it up or was he waiting for her to ask the question?

'I heard you were in trouble. Lydia has told most of the Seaview that your bloke is a cheating twat, so I wanted to check up on you. You know Niko's out and now Roman and Alexi are dead. There's some shit happening on Seaview at the moment.'

'There's always shit happening on Seaview. I'm fine, Devril. Cut the crap, I know you're a journalist now, so why are you really back?'

He shrugged. 'Just thought I'd come down for a few weeks and see what was going on. I'm not going to lie to you and say I'm not looking for a story.'

'A story on what? You can't tell me after all these years you've come back to Westbourne just "looking" for a story. What's really going on? Did Niko call you?'

He said nothing for a while, just watched her, those pale eyes narrowed and feral. 'Niko? Hell no. I'm the last person he'd call.'

'Fine. You asked if I was okay, well, I'll be even better when you get off at the next stop and piss off back under whichever rock you crawled out from. Don't you dare go thinking you can

94

rake up the past,' Holly told him, scowling. Unreasonable anger was building in her chest, and she didn't stop to think how stupid she was being to argue with him. 'I'm finished with all that, and I don't need any reminders.'

'I know about the car crash.'

'So?'

'And the kid.'

Holly took a deep breath, letting it out gently, counting to ten in her head, ordering herself to calm down. He knew the truth about her, and he had never told anyone. That would be a great story, but he hadn't used it. 'Okay I'm sorry. I know you wouldn't screw me over. It's just . . . it's just a shock seeing you after so long.'

'You're right, I wouldn't screw you over. Ever. Listen, we need to talk properly and you need to be careful walking around late at night. Did you not get a rental car until yours is fixed?'

Holly blinked at him. The conversation was surreal. She hadn't seen him for eleven years and now he was concerned for her safety? She glanced round, almost expecting to see her brother, and hell, maybe even Niko too, but the seats were empty. The couple in the back seat were oblivious to everything but each other.

Devril looked back and grinned. 'Turn you on, does it?'

'Whatever. Why were you following me? The police want to talk to you.' She tried to see if he was bothered.

He was frowning now, the shadows from the streetlights flitting across his face. 'When I came back to Westbourne I kept my distance a bit, but then I figured I might as well check you out.'

'Did you follow me to the BP garage the night of the car crash? Did you see anything?'

But he was shaking his head. 'I suppose the police caught me on CCTV. I promise it was a coincidence and I wondered whether to come over and say hi, but you had your kid, so I decided it wasn't the right time. I was over at an old mate's house in Panfield about half an hour later. The police can check it all out.'

'*Devril*, tell me why you've come back!' Exasperation made her voice sharp.

He met her eyes. 'I got a tip-off. Someone I used to know, who knew Jay, said they saw him. That's one of the reasons we need to talk properly. This is my number.' He slipped a business card into her pocket. 'I can help you more than the police. Holly, you need to give me a call.'

She couldn't process any of this. 'You're saying Jayden is *alive*?'

'Well, I haven't seen him but my source knew him pretty well and he's convinced. I trust him.'

She was shaking her head, twisting her bag handle around and around in her hands until her palms were scored with red. The sickness was rising in her stomach and the urge to get up and scream was almost more than she could bear.

'Holly?' He was leaning closer, clearly concerned. 'I'm sorry, but it's good news, isn't it?'

'For fuck's sake, Dev. You've obviously had time to get used to the idea, I'm just trying to make the jump between dead brother and reincarnated brother.' Her head was heavy with questions, none of which had any answers. Instead she saw again the candlelit vigil they had arranged as a memorial to Jayden. She saw Cath's white face, eyes red from crying, the bewildered twins solemn and scared, and Lydia dressed all in black. 'Did Jayden get Alexi and Roman killed? Is that why he came back – for revenge?'

He shrugged. 'I don't know.'

'What about his kid?'

That got him, but Devril had always been way ahead of anyone else. 'Fucking hell, the boy from the crash is Jay's boy? How has that not been leaked yet?'

She said nothing, slightly freaked now that she had blurted it out. The police hadn't told her it was confidential, but she had just told a journalist. Turning away to stare out of the dirt-streaked window, she mentally berated herself for her stupidity, but seeing Dev had knocked her off balance.

The streetlights glowed orange and yellow, striping the dark pavements with colour. The colours of the night. But her night was always striped with blue. She didn't want to talk, despite the fact she was sure he could provide some answers. She just needed to process speaking to Devril for the first time in so many years. Talking to him, with his face so close she could have touched his cheek, his body pressed lightly against hers on the seat. It seemed a lifetime ago.

'There's more going on here. I need to think. Call me tomorrow.' Devril stood up and slid away, pressing the button as he made his way to the front of the bus.

She finally turned from the window, and called softly, 'You know where Jayden is now, don't you?' It was no more than a guess, and although she couldn't see his face from this angle, his hand was clenched hard on the seat back.

The bus slowed to a grinding halt, and he raised a hand. 'Call me, Holly. You need me.'

Although part of her wanted to scream at him, to ask more, Holly watched him jump lightly off the step, and lope away into the shadows of the estate. The same walk, the same voice, and a face that had only slightly aged. This bus always took the long route around the south end of the city, past the market and back down past the station. Annoyed with herself for allowing the past to seep back in, she zipped her hoodie back up, and stared mindlessly at the dark shapes of tower blocks, which gave way to lower, squat, ugly houses.

Even hiding in the shadows of night, Seaview Estate looked nothing but hideous. The concrete, the ragged little patches of rank grass and the litter that carpeted the roads like snowfall whenever the wind blew. The estate stretched right across to the sea, and the lonely road that ran along past the breakwater. The darkness and shadows hid the junkies and the muggers at night, and in daylight mums struggled with pushchairs, spreading blankets on the pebbles and letting their kids paddle in the icy grey waves.

The bus stopped twice more and the fornicating couple straightened their clothes and jumped off at a twenty-four-hour McDonald's in Gateshill Road. It was her childhood, her teenage years and beyond. Up until Tom had swept her away from the darkness and set her up as something entirely different.

One mistake. Devril hadn't even mentioned it, but then she hadn't either. Her real mistake had been to tell Tom about her past, but who could have known? He was always so charming and charismatic, and so attentive when she had Milo. His family, initially sceptical, had also been charming, and she had allowed herself to be cut off from her past, telling herself it was what she wanted, what she needed. Telling Tom had been her letting go of her past – she just hadn't realised then that the past hadn't let go of her.

Holly climbed awkwardly to her feet, clambering off at her stop. Her injured leg had stiffened up after a long shift of sitting on her backside, and she found herself hobbling the last couple of yards to her own front door. She slipped the key into the lock, and squared her shoulders, glancing into the shadows, the dark hedges and the blackness of the alley next to the house. Nothing and nobody. She knew she would cope, because she had to, for Milo's sake. She'd done it once before, she could get through this again.

And Jayden? He could get back into his grave. Momentarily shocked that she felt this way, she shivered. But it was true. Even trying to process the fact he was alive was painful. She still felt a rush of protective maternal emotion when she thought about the child in hospital. But for her brother, that familiar numbness was spreading across her heart, insulating against the pain. Jayden must have been following her. Her brother had dumped his injured kid in her car, presumably to avoid being recognised, and left him.

So he had been following her? Had flashed his lights to try and make her pull over. For what? A chat about old times? But it made sense. Jayden couldn't afford to come back from the dead, so for whatever reason, he had come back by stealth, bringing his son.

Holly wondered, not for the first time, what Jayden and Larissa had called their son. And when – if – he woke up, surely he would tell her where his dad had been, but would he know where he was now?

Despite herself, her mind flashed back eleven years to when Devril had given evidence at the trial for Larissa's murder. He'd told the jury how he had been at his dad's house with Niko Balinta, and that Niko had left around half two. No, Devril didn't know anything about where his cousin went next, because he had then gone straight down the gym for training.

It was exactly what he had told Holly he would say, in their one phone call after Larissa had died. She shut her eyes, screwing them up at the pain of remembering the break-up. After avoiding Dev since Larissa's murder, she'd finally spoken to him during the trial. It had been a time to cut ties, move on and harden her heart to any stupid teenage dreams. It had been one of the hardest things she'd ever had to do.

'Holly? I've been trying to call you.'

'Devril, I won't contact you again, or anyone, okay? I just need to know what you're going to say?'

'It's okay, Holly, I've been trying to tell you . . .'

'What are you going to say?'

'All right. Jesus, girl! Niko and I were at my dad's and he got a call. It was obviously important news, because he wouldn't tell me anything, but ran straight out the door.'

'That's it?'

'Yeah. Holly, I never—'

'Devril, thank you. I won't bother you again. You can go travelling or whatever. Don't contact me again.'

'Fine, but—'

She had put the phone down, breathing quickly, giving him no time to say anything else. That was the last time they had spoken, although she had seen him in court, had listened to his testimony, holding her breath, deliberately avoiding his gaze as he picked her out across the courtroom.

According to the official police report Niko said he had received a call telling him where Jayden was. Still furious that Jayden had never paid his debts and ready to call them in, Niko had rung his brothers. Alexi and Roman were the family heavies. They got high and beat people up, and they enjoyed their work.

The reason Niko had not been given a longer sentence was that his lawyer had argued he couldn't possibly have known what would happen at the flat. He said he had just sent his brothers around to collect a debt, and nobody could prove otherwise. The caller who tipped Niko off as to Jayden's whereabouts had never been traced, and although there were withheld numbers on his call history, he insisted he didn't recognise the caller's voice, but it was 'probably' one of his dealing contacts.

Alexi and Roman admitted murdering Larissa but said they had taken drugs before they got Niko's call. They had no idea there was a girl at the flat, before she answered the door. They claimed they had tried to find Jayden, and when there was no money and no Jayden they had turned on the girl. Both denied even seeing a baby in the flat, despite DNA proving otherwise. Holly wasn't sure if she could ever get past the fact that one of them had murdered a baby.

Jayden had initially been a murder suspect, because his footprints were found in the blood at the flat, but eventually, it was supposed he had been out, then come back, probably between Alexi and Roman fleeing the scene, and Holly arriving, found his dead girlfriend and baby, and run.

She had always been contemptuous of this, despising him for running away again, but what if he ran away to protect his other child?

Holly turned over Devril's business card in her pocket, smoothing the edges. Not yet, she wasn't ready yet.

***

The hall light was on, dim and reassuring, as it cast a gentle warmth across the wooden floor. Milo's school bag was hanging on the banister, and in the kitchen her aunt had scribbled a note about making sure she got herself something to eat. To emphasise this there was a ready meal propped against the microwave, and a bowl of salad in Clingfilm.

There was also a parcel on the table. It was clumsily wrapped, in brown paper and tape, and addressed to Holly. She grabbed a bottle from the fridge, poured a glass of wine and sat down at the table, intrigued.

Inside was one of Milo's jumpers, and a printed note:

You have something I want, and I have something you want.

It was unsigned. The address was printed on a label too, so she couldn't check if it was Tom's handwriting. Panicked for a moment she slipped across the hallway, running lightly upstairs to Milo's room, wincing at her leg. He was sleeping peacefully, one arm around the stuffed dolphin Tom had bought him in Disneyland. In her own room downstairs, her aunt also slept, her dark hair framing her face, the striped blanket pulled up around her shoulders. Holly let out a long breath and smiled.

Was Tom upping his game, or was this about Niko and Jayden? If her brother wanted revenge for Larissa's murder, he might have figured out the truth . . . How great to have so many enemies you really couldn't decide who was threatening you, Holly thought sarcastically. She poured another glass of wine, and deciding she was starving, shoved the lasagne in the microwave.

Should she believe Devril about his 'tip-off' on Jay? Holly almost choked on her mouthful of wine. Perhaps Devril's tip-off had coincided with Niko's release, in which case where did the hell did that leave her? They wouldn't let her stay out of the game; that was becoming obvious.

A text flashed up on her phone:

Whore.

Chapter 14

Devril had saved her after her mum's death, dragging her over to Shoey's, the grubby, sweaty little gym on South Road, and encouraging her to kick the hell out of the pads, and later out of him. Boxing had become her life, and she was good. Really good. It had been something positive to get her out of bed in the morning. And then Jayden ruined her life again.

Exhausted, Holly struggled through the day, mechanically dealing with her accounts, getting dinner ready in the slow cooker for her aunt and Milo. Her voicemail was full, but she didn't feel like talking to anyone. Her mind was on DC Karen Marriot. At least she had been straight with her, no bullshit and no fake smarm, which was what her mum had always accused the police of. Despite the fact Karen worked with Harper, Holly could feel herself warming to her, even trusting her a bit.

She flicked the TV on for company, and then wished she hadn't as the news had just reached a piece about Yorke Prison. A reporter was talking to a prison official about the stabbing. It had made the main news items simply because of the horrific crime the brothers had committed.

Larissa's photograph, that beautiful smiling photograph that had been used so many times before – after her brutal murder

– flashed up on the screen and before she could stop herself Holly was slumped on the sofa, tears pouring down her cheeks. If her brother had been raising a child, she supposed he might have taken his time planning revenge, but surely the child would be a perfect chance to look forward, not back. If you got out of the Seaview alive, you didn't look back, you just kept on running. Okay, so she had only made it a couple of miles down the road, but she'd done it. And Devril had done it.

Jayden had always been obsessive, consumed by whatever took his fancy. As a child it had been online games, war figures, and then as he grew old enough to be useful in the family business it was all hacking and drugs. Donnie was so proud, grooming him to take on a load of responsibility, but still jealous of the Nicholls brood with so many sons working the patch. It was a feudal way of thinking but that's just how it was. After all this time, guilt churned in her belly. If Jayden was back and getting revenge, who would he pick off next? Did he even know exactly what had happened on the night Larissa died? She only just made it to the toilet where she threw up, gripping the cold bowl with shaking hands.

By sheer willpower she shoved the whole incident to the back of her mind, kept the TV turned off, and avoided social media for the rest of the day. Several times, she almost called Devril, but something stopped her each time she dialled the number.

By the time she went out to pick Milo up she had almost convinced herself that it was over. Alexi and Roman were dead. Larissa was avenged. But what about the child lying still in his hospital bed?

***

'You never called me, Holly. Aren't you the tiniest bit curious?'

Holly had been studiously avoiding the other mums by the school gates, waiting for Milo and scrolling through her phone as an excuse to avoid eye contact with anyone. But that meant she hadn't noticed the tall figure walk up behind her.

'Hallo, Devril, and no, I'm not at all curious.' She was lying, of course, but the fear of releasing the past that they shared made her stomach heave. To get answers she would have to allow herself to go back. Yesterday, visiting Jayden's son, feeling his soft skin beneath her fingertips as she stroked his head, she had almost been ready, but today the fire had gone out, and her fear of the past was far stronger than her curiosity.

She leant against the wall, watching Milo chatting with his friends, making his way slowly out of school. A kid with long red hair was bending down to sign his cast, a group of girls were laughing with an older woman, and, oh shit, further along the road, Tom was walking purposefully towards the school gates.

'Got to go, Devril. I will call you, but I just need to get my head around this, okay?'

'Holly, please. Do *you* know where Jayden is?'

'What? No of course I don't. I'm still not even quite sure if I believe he's alive. I thought you . . . Look, Devril, please this isn't a good time.' Tom had seen her now, and he hesitated, half turning. Today was just getting better and better. 'Okay, I'm sorry, Devril, and I do want to talk, but please could you just go away and I'll call you later. I mean it!'

His eyes glittered now, as he pulled the hood of his jacket tightly round his face, 'I'm worried about you, Holly. Christ, I thought you would have grown out of being so fucking defensive all the time. I never said a word at the trial, did I? You never gave me the chance to explain and now I'm just trying to look out for you and get some answers, and you won't even talk to me.'

Shocked and a bit guilty, she turned back to say something, but he was moving away now, disappearing into the crowds. Was she really being selfish? Or was she just trying to keep the tendrils of the past away from her son? Anyway, she told herself crossly, it wasn't her who was bringing the past back to life. Holly pulled her thoughts together, tried to stop panicking by breathing deeply, rubbing sweaty palms on her jeans.

'Friend of yours?' Tom was watching Devril disappear into the crowd of milling parents.

'Hallo, Tom.' She nodded at her ex-husband, ignoring his question. 'What are you doing here?'

'I said I'd pick Milo up today and take him to watch the match later. Remember?' He was carefully dressed as usual, in what she thought of as his cool professor clothes. The tweed jacket, tight jeans and white shirt gave him an air of sexiness. Or just made him look like a total fuckwit trying to cling on to his youth, depending on how you looked at it. He smelt far too strongly of his favourite cologne.

Holly went with the latter opinion of his appearance. 'No, you didn't. You said tomorrow. It's Thursday today.'

He was giving her that familiar pained expression, frowning like she was one of his less than intelligent students. How had she been in love with this man? 'I said today, Holly. I wouldn't get the match date wrong, and Beth puts everything in my diary.'

'Good for Beth,' Holly said lightly.

'No need to be bitter. She's very organised, and I know she'll be a wonderful mother.'

Milo was approaching now, glancing apprehensively from one to the other of his parents, sensing animosity. Holly took a deep breath, and hissed at Tom, 'Okay, maybe I made a mistake. If you're sure the match is today, I'm not going to make Milo miss out.'

Her son smiled uncertainly at her. 'Hi, Mum. Hi, Dad. I thought you said you were coming to get me tomorrow?'

Holly could have sworn a flash of anger crossed Tom's face, but he moved in quickly to hug Milo and take his bag from him before Holly could reach for her son. 'No, mate, it's tonight.' He turned back to Holly. 'Beth will bring him back for nine as it's a school night.'

'Fine.' Milo crossed over to her for a hug and she kissed him lightly on the forehead, resisting the urge to cling to his solid little body, to whisk him away from Tom and take him home with her.

But if Milo was going to be out, she now had work to do tonight. As soon as Tom and Milo had vanished into the traffic, she pulled out her phone, moving away from the crowd, leaning against the metal railings.

'Hi, Cath, can we meet up later? You're not working, are you?'

There were sounds of screaming children in the background, but her friend sounded cheerful enough. 'No, I'm not, the joys of being part-time, babes. You'll have to come here obviously. Do you want to bring Milo and sleep over, or is Lydia going to have him?'

'He's with Tom tonight. Not back till about nine. They've gone to the match.'

'Oh. And you're happy with that?'

'I'm trying to be super grown up and civilised about the whole thing. I'll come over at six if that works. I can help you get Anna and Angel to bed.'

'You are a superstar, but ditch the being grown up thing. Tom doesn't deserve it and Milo loves you just how you are. I'll see you at six.'

The stream of kids had dried to a mere trickle, now, and a few stragglers were dragging their school bags towards the seniors' block, quickly finishing up cigarettes. Holly stuffed her phone back in her bag.

'Holly.'

She swung round. She was getting used to being followed.

'Devril? I thought you'd gone.'

His expression was serious, all the teasing and cheek gone from his eyes. 'This needs to be said now.'

Holly tried to interrupt, to walk away, but he put a hand on her arm. Not forceful, but gentle, steering them both along the rain-soaked pavement to the little playground area next to the bus stop.

There were no kids playing and the rusty swing creaked, swaying slightly as the icy breeze ripped across the playground.

'Five minutes, and then I have to go.'

'We've never talked about what happened that night and I know that was partly my fault. But I tried to get hold of you and you just stonewalled me.'

She was shivering now, her breathing light and shallow. 'I don't want to talk about it, okay? I have enough problems at the moment, without bringing up the past. It's . . . It's too painful.'

He stared at her for a moment. 'You still think it's your fault, don't you? Holly, I *never told* Niko. I never passed on your message. I tried to tell you but you just cut me off. And then you walked out of your dad's place and just vanished. Holly? Say something. I never told Niko where Jay was, okay.'

'What?' Holly stared at him, her heart thundering, knuckles white on the climbing frame. She felt she must cling to something solid, something that was anchored to the ground as the flood of relief made her dizzy. All this time she had been convinced it was her fault, her betrayal that had led to the murders, and now it wasn't. Holly had made the biggest mistake ever. She'd been pissed off enough to tell the Nicholls where to find her own brother. That made her the worst grass of all. Family betrayal just didn't happen on Seaview, no matter what had gone on. 'Why didn't you tell Niko?'

He shrugged, face expressionless, framed by his hood. 'Did you really think I had? I knew you were just letting off steam, and I knew what would happen if I told Niko where to find your brother.'

Ridiculous tears started falling, and she batted them away, furiously, half laughing and unable to stop the chattering in her brain. *It wasn't your fault, it wasn't your fault* . . . 'You knew they'd kill him?'

Devril handed her a tissue. 'Of course not. I knew they'd beat him up though. There was the money after all, and the contacts he'd pissed off with.'

'Didn't you hate me for what I did though? For grassing him up?'

'Look, Holly, Jay was a mate, but I know what he was like back then. He stole money from everyone, he was an addict who didn't want to get clean, but after he'd gone that first time, I hoped, like you, that he'd grown up and got off the gear. I know why you were so angry, okay? But it wasn't us who told Niko where to find him. Niko might be my cousin but he's a stupid little fucker. It wouldn't have occurred to him that his brothers would kill a girl and a baby, I'm sure of it. I think he told the truth.'

'Fuck me.' She felt like she'd been kicked in the gut. All this time she'd believed she had Larissa's blood on her hands. The baby's blood. The relief was overwhelming, and after the initial shock, exhausting. Her legs felt weak, and her face was still wet with tears. Holly smiled, despite the cold, despite the current drama and danger. It wasn't her fault.

'You look just the same when you smile,' Devril said, his own eyes softening at her reaction.

'What do you mean?' Self-consciously, Holly touched her lip.

'You know. I always loved it when you were happy. I can see you've still got that dragon tattoo on your arm. You used to show them off all the time.' He reached over gently to her wrist, sliding her jumper up.

'Not in the winter, I didn't.' She pulled the sleeve down again, shrinking from the intimacy of the gesture. 'If you never passed on the message then who did tell Niko where Jayden was that night?'

'Niko said it was an anonymous tip-off, didn't he? He thought it was one of his dealing contacts.'

'Yeah, I suppose it could have been someone hoping to score points with the Balintas,' Holly said thoughtfully. The sweetness of guilt being lifted from her conscience, and energy returning. Maybe she could get through this after all.

'Could have been anyone. Maybe even the same person who

108

saw Alexi and Roman running away from the flat. That person was never named were they? They were just a "reliable witness".

'Suppose Niko was actually there? It kept coming up, didn't it, that he'd sent Roman and Alexi round to collect the cash, but he swore he didn't go,' Holly pointed out, leaning her cheek against the cold metal of the climbing frame. They both glanced up as a couple of skinny swaggering teenagers shambled across the far side, near the slide. The boys dodged round the swing and disappeared into the alleyway behind Tesco off into the woods.

Devril shrugged. 'No evidence though, was there? I've been asking around for a long time. It never did make sense, and Jayden was my best mate at one time, and you . . .'

Holly took a long breath of icy air. She was free. All this time. One night, one mistake, her fault. But it wasn't.

***

'So what's up?' Cath was already pouring the wine when Holly arrived. Ronnie and Sean were busy on the Xbox and the younger children were hitting each other on the rug.

Holly separated the fractious group on the floor and picked up Angel. She was a sweet kid, with huge dark eyes, and baby blonde hair, which would surely darken with age. How could Liam not want to visit a daughter like this?

'Here you go.' Cathryn passed her a large full glass, and took a gulp of her own. 'I just need a moment before we get the babies bathed and into bed. She shot a sharp look at the older twins, who were engaged in a ferocious battle, staring fixedly at the screen. 'You two need to get off there, and do your homework. Now!'

Muttering and complaining they logged off and slouched upstairs. From the back they could have been Jayden as a teenager. Tousled blonde hair, and skinny legs. Holly swallowed a wave of emotion and swigged her wine, bouncing Angel on her knee.

Twelve-year-old Kian was absorbed with his Lego, which Anna

was trying to systematically destroy. He was a quiet boy, good at school and less boisterous than his older brothers. Nothing like his dad, Niko.

'Cath, I'm sorry. I can't stay after all.' Holly took a last swig of wine for courage and stood up.

Her friend looked up from the floor, where she was picking up discarded toys. 'I thought Milo was at Tom's tonight?'

'Yeah, he is. I just think I need to go and see Lydia. She's not coping well with all this, and I should take her up to the hospital to see the boy.' It was a half lie – she was going to see her aunt, she was just visiting a few other people on the way.

'Oh, well, if you're sure. Didn't you say that the hospital only let you visit before nine? Lydia's a tough old bird but I love her to bits. Be careful though, Holly.' Cath was watching her through narrowed eyes, but Holly kept her expression innocent.

'I'll be fine.'

Holly checked her watch as she stepped outside into the cold night air. The lightness she had felt, that floating feeling, hadn't left her. It wasn't her fault, but something was going on. Time to check in on a few of her old neighbours.

She walked quickly, her trainers barely making a sound on the road. She pulled her thick coat around her to stop the icy wind cutting into her body. Her hair fanned out in the sea breeze, and the salt on her lips made her think of her childhood.

A quick call to Lydia confirmed her aunt would be ready in half an hour for a hospital visit. Like Cath, Lydia asked if Holly was okay, perhaps sensing she was up to something, just like she had when Holly was a kid.

Instinctively she cut across the playground, avoiding the high, dark walkways where the junkies and dealers lurked, keeping in the open, and staying alert. But she felt crazy, invincible, which was why she didn't stop to think just how much danger she might be walking into.

There were yells coming from the enclosed yard, quickly

muffled. The noise of a car engine revving, and cheers. Puzzled, Holly slipped into the shadows by the gate. On this side of the estate, the houses backed onto Nicholls' haulage yard. The other side of the yard was the tower block where the Mancinis lived.

Holly tried to ignore sounds from the yard. It was a big space, enclosed by a high fence constructed of solid metal sheets. No spy holes. She knew she should turn left and carry on down the road to the Balintas' place. The plan was to talk to Niko, not disturb the wasps' nest that was the Nicholls empire.

It was an easy decision, until she heard the high-pitched squeal of an animal in pain. Before she could think, Holly was dragging open the gate and flinging herself into the harsh glare of a floodlight.

There was silence as she stood, squinting round at a semi-circle of men, the huge green trucks parked neatly along the sides of the yard. In the middle of the yard a banged-up old Fiesta was parked with the engine running. A towrope was hitched to the car's bumper, and tied securely on the other end of the rope was dog.

'I don't believe it. It's Donnie's little girl.' Joey, unmistakable even after all these years, detached himself from the crowd and walked towards her. 'Have you come for a bet, Holly?'

Fury overcame any rational thought. 'What the fuck are you doing?'

Joey was close now, but instead of taking a step back she eyeballed him and had the satisfaction of seeing a flash of uncertainty cross his chiselled features. He was older now, his mop of black hair streaked with grey, with salt and pepper stubble, but the lines in his face merely added to the good looks. Donnie had always said Joey had the face of an angel and the soul of the devil, and it described him perfectly. His brother Gareth, who was the brains of the operation, hadn't lucked out on looks but had the same devil's soul. They were both evil fuckers. Gareth and Joey were dangerous in a whole different way to people like

Alexi and Roman. Still wild and unpredictable, but the Nicholls enjoyed giving pain, enjoyed their trade.

'Hey, darling, come and play with me! Another man wandered towards them. He was carrying a bottle of beer, and he staggered slightly as he reached Holly.

'Aw leave her alone!' One of the younger men was tinkering with bit of engine laid out on a couple of pallets. He sounded anxious.

'You're such an old woman. What's wrong with a bit of fresh meat?'

His breath stank and he towered over Holly. She was just over five feet five and he had to be over six feet, and solid muscle with it. But she'd faced bigger, stronger opponents so many times. Suddenly as the adrenalin crackled through her veins, the lightness, the coolness, returned. If he tried anything she'd fucking take him out. In an instant, the past was the present and nothing had changed.

Joey watched with apparent interest as the man laid a heavy hand on Holly shoulder, pulling her closer. She reacted almost without thinking, twisting her body, snapping her own arm round and up. In seconds, her attacker was lying on the stones and the mud, muttering, his shattered bottle scattering wicked shards across the yard.

'You little bitch!' He tried to get up but Joey, laughing his handsome head off, gave him a shove and he flopped back on his bum.

'Leave her alone. Piss off now, Jez.'

The rest of the crowd – there had to be about ten men still watching the action – gave her a round of applause. She heard the muttering go round, and Donnie's name mentioned. Holly was breathing heavily, but taking long, slow breaths to fill her lungs, in case she needed to fight again.

'So, Holly, what can I do for Donnie's girl?' Joey peered at her, his back to the others.

'I want the dog,' Holly said, without thinking. But then, as he laughed again, she supposed she might as well go for it. Having walked right into the fire, it was clear Joey wasn't going to hurt her – not in front of an audience, at least. 'And I want to know what's going on. Roman and Alexi are dead, someone shoved my car off the road . . .' She paused. 'Dad says you might have heard something.' Although she never used the word 'Dad' for Donnie, here it seemed like she needed to reinforce those family connections.

'You spoken to Donnie?' Joey poked his head forward, like a bird of prey judging the best place to strike. 'What did he say?'

So that had hit a nerve, but of course she had no idea what her dad said. Last she heard he'd sunk to the bottom of a bottle of White Lightning. 'He said whatever was happening you would know, because you were in charge now.' It was a major, major risk. Even as she said it, she was gritting her teeth, tensing to fight or flee.

Joey stared at her, eyes raking her face, but she met his gaze defiantly.

Behind her, Jez was back on his feet and was quietly closing the gate she had entered by. The silence was complete again, the crowd inching closer, lighting ciggies and passing round more beer. The dog was forgotten. This was a new game.

Chapter 15

'Come over here – we can talk in my office.' Joey jerked a thumb at the rusting portacabin that stood in one corner of the yard.

There was a rumble of amusement from the men gathered at the entrance to the warehouse but Joey silenced them with a look. Holly hesitated for a moment, aware of the danger, aware that Lydia would probably now be waiting for her to go up to the hospital. She weighed up her options in that fleeting moment, and followed Joey across the yard, her trainers sloshing through mud and icy water.

The door slammed shut behind them and Joey flicked on the lights. Holly leant against the wall, right next to the door, arms folded, muscles tense.

Joey gave a bark of laughter, and sat down behind the desk, a swivel chair creaking with his bulk. 'Don't look like that, girl. I don't want a black eye as well. Believe me, if that was what I'd wanted I'd have taken it years ago, but that isn't the way we work, is it?'

'Depends on your point of view, really,' Holly told him. If they could keep talking in riddles maybe she could get out of here alive. She might even be able to keep her date with Lydia. Her phone pinged, but she was afraid to break this fragile bond between her and Joey.

'You're too old for me now anyway. I like them young. Didn't your friend ever tell you? Look, Holly, I heard you might be coming back to Seaview . . .'

A wash of nausea at his first comment almost overshadowed his second. 'What do you mean? Who said I was coming back?'

Joey grinned. 'Is it true? I know old Donnie isn't up to much, but he's still got some money coming in, regular as clockwork.'

This was news to Holly, but she just nodded and played along. 'So what does that have to do with you?'

'You said that the two of you had words about me. I want to know what was said.'

'Again, why? I don't see the fact my dad is still collecting dividends being of any importance to you.'

He got up and came towards her, far too close, despite his promises. 'Listen, girl, I need to know if you're coming back to take over Donnie's business. Me and Gareth, we've got all of it except that stretch between Carside-on-Sea and Lighton.'

Holly narrowed her eyes, trying not to flinch. 'That's a pretty big area.' Her mind was frantically scrambling through memories, trying to figure out why her dad should still have this hold. She'd been convinced for years that all he had were the shops, and he'd sold most of those since last year according to Lydia. Of course, he paid her cousins to do an odd bit of illegal work on the side, but no big-time stuff. A flash of inspiration gave her the guts to push Joey. 'And if I was taking over? It's all family over there, you know, so they'd deal with me, but not you.'

Joey lit a cigarette and offered her the packet. She shook her head, and he shrugged. 'That's the whole point. If Donnie is handing over to you, I want to know if you're taking up the slack, or if you're going to sell. Because if you're selling, then I want to buy. All the contacts, all the trade and I'll give you a good price. Donnie's a stubborn old bastard, and he won't let go. I don't mind admitting I've tried buying him out, but he's always said no.'

Holly was struggling to keep up. Joey was offering to buy her out of something she hadn't actually been offered. Why had her dad kept that part of his empire? For the memory or the money? Or perhaps he really imagined that she would still take over and work the business. A crazy thought darted through her brain. Had her dad known Jayden was alive? Had he been saving it for him? 'I'd need to think about it.'

'Yeah. Look, here's my number. Call me, not Gareth. And, Holly, I heard about this kid in your car, and the crash. Nothing to do with us. I've been wanting to ask you straight up about the business, since I heard you were back. I tell you who else is back – Devril. I've seen him with Marco.'

'And Niko,' Holly said. Her phone was buzzing. Could she actually walk out of here without any injuries? She didn't believe Joey for a second when he said he had nothing to do with the crash. The only reason she was still breathing was because he wanted something. And because of that weird latent respect between the families.

'Mason's only got a few months to live, but Niko, yeah, he and I have had words.' Joey's eyes turned cold, and he chucked the cigarette down and stamped on the glowing end. 'Think about my offer, Holly.'

He opened the door and the night air poured in.

'I will.' Holly knew she should get out while she could, but the poor bloody dog was still cringing next to the car, and a light, icy rain had started to fall, numbing her face and hands. 'Joey? I still want the dog.'

He glared at her and then laughed again. 'You're something else, Donnie's girl, aren't you? All right, you take the mutt. Ring me when you've made up your mind. You've got until the end of the month.'

The amusement had died in his eyes, and his expression was hard again, so Holly marched across the soaking yard to the dog. Most of the men had gone inside, and the big warehouse doors were shut, but a couple were still working on the lorries, waterproof jackets pulled up over the heads.

She approached the dog with caution, speaking softly, half crouching, taking in the abrasions on his side, the glint of fear in his eyes. She was afraid he would snap at her, but trying to

116

hurry before Joey changed his mind, Holly began to untie the towrope. But her numb fingers couldn't undo the wet knot. She tried the other end, next to the car bumper, but failed.

'Here, I'll do it.' The man who had called Jez off earlier was crouching next to her. He slipped a knife from his pocket and cut the rope.

'Thanks. And thanks for before,' Holly said, hastily gathering the rope into her hand, and coaxing the dog with her. At least it had a sort of lead now.

'Didn't do anything,' the man said, winking at her and returning to his tinkering. He was shorter than her, with brown eyes, and a wet mop of red hair. His trousers were streaked with oil.

Joey had vanished, so Holly and the whimpering dog passed out of the Nicholls' yard without any further trouble. This was so freaky. Why was Joey so convinced she was about to take over the Hughes family business?

The dog trotted obediently at her side. It was limping slightly, but beyond the cuts and scrapes, it seemed okay. What the hell was she thinking? She couldn't keep a dog while she worked shifts. Holly called Lydia quickly.

'Are you all right? I've been calling and calling you, and now it's too late to go to the hospital! You said half an hour . . . What the hell's going on, Holly?' Lydia's voice was shrill with worry, and Holly felt instant guilt.

'I'm sorry. Can I still come round? There's stuff I need to tell you.'

'Of course, love, I was just so worried. What with everything that's been happening . . .'

'I know, I'm really sorry. I'll see you in five, okay?'

***

'And what the hell do you think I'm going to do with a dog?' But Lydia was already crouching down to the animal, gently inspecting his injuries.

'I didn't think . . . You always used to have dogs – those two rotties were lovely.'

'Jack and Daniel,' Lydia said, smiling as the dog settled onto her kitchen floor with a deep sigh. 'This one looks like a wolf, but he's a nice big lad, and when I've given him a bath we'll see what colour he is.' She turned back to Holly. 'So tell me why you were walking round the Seaview in the dark again?'

'I told you. I wanted to see Niko. I just . . . I wanted to do something instead of just sitting around wondering what's going to happen next. I didn't go out thinking I'd drop in on the Nicholls but it happened. So tell me what's going on with Dad. I've heard he's kept hold of more of the old business than I thought. Is he working again?'

Her aunt frowned and seemed to be choosing her words carefully. 'He's been a lot better for about six months now.'

'By better you mean off the booze?' Holly asked.

'Yeah. I didn't tell you because I didn't want to get your hopes up. He's got his business head back on. The little that he still owns, like the betting shops, that kebab place, and of course his slice of pie along the coast. That'll be what Joey and Gareth want, because that area runs right across county lines. It's prime dealing, and the coppers haven't caught one of your dad's blokes in years.'

'Dad's family was from down that way, weren't they?' Holly didn't think she'd ever met them.

'There's nobody left now, but the contacts are all of an age and they won't hear of selling out to anyone else. They only deal with the Hughes family, and I can't see that changing,' Lydia told her. Her black eyes were fixed on Holly's face. 'You know, your dad was pleased when he heard you and Tom had split up. He still thinks that you might change your mind and take over what little there is left. Now Devril's back, he reckons it's only a matter of time before he can hand the whole lot over to the two of you.'

Holly split her glass of wine. 'Shit! Sorry, Lydia, I'll get a cloth . . . He can't seriously imagine I'll just forget the last eleven years ever happened and move back to Seaview?'

'Just telling you what he's been saying. And now this thing with Jayden, and Jayden's son, suddenly the old man's got family back, heirs to the business, all he ever wanted.'

Holly mopped up her mess, and stood up slowly, mind whirling. 'But Joey wants to buy me out, if I take over.'

'So you say. Looks like your dad's setting up for another turf war with the Nicholls, except this time, it'll be you, or maybe even Jayden in charge,' Lydia said soberly.

'There's no way I'd go back. Whatever happens,' Holly said, but her heart was pounding as she spoke, imagining her dad the way he used to be, Jayden alive and their kids playing football together. It was a stupid dream. To achieve that, the past would have to be forgotten, and the Hughes empire would have to be rebuilt.

Joey would kill her if she didn't sell. She was under no illusions. The only reason she had walked out of his yard tonight was because she was worth something. If he had thought for a moment that she was still estranged from her dad, and therefore not part of the Hughes family, he would have left her to play with his men.

***

Holly's next shift at work was hell. A prank caller who claimed his mum wasn't breathing, some desperate mental health patients and finally a teenage miscarriage. Holly and Cath managed to snatch a quick break together and went outside into the darkness. Cath lit up and inhaled deeply, and Holly leant against the wall, the cold bricks digging into her back beneath her shirt.

'I can't believe you went over to the Nicholls' yard – you are insane! My dad says he'd never go in there unless he was carrying. You're lucky Gareth wasn't there too. He's worse than Joey. At least Joey's got the looks.'

119

'Yeah, whatever, and I'm not like your dad, with knives in every pocket.' Holly remembered Joey's passing comment. 'Cath, you didn't ever go with Joey did you, when we were younger?'

'Course not! He's an old git.' Cath stamped out her first cigarette and flicked her lighter on another. Her hand shook slightly so the flame wobbled crazily.

'Okay, okay.' There was something there for sure, but Holly knew better than to push her friend. 'Anyway, Lydia's keeping the dog. She's called him Oreo.'

'Cute. So what now?'

'I'm giving her a lift up to the hospital after work. She's desperate to see Jay's kid.'

Cath twirled a long blonde curl between her fingers, digesting the information in silence, dragging on her cigarette. Finally she sighed. 'I get that you feel a bit responsible, and hell I'd be the same, but what's going to happen when he wakes up? What if Jayden has just ditched him?'

'I'll have him,' Holly said. 'He's just a child, like our lot. And he's Larissa's child too.'

Cath's expression softened. 'Yeah . . . Just be careful, okay? Now what's going on with you and Devril? Have you seen him again?'

'I haven't seen Dev since that time on the school drop-off. I told him I need a bit of time to get my head around everything.'

'Did he talk to the police?'

'Dunno. Part of me wants to make him tell me where Jayden is, and part of me wants to pretend this isn't happening. Does that sound weird?'

'You are weird, but I do know what you mean. Too much and too fast.' Cathryn lit another cigarette. 'Plus, although Dev was always sweet on you, he's a manipulative bastard, and pretty good at stringing people along. Remember how Mason was always convinced he was working exclusively for him, and then Joey thought the same. Double pay, and as far as I know he got away with it. You know if you did ever think about going back and running the Hughes dealers, Dev would probably help.'

Holly shook her head, retying her hair into a tight ponytail. 'No chance. My dad's dreaming. You can't tear a hole in your life and then expect to put a bit of tape over it and carry on as though nothing's happened.'

'That looks like shit, put it down again.'

'Thanks.'

'Let me do it.' Cath pulled a small brush from her pocket and brushed out Holly's long dark hair, twisting and pinning whilst she spoke. 'I heard Niko is getting busy. Recruiting some of the old gang. And Mason is out of hospital again. Shame the pneumonia didn't finish the old git off. Anyway, sounds like Niko is really back in business. He was up at the yard talking to Gareth the other day, and they seemed very friendly. Colleen's seeing one of the drivers, so she tells me everything, the dozy cow.'

'Back in business. You make it sound like he was doing something legal,' Holly told her. 'Don't you start seeing any of the Nicholls lot, though . . . Actually, didn't you mention a fit bloke called Rohan a while ago? You can't be thinking of getting involved with a Nicholls. *Cathryn!*'

'It's nothing. Back to Niko, anyway. He doesn't seem that bothered his brothers have been murdered either. There, you look half decent now. He's going to have a fucking job to get back into the biz – I know Mason ran the drugs side into the ground while Niko was banged up. But now he's lost Alexi and Roman too, so with no brains and no brawn he's basically screwed.'

'Which is why Niko's hanging around Gareth, presumably. Joey seems to think Niko might work for them, or at least put some money into their business. At least, that's what I get from joining the dots on our conversation last night.'

'Right, babes. I can see what Gareth can do for Niko but not what Niko can do for Gareth, if you get me. Anyway, I'll see if Colleen can find out any more, and you need to get onto Devril. If he actually knows where you brother is . . . Come on, Holly, we could find out without the police sticking their beaks in,' Cath said enthusiastically.

'We need to get back inside.'

'Very obvious subject change, Hol. Oh, did you see that Sara has turned up with exactly the same bag as you? I think you've got yourself another stalker!'

All the team knew Holly had a pest caller. It happened to all of them occasionally. 'Has she? Whatever.' Holly led the way back into the warm building. 'I'll ring Devril tomorrow morning, okay?'

'Fine, but make sure you do it. You need to find out this stuff for yourself and screw the police. Don't trust them, Holly, they're full of shit. Oh, and you're not going to like this either, but you need to see your dad, find out what's really going on in his head.'

***

After work Holly drove straight over to pick her aunt up. Lydia had walked across the bridge to the road, so it was an easy ten minutes to the hospital.

'How's the dog?' Holly asked brightly, trying to mask exhaustion and worry with conversation.

'Gorgeous. And he's not "the dog", he's called Oreo.'

'Sorry, Oreo. I bet you've given him a bath and done his hair, and he's in dog heaven.' Holly smiled at her.

'Might have done. Suri on the top floor's looking after him this morning. She loves dogs. Used to have a Jack Russell that bit everyone.'

'I remember.' Weirdly, Holly felt nervous, but she told herself it was just too much caffeine and not enough sleep.

She dropped Lydia at the entrance and drove around looking for a space. Eventually she spotted an elderly couple about to move, so she waited, indicator flashing, drumming her fingers on the wheel with impatience.

A man caught the edge of her vision, walking quickly past the bike shelter towards the road. His coat flew out in the breeze and his head was down, but he was unmistakable. Holly stared as DI Harper vanished behind the hedge. What the hell was he doing at the hospital? Unless something had happened to the boy . . .

A loud hooting from behind her made her jump, and she blinked as a Mini dodged round her and nipped into the space left by the old couple. A couple of teenage boys gave her a V sign in triumph, but she was too worried to care. There was surely only one reason the DI would have been there . . . Holly parked illegally on the double yellow lines at the end of the car park and ran towards the entrance.

Lydia was waiting by the lifts, and Holly managed to control her anxiety until they reached the ward. She didn't know whether to expect the worst, or if they'd go in to find him awake and talking. But when they arrived, there was nothing to report. The boy was still in a private room and they sat, one either side of the bed, and watched him breathing. A quick chat with the nurse reassured Holly further. It was just a matter of time before he woke up, the nurse told them.

Holly bit her lip, relief flooding her body, making her shoulders sag. She was stupid to have even thought the DI was at the hospital in connection with the child. He must have loads of cases and loads of people to visit. It might even be a family member in here.

'He looks a lot like Jay, doesn't he?' Lydia was actually sniffing into a tissue. Gently, she touched the boy's cheek with the back of her hand, her red talons curled away from his face. The long dark lashes curled a little, and the boy's cheeks had a definite, healthy flush of pink she'd not seen there before.

They chatted across the child about this and that, and after half an hour, Holly reluctantly got to her feet. 'Sorry, Lydia, I've got to go, or I'll probably fall asleep next to him.' Without thinking she leant over and kissed the boy's forehead, smoothing his dark hair out the way, just as she had done every time she had visited.

But this time she froze, still leant over, feeling his breath on her cheek. His eyelids flickered, and the corner of his mouth twitched, before he opened his eyes with a little gasp.

Chapter 16

'Hey,' Holly said softly, smiling as the dark eyes met hers, before turning towards Lydia. It must be terrifying to wake up in a room full of strangers.

'Hallo, darling.' Lydia's eyes were bright with tears, and her hand was on his. 'I'll get one of the nurses.'

'I'm Holly. What's your name?' It was the simplest introduction and worked from childhood to adulthood, but the boy in the bed just stared at her. From time to time his eyes darted around the room, and she could see he was breathing quickly. 'It's okay. You had a car accident and you're in hospital. You're safe.'

He looked hard at her, moistened his lips, but didn't say a word. All kinds of emotions flitted across his face, like shadows on a sunny day, and he moved carefully under the sheets, until his legs were curled up, and he was on his side, facing her. Milo often slept curled up like that and Holly almost felt like crying.

Lydia came back quickly and the nurse gave them all a bright smile, before busying herself with the child's observations. She chatted away to the boy, seemingly unconcerned that he remained silent, and when she was done she drew Lydia and Holly away from the bed, towards the door.

'All his observations are normal. The doctor will be round soon

124

and there are a few more tests we need to do now he's woken up, but he looks fine.'

'He hasn't said a word. Is that normal?' Lydia asked.

The nurse shrugged. 'He's been through a major trauma and woken up to find himself in a strange place surrounded by strangers. It might take time for him to trust us. I'll have to ask you to leave now – the police asked to see him as soon as he woke up.'

***

Lydia was staying over for a few days, as she often did when Holly worked nights, and she said she would collect Milo from his after-school clubs at five. She and Holly sat for an hour with cups of tea and cake, talking about the child, speculating, arguing, until finally Holly fell asleep with her head on the table and her aunt had to shake her gently awake and shove her in the direction of the stairs.

After grabbing a couple of hours' sleep, Holly staggered down and found Lydia had tidied the house, packed up her niece's dinner for work, and left a note saying she was going home to check on Oreo, but would be back to pick Milo up from his clubs.

Holly made a coffee and sat at the kitchen table with her phone. There was a message from DC Marriot saying that she and DS Marlow had been in to see the boy, and he seemed fine, was eating and drinking but still not speaking. Holly herself kept replaying the moment when the child had opened his eyes. She had only ever seen Larissa's eyes in that photograph, but her son's were a mirror image. But the little pointed chin, the expression of wary stubbornness, reminded her so much of Jayden.

Cath texted to ask if Jayden's son had said anything yet, and Holly sent back a negative reply. The nurses had promised to ring if anything changed.

Idly she googled Devril again, and watched the results come up. She skim-read a couple of his articles, not really interested in the sordid night lives of reality stars, or dodgy fast food businesses.

Nothing really caught her eye until she came to the bottom of the results page:

Girls for Sale – The rise and rise of pop-up brothels

Holly clicked and read the full article, which was dated January this year. She knew her dad had been involved in a lot of illegal business stuff, as well as his legitimate shops and garages, but she had always managed to turn a blind eye to it. It was a source of income, and you got money the best way you could. But she had no idea he was involved in the trafficking and brothels until Larissa's death. Larissa's backstory – when the police had finally pieced it together – was sickening, but it happened, and it was over. She had found her happy-ever-after with Jayden and then it had been torn apart.

Holly read the article again. It didn't mention any names but it did quote sources from the *'south coast area'*. Could Devril be after the Nicholls?

The next article was about getting underage kids to act as mules, taking drugs across the county lines via train, and bus. Again, sources on the south coast were quoted. There was also a quote from the area police on the problem. Holly hadn't given much thought to the families after she moved out. Her dad still had the betting shop, and the kebab places, but she had been so sure he wasn't a player anymore, that he'd sunk all his money into the bottom of a beer bottle. Sure, he'd carried on as long as he could after her mum's death, but Jayden's death had finished him. But now he seemed to be staging a comeback. She really did need to go and visit. It was time for a long overdue little father and daughter chat. But first there was a phone call to make.

Dev's business card was on the shelf on top of a pile of bills. The rain was drumming on the windows, lashing insistently at the roof tiles.

'*Come on, Holly, just bloody do it,*' she told herself. The lid was already off Pandora's box, and the bad stuff was happening. She could do worse than talk to Devril. Giving herself no time to dwell on it, Holly tapped out the number, waiting, holding her breath, for him to answer.

'Devril Mancini.'

Her free hand was clutching the edge of the table, knuckles white. 'It's Holly.' She stopped, unsure whether she needed to add a surname, and if so which one.

'Hey, Holly.' There was a smile in his voice, and something else. Relief? She was used to listening to people's voices, to picking out the nuances others might miss.

'So you mentioned that you knew some stuff about Jayden. Can you talk now?'

'Sure. We can meet up if you like? Where are you?'

Letting out a long gentle breath, ignoring her thundering heart, she tried to sound normal. 'At home.' She gave him the address. He didn't ask her to repeat it. She figured he probably already knew where she lived. Especially if he *had* been following her.

Ending the call, Holly sat, slumped at the kitchen table for a while, and then walked over to the window so she could see when he arrived. Hell, she even caught herself checking out her hair in the mirror. Which was crazy and depressing because she looked like shit – old and tired. When she and Dev had been a couple, they had both been ripped from training, her dark hair had been long and straightened to within an inch of its life, and she had looked damn good. Just for a second she wished she hadn't left her box of memories at Donnie's flat.

An old cardboard box full of trophies, her magazine covers, a scrapbook of cuttings, certificates – all the stuff she hadn't brought with her into her new life with Tom. But, unlike her social media profiles, which she had ruthlessly taken down, and the photos on her computer, which she had deleted by the thousand, that box was full of mementoes you could get your hands around.

A thump on the door broke through her reverie and she ran

a hand through her hair and then hastily tied it up, pulling a few strands around her face.

'Fucking weather.' Devril had the hood of his coat pulled right down over his face and water streamed off his shoulders, collecting in pools on the wooden floorboards. 'Hell, sorry, now I've messed up your house.'

'It's fine. I haven't got long because I've got work tonight, but we need to talk about Jayden.' Holly led the way to the kitchen, unable to meet his eyes, to stand close to him, and furious with herself because she was acting like a pathetic teenager. 'I'm sorry about before. It was just a shock to see you, and with everything that's been going on, I didn't want any more shit, you know? When you told me that you never passed the message on, it was almost like I could let the past go, but someone doesn't want that to happen, do they?' She needed to stop babbling and shut up, so she started making drinks, keeping her back to him, avoiding his eyes.

'Nice place, you've got. Better than Donnie's shithole.' Devril wandered over to the kitchen windows. 'Can't see the sea from here, although I suppose you've got the woods at the bottom of your garden.'

'Devril! I thought you were a journalist, not a bloody estate agent. Tell me what's going on.' Jolted out of her nerves, Holly stood with her back to the counter, arms folded, watching him.

He turned to face her, grinning. 'Sorry, I'm a bit nervous. How weird is that? Seeing you properly after all these years . . . I'm just excited you invited me round, so I don't have to keep following you and pleading for an audience.'

Suddenly she felt better, the solid lump of worry that seemed to have lodged itself in her stomach melting a little. 'Shut up, Dev! Okay, here's your drink, so sit down and tell me what the fuck is going on and what you're doing back down here.'

'Don't I get coffee?'

Without thinking, she had made tea for them both. 'Not yet.'

'Fair enough. You're right, I'm a journalist. After the trial . . .'

He paused, glancing at her, but she remained expressionless. 'Well, you wouldn't see me, would you? The Seaview was fucked and there was a rumour I was a grass after I gave evidence at the trial. Gareth Nicholls was after my blood so I went right away. It never came to anything, and Gareth even phoned a few months after Jayden had been declared dead and apologised for doubting me.'

'Get lost!'

'No, he did. He offered me a load of money to come back and work with him.'

Wow. Dev had always done a lot of the background work, keeping track of who was dealing what and where it was going, so she supposed he had been missed. The second-tier dealers trusted him and he kept the prices high for the punters, low for the main dealers. Yeah, the Nicholls family would have taken a hit.

'I said I couldn't come back, but I might see him sometime. I didn't want to piss him off, and I knew by then that the police were going to jump on his trafficking business. Although they never had enough evidence to bust him out of business, did they? I'd always put a bit of money away, so I went off to Asia, the States, Australia and just worked my way around.'

'But you came back,' Holly said.

'After a couple of years, I knew I needed to sort my life out. I did come back down to the Seaview for a quick visit. My uncle was busy working his arse off for Gareth, and Joey and I are still on good terms. They seemed to have the whole place sewn up, and despite what the police and the papers said, Nicholls Transport was still transporting things it shouldn't be.'

'So how did you get into journalism? That's a big change from being a personal trainer.' She couldn't imagine his life after Larissa's murder, but then he probably couldn't imagine hers either.

He rested one arm on the table, propping his chin in his hand. 'Not so hard really. It's quite a recent thing. I'd been blogging about my travels, and I had a good following on Instagram. I met this bloke when I was travelling in India, and he was a commissioning editor from one of the local papers in Cardiff. He said to get in touch if I ever wanted a job. I really didn't expect him to follow through. You meet loads of people travelling and hardly ever keep in touch properly.'

'You've been living in Wales?' Holly got up to make coffee, mulling it over. 'I read some of your stuff,' she admitted, reaching for mugs. 'It was good.'

'Ta. I only stayed in Cardiff for six months, and now I'm freelance, so I still get to travel, just not to exotic places so much.' He grinned. 'But you stayed right here and got married. I would never have predicted that!'

Holly didn't want to talk about her life. Apart from Milo, she felt she had done a pretty good job of screwing it up so far. 'So go on, you're obviously back here for a story.'

'Holly, there's no easy way to say this, and I swear until the car crash – which incidentally was nothing to do with me – you weren't involved, but I had a tip-off that Jay was back in Westbourne.'

'I need to know your source. Who told you?' It came out high and sharp.

Devril waited a long moment, before saying, almost reluctantly, 'Bailey. He's Gareth's kid. You remember him?'

She screwed up her nose, thinking hard. 'Fuck, he got beaten up back then, didn't he? Outside Shoey's? And you and Jay helped him.'

'Yeah. He got stabbed but he pulled through. Bailey's a good kid and he's driving for his dad now, mostly through Europe. We've kept in touch on and off. He knows he owes me one. You know how it works.'

Holly did. People from the outside, like Tom, always thought that the Seaview was lawless and rough as hell, but it had its own rules, and the communities were fiercely loyal, sticking to their values and their families. If someone saved your life, you owed them. If someone beat the shit out of you, you owed them in a totally different way. The favours or the threats could run into future generations and grudges were passed from father to son and mother to daughter.

'Holly, I think you need to meet Bailey. After what you told me about Joey – and shit, I can't believe you walked in and out of that yard – I want you to hear Bailey's take on this. I was going to meet him later, but I'll text him now. He's got a day off.'

'Really? You want me to come along?' Holly was doubtful.

'Yeah.' Dev was already tapping out a text, and he downed the rest of his drink while they waited for a reply.

Holly's heart was hammering uncomfortably and nerves jangled in her stomach. If Bailey was snitching on his dad, Gareth would kill him if he found out. Joey's cool gaze had given her nightmares when she finally snatched some sleep this morning. The reality of what she had done, walking into the yard on her own, had hit home. But sometimes you just had to go with your gut.

'So that's me. I kind of got most of the gossip on you, but you kicked your husband out, didn't you?'

'Yeah, he was cheating on me but that doesn't matter at the moment. Do you know where Jayden is now?'

'No. I've been looking since I came back, and I honestly swear I haven't found out where he's hiding. When Alexi and Roman got stabbed, that said to me he's come back for revenge. The thing I don't get is why he brought his kid along with him.'

'Me neither. Jayden's kid is awake, but he's not talking, for whatever reason, so the police are pissed off. I get the impression they were hanging all their hopes on the boy telling them what was going on and where Jay is.'

'At least he's conscious again, that's a start. If he's anything like his dad, if he's been told to keep his mouth shut, he will. Your brother was good at keeping secrets.' His eyes rested on her, but his voice said there was more she didn't know.

'He's just a boy, Dev, and he's terrified. I could see it in his eyes. Anyway, I'm going to take Milo to the hospital to see him tomorrow after school. When I rang her this morning, DC Marriot was getting desperate to find out what's going on.' She looked questioningly at Dev and he nodded. 'The kid is the best hope of finding Jay if he is still around here.'

'What time are you going to the hospital?'

'About five. No journos allowed though, so keep your beak out – and Dev, if you put anything I've said in the papers, I will personally beat the crap out of you.'

'Fair enough,' he said, but he was smiling.

'Where are you staying?'

'Across the river in a rental flat. I figured this might take a while, so I thought I'd get settled. I'll text you the address if you give me your number. You should come and visit.'

'I'll think about it.' She said nothing about the teenage castles in the air, the dreams of an apartment across the river, but ragged reminders of those memories seemed to dance between them, unspoken and unacknowledged.

They both jumped as the gate in her back garden banged in the wind, and a spatter of hailstones slid down the windowpane.

Dev's phone buzzed, and he grabbed his coat. 'It's on. We'll take my car. Down by the river next to the old wharf; he'll be walking his dog.'

Holly hesitated, then shrugged and yanked her coat off the peg. The back gate banged again and she turned back, but Dev was already opening the front door.

'Come on, Holly!'

Sometimes the bolt on the gate worked loose, but she was never that bothered, even when Milo was in the garden, because the gate only led to the path and the woods. Hardly anyone used it, just a few dog walkers. Anyway, this wasn't the Seaview, with evil lurking in the shadows and dealers looking for secluded places to do business. But Joey's eyes were still haunting her. 'Dev, I just need to lock the back gate!'

'Okay, I'll wait in the car. It's the black BMW on the end.'

Holly grabbed her bag, checking her purse, hunting for her keys. She frowned, delving deeper, excavating biscuit crumbs, stray tissues and ancient Calpol sachets. She had two sets of keys, which had always annoyed Tom. The two back door keys were on a separate ring with a green fluffy pompom, and a black cat whose LED eyes flashed green in the dark.

The back door keys were gone. Just great, she had bloody lost them somewhere. Probably in the car, down the back of the passenger seat again. She locked the front door behind her and ran down the road to the waiting BMW.

In the car she quizzed Dev. '*Where* did Bailey see Jayden? And when?'

Dev indicated right and then accelerated, ignoring the speed limit as they drove through the old part of town. 'Beginning of the month,' he said, 'so around four weeks ago, give or take. Bailey was driving, overnighting in a lay-by on the main road, waiting until his hours were okay to carry on and deliver his load. There's a motel and a café. It's near the Eastside slip road . . .'

'I kind of know where you mean.'

'Okay. Well, Bailey went into the café about midnight to get a bacon roll and he says he saw Jay in the queue for the coffee machine. It was pretty crowded but he's convinced it was him.'

'He didn't speak to him?'

'No. And he didn't see a kid either, because I've spoken to him since your crash, since the news came out.'

'Did Bailey see where he went? His car? Anything else at all?'

'Nah. By the time he'd paid for his food and pushed through the crowd Jay was gone, but he's dead certain it was him.'

'Fuck.'

'Yeah. Look, we'll park up next to the café.'

Holly got out, the wind whipping her dark hair into tangles. The café was deserted apart from an old woman in a grubby apron laying tables. It was a desolate area, and the café was

133

frequented only by truckers heading north, mainly because there was a fuel station opposite.

They left the ugly brick building and headed across the rough grass along the side of the river. The old wharf was crumbling, graffitied and littered with broken bottles and syringes.

Dev pointed to a man in the distance, strolling along the footpath towards them, whistling to his brown and white mongrel. As he came closer, Holly squinted in surprise.

'Bloody hell, I saw him at the Nicholls' last night. He helped me. I never realised that was Bailey when you talked about him getting beaten up.'

'Yeah. He's a good lad. Not surprising he's all screwed up about working for his family,' Dev said.

***

Bailey stopped behind the remains of a crumbling grey stone tower, at the far end of the wharf. The wind moaned around them and Holly's cheeks and hands were numb with cold.

Dev made quick introductions and Bailey nodded at Holly. 'Hallo again. Joey likes you, doesn't he?'

'Not so you would notice,' Holly told him. 'Thanks for last night.'

'No worries.' Bailey ran a hand across his mop of red wiry hair. His brown eyes were anxious, and he kept darting worried glances around the water meadows. A seabird flew up, wings outstretched, screaming an alarm call, and he tensed, shoulders hunched.

'It's okay. Nobody here,' Dev told him. 'I told you I was bringing Holly and she won't say anything, so let's have a quick chat. I want to help, Bailey. I really want to get you out.'

Bailey looked at Holly again. 'Dev told you about me? About our deal?'

'Yeah. Well, kind of . . .' She saw that he had the faded remains of a bruise on one freckled cheek.

'No way I can go to the police myself, but if Dev can take what

I give, I can get out and my dad can go to hell. Before you say it, I know if they find out I was the grass they'll string me up.'

'So Dev will write a story on the Nicholls family and give information to the police that will put them out of business?' It was gutsy of him, trying to break free. But it was a big price to pay. 'Bailey, are you sure it was my brother you saw? I just mean that it's been a long time since he was around the Seaview . . .'

But he was nodding. 'I'm positive. I got a good look at him, and I'm just sorry I didn't get a chance to speak to him. Dev says he hasn't been in touch with his family?'

'Not as far as I'm aware, and certainly not with me,' Holly said slowly. Had he been talking to her *dad*? Was that the reason for Donnie's sudden turnaround – was it that Jay had come back?

'What have you got for me, Bailey?' Dev checked his watch.

The other man smiled thinly. 'This is it then; if I tell you, I'm committed.' He took a deep breath, and his dog lay down at his feet. 'Basically, Holly, I would prefer to drive other cargoes. Legal ones. I hate Dad and Joey for sucking me in and keeping me bogged down in their shit.'

'It's almost like Jay all over again, but Bailey doesn't want any part of the business,' Dev added.

'I've got some video footage. It's enough to rattle Nicholls Transport, the whole fucking lot of them involved in running the girls,' Bailey said, the words coming out in a rush.

She was afraid to ask, but equally she couldn't let it lie, not when everything that was happening could be linked to Jayden's reappearance. 'What's in the video?'

'It's still giving me nightmares, but let's just say when Niko was released, he wanted to get straight back into business, and with a whole load of prison contacts on his phone, he felt he had a lot to offer. He took the contacts list to my dad. He could see the only way back was to get in with Nicholls Transport. Dad and Joey were all for it and threw him a little party with some of their new girls.'

Holly nodded encouragingly.

135

'I was there, Rohan too, and a few of the others from the family. They were all filming it on their phones.' His expression hardened, brown eyes hooded for a second as he fiddled with his phone, as though trying to push the memory away. 'I've seen a lot, but this was what made me sure I had to quit.'

'A party? Like the old days?' Holly queried. The Nicholls had always been notorious for their involvement in the sex trade.

'Not really, it was much worse. These girls had never worked before and Dad calls them "breaking-in parties". I swear to you I made myself watch to the end because they'd have been suspicious if I didn't, but I actually almost threw up.' Bailey rubbed his face with a shaky hand. 'I've got two daughters now. If I thought for a moment that my kids could grow up and have to go through that . . .'

'If I'd been there, nothing could have stopped me beating the shit out of that fucker and his boys. It's not human.' Dev's eyes were glittering now and his breathing had quickened. 'So you see, Holly, I came down to get a story on Jay, and now I'm pretty keen to finally get enough evidence to shut down Nicholls Transport. Bailey will get a good sum to tide him over, and he gets to cut ties and run with his family.'

Bailey was nodding, pulling his coat around him, clipping a lead on the little dog. 'That's it. I've got the video, and I've taken screenshots of as much stuff as I can without going into the portacabin and going through the paperwork in there. I reckon another week or ten days and I'm good to go. It'll take a bit longer to get myself set up. My wife's not keen on moving and for her sake I don't want to tell her all of it. She's got family in Poland so that's where we'll go.'

Holly, feeling Dev tense and angry beside her, remembered him before a fight, getting ready, putting his pads on, psyching himself up. It was the same now, except he would be scrawling words on a page instead of punching an opponent. She got it, and the evil that came through from his description of the party was enough to make anyone want to hang the Nicholls out to dry.

Chapter 17

Dear Mum,

Dad says we're ready to start working on the last bit of the plan now. Is it wrong that I'm a bit scared?

When I knew that he'd got everything organised, I had one thing to do before we left. It took a different kind of planning, but I'm pretty happy with the way it turned out. They might figure out it was me, but by that time, we'll be miles away and they'll never catch us.

Dad has been really cool about training me up for our plan, and I'm a pretty good shot now. Ice cold, Dad says! He still won't tell me exactly what the plan is, but you know, I'm sure he will soon. He'll have to because he's always saying I'm an important part of it!

We still spend time at your wall every evening, and that's the only time I feel calm. The rest of the time, I have this rawness beneath my skin. It's almost like I don't have any skin, because every sound, every taste and touch makes me wince. It hurts really bad unless I'm in 'warrior mode'. Dad taught me this one, too. When he says I need to get into warrior mode, nothing can touch me, and I'm back to the crack-shot, ice-cold kid.

Dad's been a lot better lately, and he even got me an iPod and a phone. I'm not sure where he got them, but I don't care because now I feel like I've got this link to the outside world. I can stay up all night playing games online, and I've joined chat forums under different names. Finally, I can be someone different and nobody can see the truth.

So Kyle Wilson trains with the team every Thursday night after school, and they run a few circuits of the field, play some football, before he heads home through the woods on his bike. I had to take a chance that he'd be alone. I watched for a couple of weeks and mostly he went home by himself and met the boys and his girlfriend later on.

The day before we were due to leave, with our stuff all packed, and all the precious things from your wall in a flowered box, I snuck out with my gun. Dad came home with a gun for each of us a few months ago. He said we needed to keep them hidden, but that we'd need them for the plan.

It was over very quickly. Kyle came pounding down the ride, scattering leaves as he skidded to a halt, dismounted and pushed it up the steep hill towards me. I stepped out, hood pulled down around my face and he stopped, properly scared. He even dropped his precious bike in the mud. I loved that he was so scared, raising his hands, and muttering that I should calm down. I was totally calm.

I smiled at him and I could feel you near me. Did you even touch my face? I think so. I lifted the gun and aimed a shot above his head. I wasn't aiming to kill, or even hurt him – I just wanted him properly terrified. And it worked, although I think he started to say something, like he couldn't believe what was happening.

Is it like that when you die suddenly? Did you cry out? Did you know what was happening? I suppose maybe you did.

Anyway, Kyle freaked and ran off. I suppose he would've called the police, but who cares? I got back to the flat with my gun, and we made it safely away. After years of training, we've finally started on the plan. It feels like my whole life has been leading up to this. Dad says he's super proud of the way my training has gone and I kind of hope you'll be proud of me.

We're doing it for you and Dad's even sworn off the booze. It's a new start.

I love you, Mum x

138

Chapter 18

'Is that Holly?'

Oh God, she recognised that voice, despite the fact that her screen had populated with an unfamiliar set of details. Holly shivered. Her stalker had got himself another phone number. Great. She raised a hand to get her team leader's attention and carried on talking into her headset. 'What's the reason for your call?'

'It *is* Holly, isn't it?'

'Do you need an emergency ambulance?'

'I need you, Holly, and I know you want me too. You're the only person who can help me. I want you to come over here and . . .' His voice was high-pitched and his nasal whine carried traces of a London accent. His breathing grew heavier.

'Sorry, I'm ending this call now. This is the emergency line and I find your comments inappropriate.' Holly ended the call and typed up her notes, her hands shaking slightly.

Gavin was her team leader tonight and he gave her the thumbs-up. 'Logged it and reported it. Well done.'

'He freaks me out every time. It's that weird voice. It almost sounds like he's using one of those voice distorter things. Milo had one for Christmas, and when you speak into it makes your

139

voice sound like Darth Vader. But why bother? We know who he is,' Holly said unwrapping an energy bar.

Sara, perched next to her, was looking worried too, as she still did on each of her training shifts. 'Does that happen often? How does he know it was you?'

'I took a call from him a few months ago. He is known to police and social services, and he's logged as a frequent caller by us. Anyway, sometimes, if people ask, I tell them my name. It helps create a bit more empathy. Unfortunately now every time he calls he asks for me. Very occasionally he gets me. We get a few who think that 999 is a phone sex chat line, but he's pretty persistent,' Holly explained.

Ruby was explaining a CPR call to her mentee, but she chipped in, 'His name is Earl Brown if you ever get him. So far he's just been a timewaster, but there is nothing we can do. Social services are so short-staffed and the police can't do anything. Just make sure you look in the call history whenever you can. That's where we log all the information on that address or phone number.'

Sara was still looked slightly terrified, but Ruby's trainee grinned. 'It's never going to be boring, is it?' He really was very good-looking, with dark hair and skin, and amber eyes. No wonder Ruby had offered to train him.

'Not when you're with me, love,' Ruby told him before she turned back to Holly. 'Noah's going to rock this job. He already did a CPR call and got a ROSC yesterday.'

'Hi, Noah, and cool, well done,' Holly said to him, noting his leg touching Ruby's under the desk. Rubes was always a fast worker and Noah didn't seem to be in any hurry to dissuade her. She grinned to herself.

'What's a ROSC?' Sara asked, picking up her SlimFast shake.

'Why are you drinking that? You're almost as skinny as Cathryn,' Ruby said.

'Oh, well, you know I like to be healthy,' Sara said, anxiously, eyes darting from one person to the other, clearly afraid she was doing the wrong thing.

'You look fine to me,' Noah told her kindly, but with a sparkle of mischief in his eyes.

She blushed and Holly hastily explained a ROSC was 'return of spontaneous circulation', and meant the patient had a decent chance of survival.

The shift continued without any major hassle and Holly was grateful for the comforting familiarity of work. It took her mind off the shit going on at home. She was still trying to process everything in her mind. Her heart went out to Bailey. It was a dangerous game and if Joey or Gareth found out, they'd kill him with no questions asked. And what about Jay? Had he left his boy and buggered off? She couldn't imagine doing that to Milo. Was Jay there the night of the crash? And what was he doing – protecting his son or drawing hers into danger?

To add to her problems, and despite her hopes to the contrary, a text came in at one in the morning, and seeing Tom's number come up, Holly winced:

Fucking evil bitch. Don't forget I know your secrets.

For fuck's sake! What was wrong with him? He'd got what he wanted, with his new relationship and devoted girlfriend. But he didn't have Milo, a tiny voice reminded her, and that cold clench of fear, now seemingly ever present in her stomach, turned to ice. All her life people had gone missing, died, run away, and just now when, in a weird way, some of them seemed to be coming back, Tom was trying to take her son.

'Are you all right? Holly?' It was little Sara, tagging along behind her to the toilets.

'Fine, sorry. I just need the loo before I go back in. I'll see you in there.' She hoped this was a subtle enough way of saying she wanted to have a moment on her own. Sara was a sweet girl, but very clingy at the moment. It would be up to Holly to give her the confidence to get through these first difficult weeks, but for now, she needed to sort out her own life.

She went into a cubicle, put the lid down and sat on the toilet seat, scrolling through the texts. Anger surged, and she tapped out a message back:

There is no secret. I made a mistake! It never happened, I just didn't realise at the time. Dev never passed the message to Niko so it wasn't me!! BUT I will tell yours if you don't stop hassling me.

After a moment's thought she added a kiss, just to piss him off. She was free, but of course Tom would never believe that. Not that it mattered. Even if he carried out his threat and went to the police, Dev was here to back her up, and Niko would only repeat what he had said in court. The weight had lifted from her shoulders, and she felt confident enough to send the direct threat.

Five minutes passed, and she needed to get back in the control room. She frowned at her phone, and sighed. It was just such a mad thing to do, to wind up your ex when you were playing the perfect dad-to-be with your new girlfriend. Maybe they were both doing it together, having a laugh to see if they could wind her up? No, surely Beth couldn't know Tom's own dirty secret . . . or could she?

Holly walked back to her desk, automatically smiling at Sara. But there was still something else nagging at her nerves, prodding her conscience. If Jayden was going after everyone involved in Larissa's murder, did *he* know the whole story? And which version of the truth would he believe? Holly dragged her thoughts back to work.

On her left, Noah was taking a call, confidently going through the triage and concentrating hard. Ruby was listening, ready to prompt him if he struggled, still sitting a bit too close. On her right Sara was stumbling nervously over the first few questions.

'That was good, Sara, just be a bit more assertive at the beginning, yeah? We need their location as soon as you can.'

The girl nodded. 'It's really hard, isn't it?'

'You'll be okay.' It was Noah, who was now typing up his

notes under Ruby's watchful eye. 'I still brick it every time the phone rings.'

'You do?' Sara looked relieved.

'Yeah, and Colin's quit already. Colin was on our course,' Noah told them. 'Fuck, how do you spell diarrhoea?'

***

When Holly caught the bus home there was still no reply to her text, but she took it to be a good sign. Tom had nothing else to blackmail her with, but she still held his secret. She watched the darkness and the streetlights. It was nearly morning, but the blackness still stretched across the sky. Bloody winter, she couldn't wait for summer.

Holly scrolled idly through her social media, yawning. Perhaps Jay did the same. Maybe he'd been keeping tabs on all of them via Insta or something. The thought was enough to chase away the tiredness for a moment. Flicking her mind away from her family she went back to Dev. Cath was right, his Insta feed was full of him working out, muscles gleaming with sweat, and she skipped hastily over these, feeling like a perv. He'd got out and made some money, and a name for himself.

As well as a visit to Donnie, visiting Niko might provide some answers. He had previously tried to pull in both Holly and Dev when they were in the fitness industry, and if he knew that Donnie was up and running again . . . She supposed it depended on how desperate he was.

The boy in hospital intruded into her whirl of thoughts. What sort of dad had Jayden been? And where the hell had they been all these years?

She was so deep in thought that she nearly missed her stop, staggering blearily to her feet just in time. The spattering of icy rain woke her up properly as she fumbled with the front door key.

Milo was eating breakfast and her aunt was putting a load of washing on as Holly kicked her boots off and walked into the kitchen.

'Hi, Mum!' He waved his spoon, dripping milk across the table as he did so.

'Hi, sweetie. You nearly ready for school?' Holly yawned and ruffled her son's hair. 'Hi, Lydia. I've told you before, you really don't have to do my laundry.'

'I know I don't, but I can see how exhausted you are and I've got half an hour before I need to go.' Lydia was scrutinising her niece's face. 'Was it a bad night?'

'Not really, just the usual, thanks.'

'I've got karate club after school today,' Milo informed her, 'and I can't find my belt.'

'It's in your cupboard, and I only said you could go and watch again. You can't do karate with one leg in a cast,' Holly told him, making a mug of coffee to sustain her for the duration of the school run, before she could fall into bed.

'I know that, but I need to be there to watch the black belts do their grading.' Milo rolled his eyes and hoped nimbly off on his crutches.

'Fine. Don't forget we're going to the hospital after I pick you up,' she called after him.

'I know!'

'Thank goodness that cast comes off soon, he's itching to get back to normal and start working off that energy,' Lydia said, smiling at Milo, who was stuffing his karate belt into his school bag. 'Go and get dressed or you'll be late, and I've got to get home and pick up my dog!'

'I want to walk Oreo too!' Milo said, pausing on his way to the door.

'Another time. Go and get ready!'

When the boy had hopped carefully into the downstairs bathroom, Lydia turned to her niece. 'By the way, DI Harper came round earlier.' Despite the early morning, Lydia had a full face of make-up and was dressed in one of her velour tracksuits, with black fluffy mules poking out the bottom. She could pass for ten years younger than she actually was.

'He came *here*? Why this early?' Holly blinked back to full alertness as caffeine and adrenalin mixed.

'He wanted to tell me to be careful. You know he was always very kind when Jayden was in all that trouble, and he . . . he tried so hard after Sian's death to help.' Lydia paused, her cheeks reddening, although Holly couldn't see why she should be embarrassed about it. 'Anyway, he said that if Jayden was alive and he did contact me at all, to let him know.'

'Why would he come over to my house to tell you that? How did he even know you were here?' Holly demanded.

'I don't know. He said that with everything going on, he's worried that there might be trouble on the estate.'

'Lame excuse. What did he want really?' Holly asked, remembering suddenly that she'd seen him at the hospital. Was he still stalking their family?

'I'm just telling you what he said. He told me to get in touch right away if Jayden contacted me, for our own safety.' Lydia set her mouth in a thin line, and clearly wasn't going to give anything else away.

Holly sat down on a pile of schoolbooks, and hastily got up again, picking up the top book and shoving it in Milo's bag. 'Have you thought about what we're going to do if Jayden doesn't come back for his son?'

Her aunt pushed a stray strand of hair back behind her ear, fiddled with her watchstrap. 'Alexi and Roman are dead. If it was a revenge thing then it's done now. There's nothing to stop your brother coming back to claim his son.'

'I'd say there were loads of reasons! Firstly that he's officially dead, and secondly the Balintas will take him out if he sets foot on the Seaview. And that's just if Gareth and Joey don't get there first.'

'They left you alone. It's still giving me nightmares that you went to their yard . . .'

'That's because they don't have any grudges against me, and they think I have something they want. Jay took one of their girls, and a load of contacts. Niko said some of them were Joey's customers too. Granted he could do a bit of bartering with them, but I'm pretty sure they'd enjoy hurting him first. Anyway, my head's a mess at the moment. Don't leave for Spain just yet, will you, Lydia? Let's get this sorted first.' She smiled at her.

'I said I'd only go when you're settled, Holly. As soon as things are easier for you, you're happier about everything, and Milo is a bit bigger then I'll go. You could always come too, you know.' Her aunt smiled, folding clean school shirts into the ironing basket. 'In the meantime, the rental makes me enough cash to live on. I wish I'd got into the rental market earlier, you know. If I had, I'd have a whole string of villas in Spain by now! But it was never easy for a woman to take control of business interests in our family. Your mum tried after she left home, to get into property development, but then of course she married young . . .'

Holly, tired and emotional, didn't want to talk about her mum, but filed this piece of information away for future reference. Her mum had never mentioned it. 'Thanks, Lydia, but we'll just be the ones who visit all the time. I need to sort Tom out too. He had a total hissy fit when I even mentioned the idea of moving out there with you, and I can't afford any more legal fees.'

'I know, love. Right, if you're okay, I'm off to walk Oreo. It's good having a dog again, so you did me a good turn even if you did nearly get yourself killed. All right, I won't say any more about it! You're working another late shift for overtime this week, aren't you? Is it Thursday?'

'Half six till half six, but then I've got my five days off, thank God.'

'You need some rest. You need to look after yourself, Holly,' her aunt told her sternly.

'So do you.'

'Yes, well all this business isn't helping. I don't like looking back and dragging up the past. There's nothing like being told your dead nephew is alive to fry your brain!'

'I'm sorry.'

'Not your fault, is it?'

Holly nodded, then shook her head, her brain foggy and exhaustion shutting down her body. But she had no intention of getting more than a couple of hours' sleep. It was time to visit Donnie.

***

Cath was at the school gates, dragging her kids along behind her. 'Hey, you got a car!'

'Insurance company finally came through on the rental, and my leg's okay now. Christ, I can't wait to get into bed. You aren't working tonight, are you?'

'Nah. Two days off. It's all right for us part-timers.' She was grinning through her exhaustion.

'I don't know how you do it all with all your kids,' Holly told her honestly.

'Yeah I'm just Wonder Woman. Right now, this superhero needs a kip. I'll ring you later, babes.' She pushed the older kids through the gates, kissing them, adjusting collars, stuffing a stray glove into Kian's backpack.

Holly waved Milo off, and watched Kian, Ronnie, and Sean march off towards the senior school, while the younger ones followed Cath towards the nursery and primary school. Someone jostled her in the crowd and she fell against the chain-link fence. Blinking, expecting an apology, she looked over her shoulder, but the throng of milling parents hid the culprit. Just for a second she almost thought she saw Dev, but dismissed it as her imagination. Holly rubbed her shoulder, pulling the strap on her bag higher up her shoulder. Must be just a latecomer hurrying off to work.

A kid with red hair and freckles reminded her of Bailey. Her heart went out to him. It took courage to break free, and he wasn't just running, he was grassing his family. A brave man or a stupid one?

Ignoring the rain, which had now become a downpour, she made it back to the car and dumped her bag on the passenger seat. A ten-minute drive and she could grab a hot shower and fall into bed for a couple of hours. Her phone buzzed with a text and she automatically delved in her bag for it:

You killed her.

Right, that was it. Exhaustion, the stress of the last few weeks, and worry about the divorce all coiled up inside of her, finally exploded into fury. Enough. She called Tom, but his phone went to voicemail, so she tried the landline.

'Beth, it's Holly. I need to speak to Tom urgently. Is he at home?'

'No, he's on campus today. Is Milo okay?' Her voice was pretty, light and childish.

Holly took a deep breath, felt dizzy and leant her head against the coldness of the car window. 'Look, Beth, I've been getting texts from Tom's phone for the last few weeks, really vicious weird stuff.'

'Did you ask Tom about it?' Beth was wary. 'Because I can understand that this isn't an ideal situation for us all.'

'An ideal situation? It's a fucking nightmare. I love Milo, and all I'm doing is trying to keep some sort of a life going. You know I didn't have a clue Tom was seeing you. It's funny, isn't it – I thought he might be planning a holiday, or a day out or something, and that's why he was being all secretive, but all the time he was meeting you.' This was not a good idea, Holly thought suddenly, but she couldn't stop herself. She had never really talked to Beth, had no idea what Tom had told her, but it wasn't going to be good.

'I . . . I'm sorry but these things happen. I don't know anything about any texts, but I can ask Tom if you like.'

'Don't bother; he says he didn't send them. But they came from his phone . . .'

'You think I sent them?' Her voice was sharper now.

'I don't know, did you?'

'I don't even touch his phone, Holly, and I trust him a hundred per cent, so if he says he didn't send the texts then he didn't. There must be some kind of mistake . . . I need to go now. I'm sorry you're upset, but I want us all to be . . .'

'Friends? Please tell me you weren't going to say friends.' Holly ended the call, shaking. Beth was either totally naive, or sharper than she had imagined.

The girl on the phone today had alternated between uncertainty and something harder, sharper. But then she was pregnant; it made you feel odd things, and certainly made your emotions all over the place. Holly mentally shrugged it off, but she sat and watched the rain pouring down her windscreen in gushing channels for a good few minutes before she found the energy to drive home.

***

When she woke, just after lunch, she felt groggy and slightly dizzy but at least able to think straight. Bloody night shifts were just hell on earth, but she needed to sort out dinner for Milo, get her stuff ready for tonight and get over to the Seaview. She poured a coffee, made a bowl of cereal and took them over to the sofa, curling her legs under her. Daytime TV was crap but strangely comforting, so she flicked across the channels to find a chat show.

Her phone had two voicemails and she quickly checked them whilst she ate. The school had her home phone number, which had a ring to wake the dead, but it was always her first thought.

DC Karen Marriot was her first caller, merely saying that she wanted a chat about Jayden's son, and to ring back when she had a minute. She added that it wasn't urgent.

Tom, clearly alerted by Beth, had left a message saying he was fed up with her bitterness, but he thought that someone must be using his phone. It was his old number and although he had updated the school, he had forgotten to tell Holly. He reeled off a new number as she rolled her eyes. Did he really think that was even remotely plausible? It was a pathetic attempt to explain his behaviour.

But the messages had never come this early in the day before. Holly finished her cereal and flicked back through the messages, checking dates and times, pleased that she had had the sense to keep them. No, there was really only one explanation, and she shivered slightly at the thought. It wasn't her going crazy, it was her ex-husband.

***

The rain was still spitting sullenly as Holly made her way to her dad's house. It was strange and familiar at the same time, following the muddy path, taking the cut-through that led round the back of the recycling centre. Her legs carried her all the way to the front door, without her having to emerge from her thoughts. Discovering she was shivering, despite her coat, Holly told herself firmly to grow some balls and get on with it.

She thumped on the door, watching through the glass panels as a distorted figure approached, hearing them fumbling with a lock and chain.

The two shops next door were closed, and the kebab store had a broken window behind the rusty security bars. Litter circled the scrubby bit of grass outside the house, whirling into a tidal wave of filth as the wind caught it.

'Hey, Holly.' He was grinning at her, dark hair shaved close to his head, his face grey in the murky afternoon light.

'*Niko!*' Holly found herself checking she had come to the right house. What the hell was bloody Niko doing here?

150

Chapter 19

'Niko? Who is it?' Donnie appeared behind the other man, his bulk filling the doorway. If he was surprised, he didn't show it.

Holly, having mentally prepared for a showdown, was totally floored by the fact Niko was apparently having a cosy chat with her dad. She cleared her throat. 'Hi, Dad. I thought I'd come round and see you because . . .'

The big man smiled. 'Because Jayden is back.'

His face was still mottled with red veins, and the whites of his eyes looked yellow, but the stench of booze was gone, and he was standing up straighter than he had for years. She had left a hunched old man, ready to end his days at the bottom of a bottle of White Lightning, and now . . . Donnie was dressed in a clean rugby shirt and chinos, his expression somewhere between amused and apprehensive.

Niko opened the door and she stepped inside, biting her lip to stop it trembling. What was going on? Niko didn't seem bothered that Jay was back. In fact, he was still smiling at her.

'Niko, I've got no idea what's going on with you, but I was kind of hoping for a private chat with my dad,' Holly told him.

'That's okay I was just going.' He shrugged, and punched Donnie's shoulder in a gesture of affection, before leaning in as though he was going to kiss Holly's cheek.

She pulled back. 'Fuck off, Niko. Don't you remember what happened last time you tried to kiss me?'

His eyes flashed, and the darkness returned to his face for a second, but then he laughed. 'Things have changed, Holly.'

'Been to see your kids recently, have you?' she prodded.

'Not that it's anything to do with you, but I'm actually going to see Cath now.'

'Don't upset her.' Holly was torn between wanting to protect her friend, and desperation that she needed to get this long overdue talk out the way.

Donnie led her into the lounge and she noted that everywhere was clean and tidy. The ashtrays were empty, and the bottles that used to clutter the table and sink were gone. She thought some of the furniture was new, and the kitchen lino had been changed for grey tiles. Someone had come into some money.

'What can I do for you, Holly?'

Holly found she hardly knew where to begin. She hadn't seen him for ages, hadn't contacted him for months unless you counted the quick text about Jayden's son. 'Why didn't you come and see me?'

The big man shrugged. The intelligence had returned to his face, despite the physical scars of alcoholism. 'I wanted to wait until I was sorted properly again. Lydia knew, but she promised not to say anything until I was sure I could do it.' His hazel eyes rested on her face. 'You're looking good, Holly. How's Milo doing at school?'

Holly leant forward eyeballing her dad across his shiny new coffee table. 'What's going on, Donnie? You've taken fuck-all interest in my life, or your grandson's for years. In fact, in case you'd forgotten, you were so pissed you tried to hit me when I walked out after the trial. You've been a sad old drunkard for years, wasting your life and doing bugger all, and suddenly you're going to pretend everything's normal again?' Her voice rose, and her throat clogged with tears. It seemed at the moment that everything she thought she knew was a lie, and she wasn't sure how to cope. 'You think, what, that because Jay is back, we're going to go back to how we were?'

Donnie shook his head. 'Give me some credit, Holly. If you want the truth, I haven't seen Jayden. He sent me a text to tell me he was coming back a few months ago, and a few others . . . We got chatting. Before you ask, I haven't heard from him since the crash, and yes, I already knew he had a son.'

'Jesus! You never told us? The police?'

He snorted with laughter, which turned into the deep belly laugh she remembered from childhood. 'You're joking?'

'Yeah.' She was quiet for a moment, listening to the rain drumming on the window, inhaling the smell of furniture polish and lingering cigarette smoke. 'Don't think I'm not pleased you seem to be off the bottle. I am. It's just a bit of a shock. Go on, Dad, give it to me straight. Don't fuck me around. What have you got planned?'

He lit a cigarette, and smiled, showing stained, yellow teeth. 'First up, I'm an alcoholic. Always will be. I've been to those meetings, and they helped me get sober but I can't ever touch a drop again. Doctor reckons I've done some permanent damage to my insides with all the grog too.'

Holly opened her mouth to ask, but he held up a large, rough hand, silencing her.

'Lydia was the one who got me to the meetings. She's been trying for years, been such a help ever since Sian died . . . Anyway, I didn't tell her about Jayden getting in contact, but once I got back on my feet I knew I had to sort things out. Your husband was a wanker, Jayden had been driven away by the Balintas, and there were grandsons to think about now.'

'Oh God, I'm getting family business vibes again,' Holly told him, fidgeting with her phone.

He grinned, unperturbed. 'Devril Mancini's back too. Did you know? I'm sure he's looked you up by now. He's a good lad, and because of you he's more Hughes than Nicholls – whatever his Uncle

153

Marco thinks. So here we have it. A bigger family than I thought, and now I've spoken to my contacts, a bigger supply chain than I thought.'

'You know Joey and Gareth want to buy you out? That's a prime chunk of business you've hung on to, Dad. And if you won't sell, they'll go to me or Jayden?' It fell neatly into place. Her dad getting ready to play the big man again, both him and Niko claiming to have hidden funds, the Nicholls getting worried that their reign might be challenged . . .

'I know.' He tapped his cigarette ash carefully into the glass dish, and then sat back, watching her. 'It's all in place. The shops are sold, so I've got a bit to invest in merchandise, but I've kept this place, and there's still money from my old patch. That's what we'll concentrate on. Dealing's how I made it in the first place. I should never have been distracted by the bloody girls. Your mum was right, you know. She told me to stick to what I knew.'

Holly blinked hard at the mention of her mum, but managed to ignore the comment. 'Just to get this straight in my head – you want me, Jayden, Dev and Niko to go into business with you? You want us to play drug barons?'

Her dad stood up, moved over to her side of the room and looked down at her, his eyes bright. 'I want you to come home, Holly. Move back to the Seaview, where you belong. Your friends and family are here, and we can raise the kids between us, while we build the business. It's solid.'

'It's illegal! The whole business ruins lives, kills people, causes families to break up. It's blood money, Donnie, and you fucking know it. Stop trying to convince yourself it's all okay.' She was breathing fast, fists clenched.

He shrugged again, dismissing the problem. 'There will always be drugs. Just because I go straight, doesn't mean anyone else will, so there's no point. It's a question of supply and demand, and if the coppers didn't catch me before, why should they catch us now? I'm offering you a chance to earn a lot of money, get respect, and with my full backing. You can't say no to that, can you?'

Chapter 20

Dazed and furious, Holly walked home through the driving rain. She didn't even bother to put her coat on, but carried it under one arm, perversely enjoying the fact she was soon soaked and freezing. What the hell was going on? Fucking Donnie was in cloud cuckoo land. How dare he tell her she had no other options.

Banging the front door on her way in, her phone buzzed and she dropped her sodden coat in a heap, dripping onto the carpet. It was Karen calling. 'Hallo? Sorry I didn't get a chance to call you back. Is the boy talking to you yet?' It still felt so wrong they didn't even know his name.

She could hear the exasperation in the other woman's voice. 'No. The tests have all come back fine, so there doesn't seem to be any physical reason for him not to speak.'

Holly was silent for a moment, digesting this, pushing Donnie from her mind. 'DI Harper came to see my aunt this morning. He came here, to my house, because she was looking after Milo until I finished work.'

'Okay. And?'

'And he told her to make sure she contacted him if Jayden tried to get in touch, told her to be extra careful and slightly

155

freaked her out. But she thinks he's just trying to help. Did you know he was round here?'

'No, I didn't, but I'm not his keeper. It's natural he would take an interest in the case because of the history, and natural that although he's taking a back seat he wants to look out for people like your aunt.'

Holly still wasn't sure. It seemed slightly out of kilter to her and she filed the thought away for future reference. She almost said he'd been at the hospital that one time too, but dismissed it before the words came. It was easy to be a bit paranoid when she was this tired. 'We're going to the hospital about five. I thought I'd take Milo and see if he can talk to the boy.'

'Good idea. I might be back there myself. I need to get this case moving, so any little detail that Milo might let drop, if he remembers anything, or if the boy *will* talk to him, I need to grab that chance. DI Harper and I have a meeting with the DCI on Thursday, and they will both want a progress report.'

Holly thought she understood. The bosses were riding her arse and wanted results. It explained why Karen was being extra nice to her, why she kept dropping around, keeping her updated. It was because she was desperate for a result. 'Fine, I'll see you later.'

***

It was raining again as Holly pulled up outside the hospital. After six hours' sleep, and a bacon sandwich for lunch she was feeling like shit, running on adrenalin and wishing she hadn't said she would do this. Milo sat in the back, wide-eyed and excited, clearly delighted to be part of the action.

Holly turned the engine off and glanced back at her son. 'Are you sure you want to see him?'

'Yeah, of course I do. I want to ask him loads of things.'

'Just be careful, because he may not talk to any of us. And you know that the police officers will probably sit in on our chat?'

'I know, I'm not stupid. But if I ask him lots of questions he might answer them, mightn't he? Hey, Mum, can we get my cast off today as well?'

'Not yet, you know that. Just a couple more weeks and your leg will be mended.'

She parked the car and waited whilst Milo hopped out with an 'I can do it by myself!' when she tried to help him. The rain had stopped but the sky was leaden with the promise of more and the wind chilled her bones. They walked slowly up the path towards the main entrance.

Devril was waiting next to the bike stand, his collar hunched up, hood pulled down. Holly stopped, standing in the pouring rain, staring at him. He smiled, and she frowned at him. 'Milo, this is an old friend of mine, Devril Mancini. Dev, fancy seeing you here. I'm sure I said no journos allowed.'

Milo studied the man warily, and gave a small smile, but said nothing. Devril grinned at him, then turned back to Holly. 'Relax, I'm doing family stuff. This is nothing to do with you.'

'Right. Despite the fact I told you what time I was visiting . . . What are you really doing here?' Holly pushed a wet strand of hair out of her eyes, peering at him.

'Family. My aunt had a check-up in Outpatients. I'm waiting to give her a lift home.'

'Really? I didn't know you were so close to Cerys. I thought you never even spoke to her.'

Dev shrugged. 'Okay, I'm here because I had an hour to kill and I'm still chasing my story. The news will leak somehow and my colleagues will be chasing after it, so I'm here first. Happy?'

'Not really, but I appreciate you being honest with me,' Holly told him. Bastard! To think she'd been going to level with him about her chat with Donnie. Not now, he could bloody well find out for himself what was being planned.

'Muuuuum, I'm getting wet!' A squally shower was soaking them all, and Milo was hopping around waving his crutches.

'Sorry, Milo,' Holly told him. 'Dev, we might be ages, so enjoy your chill in the rain, won't you?'

'I've been in worse places,' he said, pulling his coat collar up. 'Come over to mine afterwards for a chat. Just give me a call when you're done.'

'So who is Devil, Mum?' Milo asked as they pushed carefully through the crowd of walking wounded, visitors and staff, all streaming along the wet concrete, heads bowed, colourful umbrellas bashing the unwary.

'A friend. And it's Devril not Devil.'

'Devil is a way cooler name. Is he your boyfriend? Dad says—'

Holly cut him off quickly. 'No, I don't have a boyfriend. You're a smart boy, Milo, and you know things have been a bit weird since the crash, but I'm really proud of you.'

He nodded, slightly puzzled. 'Cool . . . Mum, can I ask you something?'

They were walking in through the automatic doors now, heading for the main reception desk. Milo scooted along on his crutches.

'You can ask me anything, you know that.' Oh God, she really hoped it wasn't going to be an awkward question about Beth and Tom.

'Mum, if someone asked you to keep a secret would you do it?'

They joined a long queue of patients and families, waiting to be seen at the reception desk. 'Depends what kind of secret. If it was something bad, I'm not sure I would keep it quiet . . .' She kept it light, but her brain was running over possibilities. His little face was deadly serious, and he was looking intently at her, as though this really mattered. 'Depends who asked me, too . . . Is it a friend from school?'

'Um . . . No. I . . . Oh look, Mum, there's Steph, that police-woman. And she's waving at us.'

Silently cursing, Holly extracted them from the queue and went over to join DS Harlow.

'Is . . . Is Karen here?' Holly asked. It was still hard calling them by their given names. She felt uncomfortable, like the barriers were coming down and she didn't know which side everyone was on. It made them human, she realised, and she didn't like it. Especially after talking to Donnie. It was like having a foot in both camps.

Her dad had raised them to hate the police. They were pigs, always picking on the inhabitants of the Seaview, he'd told his kids. And here she was talking to the police, helping with an investigation even, just hours after her dad told he that he wanted her to run a drugs op. No wonder her brain was fried.

'She got called away, but I'll sit in with you, just in case we get anywhere.' Steph smiled at Milo, holding the door open for him to hop through.

They took the elevator to the fifth floor and signed in on the ward. The boy was in a cubicle as usual, and the room was crowded once they had all piled in.

Jayden's son was pale, but alert as Holly dumped her bag next to the bed. Milo, who was swinging along on his crutches, studied the other child with interest.

Sitting up, the boy looked skinny, but wiry and muscled rather than malnourished. There was a hardness in his expression that sleep had hidden, and the vulnerability that had shown in his face when he'd first woken was gone. A child with secrets and perhaps not one accustomed to an easy life? Seeing the two boys together Holly's heart gave a twist and she bit down hard on her lip. He was just a child. Larissa's boy. Jayden's son.

She sat down carefully on the chair next to his bed, and Milo leant against her, perched on the bed itself. Steph, sitting opposite, scrolled through her iPad. It felt crowded, claustrophobic, and massively awkward. The air was stale and the scent of disinfectant pierced the general mugginess of sweat and urine.

'Hi again.' She felt stupid but she had to say something. 'Do you remember I was here when you woke up? I'm Holly and this is Milo, my son . . .'

The boy shrugged, and met her eyes briefly, before resuming

his careful sweep of the room. He was clearly indicating he had heard her, she thought. But his black gaze was resting on Milo now. She would have said his expression registered interest, but this was quickly shut down into blankness.

Again, emotions crashed through her. A child shouldn't be able to look like that, shouldn't be able to crush his own feelings, his expressions like that. Bizarrely she was reminded of her dad, today, when he asked her to move back to Seaview. His blank expression hadn't matched up with the brightness in his eyes, the hope in his voice.

'You were in the car after it crashed,' her son said, leaning forward to rest his hands on the white sheet. 'Who was the man? Was it your dad?'

The boy in the bed said nothing, but kept looking at Milo, searching his face. Holly looked helplessly over at Steph, who nodded encouragingly.

'What's your name?' Holly asked gently.

The thin lips parted, he moistened them with his tongue, but then his mouth clamped shut again.

They sat down, and Holly told her son he could ask any questions he wanted.

'I'm really glad you woke up!' Milo told him, completely unabashed. 'Look, I brought you some books to read. Do you like David Walliams?'

There was no response from the bed, but Milo chattered on, scattering the books he had brought, across the bed, telling the boy about karate and rugby and his school friends. All the time he looked hopefully at the boy's face, apparently willing him to speak.

At half past five, DC Marriot entered the room, smiled at them all, and dragged a chair over to Steph's side of the bed.

Although Karen looked her usual immaculate self, Holly could see shadows under her eyes, lines under the make-up, despite the brave red lipstick. Clearly there wasn't any more news on Jayden.

'Did you speak to the doctors earlier?' Steph asked.

'Yes. They say that there are improvements.' Her gaze rested on the boy, but his concentration seemed to be focused on Milo.

Whilst Milo chatted away, Holly moved round and asked quietly if there was any news on the deaths of Alexi and Roman.

'We are still investigating, along with the prison service.' Karen's pursed her lips, and added, 'Alexi had two visitors in the week before his death, and one of them has been untraceable.'

'You mean he had a fake ID or something?' Holly asked.

'Possibly. We sent officers to his address and it's a rental flat in Marshford. Landlord says the bloke paid cash for a six-month rental but he's hardly ever there. The name on the visitor's book, and on the ID was Arron Carter. Don't suppose that rings any bells with you?' She looked hopefully at Holly.

'No. Sorry, I've never heard the name mentioned.'

The adults lapsed into silence and Milo, apparently unaffected by one-sided conversation, chattered on, his leg propped awkwardly out to the side as he leant over the child in the bed.

'What's your dad's name?' Milo asked suddenly. 'My dad's name is Tom, but he doesn't live with us anymore.'

'Did you dad ever talk about his family?' Holly asked the boy, gently, but he drew back, frowning. 'We think that I'm your dad's sister.' His eyes widened, but he controlled himself again, and went back to staring at Milo.

'That would mean your dad is my uncle. We're cousins!' Milo told the boy, his eyes lighting on the pile of books next to the bed.

'You understand we are very concerned about you,' Karen told the silent child. 'You won't get anyone into trouble by answering our questions. We're worried about your dad, too. He might have been hurt in the car accident.'

The boy shrugged again, as if to say, 'whatever', and looked back over at Milo.

Holly searched for something that might establish a connection, anything that might prompt the boy to start talking, but she could think of nothing, and gradually Milo ran out of chatter too. They had failed.

The boy was eerily calm, registering no emotion in his pale face. Again, she thought how unnatural it was for a kid that age to be so cool and closed off. He must have been terrified to wake up in hospital, and he must be wondering what the hell happened to Jayden. Perhaps he was simply too terrified to talk. His eyes were shiny black pools, and he sat tense and still now, one thin hand holding the sheet around him.

She laid a gentle hand on the bed and squeezed his hand. There *was* something else in his gaze. Holly thought that maybe he wanted to speak but somehow he couldn't. Perhaps he was scared of getting Jayden into trouble. She wanted to ask him so many things, to persuade him to communicate with her, but that hard exterior was shielding him from her emotions. Or was it fear *of* Jayden?

A nurse came in and gave him some medication, which he took obediently, gulping the water, his eyes fixed now on a place just below the ceiling, straight in front of the bed. Holly forced herself not to let her frustration show, and she took a deep breath, trying desperately to think of words that might pierce that shell. But nothing came, so she simply told him again about the night of the accident, reassuring him he wasn't going to get into trouble, and she was just worried that Jayden might need help.

Before she left, Holly again bent and kissed his cool forehead. The skin was soft and his hair brushed her cheek, and his face showed that flicker of something.

Once again, in the shape of his face and the stubborn tilt of his chin, she saw her brother, but the lips remained firmly closed.

'Maybe you'll feel like talking next time we visit?' Milo suggested, before hopping towards the door. He paused. 'Or I know . . . If you can't talk you can write me a message, can't you?' He balanced on one leg, delved into his pocket and produced a grubby pencil and a bit of paper, which he placed carefully on the end of the bed.

The boy made no move to take the paper, and just stared at Milo, face impassive and controlled.

Outside the room Karen outlined her plans. 'Thanks for trying anyway. He will have to stay in for a couple more days, but the tests are reassuring. He was incredibly lucky. If he still doesn't tell us anything, and there are no further developments, we'll have no option but to place him with an emergency foster care until we can locate his father.'

'Why don't you send him home with us?' Milo asked artlessly. 'I bet he'd have to talk when we get home. Like . . . He might hate peas but get given them, or he might need to know where the loo was, and he'd have to ask or he'd wet himself, wouldn't he?'

Holly grinned, and even Karen half smiled. 'I'm not sure that would be a good idea. You have enough to cope with at the moment and he might need specialist care. We have someone coming in later who specialises in trauma cases, so he may well open up to her.'

'He could stay with Lydia?' Holly suggested. 'When she finds out she'll want to look after Jayden's son.'

'Holly, we need to proceed with caution. We don't know that your brother isn't behind the recent events, and we have no idea of his state of mind, so his son needs to be kept safe. Legally, at this stage all we can offer is foster care. Long term, depending on whether Jayden does come back, we can discuss further possibilities.'

'Where's DI Harper? I thought you were both on this case . . .' Holly was trying to stop the churning in her stomach, the urge to take the child out of the hospital bed, into her car and take him home. The first instinct had been a protective one, when she discovered him injured in her car, but now he was family she felt a tidal wave of emotion. She would look after him if Jayden wouldn't.

'He's . . . He's taken a back seat on this one. We both know your history, and we all felt, the DCI included, that it was better if DI Harper was less involved.' Her face was blank, and Holly frowned.

'He told me Jayden was dead, and he worked Larissa's murder case. You'd think he'd be bursting at the seams to talk to Jayden's son. To Larissa's son. This boy must be terrified, and we don't know what Jayden has told him about his past.' Holly took a calming breath, glancing at Milo, who was watching a kid on the ward playing with his laptop.

'It seems strange that your brother would risk coming back with his son after what happened. Why would he put his son in danger?'

Holly bit her lip, her mind whirring over possibilities, considering, discarding theories. She should really come clean about Donnie, but she couldn't. It was years since she'd had the conflict between family loyalty and the law, but here she was again, walking the dark side, shutting the police out, when they just might be able to help.

But what could she do? Grass on her own dad, when he'd just got sober? Eventually she shook her head. 'I would guess that Jayden is desperate to make sure his boy is safe and looked after, but after that, who knows . . . Have you got kids?'

Karen shook her head.

'Well, if Jayden does still care I reckon he'll be in touch,' Holly finished lamely.

'Point taken. Ring me when he calls, won't you?' There was a glimmer of amusement in the other woman's eyes.

Holly made sure Milo was inching nearer to the laptop, his attention fixed on the screen, before she told DC Marriot about the phone call she had made the night of Larissa's murder. This was information she *could* share.

'Right. Can I just clarify, on the night of Larissa's murder, you told Devril Mancini where Jayden was?'

'Yes. He was at Niko's place. Dev said Niko left his house about 9 p.m., and he didn't see him again.'

'So if we assume that someone did phone Jayden and tip him off, Devril also knew where to find Jayden at this point?'

'Yes.'

'You never mentioned this initially. Were you afraid Devril would tell the police when he was interviewed? Why didn't *you* just tell us?'

Holly sighed. 'It was a terrible thing to do. I was terrified that I was the reason Larissa and her baby were dead, and most likely, my brother too. When I kept quiet, I thought I'd wait until they found out. But they didn't and nobody ever asked me. I didn't know why, because Niko wouldn't protect me.'

'But Devril would?'

'Yeah, I thought so.' Holly picked up her bag. 'I'm not sure we were much help in there.'

'Thanks for trying. I'll keep you posted,' Karen said wearily, and Steph, who was tapping out notes on her iPad, raised a hand and waved.

When they walked out, back though the crowded reception area, Milo said, conversationally, 'If the boy does start talking, he might tell us more about the man in the car.'

Holly stopped suddenly, blocking the way and causing the people behind to swear at her. She drew her son to one side and bent down to his level. 'Milo, do you mean the man who was in the car after we crashed? The one who stroked your face? Have you remembered something else?' For a moment his freckled face twisted, lips pursed.

'No. I don't *know* anything else. I was just *saying*. . . Let's go to Devil's house. He did ask us, didn't he?' Milo said, shoving the push pad for the automatic door.

Holly sighed, plunging back into the stream of people, dodging wheelchairs and small children.

The icy wind hit them as they stepped outside, and Holly leant over to pull Milo's hood up. Annoyed, he shook it off again, hopping proficiently along next to her. If Jayden had found Larissa and his baby daughter murdered, gathered up his son, taken the money he already had, and just driven away, where the hell had they gone?

Perhaps he had hidden out until that small-time dealer, Luke Hastings, told the police he was dead, and then gone abroad . . . The fifteen grand would have probably nabbed him a pair of fake passports. She thought about the man visiting Alexi before he died. It wasn't hard to get fake IDs, she knew from experience, but good ones were pricey. Donnie had previously made a fair bit from that line of trade. The passports, she remembered suddenly, were usually real, and stolen from the deceased. It was easier to steal identities if the victim wasn't alive to kick up a fuss.

But Arron Carter could not be Jayden Hughes, because he would have been recognised on the CCTV. Not to mention Alexi would surely have gone mental if Jay had turned up to visit . . .

'Milo, the man in the car wasn't the person who asked you to keep a secret was he?' Holly looked down at her son. They were walking down the footpath to the end of the car park now, where Devril was still standing under the bike shelter, absorbed in his phone.

'Nope. Devil's still here, Mum.'

'I can see that, and I guess he's waiting to see if we have anything exciting to tell him,' Holly said with a sigh.

A crowd of people pushed past them, a mum with a baby, and a few men arguing. Away from the bright lights and stuffy warmth of the hospital, the darkness was pierced only by a couple of streetlights, which lit the rain-glossed concrete with a feeble yellow glow. A couple of people were standing, hoods up, smoking near Devril. As Holly and Milo approached one of them turned quickly, shoulders hunched against the rain and the cold.

Milo gasped. '*Mum*, that's the man in the car.'

'*What?*' Holly forced herself to keep walking towards Dev, although her eyes were darting, trying to see where Milo was looking. 'Where? That man in the blue Nike jacket or the one leaning on the bike?'

'No, the younger one with the black hoodie. He was just behind Devil. Mum, he's looking right at us *now*.' Milo's voice rose a little, but she grabbed his hand and tried to see through the rain. The man's face was almost obscured by his hood, but she thought she caught a glimpse of blonde hair.

'Jayden?' The name tasted unfamiliar, and she called again, louder. Was it hope or fear that made her spine prickle with ice?

She saw Devril spin round, puzzled. Too late, the man had moved, shoving into the crowd, walking swiftly across the rain-sodden plants behind the shelter and into the road.

'*Devril!*' Holly had reached him, grabbed his arm, her heart pounding. 'Quick, that man crossing the road, black hoodie, blue jeans and Converse. Milo says he's the man from the car crash. Fuck, is it Jayden? I can't leave Milo but can you follow him?'

'Okay, I'm on it.' Devril pulled his own hood up and jogged after the man.

Holly wavered for a split second, phone in her hand, and then followed, slow enough for Milo to keep up on his crutches.

'Are we going to chase him?' Her son's voice was a squeak of excitement, and he was hopping as fast as he could.

'Kind of.'

'Shouldn't we call the police? Steph might still be at the hospital.' He was breathless now, and she slowed down.

'No, not yet. Milo, are you completely sure that was the man who was in our car after the crash?' Holly could just see Dev running further down the road, and then he made a sharp left, disappearing into the shadows.

'Of course. I'm not stupid, Mum.'

'I know, but you had just been in a car crash and you were hit on the head. And we were just talking about him, so you must have been thinking about him.' She was breathless too now, but not from exertion. What if Jayden was right in front of them?

'It *was* him!' Milo insisted.

They paused at the point in road where Devril had vanished. It was a pitch-black, overgrown path and Holly hesitated, but Milo plunged onwards.

'Come on, Mum!'

She half recognised where they were as they stumbled along the narrow footpath. The darkness and the rain seemed to have driven everyone indoors, but the trees dripped spookily and Dev and his quarry seemed long gone.

They rounded a corner and saw the playground where the drug dealers did their thing. The slide and swings gleamed in the light of the houses behind the line of trees. At the same time Holly could hear the distant roar of a train and remembered the railway line ran along the back of Denne Road, crossing by an overhead bridge on its way down to the coast.

'Holly!' Devril was breathing hard. His clothes were muddy, and he had a streak of dirt on one cheekbone.

'What happened? Where is he?'

'He went off over the railway line. Straight in front of the train. Don't worry he made it, but I couldn't exactly follow and now he's long gone.'

'Do you think it was Jayden?'

'It could be. Same height and build. His face, what I saw of it, was similar, and he would have changed a bit in eleven years, wouldn't he?'

'Yeah.'

Frustrated, Holly finally made the call to the police.

Karen practically blasted her eardrums. 'You just *saw* him?'

'At the hospital. Milo says he was the man in the car. He's just gone across the railway line at Standen Point – you know behind Denne Road. Devril was with us and he chased him.'

'He chased him?' Holly could hear muffled voices in the background and running footsteps. 'Are you sure it was Jayden?'

'No! It could have been though.'

'I'm on my way.' Her voice was sharp, angry, and Holly couldn't blame her. If she had called when they first spotted the man the police would already be here. As it was, she had been so desperate to see him, any thoughts of calling in the law, who he definitely wouldn't want to see, had been firmly banished. Wrong call.

'She pissed off with you?' Devril was staring out across the railway line, as though his gaze could pierce the darkness. 'So if that was Jayden I think we can assume he has been checking up on his son. Funny, he was right behind me and I never noticed. That freaks me out.'

'You think it was him, don't you?' Holly asked, aware of Milo, breathless with excitement behind her, wobbling on his crutches.

Dev shook his head, moving closer to her, his hands gentle on her arms. 'Holly, I don't know. I'm sorry but I really couldn't tell. He was about five nine, blonde and the same build as Jay always was, on the skinny side, but that doesn't mean it was him.'

She could smell his sweat, his aftershave, and feel his body against hers, his chest still heaving after the run. Emotion bubbled treacherously in her chest and she turned to look at her son, who was watching with interest.

'Milo says he was the man in the car after my crash, even if he isn't Jayden.'

The police arrived ten minutes later, and Karen told them she had another team searching across the other side of the railway. Milo answered her questions unwillingly. He was getting tired now the excitement was over and Holly wiped the wet bench with her coat and sat him down. Dev added his hoodie and wrapped it round the boy's shoulders.

A couple of uniformed officers were questioning Devril now, and Holly was torn between waiting for them to finish and getting Milo home and warm. Finally Dev broke away from the group, and walked back towards them, shaking his head.

'What's up?'

He grinned. 'I got a bollocking for chasing him. I feel like that naughty kid at school again.' His light grey eyes held hers briefly, invisible messages passing between them like an electric current. 'You get Milo back and I'll stick around for a bit. DC Marriot wants to talk to me apparently. Is she a bitch?'

Holly thought for a moment, one eye on Milo. 'No, she's all right.'

'Never thought I'd hear you say that about the police.'

'Well, I'm all grown up now and I don't belong to the Seaview anymore. I'll call you tomorrow,' she told Devril. 'Sorry you had to get caught up in that.'

He shrugged. 'It's fine. If I've pulled a hamstring I'll make sure you know about it.' He grinned again. 'I'm kidding. Seriously, we need to chat some more, so make sure you do ring tomorrow, okay?'

She nodded, dragging Milo back down the footpath, past the dog unit, which had just arrived, to the hospital car park. Whatever had just happened, she imagined Dev could turn it into a great story.

Chapter 21

After a night of broken sleep Holly called Dev first thing the next morning.

'They didn't find anything. Even the dog team couldn't get far and it was pissing down with rain. DC Marriot gave me a bollocking and some PC told me to go home so I did. Sorry, I can't believe we were so fucking close!'

The thought made her ball her fists with frustration. She was tempted to ring Karen or Steph and ask if they had any news. But she knew Karen was pissed off with her for not calling the police as soon as they saw the man, so she forced herself to calm down, shoving Jayden to the back of her mind. 'Not your fault, and I don't think DC Marriot, Karen, is even speaking to me now.' The disappointment was still biting hard, but it was surprisingly easy to talk to Dev now. She bit her lip. 'Are you around this weekend?'

'Maybe. I'm home but I've got some work to do, following up on a couple of leads.'

He didn't elaborate and she didn't ask, forcing herself to be nonchalant. 'Okay, I'll ring you if I hear anything.'

'Yeah me too. How's Milo?'

'He's okay. He thought it was cool. And he also thinks your

name is Devil. He wouldn't listen when I corrected him.' Holly smiled and could hear amusement warming her voice.

'Do you still get down the gym?'

'Shoey's? Not for years . . .'

'We could have a workout next week if you like? See if you can still fight, get the pads out. Go on, you know you want to.'

She did. The thought of releasing the tension, working out until her muscles screamed and her bones ached was strangely appealing. 'Deal. About ten on Monday?'

'Deal.'

Saturday morning and despite everything, Holly savoured the thought of a weekend off. When she checked her messages, there weren't any more crazy texts from Tom either, which subconsciously made her relax a bit more. It would be okay because she would make things right, would fight through whatever was thrown at her. *'Everything will be okay.'* She could still hear her mum saying the phrase whenever something bad happened, and because of who she was, she had ended up saying it pretty often. When her mum was killed, Holly stopped believing and started taking matters into her own hands.

She called Milo downstairs. Her first proper day off in ages, and she was going to take him to the park near the beach. It was on the fringes of the estate, but she didn't figure she'd get any bother. Especially not with Cathryn there too. She had an hour to kill as her friend needed to take Angel for an eye appointment at the hospital, but she was restless and Milo would be happy enough chilling on the beach. Refusing to let anything ruin her day, shoving away thoughts of Jayden, the silent child in hospital, and the police hovering like hawks waiting for a kill, she made pancakes for breakfast.

'These are lush, Mum,' Milo said, stuffing a pancake dripping with butter and honey into his mouth. 'And you didn't burn them this time!'

Holly grinned, treasuring the time they spent together. Time when she didn't feel guilty about being at work, about missing clubs and matches and bedtime stories, was precious, and today, for the first time in ages she felt like a proper mum.

The sunlight was pouring through the bay windows in the living room and, in the back garden, a few tentative green spikes were starting to appear in the flowerbeds. Beyond asking if the police had caught the man from last night, or if the boy in hospital had said anything yet, Milo seemed to have lost interest in the proceedings, which suited her just fine.

They were just pulling their coats on when Lydia turned up, tottering along on her high-heeled boots and dragging two shopping bags and a dog. Her dark curls were blowing in the breeze and her lipstick was bright pink. 'Thanks so much for saying you'll have him today, Holly. I'll be back around eight so just bring him back tomorrow if you like. I left enough stuff in your cupboard for him when I was here last and Anita sent you these chocolates to say thanks for her birthday flowers . . .' She shoved a box of Cadbury's Roses into Holly's hands. 'Holly?'

Holly stared at her, then at the dog. Oh God, she'd forgotten she'd offered to have Oreo. The dog wagged his tail, and automatically she fussed over him.

'If it's not convenient I can ring Jackie and see if she'll have him . . .' her aunt said, her voice trailing off, sensing Holly's confusion.

'No, it's fine. We'd love to have him, wouldn't we, Milo?' Milo was already down on the ground, his arms around the big dog. Oreo looked far more presentable now, and he was a friendly, clumsy great lump of a dog. 'It's fine, Lydia, you go out and we'll be fine. Sorry, I am a total idiot, it went right out of my mind.' She hesitated, wondering if she should say anything about last night, before deciding not to ruin her aunt's day out. 'I'll bring him back tomorrow morning.'

'If you're sure . . .' The relief in her aunt's voice was palpable. 'I might be able to pick him up tonight. Oh and, Holly, we need to have a proper chat. There's a few things you need to know, love.'

Before Holly could grill her, she was gone, tottering away down the road. Holly stared after her for a long moment, good mood evaporating. Too many people keeping secrets. It was rapidly becoming a farce and she didn't know who knew what, like some crazy child's guessing game. She bundled boy and dog into the car and cursed the dark clouds gathering on the horizon. Still, they had coats and boots and Oreo, with his thick fur, wouldn't be bothered by the rain.

The car park opposite the beach was almost empty, and just a few desolate dog walkers trudged along the windswept stones. The ice-cream kiosk was boarded up for the winter and covered in graffiti. Waves, whipped into a frenzy by the recent high winds, spat froth up as far as the tussocky grass that ran along the footpath.

Keeping the dog on the lead, they crossed Beach Road and wandered along the footpath, Holly keeping a look-out amongst the rubbish for needles and broken bottles. Milo hopped ahead, football under one arm, and, satisfied it was safe, Holly unsnapped the dog's lead so he could run along the beach.

She never heard them approach, but Oreo let out a warning bark, and rushed back from the bit of seaweed he was exploring at the water's edge.

'Hey, Holly.'

Her heart gave a sickening jump and she spun round, calling to the dog, holding his collar as he growled at the newcomers. Milo was kicking his ball against an upturned wooden boat, letting it bounce back and kicking it again with his good foot. He glanced up, studied the strangers, but when Holly didn't react, carried on with his game. 'Niko. Gareth, haven't seen you two in ages.'

Niko with his shaved head and an air of insolence, in contrast to his friendliness yesterday, ignored her. Oreo sniffed him, but didn't run off again immediately. Instead he sat close to Holly, watching the other man intently, pale amber eyes fixed and wary, teeth bared in a warning snarl.

'Joey told me he gave you the dog.' Gareth, tall, slim and muscular, with his grey hair tied back, still had the same smile. The baring of teeth, that never reached his cold sea-blue eyes. Everyone said he smiled while he killed. 'Didn't expect to see you here, but I was just saying to Niko, I think you and Holly need to have a chat, and here you are. Old friends and all that . . .' He was wearing jeans and a grubby bomber jacket with NICHOLLS TRANSPORT stencilled across the front.

'I don't have anything to say to Niko,' Holly told him. 'Cathryn's on her way down.'

Niko rolled his eyes. 'Holly, we just need a chat.'

'You should go,' Holly said shortly, just managing to control her emotions. She could handle Niko, but Gareth was another matter. Did Gareth know Niko was getting cosy with her dad? She could drop him right in it, but she'd look pretty stupid if he already knew.

'I'll carry on with my walk, then, and leave you two to catch up,' Gareth said, giving Niko a hard stare. 'Nice to see you again, Holly. You're looking—' his eyes flickered over her body in a cool appraisal '—good.'

For hers and Milo's safety Holly refrained from telling him to fuck off and just nodded. The icy terror she had felt whenever she had encountered Gareth as a child, had faded to a healthy dislike. But she wasn't stupid, and it would do no good to antagonise such a powerful player.

Niko waited until Gareth had strolled towards the water's edge. 'Look, Holly, the police have been round a couple of times and I just don't need it. What the fuck is going on with this kid in hospital? Alexi and Roman are dead, and your dad's on about taking on the Nicholls? It's Jayden, isn't it? All this has happened because he's come back?'

She stared at him, seeing his pallor, the shadows around his black eyes, and the way his face was too sharp, the jawline too pronounced. His massive Puffa jacket encased his skinny body like a red shroud, but the old Niko was still there, with those black-lashed eyes fixed on her. The dog growled again, still watching Gareth, but they both ignored him.

'I don't know what's going on,' she said finally, satisfied he wasn't about to launch an attack on them, shifting her gaze to the sea. Far out on the horizon a glimmer of pale gold set the waves shimmering and dancing. Gareth had walked over to the next breakwater, and was strolling along, smoking. 'I didn't know you were mates with Gareth, or my dad.'

He scowled, changing the subject. 'Luke said Jayden was dead. Alexi and Roman swore they never touched him, but you know nobody saw him after that night.'

Luke Hastings, the dealer who swore he'd helped dispose of Jayden's body, pinned the murder on Larissa's brothers. There had never been any evidence to charge Alexi and Roman with Jayden's murder, except for Luke's confession. Luke said he didn't know when Jayden was killed, but when he went in the sea he had definitely been dead for a while. Coincidentally Luke died in a car crash soon after he gave the police this snippet of information.

'Niko, I don't know any more than you,' Holly told him. 'What are you doing with Gareth, and why does he want us to talk? If you go in with him, you'll just end up back in prison again, for fuck's sake. And why are you talking to my dad?'

'Like you care. The boy's woken up, hasn't he? The one in hospital. Has he said anything?' Niko was clearly pursuing his own lines of inquiry.

'Niko, come on, why are you so worried if Jayden's back? What's it to you and Gareth? I can see that my dad is empire building, but not where you fit in.'

Niko's face contorted in anger, his eyes narrowing. He looked like some evil forest creature. 'Holly, you should know that if Jayden's back he still owes me money.'

So that was it. 'Fuck off, Niko, you can't be serious. After everything that's happened!'

He took a step closer and the dog growled. 'He owes me fifty grand, and if he's alive I want it back.'

'What the hell are you talking about? It was never fifty grand! You said fifteen hundred tops before Larissa was killed.' What the fuck was he playing at? Holly's fingers tightened on the dog's collar as he reacted to the change in her voice. She licked her lips, tasting salt, realising how cold she was, shivering in the wind. Milo was still playing ball, and a car drove past, music blaring.

Niko came closer, keeping a wary eye on the dog. 'This is money that's gone since I've been away. It was in an account . . . Look, there was no fucking way anyone could have access to that account except me and Dad, but it's been emptied out. He left me a pound in there! I've been banged up for years in that fucking hole, but now I'm out things need to get to how they used to be. I need the money your brother stole from me. If he won't give it back then the debt passes to you.'

'How do you know it was Jayden who took the money?' Her heart was pounding again, her jaw clenched with cold and shock. Jesus, that was a hell of a lot of money. Perhaps Jay had been living the high life all these years. 'Is that what you were talking to Dad about?'

'You know what he was like with computers – a fucking genius. He helped us hide all the money before he went rogue on us. This is down to him. When I heard about all the shit that's been going on, and then the boys got taken out, I knew he was back.' Niko had calmed down now. He wiped a skeletal hand across his face, which was reddening in the icy wind. 'Luke's long gone or I would have tracked him down. Someone must have paid him off to say Jayden was dead.'

'It's not like your family has lots of friends. How do you know that it wasn't the Nicholls family who stole your money?'

'Because I do know. Soon as I was out Gareth was on the

phone, asking me to come in with them, to put some money into the business. Why would he do that if he'd already stolen my money? Besides the Nicholls don't do cyber stuff, they can only just figure out how a cash point works.'

Holly's mind was spinning. Nearly ten grand from Lydia, and then fifty grand from the Balintas. Well, that was probably enough to live on for a few years. 'Do I look like a millionaire to you? Fifty grand, Jesus, Niko, I don't make that in a year!'

'You got a house. Your aunt's got business interests and you got a rich husband. I told your dad Jayden owed me, and he said that we'd sort it all out, if I come in with you. Your dad reckons he's got money to set up properly again, but what if I just want to take the money and go? Who's paying then? You maybe?'

'Hell, Niko, we don't have any money. Why didn't you ask my dad to give you the cash, if you're so sure Jayden stole your money?'

'He won't give me fuck-all unless I go in with you.' His eyes glittered again, another quick mood swing, and she wondered if he'd taken something before they met. 'And what happened to your husband? Did he find out you were a frigid bitch too?'

Holly moved her hand an inch and Oreo snarled again. 'Cheap insults Niko. Pathetic. We aren't at school anymore, and I don't have any money. And I don't know where Jayden is.'

Niko's gaze shifted to Milo, still kicking his ball, hopping and dodging on his crutches. 'Got a bit of talent your kid, hasn't he?'

'Stay away from me and stay away from my kid. You can't threaten us anymore. Whether Jay's alive or dead, none of us will be paying his debts. Do you get that?'

He stared at her. 'You can't fucking walk away from me, you know. I need this money one way or another. Either I go in with Donnie and we work together, or I've got to get something to offer Gareth. He thinks I'm talking to you to find out where Jayden is, Holly, c'mon. Dev's back too, isn't he? Have you seen him? This isn't going to end well for Jay and your family unless someone settles the debt. You need to watch yourself, Holly.'

'Jesus. Look, Niko, why do you think Jay's come back?'

'To take out Alexi and Roman? To dump his kid on the family? I dunno.'

'Why now? Maybe he waited until you were out and walking around free and happy, because it was too hard to get you killed inside as well. I think Jay's after *you*, Niko.' Holly tried to sound confident. Niko clearly didn't believe her when she said she didn't know where Jay was or what he wanted, so she might as well call his bluff. It was all she had left to threaten Niko with. 'If he stole money from you, haven't you thought that perhaps he was a tiny bit pissed at the fact you basically murdered his girlfriend and baby?'

'I didn't . . .' But the shock showed in his face and it was clear he had been so fixated on the money, and going back into business with the Nicholls, that his own safety hadn't crossed his mind.

'Whatever. You told them where to go, and what to do when they found him. Come on, Niko, admit it.'

'I need that money. Even if he is alive, Jayden wouldn't dare touch me.' He studied her. 'You work nights sometimes, don't you, Holly?'

Gareth was walking back towards them, slowly, hands in pockets, his eyes flicking from one to the other. The dog barked furiously as he approached but Holly held tight to his collar. 'Did you have a nice chat, kids?'

'More of a misunderstanding,' Holly told him, glaring at Niko.

Gareth shook his head. 'Stupid girl. You're as bad as Niko's ex. Years ago, when you were young enough, I said to my brother, those two girls are stupid, but he says to me that one's hot and one's got brains. Guess which one he had?'

'What do you mean?' Holly had an inkling but couldn't bring herself to believe it. It was like being punched in the guts. Gareth, she remembered, liked to talk in riddles, clearly believing himself more intelligent than anyone else.

'Listen, Holly, we always get what we want, and just now it's

178

that slice of land Joey mentioned. One way or another, it won't be Hughes-owned for much longer, no matter how big an army Donnie's building for himself. You tell him that, kid.' He leant towards her, careful to avoid the snap of sharp teeth, as the dog pulled against Holly's restraining hand. 'Every time it gets dark, Holly, you think of me, and remember that I know where you are. And I know where your kid is.'

For a second, she stood, hypnotised by his words, his air of menace. Joey, she could understand, he was like all the others, but Gareth was truly evil.

He smiled at her now, still far too close. 'Every time, Holly, I'll be watching you.'

Chapter 22

'Fuck off!' She turned and stalked away, tugging the angry dog, yelling for Milo, who caught the ball neatly in one hand and tucked it under his arm.

They left the beach, crossed the road and walked quickly across the winter-browned grass to the playground. When she glanced around Niko was striding across the pebbles with Gareth gesticulating wildly.

'Who was that man, Mum?' Milo wanted to know.

'Nobody. Just someone I used to know,' Holly told him shortly. 'Do you want to get on the zip line before the others get here? Can you manage with your leg?' When she turned back towards the beach, Niko was gone. Jesus, fifty grand . . . She couldn't get her head around that. Niko was right, her brother had been a right tech nerd when he wasn't using. He'd spent nights gaming, scanning the internet for opportunities to make a quick bit of cash, testing himself by hacking high-profile websites . . . It fit, but she didn't want to believe it. It was another layer of complication.

Cathryn was pushing the stroller across the path towards the climbing frame, a gaggle of fretful children tagging along behind her. 'You really want to be out in this, Holly? Hey, what's wrong?'

She waited until the kids had fussed over Oreo, then swarmed across to the climbing frame. The youngest two were busy toddling round the swings. 'Bloody Niko was here, with Gareth.'

Cathryn's expression changed, her thin face twisted. 'With *Gareth*? Why? Did he talk to you?'

Holly, leaving the kids to play, gave her the gist of the conversation, and told her about the possible sighting last night.

'Fucking hell! And I suppose the Nicholls thought they might get a shot of cash if they welcomed Niko on board?' Cathryn was scowling. The kids yelled and chased each other down the slide.

'I suppose Niko didn't come and see you?'

'See me? You're having a laugh?' Cath was scornful. 'He hasn't been near me or his kid since he got out. Why?'

Holly hadn't mentioned her conversation with Dev, and she figured that she could hardly tell Cathryn about the Nicholls' real welcome home party without putting Bailey in danger, but she filled her friend in on Donnie's plans.

'If Niko allies with your family, then where does that leave the Mancinis, or my dad? They all work for the Nicholls now. It'll turn nasty like it did before, when your mum died and your dad lost it.' Cath's face was pale and worried, and she was twisting a long strand of blonde hair between her fingers.

'Yeah, I know. Jesus, there's just too much going on, Cath. I know it must all fit somehow but I can't work out how. Oh, and are you sure you never had a thing with Joey?' After he'd hinted the other night, and Gareth had just mentioned something on the beach . . . Holly looked carefully at her friend.

Angel was whining, and Cathryn busied herself fumbling for a bottle of juice. 'Here you go, sweets, and you better have a rest now.' She swung her daughter into the stroller and strapped her in. 'Holly, you know I love you, but just don't ask about Joey, okay? Please? It was a massive mistake and a long time ago.'

Holly watched her as she stroked her daughter's hair, fussed with her blanket. 'You slept with Joey?' When would that have happened? Cath and Jayden got together when they were still at school, around thirteen or so. She and Cath had always been close, but after her mum's death, the two girls had been inseparable. It was Cath and Dev who had kept her going, kept her fighting . . . She thought she knew every crush, fling and one-night stand Cath had had.

'Holly!' Cathryn tried to light a cigarette but the wind whipped it away. 'Shit, all right. Once, we did it once when I was thirteen, because I thought he was this hot older guy, and I suppose I was flattered he wanted me. Happy? And before you ask it was before I went out with Jay. Now, did Niko say anything else?'

Holly, still shocked at the revelation, accepted the subject change. 'Not really.' But inside she was nauseous. If Cath had been thirteen, then Joey would have been in his twenties . . . He had a reputation for liking young girls, of course, so she supposed it fitted.

Cathryn forced a laugh. 'I can imagine. God, if my family saw Niko in the street outside they'd probably lynch him anyway. You know, it's so weird, I actually thought he'd be a good dad. He was so excited about having kids, you'd never believe it. He was different to how he is on the outside.'

'I can't even get my head around the fact you had sex with that bastard,' Holly told her, pushing back stray strands of black hair, which whipped across her face, making her eyes water. Or with Joey, she added silently to herself. Had Joey forced her? There was something about the way Cath had slammed the subject shut, the fear in her face. Normally she was happy to ramble on for hours about her sex life, and Holly thought she knew every detail of her conquests.

'Probably just as well. You wouldn't understand.' Cathryn grinned properly now, colour returning to her face. 'Word is already around the Seaview that Niko thinks he can just open for business again and go back to how things were. But if he's playing games with Gareth and Donnie, they'll find him floating face down somewhere. He obviously hasn't learnt anything inside.'

'Jesus, Cath, that's pessimistic.'

'True though.'

***

Back at work after her days off, Holly was seriously struggling to keep her mind off the hassles at home. Kev was on security duty again and he offered her a plate of cakes as she passed. It was a bit early, but Kev was an ace cupcake maker, so she accepted one and tucked it in a napkin for later.

Ruby and Noah were already making coffee in the tiny kitchenette, as she shoved her dinner in the fridge for later.

'You all right, Holly?' Ruby asked, adding another cup and passing it over.

'Yeah, just a bit knackered. Ta.'

'I'm wrecked with all this night work. Seriously, how do you cope with this all the time?' Noah yawned and attacked an energy bar.

'What did you do before?' Holly asked.

'My dad's got a building firm so I used to graft for him. What I really want is to go out on the road as a paramedic, but I don't have the exam grades to go straight in, so I hope this is a good place to start,' Noah explained.

'Yeah loads of people do that,' Holly said, frowning as Sara made her way across the control room, towards the kitchen. She obviously hadn't spotted them yet and was scurrying along in her usual timid manner. 'Cath was right, she's only got the same bag as me!'

Ruby giggled. 'Come on, Holly, just be flattered. She doesn't mean any harm.'

'I'm sure she doesn't, but it's just weird.'

'Well, Ruby keeps nicking all my shirts, and I swear she's borrowed my pants tonight,' Noah said, his eyes dancing with mischief. 'Maybe it's that special mentor relationship.'

183

Ruby gave him a slap on the butt. 'Come on, we're going to be late. Hi, Sara!' And she breezed out towards the workstations, dragging a still-grinning Noah with her.

Not wanting to be left with Sara, Holly mumbled a brief 'Hallo' and fled after them. She set up quickly, and when Sara slid into the seat next to her she was ready for the first call. 'I'll do a couple to start off and then you can take over for a bit, okay?'

'Okay,' Sara whispered, clutching her hot cup with both hands. She had dumped her bag, which was a perfect match for Holly's, under the table next to Ruby's Tesco carrier and Noah's green Adidas holdall.

Holly hit the button on her keyboard. 'Ambulance service – is the patient breathing?'

'Oh God, you've got to send someone. There's this man just lying on the ground in the car park. He's got no shoes on and I think he must have jumped from the block of flats. There's a window open and curtains flying out in the wind three floors up.'

Holly went through the triage as quickly as possible, passing the information across to the dispatch desk. It was definitely major trauma so the HEMS desk would send helicopter assistance.

Sara, next to her, was actually shaking. 'Do you think he'll make it?'

Holly muted the sound on her line after delivering care instructions for the patient. 'I don't know. He'll probably have massive internal injuries if he did jump from three floors up, poor bloke.' She checked the maps. 'Look, they'll be with him soon. We can check later and see how he's doing if you like.'

Noah was leaning in, watching the moving icons on the map. 'I definitely need to get out on the road. Maybe they'd let me in the helicopter.'

'Maybe not if you don't take some exams,' Ruby told him, finishing her own call and typing up the notes. 'You said you dropped out of school, didn't you?'

Another call came in before they could carry on the

conversation. Holly was used to sentences broken off mid-way, stories half-finished and questions unanswered. She switched smoothly back into work mode.

'Ambulance service – is the patient breathing?'

***

There was a lull around two o'clock in the morning. 'It's that time when the clubs have just closed, and the patients in the care homes haven't woken up yet,' Holly told Sara. 'I'm going to take a quick break if that's okay?'

'Yeah . . . I'll go last if you like?' Noah offered. 'Then it's nearly time to go home.'

'You wish,' Ruby said. 'Hey, Noah's having a party next week, and we're all invited.'

He rolled his eyes at her. 'It's not totally sorted yet but it will be probably Thursday or Friday as we're all on our days off, still. I'll text Ruby the invite and she can send it round.'

'Cool. I've got to admit these days my nights off usually mean straight into a bubble bath after Milo's in bed. Instead of putting on make-up and party clothes, I'm locked in the bathroom with a large gin by half eight.' Holly smiled, just slightly wistfully. God, she felt totally middle-aged and boring compared to this lot, despite the fact Noah and Ruby couldn't be more than a few years younger than her.

'All the more reason for you to get out, mate. It'll be fun!' Ruby told her.

Holly wandered off to heat up her curry dinner. The darkness outside was punctured by the regular synthetic glow of the lights in the car park, and the wind was howling around the building.

Out of habit she checked her phone, sighing as Tom's message flashed up on the screen:

I'll fucking get you.

Well, that was charming. She found the longer it went on, the

185

less power the texts had to hurt her. They still made her bite her lip, but the fear that he could expose secrets was gone. It hadn't happened. It wasn't her fault. The relief still overwhelmed her and every time the thought crossed her mind she felt a bit teary. But now Tom had no hold over her, should she tell his secret?

Despite the bitterness, she had been married to him for nine years, and there was a vestige of something left in her heart, buried deep down. The funny thing was, he had so much more to lose, and yet he was the one who kept bringing up the past. She glanced back over the texts, concentrating, ignoring the 'ping' on the microwave. The messages were vile and abusive, but poorly constructed. Tom was a stickler for punctuation, even in a text, and these had none that made sense. There was even the odd misspelled word, probably due to autocorrect. Was he sending these texts when he was drunk?

***

The next morning Lydia was waiting when she got home from the school run, sitting at the kitchen table with a mug of tea and the biscuit tin.

'I thought you would've gone home by now,' Holly told her, surprised.

Her aunt's face was minus its usual plastering of thick orange foundation. She'd even left off the lipstick and her eyes were red, as though from lack of sleep. 'Holly, you know I said there were things I needed to tell you . . .'

'Yeah.'

'I should have told you before. When Jayden disappeared the first time, I knew he was okay. But before you say anything, I didn't know about the kids or the girlfriend.' Her fists were clenched on the table in front of her, as though preparing herself for battle.

'Fuck.'

'Don't interrupt and stop bloody swearing. I've had another

186

chat with DI Harper, George, and he agrees I should be the one to tell you. He's already spoken to his colleagues investigating the case.' She took a deep breath. 'Your mum was having an affair with George Harper. She was one of his informants, and things got out of hand. He was in love with her, but she felt she couldn't leave Donnie and you and Jayden. Don't say anything yet.' Her aunt held up a hand and Holly shut her mouth again. 'The affair had been going on for years. She kept breaking it off – going cold turkey, she called it – but she'd always go back to him.'

'Bloody hell, Lydia. It's okay, I couldn't string a sentence together if I tried. I can tell there's more, so hit me with it, before I recover from the last bit.' Holly felt like she'd been hit in the stomach, blindsided by her own mother. *George Harper?*

'Right. Yes. Jayden is George Harper's son, not your dad's.'

Holy opened her mouth to speak and closed it again as the room spun round. She rested her head in her hands, rubbing her temples. She wasn't just being kicked in the gut, she was being trampled by a rugby team. 'Did my dad *know*?'

'Not to my knowledge. He's never given any indication of knowing,' Lydia said, frowning. 'Sian was good at keeping secrets. Obviously, George wanted to help when he saw Jayden struggling after your mum's death . . .'

'So why didn't he find out who killed her? If he loved her? If he loved Jay?' The questions rattled out, and she clutched the edge of the table so hard her knuckles went white. She couldn't imagine her mum as an informant, let alone being in love with that bastard and to have his child . . .

Her aunt laid a gentle hand on her arm. 'Holly, I'm – we're – fairly sure one of the Nicholls brothers killed Sian. I'm so sorry, and I know George was desperate to gather enough evidence to prosecute, but there simply wasn't a shred to tie them to the hit and run.'

Holly found she couldn't speak. She ran her tongue round her lips, tried to swallow. 'Why them? Oh, wait, I get it, she was spilling stuff about their operation?'

Lydia nodded. 'When your dad started out, it was just about the drugs, but when he got mixed up with the Nicholls, she really couldn't cope with the trafficking of young girls. She and I . . . We didn't have the best childhood, as you know, and it hit a nerve for her. She went all out to try and stop Donnie from getting involved, and when he didn't stop, she said she would take down the Nicholls.'

'But she never seemed bothered about any of it! Always told us the police were vermin. Fuck, I sound like my dad. He must have guessed though . . . Although I suppose not if he's rolling out the red carpet for Jayden now, and going on about all this family stuff.'

Lydia shook her head. 'Your mum cared about the girls, Holly. She hated what was going on. But somehow, the Nicholls found out she was a grass. George is convinced one of them followed her. George always dropped her off in the same place on Beach Road, at the same time, because she insisted on it, he said.'

'Okay . . .' Holly was thinking it was a good thing she hadn't known this before her recent conversations with Joey and Gareth, or she would have been tempted to smash their faces in. 'And Jayden? Does he know who his real father is?'

'Yes. Sian always said that if anything happened to her, she wanted her son to know the truth. Harper told him after your mum's funeral. You know your brother went off the rails a bit, but later he knew Harper was his best chance of getting out of here. Jayden asked George for help to get away with Larissa and his family. George agreed to put him in touch with a contact who could get them a new identity, and a place to live. For a price.'

'Hang on, DI Harper, sorry, *George*, knew Jay had two kids but he never told you?'

'Yes. The money Jay took from me was for the new identities. George was able to pull some strings with a mate in Witness Protection and get them. The night of the murders, the final payment was due. George had no idea of course. He'd done his bit and stepped back. He made Jay promise to keep in touch, and that was it.'

'The money wasn't for drugs? Or for Niko?'

'No. It was for his family.'

Holly stared blindly at her aunt, tears cascading down her cheeks.

'I told you, he was due to leave the day after Larissa was murdered, which is why he was desperate to get the money together and collect the new identities,' Lydia said. Her shoulders drooped and she sagged in her chair, exhausted by the revelations.

'And I told him to fuck off. Why didn't he *tell* me?' Holly whispered. She'd made the wrong decision. Again. She'd failed the little family and Larissa and the baby had been murdered. 'If I'd got the money when he first asked me it might have made a difference. He'd have gone before the Balintas found out where they were.'

Chapter 23

Dear Mum,

Isn't it funny how I can see you more clearly when I close my eyes? I've been doing that a lot and keeping really quiet since we got here, because just between us, I don't trust Dad's friend.

It's been just you, me and him for so long that I couldn't see how he let someone else in. But Dad's clever so maybe he has another plan that he hasn't told me about yet. I'm sorry we can't make a new wall for you, but we're moving around a lot.

I've got my book though, and I've got loads of your pictures on my phone now. I've wanted a phone for ages but Dad said I was too young. Now we've moved he's been so focused on the plan that he isn't noticing what I've been doing so much.

Once we've finished with the plan and it's all over, we'll be moving again. Dad says we'll be living on a boat for a while, and just sailing around.

Dad's friend wasn't part of our plan, but now he seems to be tagging along the whole time. He's always nice to me, and buys me chocolates, laughs at my jokes, but I can't tell what he really wants.

One thing I do know for sure is that Dad will kill him if he screws with the plan.

I love you, Mum x

Chapter 24

After Lydia had left, Holly made herself sit down and get all the bills out. She needed something to focus on, to distract her from the questions whirling in her head. But it made depressing reading, and she was going to have to admit defeat on the mortgage repayments unless Tom helped out. Which he had already made clear he wouldn't. At least he was paying child support, but it was a tiny amount compared to what it took to keep this house. Perhaps she should move to another part of the country? Or even go to Spain with Lydia after all, and start again . . .

The news that Jayden was DI Harper's son still made her feel ill whenever she thought about it. How had her mum done that? Maybe Donnie had found out after she'd died, and that was why he took to the bottle?

Niko could go to hell, with his stupid threats. She knew he had been shocked at her suggestion that Jayden might have come back to settle the score. She had seen the fear in his eyes. Once, Niko – backed by his brothers, and well in with the Nicholls – could have relied on a whole gang of people to protect him. Now, with his skinny, pale body hunched into the red jacket, he seemed kind of ridiculous. But she couldn't write off the Nicholls as easily. Had Gareth or Joey really been responsible for her mum's death?

Her thoughts spun back to Jayden. He was clearly good at hiding, so much so that he and Larissa had lived just a few miles away for over a year before it had all kicked off again. With a new identity they could have been anywhere. A headache nudged at the base of her skull and she rubbed her sore eyes. She remembered how terrified she had been at the trial, and before during the endless police interviews. Everyone asking where Jayden was . . .

Holly's phone rang and she took the call from Karen.

'Just wanted to let you know that the boy has been released into foster care. The hospital will still need to see him as an outpatient, but he's doing well.'

'Thanks . . . Can I still go and see him? Did he say anything yet?'

She could hear the sigh down the phone. 'Let him settle in a bit first and then of course you can visit. The more contact he has with his family the better, but foster care is the only answer until we find out what's happening with his dad.'

'Okay . . .' A tiny part of Holly wanted to ask Karen if she knew Harper was the boy's grandfather, but she shut down on the secret. Now wasn't the time. She said goodbye and ended the call.

Stretching her aching limbs, feeling the bolts of tension run through her shoulders, Holly recalled Dev's offer and suddenly knew exactly what she needed.

***

Dev suggested they have a workout first and then they could talk properly afterwards.

Holly drove down to Shoey's, the rundown 1960s gym next to the Seaview. She didn't have any proper workout gear anymore, so she'd settled for tracksuit bottoms and a tight, cropped T-shirt, wincing at her lack of muscle.

A few lads crowded out the doors as she went in, but there was no banter. Shoey's wasn't some fancy gym with a stage and mums doing yoga. This was a boxing club and martial arts haven, and you only braved the stench of sweat, and the filthy changing rooms if you were serious about your sport.

Memories came roaring back, taking her by surprise, as she turned right then left to the women's changing rooms without hesitation. She even went to chuck her bag and coat into the same battered locker on the end of the row.

So many years had passed since she had practically lived in this place, sparring with the best of them, arguing with Shoey himself. God, she had been an arrogant kid, but a talented one. Then when Larissa was murdered she had run away from everything that reminded her of her old life, turning her back on a good career, and signing up for university instead.

It had been blind panic and determination to change into someone totally different, someone she herself didn't recognise, that had led her to the uni course. As it turned out she'd met Tom in her first term and proceeded to screw up the new version of herself too. Funny how life turned out, and here she was, peeling back the layers to find 'old Holly'.

Donnie had been proud of her boxing skills, although he was less keen on her choice of men. He liked Dev but saw the Mancinis as pretty far below him and tried to encourage her to see one of the Nicholls boys, or the Balintas. Holly snorted to herself as she tied her laces. The closest she'd ever got to getting physical with any of the Nicholls boys had been here at the gym. There had been a nasty little incident when one of Joey's nephews, Charlie, had gone down to her in the ring. He'd waited for her late one night after that as she walked back from Dev's place, grabbing her arms, forcing her back against the wall.

She'd almost forgotten about it, but now she smiled as she recalled the round kick that had sent him flying. As well as boxing, she'd done a fair bit of martial arts training. Her world had been so different then.

There was a stained, chipped mirror still up on the end of the lockers and before she went out for her session she looked hard at the woman in the mirror. Black hair scooped up in a high ponytail, green eyes and olive skin, nothing like her fair-skinned, blonde brother, who she had always thought took after Donnie. Had George had blonde hair at some point? She only remembered it as grey . . . Back to the mirror, blocking out the thoughts. Holly was tall, solid, and there were still muscles, but they were slack from lack of use. She flexed an arm and smiled, feeling blood rush as the anticipation hit.

'Well, look who's back?' A man shuffled into the changing rooms, giving scant regard for the fact that this was the women's area. His face was shrivelled, head bald and shining, but whilst his skin was wrinkled and creped in the folds of his joints, a grubby red vest and black gym shorts showed off a sinewy body and bulging muscles.

Holly had often thought about coming back here, had wondered how awkward it would be coming face to face with her old mentor, but now the time had arrived there was only one thing to say: 'Looking good, Shoey.'

'Yes, I know, darling.' He ran his eyes over her body, profes-sionally assessing. 'You look like shit. Still, we'll soon get you ripped again. Get your arse out in that gym. Dev's been in for an hour already, so don't be surprised if he knocks you out in the first round.'

'Yeah, whatever. We're not competing anymore – this is just pad work.'

He laughed, strange and high-pitched like a hyena. 'You two was always in competition, darling. It won't be any different now.'

She smiled, and as she went past him, he closed a hand on her wrist, bringing her to a gentle halt, his voice a mere breath in her ear. 'Be careful, darling, something's going down and you need to watch your back. You're okay here. Nobody fucks with you in my place but take care of yourself. Especially round Gareth.'

He released her, patting her back, sending her on her way before she had a chance to reply, and when she looked back at the door he had gone. A shiver of fear slid across her spine, making her hunch her shoulders as though a blast of cold air had taken her by surprise. She had managed not to think about Gareth's warning most of the day, but his face was often there when she woke at night.

Dev was in the corner, lifting weights, and she watched him for a moment before walking over.

'So you have you come to work out properly, or did you just come to perv over my fit body?'

She grinned, despite herself. 'Get over it, Dev. Listen, I've got something to tell you. You want to grab a drink before we start?' They wandered over to the water fountain, dodging grunting and straining combatants. The stench of sweat, and rubber, the whir and cough of the broken air conditioning unit, and the mats underfoot, all came back in an instant. She felt more at home here than she ever had at university.

After she'd told him Lydia's revelation, he bent down and took a gulp, wiping water from his face and neck. 'So what are you going do now?'

She took a swig, licking the excess from the corners of her mouth, and wiping her own face with her towel. 'No idea. You don't seem that surprised about Jayden?'

'I sort of guessed there was something between him and DI Harper. Harper kept bailing him out, looking out for him. I'm not sure anybody else noticed, but I was with Jay so much . . . I never would have guessed about your mum though. How do you feel about that?' Devril ran both hands across his head, then leant down to a rucksack and pulled out an energy drink.

'Weird. I mean, she's this totally different person to who I thought she was. She was shagging Harper and trying to take down the Nicholls, and none of us ever noticed? Which reminds me. Have you heard anything from Bailey?'

'No. He's gone a bit quiet, which is a bad sign. He was just about ready to go.'

Shoey appeared in front of them, treading lightly across the mats with his elastic gait, his expression thunderous. 'Lazy fuckers, get over there and start warming up. Come on, Holly, I'll start you off!' He was grinning now, watery grey eyes alight with mischief and challenge, and Holly felt a lump in her throat. God, she'd missed this. It was like stepping back in time.

By the time she was on her sixth rep she remembered the muscle burn perfectly. Her breath was coming in gasps and Devril was drawing ahead, the bastard.

After an hour they got the pads out, and Holly surprised herself. She might be unfit but the muscle memory was there, and Shoey had stopped shaking his head in despair at her lack of fitness.

After eighty minutes she was dripping with sweat, every single fibre of her body hurt, and she felt great. 'I've had it now, Dev. I need to do some stretches and grab a shower.'

Shoey drifted off to yell at some women on the mats in the far corner, leaving Holly and Dev to warm down in silence. Gradually, as she pulled her body through the half-remembered stretches, Holly's heart rate began to slow and her breathing returned to normal.

It felt so natural, leaning out over the mat, feeling Dev next to her doing the same, knowing that instead of a gushing hot shower, there would be only a trickle of cold water, and she would have to pick her way around the patches of grime on the floor.

'Do you want to come back to my place for lunch?' Devril asked now, grabbing his kit bag, shoving his gloves back inside. Holly had left hers behind years ago, and had to suffer the humiliation of borrowing an ancient threadbare pair from Shoey. It made her feel like a beginner again. She resolved to invest in some decent kit as soon as she got paid at the end of the month.

Before she could answer, Shoey yelled happily across the gym, 'Showers are fucked again so go home and use your own!'

'Bailey's left a voicemail. He thinks Joey is onto him.' All the amusement had faded from Devril's face, leaving his pale grey eyes blank and worried. 'Fuck, this is bad. How can Joey know?'

Lowering her own voice as they went into the corridor, Holly replied in a whisper, 'I don't know. What are you going to do?'

'I'll wait until he makes contact. It's what we agreed if there was ever any trouble, just in case the Nicholls got hold of his phone. He's super careful, and I'm stored under some random name, plus he deletes everything as soon as he's read it.'

'He's got kids, hasn't he? And what about his wife?' Holly felt sweat start again, beading her face, moistening her palms.

'Yeah. *Shit*.' He slammed a fist against the wall, and Shoey, always on the lookout for trouble, shot into the corridor, spinning round in fighting stance.

'What's up with you? Don't you go trashing my place, Devril Mancini,' he said aggressively, but his expression was concerned and he lowered his fists. 'Okay, off you go home! Go and jump in your own showers.'

'What now?' Dev asked, as they walked towards the changing rooms, dodging a group of sweaty lads.

'I'm going to talk to Niko again.'

'Not by yourself, you aren't.'

'He's not going to hurt me. He's as curious as the rest of us about Jayden's son, and he's after the fifty grand he says Jayden owes him.'

'Fifty? Since when?'

'He says Jay took all the money out of his secret account or something. Reckons it was stashed away ready for his release, and now it's all gone. That's the only reason Gareth is so interested in him and when he finds out Niko is as broke as the rest of us, *and* getting cosy with Donnie . . .' She left the threat open-ended, but Dev nodded in agreement.

He pushed a shoulder to the door, pausing to look down at Holly. 'True. The Nicholls won't even spit on him when they find out he's got no cash to bring into the business.'

'Yeah, which is driving him crazy.' Holly couldn't help a quick grin. 'But seriously, I want to talk to him. He was shitting himself when I mentioned he would be on Jayden's hit list for sure. I don't think it had occurred to him.'

'You think Niko's next in line?' Devril was sceptical. 'Maybe he's done Roman and Alexi and that was it.'

'No, he would want to get Niko too. Without him sending his idiot brothers over, Larissa and her baby would still be alive.'

'Point taken. But his other kid is still in hospital. When he's finished and got revenge or whatever, he won't leave without his kid, Larissa's kid, surely?'

'Yeah, I thought that too. But if Jayden doesn't – or can't – come back for his boy, then I'll fight to adopt him or something. He's just a kid and I feel like I owe Larissa. But I need to sort out this shit with my ex first – it's driving me crazy. I've got to run and pick Milo up, but I'll call you.'

He was pushing his way into the changing room. 'Sure. Call me anytime.' Dev flung the words over his shoulder, and the door banged.

She felt herself blushing. Crazy. There was no way she was going to get involved with Devril Mancini again.

***

Holly picked Milo up from school, cheering him up with the news that they could go to the hospital for a check on the twenty-ninth, and if all was well, his cast could come off in two weeks' time.

He didn't seem as pleased as she had expected. 'Are you all right? Did you have a bad day?'

He shrugged in the back seat, looking out of the window, so she waited until they were home, and she was taking his empty lunchbox out of his bag. 'What's up, Milo?' Holly dumped the water bottle on the countertop, walked over to the sofa and pulled him close, but he wriggled away, eyes downcast.

'We did this thing at school today.'

'Mmmm.'

'A man came in to talk about drugs and how we didn't have to take them if we didn't want to, even though lots of people on the Seaview do.'

'Okay.' She really couldn't see where this was headed so she just let him talk.

'You know I said about having a secret a while ago?'

Holly cast her mind back. 'I do. But wasn't that about the man in car?'

He shook his head.

'You can tell me anything, sweetie, you know that.'

'Dad said I wasn't to tell you.' The words came out in a rush, and he looked up, big green eyes filled with tears. 'He said not to tell you, and if I kept his secret I could have a new toy every month.'

Holly's heart was thumping so hard her chest seemed about to explode, and blood seemed to be filling her brain. '*Dad* said that? It's okay. You can tell me . . .'

'I wouldn't have told, but when I went to stay with him, you know, last month? When Beth was out visiting her friends, he put a film on. It was the new *Star Wars*, and it was great.'

'I'm sure, but what upset you?'

'I was watching the film with a bag of sweets, and I heard Dad's mobile ringing, but I couldn't find him, or the phone, so I followed the noise up to his office.'

Tom had converted a large spare room in his new place into a palatial office, stocked with every electronic gadget known to man. Holly had only seen it once, when she dropped Milo off and Beth had insisted on showing her around 'their' new house.

'He was doing the same as last time . . . He was snuffling up white powder. It went up his nose.' Milo sounded a little puzzled. 'Last time he saw me and he said it was an adult's thing, and that it was a secret.'

199

'But you knew it was wrong.' Holly was so angry she wanted to march straight round and batter her ex-husband senseless.

'Yes. He didn't see me this time, and he was so angry last time, before he said about keeping the secret, so I just snuck away, and went back to the film.'

Holly pulled him close. 'You did the right thing telling me.' She felt a terrible thud of darkness, of guilt. She had caught him at a party once, when she was heavily pregnant, snorting cocaine, and he had promised it was a one-off. A part of her was even relieved that she had a secret to keep for him, a confidence in return for what she'd told him. 'A one-time thing', he'd called it and she had never caught him again, and had chosen to believe him, despite having had a pathological liar and addict for a brother.

How could she have been so stupid? How could Tom still be doing coke? And while he was meant to be looking after Milo. That was the worst thing. He was supposed to be looking after their child and he was doing a line in the next room! She had kept his secret as he had kept hers. But now, all bets were off.

Chapter 25

Holly rang Cathryn as soon as Milo had gone to bed and she was sure he was fast asleep.

She ran through everything Milo had said, but Cathryn, although she agreed Tom was a fucking wanker, seemed distracted. 'Sorry, Cath, have you got someone round?'

'Yeah. Look, don't do anything yet, okay? You need to work out whether to go and have it out with him and tell the bitch girlfriend, or just go straight to the police or hell, even that cow from Social Services. She nailed it when Liam was giving me trouble. I've got her number somewhere. Don't do anything until tomorrow, okay?'

Holly went straight to the fridge and poured a large glass of wine. She hoped Cathryn wasn't getting back with Liam. She was sure she'd heard a man's voice in the background and her friend had been dead keen to get her off the phone, so it wasn't a family visit.

Despite flicking on the TV and scrolling through social media, Holly couldn't settle. She was actually shivering with rage, and guilt. How could she have let this happen? Tom had always been able to argue his way out of anything. He had managed to convince her that for him, the drug use was a novelty, a fun way to pep up a party.

Of course she had told him exactly why drugs ruin lives, had cited the dealers and addicts she had known since childhood, had explained about the Nicholls, her father and the rest. But she had been heavily pregnant, clinging to a relationship, to a marriage that she thought would change her for the better. And so she had forgiven him and he had laughed, telling her that now they knew each other's dirty little secrets.

Her phone rang halfway through a rerun of *CSI*, but when Lydia's number came up, she ignored it. She couldn't trust herself not to blurt out what had just happened, and her aunt had enough to cope with at the moment.

Milo was slightly subdued the next morning, but she reiterated that he had been very brave to tell her, and there was no way he would get into trouble for it. Poor kid, carrying this around for weeks, and putting up with the aftermath of the accident. Every time Holly thought about it, it felt like a kick in the gut. Regret and stupidity would do nothing now though. Action was needed.

She dropped her son at school and called Dev on the way home. Despite his teenage years running dealers' supply lines, he'd never touched the stuff himself. He'd seen what the drugs had done to Jay and countless other kids on the Seaview, and had known not touching the goods was the only way he'd get out of the estate. But Dev agreed she should get advice from her solicitor, and made it clear she should also refrain from going round and confronting Tom until she'd calmed down.

'Any news from Bailey?' Holly asked before she rang off.

'No. It's like he's dropped off the planet. I'm seriously worried.'

'Yeah. Have you got his wife's number?'

'I've been ringing his mobile and his home number for the last couple of days, and I found out his address so I went round, but it looks like the house is all shut up, like they've gone already.'

'Maybe he got cold feet and just took his family and ran?' Holly suggested.

'No, I don't get that feeling. He was so determined to help take down the Nicholls . . . We'd got too close to give up.'

Having extracted Milo from his after-school club that night, Holly drove home, put him to bed, then took a deep breath and picked up her phone. Her rage had been festering all day, and she realised she should have fitted in a quick trip to Shoey's to work off her anger.

Tom wasn't answering his mobile, so she tried the landline.

'Hi, Beth, is Tom there?'

Beth's voice was wary. 'Yes he is.'

'So can I talk to him please?' Holly made her words exaggeratedly polite. She had a glass of wine on the table next to her, and she wrapped her fingers around the stem, pressing the cool glass so hard that her fingers turned white.

Tom took ages getting to the phone. 'Holly? Is Milo all right?'

'He's fine. Look, Tom, I need to discuss something with you. Can Beth hear what I'm saying?'

A moment, and his breathing came quicker. 'Let me take the phone into the office.' He put a hand over the receiver and she heard him call something to his girlfriend about legal divorce stuff.

'Okay, Tom, I'll make this quick. Milo told me that he caught you snorting coke. Firstly, what the *fuck* did you think you were doing? Secondly, we need to talk about what happens next.'

There was a long pause, then: 'You fucking bitch.'

He was like a cornered animal, furious but unable to hurt her now. 'Bad choice of words. Tom, I can't believe you snowed me like that. Were you using the whole time we were together?'

'Of course not! And "using" is such a pathetic word. I'm not some addict on the streets in a cardboard box or some loser from the Seaview.'

'If you are taking drugs it doesn't matter if you're on the street or on the lecture circuit staying in five-star hotels. You've got this wrong, Tom, it isn't where you are, it's who you are.'

'So what are you going to do?'

'Depends on you. I want a deal. You leave Milo to me and stop trying to go for full custody. Stop the shitty texts and threats, and keep paying child support. In return, I'll get Milo's evidence, and mine, all filed away neatly with my solicitor, and you won't hear about it again. Neither will Beth.'

'And if I don't? Don't forget I've got stuff on you too!'

'Not anymore. I told you it was a mistake. I've already told the police. Do you get it? The message was never passed on, so I wasn't involved in Larissa's murder at all. And before you start, I have someone who would swear it in any court, so no, you have nothing on me. You took drugs in front of our child, Tom. Nothing else matters to me except Milo. You should know that by now. I've got this great journalist friend too, and I bet he'd love the story . . .'

'All right! I'll speak to my solicitor tomorrow.'

Satisfied, Holly put the phone down. Horrifying though it was to think her child had been exposed to drug-taking, she had no wish to go through with her threats and hurt Milo in the process. As long as the messages stopped and the threat of a custody battle vanished, she'd stay quiet. Tom would have to get help in his own way, if that was what he needed. How had she married a drug user? After everything she'd seen and done, it stung, painful and sour in her middle. Was she really that blind? She had no doubt he would try to get some little petty revenge, but with this evidence she could destroy him and everything he cared about. His status and the adoration and flattery would all take a nosedive if it ever came out that he had taken drugs in front of his eight-year-old son.

Emptying the last of the wine into her glass, she made another call, but the phone went straight to voicemail. After a second's hesitation she left a message. 'Hi, Dev, just checking to see if you wanted to meet up tomorrow. I . . . I'll try you again in the morning.'

It didn't feel right to leave any details of her conversation with Tom, although she felt like celebrating. To have the threat of losing Milo lifted was like winning the lottery. Shame she couldn't manage that too, then she could keep the house.

Outside, the wind had worsened and the back gate was banging again. She really must find those bloody back door keys. Frowning, Holly glanced back down at her phone as it buzzed. There was a message on the screen:

You haven't won. You have no idea what might happen next.

Tom's threats didn't bother her as much now, but for some reason she thought of Gareth and his cold, soulless eyes. Moving quickly around the house she checked the doors and windows as usual, emptying out two drawers in the kitchen cupboard in an effort to find her keys. But there was nothing but the usual muddle of receipts, broken pens and sticky rubber bands. At least the door was locked, she reasoned with herself. She may not be able to open it, but nobody else could either.

***

Holly's next shift was an early one, so she made sure Milo's lunch was done the night before. Lydia was coming over at six to take over whilst she snuck out of the house and drove to work. Whilst she drove, she put in a quick call to her solicitor, leaving a message saying she wanted an appointment booked in for tomorrow afternoon. She was fairly confident she could coax Milo into repeating what he had said for the record, and then it was done, and ready to be used if Tom ever turned nasty again.

The rain was pelting down, bouncing off slick roads, and clogging her windscreen with torrents. After very little sleep, her mind was bouncing around all over the place. Niko, Gareth, Jayden and Tom's faces were jeering at her, and she almost perversely enjoyed getting soaked on the short walk from the car park to the main building.

Holly's phone rang, and she frowned, surprised as Donnie's

number flashed up. Since when did *he* call *her*? 'I'm just going into work.'

'Won't take long. I need to know if you've had any thoughts about my offer?'

'Plenty, but I've got a lot on at the moment. Don't push me, Dad.' It seemed safer, with the Nicholls hounding her, to hedge her bets. There wasn't a chance in hell she was going back to run a drugs op on the Seaview, but if playing along got her access to her brother, and kept her in Donnie's confidence, she could at least keep up a pretence.

He was laughing. 'Well, that's a turnaround. Or are you just keeping me sweet for another reason?'

Nobody's fool now he was off the bottle. 'Whatever, Donnie. I need to go. Have you spoken to Jayden?'

'No, but he'll have his reasons. I went to see my grandson in hospital, though. I saw him just before they took him to that foster carer.'

'Why?' Donnie hadn't ever bothered with his other grandson, and she was indignant on Milo's behalf. She was also freaked by the thought that her dad was all excited to play happy families, without knowing that Jay and his son weren't actually related to him. Clearly Jay hadn't thought it was necessary to tell Donnie this little detail.

'Just to see him. It's nice to have family again isn't it?'

Holly couldn't decide if he was being sarcastic or not, so she muttered about going to work and killed the call. So if Jayden hadn't contacted anyone since the crash, what was he doing? And Bailey was missing too . . . Could there be a connection?

Dragging herself from her tangled thoughts, Holly realised she still standing outside in the pouring rain. Her hair was soaked, and she was going to be late. She dived into the toilets to sort herself out, dragging a comb and some make-up from her bag to repair the damage.

'Hi, Holly. What are you staring at?'

206

She was leaning over the sink trying to rub foundation under her eyes to cover the dark shadows.

'Hi, Rubes, how's it going?'

'Yeah, you know, got my little trainee to keep me company again today.' Ruby winked, and added another layer of mascara to her own thick black lashes.

'Are you seeing him properly, or just playing around?'

'Oh, I've seen all of him, and he's gorgeous,' Ruby confirmed with a wicked little grin. She added a slick of scarlet to her full lips and smoothed her long black ponytail. 'It's not serious, but I'm happy with that. Last thing I want is a proper relationship after all that shit with my ex.'

'Fast mover.'

'Of course. How's your girl doing?'

'Well, I'm not sleeping with her. She'll be fine. She's a bit nervous, but she'll get there.' Holly added lip gloss and pulled a face in the mirror. She still looked like shit.

'Glad to hear it. You've got enough on your plate at the moment. Come on, we'd better move it.'

They swiped into the control room and found empty desks next to each other. Noah pitched up with five minutes to go, clutching a cup of coffee, his wet hair flopping over his eyes.

'Can anyone take a red call?' The team leader was looking down the table, poised for action.

'I can, I'm logged in now,' Holly answered, and then wished she hadn't.

'Okay, it's a hanging. A twenty-year-old male.'

The red telephone was used for queue-jumping calls when the operator was given sufficient information to make the caller high priority. The red calls were generally CPR ones, and Holly went straight into her triage, adrenalin pumping.

'My brother is hanging from the banister rail. Oh my God, help me!' The pain and horror in the caller's voice made her indistinct as emotion took over.

'Listen to me carefully . . .'

After the crew had arrived at the address, Holly killed the call and typed up her notes. She felt emotional herself, now, her throat a bit choked, her heart still pumping. 'I need a break.'

'You okay?' Her team leader was Alex today, and he was a sweetheart. 'That was a tough one. Take ten minutes.'

Ruby, next to her, was in the middle of a complex mental health call, with Noah listening in and taking notes, but she had clocked was happening and stretched out a hand to squeeze Holly's shoulder.

In the break room, Holly made another coffee and opened a packet of crisps. The adrenalin rush was slowing now, leaving her drained and exhausted. It was important to move on after a call like that, to not dwell on what might have been, or hear the screams in your dreams. You couldn't afford to let it get to you, but it was okay to take time out to recover. After all, if you didn't care, you shouldn't be working for the ambulance service.

It had been said many times before, and Holly was used to dealing with horrific trauma calls, she just needed a bit of time and space. But today tears were running down her cheeks, and she hastily wiped them away.

Sara drifted in, her red curls soaked and dark, her coat dripping water onto the floor. 'Hi, Holly! Oh, are you okay?'

'Yeah, I'll be all right, thanks. You?'

'I'm fine. Before I forget, are these yours?' She was rooting around in her bag, which was the exact match of the brown leather bag that Holly owned. 'I found these keys after the last shift and I wondered if you had shoved them in my bag by accident . . .? All the bags get thrown under the table don't they, and it would be easy to muddle them up.' Her eyes were bright, her expression the usual mix of slightly anxious and eager to please.

Holly watched as she dangled the keys, with their silly black cat LED and the random ball of green fluff. 'They're mine. They're my back door keys.'

'Oh! Oh, I'm sorry, but our bags are so similar, aren't they?' Sara was still smiling, apparently unaware of the awkwardness of the situation.

'Thanks.' Holly held out a hand and caught the keys neatly in one fist as Sara chucked them across the room. All thoughts of her last call were banished from her mind, and she watched Sara as the girl went into the little kitchen area, unpacking her meal for later, boiling the kettle for tea. Had she really put her keys in the wrong bag, or had Sara taken them? It was . . . weird.

But then Holly let out a long breath and forced a smile as the girl came back into the room with a mug in one hand. Perhaps she was just jittery with everything that was going on at the moment. Sara wouldn't nick her keys, and if she had, she clearly hadn't done anything with them. Did she even know where Holly lived?

Exactly ten minutes later, she was back at her seat, sharing a packet of dolly mixtures with her side of the desk. 'Ambulance service – is the patient breathing?'

***

It was better getting home at seven in the evening than seven in the morning. She always looked forward to the bedtime routine, and as Milo got older it got better. He was an amusing companion now, and although he still insisted on her reading him a story as he drifted off to sleep, she could see that soon he would be all grown up. Although there was a little pang, when she looked at baby photos, or held someone else's newborn, she had never wanted another child, and almost looked forward to the time when Milo was an adult and she could see what he had become. Unless he turned out like the rest of her family, of course.

Her mind drifted back to her teenage self being told the news about her mother. The police had been arguing with her dad, which wasn't unusual. But this time the chaos wasn't familiar, it was devastating

209

Donnie, forcibly taken down to the police station and questioned, had maintained the ferocity of a caged bear during his interrogation. He said Sian had gone down the Bingo for a few hours. But she had not been at the Bingo, or anywhere in town that anybody could trace. Rumours were rife that she had a lover, but it was never proven. Suppose Donnie *had* found out about Jay's parentage, and had one of his men take her out of play?

But Donnie had spent a few months ordering beatings and pulling in all his contacts to try and find out who had killed his wife. In the end, though, he had no more luck than the police.

Holly and Jayden, once so close, had drifted apart after their mum's death. Jayden took on a more active role in the family business, shoving a lot of coke up his nose in the process, and Holly spent her time in the gym with Shoey and Dev. Cath, previously slightly distant, had been with her constantly when she needed it, instinctively leaving her alone when she needed to grieve.

The local families had been supportive, too, and banded together to help out. That was the side of the Seaview she missed, the side that outsiders would never see. Alongside the crime there was a staunch loyalty and a sense of belonging.

Smiling a little sadly to herself now, Holly remembered that even Niko had slipped an arm round her shoulders one night when he found her crying and punching the fence on the footpath. It had been weird and a tiny glimpse of the person Niko might have been if he'd not had Mason as a dad, perhaps. She'd been so sure he was going to try something, but his solicitude seemed to have been genuine.

Niko's dad was a bastard, but his mum, Bev, had been okay. Cathryn in particular adored her, because she was always glam, in full make-up with loads of jewellery and expensive sunglasses. She'd had a good heart and was always a shoulder to cry on for any of the kids.

Bev had been one of her own mum's best friends, and six months after Sian had been killed, Bev had taken off with another man. Nobody blamed her, and Mason just moved one of his junkie girlfriends into the house.

What would her mum think of her current situation? What would she think if she knew her secrets had been exposed to Holly? Sian had never been the type of mum to tell her kids she loved them. She'd been kind of guarded and careful around all her family, including Donnie.

As she poured a glass of gin and tonic, Holly looked at the bank of family photos arranged on the dresser. She only had a couple of her mum, and her favourite was a back view of the two of them, standing on the beach on a grey day. Their arms were around each other and their dark hair was blowing in the wind. Her mum's charm bracelet glinted on her wrist. Holly must have been about twelve.

Holly touched the photo with her fingertips, lightly, smiling again at the memory. It still hurt but she had learnt to live with the hurt. There were some good memories, and it was better to hang on to the good than the bad. Right now, she needed some chill-out time. She padded upstairs, checking on Milo as she went. The luminous numbers on the clock in his room said eight-thirty. He was snoring peacefully, so she went into the bathroom, closed the door and put some music on. It was her ritual.

She pushed away the thoughts of Jay and his son, the stress of work, the worries over her finances, and hid under the bubbles from the faces that danced through her mind in endless repetition. The music soothed her, and the drink made her sleepy.

The water was cold by the time she hauled herself out, an hour later. After dragging on her pyjamas she untied her hair from its bath-time knot and shook it out. She wandered back downstairs, peeking in on Milo again, as she always did. He generally slept curled into a ball, his soft toys gathered around him.

Her eyes adjusted to the light and she peered carefully into his bed, seeking out his pale little face. But there was only a tangle

211

of duvet and a mountain of soft toys. Her heart began to beat faster, scanning the bed, the room, pulling away the covers. Milo wasn't there.

Chapter 26

Several teddy bears tumbled to the floor, as she spun round, checking the room, glancing stupidly at the tightly closed curtains.

Holly couldn't breathe and her chest was hurting as she flicked on the light, calling his name. He must have gone down for a glass of water . . . Yes, that was it. She was being silly. But she still called his name and nobody answered. Maybe he was sick or had fallen with his cast? He was pretty good at going down the stairs on his backside, but perhaps he had slipped?

'Milo!' Her voice echoed around the house, the thud of her bare feet amplified by the emptiness. She checked the empty rooms, the kitchen, the downstairs bathroom, the spare room, and opened the window, yelling his name, crying now, unable to believe he was gone. A dog was barking a few doors down.

The front door was unlocked, no safety chain across, but she never locked up until just before she went to bed. She opened the door, peering into the road, squinting into the darkness.

Now the back door – dear God, the back door keys were still in her bag. She wrestled with the door, screaming his name, yanking the door open and running out onto the grass. Her bare feet were icy in the mud, and her pyjamas flapped around her legs, but she barely noticed.

Their garden backed onto woods via a wire fence. The gate swung out onto the narrow footpath that ran along the back of the woods. All the houses along this road had one, and it was a nice extension to their gardens. It wasn't an area known for its crime, despite the proximity to the Seaview Estate, so the wooden gate was secured by nothing but a couple of bolts. Except it hadn't been, had it? It had been banging in the wind for the past few days, unsecured and wide open.

Holly could see nothing in the woods, but blackness amongst the swaying rain-filled trees, and she yelled again and again. Her throat hurt and blind panic sent her hurtling back across the grass. Panting back through the house, she ran to the front again, unable to believe it.

'*Milo!*' She hauled the curtains to one side, wiping the window with her sleeve and staring out of the living room window. But there was nobody in the road, apart from the odd car swishing past, headlights dazzling and fading as each vehicle passed.

She dragged the front door wide. Her car sat parked neatly next to the pavement, along with numerous others. There were a couple of people hurrying along under umbrellas now, and a few more cars whizzed past, splashing up dirty water onto the glistening pavement. There was no sign of a child. Heart pounding, her whole body shaking with cold and fear, Holly ran back inside and scrabbled for her phone.

But she was met only with her ex-husband's voicemail. '*Tom!* Have you just been and taken Milo? Pick up the bloody phone.' She could hardly speak, waves of terror breaking over her, making it hard to breathe. Emotion was clogging her throat, heartbeat loud in her head. She tried the landline.

'Holly?' Beth picked up, her voice high-pitched and anxious. 'What's wrong?'

'Milo's gone. I need to know if Tom took him. Where the fuck is *Tom*?'

'He's . . . he's out at a meeting. He said he'd be late, but he should have his phone with him.'

'*Fucking hell!* I've just tried it but it's switched off as usual. Come on, Beth, has he taken Milo?' She was crying now, shaking violently, unable to hold it together, but sure that Tom had finally cracked and taken her son.

'*No!* Why would he? You're being crazy. Holly, is Milo really missing?'

'No, I made it up for a laugh. My fucking son has disappeared. Somebody has taken him right out of my house while I was in the bath, and if it wasn't Tom, I really don't have . . .' She dropped the phone. Niko, standing next to her watching her son play football. He had threatened her. Gareth, looking into her eyes with such evil he'd made her shudder and telling her to think of him in the darkness. Sara, passing her the back door keys, smiling and saying they must have been put in her bag by accident. Jayden, lurking in the shadows, watching his own son lying in hospital, definitely still grieving over the loss of his daughter. Could he have taken Milo to show her what it was like to lose a child?

Picking up the phone, she ended the call to Beth and dialled Karen's number instead. 'Someone has taken my son! I need your help . . .' She was sobbing now, gasping and trying to pull on her coat at the same time. Although she had no clue where she was going.

'Holly? Taken by who? Are you at home? *Holly! Calm down.*'

She managed to give details, although her teeth were chattering from the effort required not to just scream with terror. Afterwards, she opened the front door and began to run along the road in the pouring rain, still shouting his name, until the police arrived and their appearance cut through her hysteria. Milo's coat hung on the hook next to the door, his wellies and trainers in a basket next to hers. Her mind was numb, and her clenched fingers scored red marks into her palms.

Three cars, with uniformed officers, plus Karen in a separate unmarked vehicle pulled up outside. Holly showed them in, trying to be as quick and lucid as possible. Every second counted.

Karen was efficient, wasting no time in greetings, and the uniformed officers spread out to search the house.

'I already looked . . .'

'Standard procedure. We've had missing kids crawled in wardrobes, hiding under beds before now. Before you say anything, I just need to tick it off, and then we'll start outside. How long were you in the bath for?' Her face was a mask of concentration, energy crackling from her fingertips as she took notes on her iPad.

'Maybe forty-five minutes . . . I had the door shut but not locked, just in case Milo needed anything. I had music on, but not too loud. The TV was on downstairs, but again it wasn't loud. When I went to check on Milo after my bath . . .' She gripped the edge of the sofa, clenching her jaw to stop herself from screaming.

'You said on the phone you thought your ex-husband might have taken him. Why do you think that?'

'We've argued a lot. He thinks Milo would be better living with him. He . . . he's been sending me abusive texts late at night saying that I'm a bad mother and not fit to have a child.' She couldn't stop shaking, and icy sweat made her face wet to touch. The metallic taste of blood in her mouth told her she'd bitten her lip.

'Does he give any reason for this?'

'What?'

Karen leant forward, holding Holly's forearms gently. 'Holly, I can't imagine how tough this is but you need to focus and help us find Milo.' She repeated the questions.

'He denies sending them, but they came from his bloody phone! I found out that Tom took drugs whilst he was supposed to be looking after Milo. Milo told me, and I . . . I rang Tom and told him if he didn't tell his solicitor to back off I'd tell you and his boss about his drug-taking.' Holly didn't care about anything else now. Everything was blown apart and she would do or say anything to get her boy home safe.

216

DS Steph Harlow came into the room, gave Holly a quick greeting and sat down next to her colleague. Karen continued, 'This happened yesterday, you threatening to expose him?'

'Two days ago. I made an appointment for me and Milo to see my own solicitor tomorrow afternoon. I don't know what's going on with Tom, whether he's taking drugs on a regular basis, and I don't care. I just knew that Milo shouldn't be exposed to that.'

'Has he ever taken drugs before?'

'Yes. I caught him once when I was pregnant with Milo. I swear if I knew it was a regular thing I would have left him straight away, but he said it was a one-off and we were at a party. I believed him. How fucking stupid am I? Do you know I was so angry when Milo told me he had seen what Tom was doing, but when I realised I could use it to get him off my back, I was that relieved.' Holly felt her own temper flare, a welcome flame to keep her going. 'He was furious, of course, but I haven't heard anything from him since.'

'Does anyone else know about the drug-taking and your threats?'

'Devril Mancini. I saw him yesterday. Cathryn, my best friend. Not Lydia yet . . .'

Karen gave her a quick, unreadable look. 'You say you spoke to Tom's girlfriend, Beth, this evening?'

'Yes. Tom was the first person I rang, on his mobile, then his landline and Beth answered. She said he was in a late meeting on campus.'

'In your opinion, does she have any idea that Tom is a regular drug user?'

'I really couldn't say.' Holly found she was hunched forward, hands clasped tightly together, shivering. More than shivering, she couldn't stop shaking. 'Why is that important?'

'It might not be, but we're trying to get as much information as we can. We have sent a car over to the university to locate your ex-husband, and we have officers interviewing Beth at the moment.'

Despite her encouraging words, Steph looked grim. 'Can you think of anyone else who would want to harm you or Milo?'

'Niko Balinta threatened us,' Holly said promptly. 'He says that if my brother is alive, he owes him money and if he doesn't pay he wants me to. Gareth Nicholls was with him on the beach and he told me to watch out for him.'

'Okay. Tell me exactly what they said to you.'

She did, trying to remember the conversation word for word. When she was done listing pretty much everyone she knew, Steph, without the slightest hesitation, added Sara and Jayden to her possible suspect list. And Dev . . . Holly tagged his name along too. She couldn't afford to trust anyone.

Another uniformed officer came in through the open front door and there was a rumble of conversation as his colleagues updated him. Holly watched, fidgeting with her phone, waiting for something to happen, for the call from Tom to say he'd taken her boy, that he was safe at least.

'Holly, we'll do everything can to find Milo, but anything you can think of, even if you don't think it's relevant, may help,' Steph said.

She studied the other woman's boots, unable to lift her head suddenly. 'Just find him and bring him home safely,' she said. Suddenly she remembered Lydia sobbing after Larissa's death, saying the same thing about Jayden. But her brother was an adult – a liar, a thief and a cheat. Milo was an innocent child.

Karen was talking to another officer, occasionally glancing in Holly's direction as she spoke.

Steph glanced at her notes. 'Niko wants you to pay back some debt, is that correct?'

She nodded.

'How much money did Jayden owe?' Steph's voice was low enough to be lost in the general buzz of conversation and crackle of radios, but her gaze raked Holly's face. Her attention was focused entirely on Milo, and Holly felt a thud of emotion, of gratitude. They would find him. It would be okay.

'Fifty thousand. Niko says whilst he was doing time, Jay cleared out this bank account he had set up as his "getting out" fund,' she said. She glanced down at her phone as she spoke, quickly texting everyone she knew, asking Cathryn to start people looking on the Seaview. Her thumb hesitated when she got to Donnie, but she hit 'send' anyway. After all his comments about family he could bloody well prove his own family values now. 'I told Niko to fuck off, of course. I don't have any cash. The Nicholls think I'm going to set up business with my dad, and they're worried about a turf war.' Holly bit her lip again, still shivering. Things were so complex, this was the best way to describe things quickly.

'Okay.' Steph went over and spoke quickly to Karen, gesticulating and nodding at her colleague's replies.

Holly's temper, fuelled by terror, made her snap at them. 'So go and arrest Gareth! Or Niko. Or get Tom or do something to find my son, instead of asking me about some fucking money!' she said, raising her head from her text messages.

Karen stepped back into the kitchen. 'Holly, we are trying to establish whether this is an abduction, possibly initiated by your ex-husband, or if another player could have planned Milo's kidnap. If it's the latter we should be hearing from him, or whoever took Milo fairly soon, demanding money as a ransom. That's why the money is relevant, because according to you, the Nicholls and Niko believe that in some form, you owe them. This may be a way for them to get it back.'

'Jesus!' Holly whispered, biting down hard on her bottom lip to stop herself from screaming. Her phone was ringing, but it was Cathryn.

'Babes! What the fuck is happening?'

At the sound of her best friend's voice Holly burst into tears again, but managed to gasp out the essential information.

'All right. Look, do you want me to come over? I can get Colleen round?'

'No. Thanks, Cathryn, just get everyone out looking, spread the word. Go to Aisha's and tell Josef – he's got his dogs still, hasn't he? If I hear that bastard Tom has got him I'll let you know where . . .' Holly was suddenly aware of Steph listening to her call, hastily remembering she wasn't in any position to tell Cathryn to get the Seaview boys to 'do him over' if they found her ex. 'I'll let you know if anything happens.'

'On it, babes. Love you!'

Donnie's number flashed up. 'Holly? What happened to the boy?'

Too distraught to protest that he had a name, Holly explained.

'Bastards. I'll get things started my end, and go and have a little chat with Gareth. And I won't go on my own. You never told me he threatened you, or Niko. They'll regret fucking with the Hughes family again. Sit tight, girl, and I'll find him.'

Another flash of fear as he ended the call. He was taking on the Nicholls and the war was starting. But she didn't care, didn't care about anything except her son. As soon as she could, she would be out there looking with the rest . . .

Over by the door there was a hurried conversation and Lydia ran into the room, blinking in the light. She went straight to her niece and put her arms around her. Holly rested her head on her shoulder, breathing in hairspray and that knock-off Chanel perfume that Lydia adored. 'I only went up to have a bath!'

'It'll be okay, love. I'm sure he's with Tom, and if not, I'll have the whole bleeding estate out looking for him.' Lydia's eyeliner was wonky, her lipstick bleeding into the wrinkles around her mouth, but her brown eyes were flashing. 'Family's the only thing that matters, love, and we'll find him.' She gave Karen a scathing glance.

But the radio crackles informed them that Tom had been located and denied all knowledge of seeing Milo today. He rang Holly's mobile and all trace of the bastard ex-husband was gone. His voice was shaking with emotion. Tom added that he and Beth would come straight over, and much as she hated them both, Holly agreed. She would have teamed up with the devil himself to get Milo back.

The police were now busy with search teams, and the dogs were already out in the woods behind her house. Every call, every crackle on the radio grazed her nerves like sandpaper on an open wound. She felt raw and bleeding, and was surprised when she looked down and saw her skin was actually intact. The helicopter was whirring overhead, powerful beam of light illuminating the wooded areas around her house.

Texts made her phone buzz, but they were all messages of support. The residents of Seaview, all feuds pushed aside, were apparently searching along Beach Road and across to the end of her street. Holly mentioned this to Karen, who shrugged, but said nothing. Clearly she wasn't stupid. Whatever anyone thought of the crime-riddled, drug-soaked community that bordered the coast, they would band together for a missing child. There was still a strong sense of family, and community and for the second time, Holly felt a twinge of positive emotion towards the Seaview.

There were no texts from her dad, or from Devril. A chill ran along her spine and she stood, forehead pressed to living room window. Jayden. Jayden and Devril. What if she had been wrong to trust Dev, and he and Jay had taken her boy? She spun from the cold glass, and pushed her way through knots of people to the door.

There were police everywhere, and a few groups of bystanders. She studied the latter carefully, and noted camera equipment being unloaded from a white van. Press. Although her stomach clenched at the thought of reporters crawling all over her story, it was good. The word would be spread quickly. Holly found she was searching the crowd for familiar faces.

If her brother was still around, he would surely hear what was going on? And what would he do? Wrapping her arms around her, Holly acknowledged the fact that her own brother might well have taken her son. After all, if Jayden thought he knew she had betrayed him, and he was back for revenge, what better revenge than to take a child?

Chapter 27

Desperate for progress, Holly found Steph and explained her theory on Jayden. 'You need to check Jayden's son is okay too. He's only been out of hospital a couple of days and you said that foster care was the answer. What if Jayden is furious with me for not taking him in?'

'Holly, calm down. Sorry, I hate it when people say that to me, but you've got to stay in control. We've got the team going over everything you've told us, following up every lead, not to mention searching the town and beyond. This is a massive operation, and we are very aware that Milo is our number-one priority. I will check on Jayden's son, but bear in mind if something had happened his foster carer would have called us. The last we heard, he was still unable – or refusing – to talk.'

'Okay.' Holly wanted to say more but she could hear familiar voices.

Tom and Beth had arrived and were quickly brought into the living room by Lydia, who shot them a murderous look before marching straight back into the kitchen and bustling around making cups of tea for everyone.

'Tell me exactly what happened,' Tom said. His face was ashen, his tie askew, and his hand in Beth's was shaking. 'I hope this isn't anything to do with your family, and I hope you one day know exactly what it feels like to be ripped out of a meeting and told not only that your child is missing, but to be interrogated like a suspect as well.'

Shocked that he could still be playing the arrogant wanker when his child was missing, Holly told them, going through everything that she'd already said to the police, watching Beth more than her ex. The girl sat knees together, shoulders back, her lips pursed. She didn't look especially pregnant, but she was wearing a loose-fitting jumper dress over expensive boots, so Holly gave her the benefit of the doubt.

She leant forward now, her dark hair swinging off her shoulders in a shiny curtain. 'I'm so sorry, Holly. About Milo I mean.' Her brown eyes held Holly's for a second. She had very big eyes, a beautiful shape and the same colour as her dark brown leather boots.

Holly didn't bother to answer, and they sat in silence, Tom clearly still simmering with rage at what he saw as an injustice towards himself. But Holly caught his eyes straying towards Milo's pictures on the wall, lingering on the box of Lego on the coffee table.

The clock on the wall was showing that it was just past midnight. Milo had been gone for at least three hours. Holly stuffed a fist into her mouth to stop herself from crying out, and quickly got up. Lydia was making bacon sandwiches and more cups of tea. In between this domestic efficiency she was scribbling on a list in her rose-patterned diary.

The house phone was propped between her chin and shoulder, and as Holly watched, distracted for a moment, she snapped goodbye and hung up. 'Any news?'

Holly shook her head, and her aunt's mouth trembled, but then set in a hard line. 'I've got a few more to go, but that's everyone I know as far as Panfield, Gothfield and Havering. Most of them are family. I got hold of Joey's wife, you know that tart Sammie . . .'

Lydia paused for breath and Holly saw she had swapped her patent heels for the fluffy mules she kept around the house. 'Anyway, the Nicholls are right sneaky fuckers, but Sammie understands that there's a kid missing and it's one of ours, so they'll put the word out to their drivers.'

'Do you think she'll even tell Joey?' Holly tried a slurp of tea, almost retched and hastily put the mug back down on the table.

Lydia fixed her with a gimlet eye. 'Course she will. There's some things that cross the lines and this is one of them. Oh, I know Joey and Gareth and that won't care about Milo, but they'll have to do something, 'cause most of their drivers have got family on the Seaview and if word gets around they did nothing . . . Well, they won't want trouble will they?'

Holly knew what her aunt meant. This wasn't just a bit of trouble, this was something that mattered. Oddly comforted she checked her phone and found a message from Shoey:

Heard what's happened. Call you tomorrow if I get anything. Don't trust the coppers, babe x

Steph came back in from the garden, but quickly shook her head when Holly looked a query at her. They went back into the living room, where Tom and Beth were huddled over cups of tea.

A uniformed police officer was in the hallways, relaying information as it came in from the search teams, and an incident van had joined the cars and journalists outside. Steph pushed back a strand of grey hair and addressed them. 'We can't find Sara Michaels at her address. Her landlord says she's often out and he thinks she stays away with family when she's not working.'

'I don't really think she's taken Milo,' Holly said, frowning. 'She's so little and nervous, but it does seem weird about the back door keys.'

'Okay. We'll keep trying to find her. I've just asked your aunt to keep the landline free in case this is a kidnapping, and you get a call confirming that the kidnapper is looking for a ransom. Try not to keep your mobile busy either.'

Tom moved convulsively, his hands, shaken free of Beth's and clutching at the sofa cushions, his eyes bright. 'Do you really think that might be what's happened? That someone has kidnapped my son for money?'

Karen came into the room, speaking quickly into her phone, and disappeared into the kitchen, while Steph answered carefully, 'We have to keep our options open at this stage. Because there is money owed, we have to keep an open mind, but if we don't hear anything, we will treat this as an abduction.'

Beth was nudging Tom, who was shaking. He shook his head, and mumbled, 'I can't . . .'

'Mr Kendal? Tom?' Karen came back into the living room, a cup of tea in one hand, her iPad in the other, her eyes flicking from one person to the next. As before, Holly could almost feel the electricity crackling from her perfectly pressed suit. 'Do you have something to tell us?'

Tom said nothing, but Beth coloured slightly, and then nodded. 'Tom has admitted to me that he has been taking drugs.' She paused to moisten her lips. 'He uses cocaine occasionally and . . .' She looked at her boyfriend but he just shook his head, shrinking back into his tweed jacket. 'Tom owes his dealer some money.'

Holly stared at them both. Beth knew? Since when? Surely she was far too calm to have been let in on Tom's dirty little secret just a few hours ago.

'That's useful information,' Karen said, exchanging quick glances with her colleague. 'Tom, I need the name and contact details of your dealer. You might find it easier if we go through to the hallway and have a chat.'

Tom shuffled away, whilst Holly fought an impulse to leap up and scratch his eyes out. Instead she turned to Beth. 'How long have you known about this?'

Beth took a shaky sip of tea and put the mug down carefully. 'A few weeks. I knew that Tom did a line occasionally. I met him at SugarFree in Addington, and everyone does a little bit at a party, don't they?'

Holly knew SugarFree was a club along the coast, well known for its celebrity and upper-middle-class clientele. If wasn't somewhere she would dream of going. In the same way that polished Beth, would probably never want to see the inside of Shoey's gym.

Tom slid back into the room half an hour later and Holly glared at him. 'Who's your dealer, Tom?'

'I already told DC Marriot. I don't need to go over it again,' he said defensively, but she pressed him.

'It might help to tell me because I might know something about them,' Holly snapped.

'I thought you'd left all that behind? Christ.' This as she lifted and arm and her loose top slid back, exposing her artwork. 'Have you gone and got yourself another tattoo?' He blinked at her.

'No, it's always been there, you idiot. Who's your dealer, Tom?'

But it was Beth who spoke. 'His name is Rohan Nicholls, and Tom meets him behind The White Dragon in the kids' playground when he wants to buy some gear.' She ignored the furious look on her boyfriend's face and added, 'Just in case anybody is wondering, I don't take drugs. I might smoke and I like a bit of a drink, but I've never taken drugs, not even a few pills.' Her dark eyes were steady, and although she was a bit pale now, she was calm and resolute.

Holly was clutching her mobile phone, glancing down every time a message came in. A Nicholls player. Well, that wasn't really a surprise. The police would never get hold of them, so that would be down to the strength of the rest of Seaview to find out if the Nicholls had her boy. Cath might be able to help there too . . . Holly sent her a quick text about Rohan.

'I would say that this Niko Balinta seems the obvious choice. Has he been arrested yet?' Tom asked, exchanging unfriendly eye talk with Beth, and clearly rallying slightly.

'I have officers at his address now,' Karen said, smiling thinly at Tom's look of surprise, 'A missing child is a major incident and we do have some expertise in these matters.'

'And Jayden? What did you mean when you said that the boy from the crash is Jayden's son? Your brother is still alive?' Tom rubbed his face. His eyes were sore and tired, and Beth, beside him was pale. She was picking at a sofa cushion with nervous fingers.

Lydia came in, notebook in hand, her own eyes red from crying. She sat next to her niece, pulling her close. 'They'll find him, Holly. I know they will.'

'They never found Jayden,' Holly pointed out. She felt strangely cold and drifting, as though she was observing the drama from some lofty point on the ceiling.

'That was different. He was an adult. Milo is a little boy.'

***

Later, as the clock ticked towards five in the morning, and the police operation continued, more press were gathering outside Holly's house. Her phone rang.

'Holly! Jesus, has Milo really gone missing? I just got a call from a mate who works for the *Echo* and he filled me in.' Devril's voice seemed genuinely anxious and Holly decided she had no reason not to give him the benefit of the doubt. 'I haven't had a phone signal all night so I only just got your messages.'

'Someone took him from the house while I was having a bath. The police are searching; the whole of Seaview seems to be out . . .' Her voice trailed away, because she was afraid she was going to cry again. Time was slipping away, and she watched enough TV to know that the precious Golden Hour had been and gone. Milo had been missing for over nine hours now.

'I'll come over . . .'

'You don't have to. Where have you been anyway?' Holly was aware that Lydia had roused herself from dozing on the sofa and was listening to her conversation.

'Tell you when I see you. It was just to do with what we were discussing earlier this week. I'll come over now. I can help you anyway, because the press, my mate included, are camped outside your house.'

Holly peered out the window and saw with a stab of fear that he was right. But her mind also told her that this was a pretty good story for Dev to get the inside scoop on too. 'Okay.'

Lydia staggered into the kitchen. 'Sorry, love I heard the phone ring and thought maybe it was news of Milo.' She flicked the switch on the kettle and squinted at her niece. 'You had any sleep yet?'

'No chance.'

***

Dev arrived within half an hour and she watched as he pulled up and exchanged a bit of banter with the other journalists, before running up to her front door.

'Jesus, Holly, I'm sorry. I got back to the flat late last night and saw blue lights all over the estate. Then when my phone had about ten voicemails including one from Casey at the *Echo* and those texts from you . . . Niko was on the phone asking me what the fuck is going on, and saying to tell my girlfriend he hasn't got her bloody kid. The police have been round at my place too, just before I left. Barry at Mason's garage was up, and he said they've been out looking for Milo. Reckons the police have taken Niko for questioning, and there was a stabbing at the Nicholls' yard last night too.' Devril ran a hand over his shaven head. 'So what can I do? Tell me what will help get Milo back.'

Holly was watching him closely, but he seemed totally genuine and Christ, she could do with his extra help. 'Who got stabbed?'

'Rohan, I think.'

Holly was about to dismiss this, except that Rohan had been Tom's dealer . . . Was he stabbed before or after Milo went missing? Her dad would be another inside link to the estate, but he hadn't answered his phone when she called earlier. Hopefully he hadn't gone missing too. 'Niko knows I'm not your girlfriend, doesn't he?' She could do without any added complications.

'Yeah, he's just pissed at being hauled in so soon after he got out, the stupid wanker. No news then?'

'No.' Briefly, she told him what had happened. As Lydia fetched the inevitable cups of tea Holly realised what was making her stomach roll uncomfortably. It wasn't the fact Dev might be sucking it up to write a story on Milo, it was that Devril had been just like this when Jayden first went missing. He had asked what he could do to help.

And now? Her own child was gone, and she would do anything to get him back. She would form an alliance with whoever offered it if it meant Milo came home safe.

Holly registered the noise of the search outside as the helicopter flew overhead again and told herself every effort was being made to find her boy. They were looking for him, and that was all she needed to know. Milo's disappearance was trending on social media. The more people who knew the more likely he was to be brought home soon.

Dev was tapping away on his iPad. 'Here. You need to speak to DC Marriot, but I've done a quick story on Milo's disappearance . . .' He studied her face. 'You don't have to do this but it will help if the facts are correct. They'll write something anyway, but this way you can control it to a certain extent.'

Holly scanned the story. It was the usual tabloid style and it make her sick to her gut buts she nodded. 'I need to find him, Devril, and I'll do whatever it takes. If Niko wants money I'll get it somehow. If it's Jayden, I don't know what he wants, but I'll find out.'

'You said your ex was getting gear off Rohan Nicholls? He's not dead, by the way. You never asked when I told you, but he's in hospital. I can chase that up if I ever find Bailey.'

'Is he still missing too?' But she wasn't really interested. Her world had narrowed to Milo being found and any tiny bit of energy not concentrated on that seemed like a waste.

'Yeah. That's where I was last night, down at his wife's sister's place. I finally tracked her down, and she's freaking out. Bailey told her to get out if he didn't come home one day, that she needed to just go, no questions asked, but she's been dithering, staying with her sister, hoping he'll turn up. I told her to go, so she's packing up and driving to her dad's in Bradford with her kids today.'

'Did she tell the police he was missing?' But Holly knew the answer even before he shook his head.

'He told her not to. Said it would get him into worse trouble. Of course, once she's gone I'm going to tell DC Marriot what was going on. It's gone far enough that it's the lesser of two evils.'

'Yeah.' Holly dropped her eyes, fiddling with the cuff of her hoodie. Her phone buzzed with another message, but it was just Cathryn telling her that her brothers and their cousins were going over to St Peter's dock to search the warehouses. 'Where the hell is my son, Dev?'

'I've been thinking, Niko's old man still owns a load of lock-ups near the station where he used to stash gear. I really can't see that it would be Niko but you did say he's been on at you about Jayden's debt again? You haven't had any ransom demand or anything?'

Holly shook her head, thinking about the old lock-ups. The same warehouses they had played in as kids, on the same industrial estate where Jayden and Cathryn had torched one of the buildings. 'You think he might have taken Milo there?'

'We can try.' He flicked a glance at the kitchen, where Lydia was sitting at the kitchen table concentrating on her phone, texting with great efficiency. 'You going to tell the police about the lock-ups?'

Holly hesitated. 'Yeah. Anything that might help. I'll tell Steph now. She's out the back. I need to go out too, I need to be searching . . .' Her voice cracked and Dev pulled her close.

'Wait till it's light. Look, two hours' sleep and we can go anywhere you like,' he suggested.

'I can't sleep.'

'Watch TV then, just get some rest.'

'Are you serious?'

'Okay, okay, we'll go now. You got a torch?'

Holly got up and went to the drawer in the hallway, thinking hard. When she turned she went into the kitchen, told Steph about the lock-ups and then ran upstairs to where Lydia was crouched on her bed, phone in hand, muttering as she checked off a pile of lists with her pencil. 'Lydia, I'm going out looking for Milo with Dev. I'll take my mobile so you can call me if there's any news.'

The older woman nodded, without any hesitation. 'You go. Look anywhere you think the police won't.'

'We're starting up near the station.' She turned towards the hallway, ready to yank her trainers on, when Dev put a hand on her shoulder.

Steph tried to persuade her to stay at home, but Holly was determined. She was not staying inside when her child was missing.

'Holly?' Dev said gently.

'What?'

'You might want to put some clothes on. It's fucking freezing outside, not to mention those journos are camped on the road, and all you're wearing is pyjamas and a hoodie.'

Chapter 28

The blackness of the night was punctuated by the odd police car screaming past. Holly was comforted to see uniformed police patrolling the street, near the house, and to note a dog unit van at the entrance to the woods. Surely Milo was somewhere nearby. She strained to sense him, to comfort him. Mother and child had an invisible connection, she was sure. She would *know* if he was dead. The tearing, clawing pain inside hadn't lessened since she found him gone, and she fought to keep her thoughts in check, to stop her imagination from flinging darker thoughts into her consciousness. His pain. Her pain. Any mother would kill to protect her child, and Holly knew she was no different.

This present evil had come from the estate, and with all the puzzle pieces she had, it made sense that Milo had been abducted for use as a ransom token. With this, negotiation was possible, a tiny chink of light. Whoever had him wouldn't hurt him whilst he had this value. Jayden, Gareth, Niko? The names danced in her head, branding the night sky in front of them. What a bloody joke that her own ex-husband had been buying gear from them.

Dev drove to the station and pulled over. 'We can just cruise around if you like? Unless you want to go somewhere in particular?'

She shook her head. 'I just need to be out looking.'

'Okay, that's fine.' He was about to pull out when his phone buzzed with a message. 'It's Bailey!'

Holly watched with dull eyes. The pain in her chest, the horrors flickering through her mind, did not allow for distractions.

Dev studied his phone, and turned to her, brows knitted. 'Bailey says he's got everything ready for us and to meet him behind Kelly's Transport Café. Thank Christ for that. No mention of the disappearing act or his family . . . It's only two roads down, and he says he's out the back parked up for the night with one of the Nicholls' lorries. What do you think?'

'Yeah, whatever. Tell him we'll come over.' Holly tried to work up enthusiasm for the Nicholls' take-down, but all she could think of was that Bailey was safe and Milo wasn't. What would Gareth do to a child to torture his mother?

Donnie sent a text to say he was still looking, and to let him know if there was any news. It was so weird having him act like a dad again, but the only emotion she could summon up was passionate relief that one more person was out searching for her boy.

Out on the main road, they were overtaken by two police cars, sirens screaming, blue lights flashing and Holly clutched her chest, constantly checking her own phone. Surely somebody must have seen him. Whoever took him must have had a car so maybe . . .

'It must be this way round the back. Do you think?'

She saw with a jolt they had reached their destination. Dev drove slowly past the café, and across the bumpy lay-by to the big square of gravel and dirt at the rear. It was a big area, well-used by the lorry drivers, and the café was open all night, its lights shining a cheery yellow across the shadows.

'You sure you want to be part of this?' Dev drove down to the far end of the pull-in. 'Maybe you should stay in the car and I'll go and chat to Bailey.' Huge shapes of lorries, most of their cabs in darkness, were parked in neat rows. The parking area backed onto woods, and the branches of trees hung menacingly, pointing their twisted fingers towards the vehicles.

'Of course I am. Stop asking.' Holly knew this wasn't helping but she couldn't just sit and wait, leaping every time her phone rang, watching the drama unfold on social media. 'I just thought, Tom has a place near Highton Downs. He sold the house but he still has the piece of land. He rents it as an allotment, but there are a few buildings on there too. I'll ring Karen and tell her.' She scrolled through her contacts as passed on the information, ignoring the other woman's instruction to wait at home.

'I thought you said Tom wasn't a suspect?' Dev still hadn't got out the car. He was watching her carefully, anxiously.

She shook her head. 'He was in a late meeting when Milo was taken, but until we know for sure, and especially now I know the shit was getting coke from Rohan, I can't trust him. Let's find Bailey and get this over with. If he gives us the information to take down the Nicholls we can go straight to the police. They can pull Gareth and Joey in and if they've got Milo . . .'

He didn't answer, just covered her cold hand with his, driving with one casual hand on the wheel. They pulled up in the shadow of a derelict shed and Dev killed the headlights. 'There's his lorry – he's got a collection of furry dice in the window.'

They followed the light of Holly's torch, circling the other vehicles. There were two brick garages, both derelict now, and the parking area was brown with dead weeds, a maze of muddy cracks. Nature was slowly reclaiming the space. A train rattled in the distance, gathering speed into the darkness and behind them the lights of the café shone a little duller as it spilled into the early morning.

They rounded the green lorry, peering into the shadows. At first Holly didn't register the pair of feet at eye level, but Dev shot a hand out to stop her walking.

A pair of scruffy white trainers swayed in the breeze, and her first terrible thought was that it was Milo. As her gaze travelled upwards, reality returned and she let out a long shaky breath. It was a man, and he was hanging by his neck from one of the overhanging tree branches, limbs dangling uselessly, red hair plastered wetly across his downturned face.

'Fucking hell! *Bailey!*' Dev shouted. 'We need to get him down!'

Holly was already tapping out 999 on her phone, speaking to one of her colleagues. The nightmare of being at the other end, of dealing with the patient, being the person who was screaming for help, jarred her brain and she fumbled over her words.

Trying to answer the questions, she looked around wildly for Dev, whilst explaining to one of her colleagues that there was currently no way of getting the man down but they were going to try.

Whilst she had been talking, Devril had roused a few other drivers and half the occupants of the café surged towards the crime scene. Dev shoved a stepladder into position and balanced on the top rung, producing a knife from his back pocket, slicing the rope that held the body.

Three men helped to lower Bailey to the ground, removing the cord from around his neck. Holly stood on the outskirts of the group. She wanted to help, but her limbs felt leaden, her brain uncooperative. She should help; she knew exactly what to do. It was Larissa all over again, but this time, she couldn't even try. Another driver was starting chest compressions and the scene was being managed with great efficiency, so she relayed this information to her colleagues, leaning helplessly against one of the HGVs.

An ambulance turned off the main road and followed the men waving it towards the lorry park, followed by another police car.

The tiny flicker of relief she felt at the sight of her colleagues, and the hope that perhaps Bailey wasn't dead, wasn't enough to give strength to her trembling legs. She slid to the ground, sitting on the wet gravel, arms around her knees, watching, hoping. How had this happened since he had texted – what? Ten minutes earlier maybe? He had told them to come. But of course, he couldn't have sent the text. It had all been too easy, and she and Dev, blinded by the worry of Milo's disappearance, had fallen for it. She watched the continuing CPR with a mixture of fury and terror, mingling with the dull leaden conviction that Bailey could have been up there for an hour or so, or even murdered elsewhere and hung from the tree like a crow scarer. They would have known she'd come, her and Dev, and they wanted her to see what happened.

It was both a warning and punishment. Gareth and Joey had taken action.

***

By the time the sky lightened to proper morning, Holly was back on the sofa, mug of coffee in her hand, phone in the other. There was no news from the search teams. She had passed on her thoughts about Tom's old allotment and was told it would be investigated, but Tom was not currently a suspect as his meeting had given him an alibi.

Dev, shaking with suppressed emotion, had gone home to shower, change and file his story on Milo's abduction. He promised to come back this afternoon and she had agreed. It was weird how they had suddenly become so close after years apart, but she was too exhausted to examine his motives. His concern was obvious and she was grateful.

Bailey was confirmed dead. His neck had been broken before he had been strung up, and his phone was missing. When the police interviewed them, Nicholls Transport expressed shock and grief at the news of an employee's death. They also apparently denied Bailey had been going to grass them up. Holly and Dev had told the police everything but there was no evidence with Bailey dead, and his phone missing.

Karen had shared her frustration that Bailey didn't have the chance to hand anything over. Bailey's wife had vanished with the two children and Holly couldn't bear to think about them, beyond a swift hope that they had run before Gareth got to them. Dev had said Bailey's wife didn't know what was going on, anyway, just that her husband was getting out of the danger zone.

Karen, her face grey with exhaustion, had been back to see Holly, assuring her that everything was being done, but no, they had no idea, as yet, who had taken Milo or where he could be. The Nicholls' yard had been searched, and Rohan was off the critical list. He refused to tell the police who attacked him.

They had found and questioned Sara, and although it was a hell of a coincidence the keys had ended up in her bag, there was nothing to suggest Sara was involved in Milo's disappearance. Steph had gone back to the station but promised to return later.

'Holly, I made you a bacon sandwich. You need to try eat and get some rest.' Lydia came in with a plate. Her eyes were red from crying, and her wild black hair was sticking up on one side. 'The police will call us if they get any news and I'll wake you straight away. Cathryn called on the landline while you were in the bathroom. She said she'll be over later but call her if you need anything.'

'I can't sleep,' Holly told her. 'But thanks.' It was more than that. She almost felt if she slept that Milo would slip away from her. By staying awake she was with him, keeping his face in her mind, willing him to be okay.

DI Harper was summoned from another case, but Holly couldn't face seeing him, and retreated to the sofa, flicking through the messages on her phone, racking her brains to try and figure it out. She found herself almost willing her phone to ring and Milo's abductor to demand money. Then at least she would have a starting point, to feel she was doing something, had a hand in all of this. So many questions for George Harper, but none she wanted to ask now. He had his own reasons for wanting the Nicholls destroyed, and she hoped he would succeed, but all she could think of was Milo.

Despite her intentions Holly eventually fell asleep where she was on the sofa, a crumpled heap of clothes and her coffee mug overturned on the floor.

By midday she was awake and showered, Karen was talking about a press conference, a TV appeal, which would also add to the social media hype. It was good, Holly thought, the more people who saw his face, who heard he was missing, the more chance there was of someone seeing him, or remembering something odd about last night.

She was flicking through the TV channels, seeing nothing but Milo's face on the screen, when Cath rang back.

'Sorry, babes, I went straight to sleep on the sofa after school drop-off and didn't check my voicemails. Jesus, it's all kicking off isn't it? Bailey's dead and Rohan's in hospital . . . I'm coming round now but I just need to get dressed. Colleen's got the kids . . .'

'You don't have to . . .'

'Of course I fucking do. Ten minutes, babes.'

Despite her feeble protest, Holly waited by the window for Cathryn to arrive. She was shivery now, earlier positivity vanishing. So far she had resisted the urge to go into his bedroom, but the photographs she had given the police and Devril were plastered everywhere.

The doorbell rang, and she rushed to answer it. Lydia had gone home to get some more clothes and take Oreo out for a walk. She was also going over to Donnie's to update him. Holly rubbed her gritty eyes. Hopefully her best friend could stop her from going crazy.

But it wasn't Cath, outside on the step, it was Beth.

'Is there any news of Milo?' She was wearing a red wool dress and black shiny boots, her dark hair drawn back by two gold slides. Holly couldn't help but think after a sleep-deprived night she looked the perfect, polished mum-to-be. The bump that had been carefully hidden last night was proudly on display, and quite big for three months gone . . . She hadn't noticed it all last night, but now, in daylight, it was obvious.

'Sorry, Beth, I'm expecting a friend over. No news. Where's Tom?'

She twisted her handbag strap between nervous fingers and bit her lip. 'Oh, he's gone into work. He said he can't sleep knowing Milo is missing and he went onto campus at five this morning. The police spent a lot of time questioning him about his dealer and all that stuff.'

'Okay.' Holly processed this information, skin prickling. But no, Tom had an alibi for last night. God, was it really only last night? It felt like weeks had gone by since she last held Milo. To her horror she felt tears slid down her cheeks, hot and wet. 'I'll call you if I get any news, okay?'

'Holly, can I come in, just for a minute? Please, I've got something to tell you.'

She held the door open, reluctantly. 'If it's anything important you need to tell the police.'

Beth stood awkwardly in the hallway, still clutching her bag.

To hell with being polite. 'Come on, Beth, what is it?'

'I . . . Can I sit down?'

She did look a bit pale, Holly thought, offering her the sofa. The room was a mess of mugs, tissues and muddy footprints, and Beth sat neatly on the end of the sofa, knees together, hands folded in her lap. 'So tell me?'

'Tom . . .' She frowned, forehead wrinkling. 'I wanted you to know that I had no idea he had a major problem. It wasn't anything to do with me, because as I said, I don't do drugs.'

'Yeah, you said last night. Sorry, Beth, but I really am expecting a friend . . .'

Beth brushed her interruption aside so Holly stood arms, folded, towering over her. 'I have noticed in the last couple of months, since we moved in together, that he does seem to do a lot of coke. I knew he liked a bit, of course, and he always said, who hasn't tried drugs? He never seemed like he was an addict, but I realise now he was hiding it from me . . .'

239

'Me,' said Holly grimly. 'I'm like you. I've never done drugs. It isn't fucking given that you have to try everything you get offered. So what are you telling me? He's a regular user now? I don't really care. I only cared when it affected Milo.'

'The texts he sent you. He takes something and then he gets really weird, like he isn't himself at all. He's paranoid about everything. He starts thinking you're trying to stop him seeing Milo, or that people at work are out to ruin his career. Weird stuff.'

Holly thought about this. It made sense. It was a slippery slope from party use to addict. Fuck, she knew that all right. But Tom had always seemed so together, with his perfect career, money and lifestyle.

'What are you thinking?' Beth asked her coolly.

Holly was surprised. She'd always thought of Beth as a bit of a vanilla character – young, inexperienced and blown away by Tom. Uncomfortably close to her younger self, probably. But now the girl was showing a tougher side. 'Is there any way he could have got out of that meeting and taken Milo last night? Is there anything that you've seen recently that would suggest he was planning to take him? Come on, Beth, this is really important. Imagine if it was your baby who had been taken.'

Her carefully made-up big brown eyes opened wide, but she was shaking her head. 'No. I've been trying to think since the police questioned me, but the only difference is he seems to be getting more of these weird times. Occasionally he'll get all twitchy, make a phone call and disappear for half an hour.'

'You think he's goes to find his dealer? Did you tell the police about this escalating drug use?' Holly's voice was hard.

'Of course. I mean, you had already told them so I just confirmed what they already knew. He isn't the person I thought he was, Holly.'

'Really? You do surprise me. Is that it?'

Beth stood, flicking specks of dust from her dress. 'Yes. I just wanted you to know. I also wanted to say goodbye. I'm leaving Tom.'

Holly couldn't help but feel a sneaking respect for the girl. 'Have you told him?'

For the first time her composure shook slightly, just a slight change but noticeable, like thin ice sliding across a puddle. She covered it by pulled her bag over her shoulder and turning to go. 'No. I'll text him later when I'm far enough away from this place. He isn't a fit father for my child, and he certainly isn't a decent boyfriend. I'm not marrying an addict. Oh, and Holly, I'll drop in at the police station on my way out, and tell them about the text messages and well . . . everything.'

Hammering on the door indicated Cathryn's arrival, and Beth jumped slightly. 'Good luck then.' Holly found she couldn't actually say 'fuck off' because, really, this girl had guts.

The other woman paused in the hallway. 'Thanks, you too. I hope you find Milo.'

'I will.'

Chapter 29

She opened the front door and Cathryn staggered through, cigarette in one hand, a carrier bag of groceries in the other and her vast handbag balanced somehow on her shoulder.

Beth strode away down the road to her car, and Holly watched her thoughtfully. The other woman climbed carefully into a shiny red Golf and pulled away into the traffic without a glance backwards. A yellow Battersea Dogs Home sticker and a row of silver stars were stuck on her back window. She indicated right at the traffic lights and vanished behind a white van. Beth was gone.

'Who was that?'

'Beth, Tom's girlfriend.'

Cathryn studied her best friend's face and then shrugged. 'Bitch is way more than three months gone.'

'Yeah.' Holly burst into tears properly and sobbed whilst Cathryn cradled her. Finally she sat up, sniffing.

'Here you go, babes, you got to let it all out,' Cathryn told her firmly, offering a wad of Kleenex. 'I've got you bread and milk, pizza, wine and all that shit. Have you sorted out work?'

Holly shook her head and sat docile as a child whilst Cathryn rang the control centre and explained. She rang off ten minutes later. 'All done. You get an indefinite leave of absence, and you'll even be paid for a certain amount of time. So don't think about work.'

'Thanks. Karen says we need to do a press conference later. She's going to arrange it for about four. Can you stay?'

'Course I will. So tell me what the fuck is happening, babes, coz I can't believe this shit. Milo missing and then Bailey hangs himself! And I don't mean to add to your problems but the Nicholls are blaming Donnie for Rohan's stabbing.'

Holly sighed. 'Bailey didn't hang himself, he was killed before he was strung up. I feel like I don't understand anything anymore. Donnie's playing the good dad, and I know he sent his boys out looking for Milo, so if Rohan got in the way, I don't care. He won't talk.'

'Jesus. What a fucking mess.' Cathryn pulled a bag of crisps out of the grocery bag, tore the packet open and shoved them across to Holly. 'Share.'

'I can't. I need to get back out there.'

'Sure. Where do you want to go?'

Holly frowned. Terror made her unable to sit still for long, and at least if she was out there looking she was occupied. 'The woods. I know it sounds crazy but I want to walk through the way he was probably taken.' Her voice broke and tears poured down her cheeks again. She laid her head in her hands, listening to her own sobs and the thumping of her heart.

'Holly?' Cath had her arms around her. Thin, wiry arms that hugged her with a surprising amount of strength. Just as they had when her mum died, when Jayden was declared dead, and all the other times when Holly had needed it. 'Come on. We'll go out now and be back by two. That gives you time to get ready for the press.'

Holly nodded, sniffing. Cath always loved everything to be in order. Her own calendar was ruthlessly organised, which was really the only way for her to be as a single mum juggling work and five kids.

***

The woods were dank and dripping after the recent downpour.

Holly banged the gate shut behind them, 'Whoever took him came out here and walked to the footpath.' Her fists were clenched, and she was shivering. It had been a cold night and Milo had only been in his pyjamas. She concentrated fiercely on the muddy path.

Cath wiped raindrops from her face and pulled her hood closer around her hair, 'Okay, so suspects. First is Tom. A total fucker, and now we hear a bit of an addict too. But would he take Milo? Granted you say he's been hassling for custody and he sends you texts when he's high, but would he actually take him?'

'He was in a meeting last night. The police checked. He was the first person I thought of when I found Milo gone. He probably still has his keys, Milo would go with him without crying out if he made up some story, and he knows my routine in the evening when I have days off.' Holly led the way along the path and paused at the main track. 'Straight on or turning right?'

'I reckon straight on. It's quicker and you can leave a car right by the road without being too obvious. The other path comes out right on a bend. Whoever took him wouldn't have wanted to be walking along the road with a kidnapped child, would they?' She paused and swallowed hard, 'Back to Tom. He has an alibi. At the moment. Next one, Niko, another fucker. I don't think Niko would take a kid, though, even with money involved.'

'Really? He threatened us down on the beach, and he even said something about Milo.' Holly was surprised. 'The police said if it was to do with owing money then the kidnapper would be in touch with a ransom demand.' She tried to speak slowly, carefully, but her words kept getting choked up, and tears escaped again.

'But nobody has been in touch, right? When Kian was born, he was four weeks early, wasn't he?'

Holly nodded, remembering the panic.

'So Niko was totally different then. He was how he used to be when we were kids, you know funny, a bit cheeky, and he looked after me and the baby so well. For a while.'

They were nearly at the road now, and Holly could hear the swish of tyres on wet tarmac, the monotonous hum of engines that permeated the quietness of the wood. She indicated the row of houses behind them. 'The police searched all those. Karen said they wanted to check if Milo'd been hidden or something.'

'That would be weird. Even weirder is you on first-name terms with a copper.' Cath gave her a sideways glance through her wet lashes.

'Whatever. I reckon Joey or Gareth have got Milo.' Just saying it out loud seemed to make it real, and the icy fist inside wrenched at her guts. 'Bailey was a warning, and maybe a bit of fast revenge for Rohan. They're showing us how hard they play to get what they want.'

Cathryn sighed, fiddling with the rings on fingers. 'Bastards. And they really want that slice of business, don't they?'

They reached the road and stood staring at the traffic as exhaustion began to kick in again. 'So that leaves Jayden then,' Holly said softly. 'My brother comes back, and swaps his kid for mine?' The pain inside was getting worse. Every second her boy was missing, every time the clock hands crept round to indicate another hour had gone past, meant he was getting further and further away from her. She clung to the thought he had been taken for ransom. There was no point in hurting a human bargaining chip, was there?

Cathryn shivered. 'Let's go back. Is Jayden's kid in foster care now?'

'Yeah.' Holly took the lead and picked her way through the mud. Her eyes darted from one side of the path to the other, peering deep into the trees, even though she knew the search team with the dogs had already covered every inch of this area.

***

The press conference was in the local scout hall, and Holly, clinging to Cath's hand, stood up to make a plea for her son.

245

By this time anger was taking over, consuming her. Anger that someone was messing with her life, had taken her child. She was behind a table, flanked by DC Karen Marriot and DC Steph Harlow. Cath squeezed her hand.

Devril had texted her to say he'd be there, but she couldn't spot him in the crowd. Outside there were TV broadcasting vans, and so many people gathering. Lots of locals were holding up banners and #FindMilo was trending on social media. It was good, it was all good, Holly told herself. And the least she could do was to speak out and say her piece without crying.

She got unsteadily to her feet, taking up her position next to the microphone. 'I just want Milo home safe. Whoever has taken him, for whatever reason, he's just a little boy. My little boy. If anyone has heard or seen anything please, please tell the police. Thank you.'

'Do you think your brother is alive, Holly?'

'Is this about Larissa Arnolds?'

'Holly, did you know your ex-husband was taking drugs?'

Holly bit her lip. 'My son is everything to me, and I just want him home safe.' She could feel Karen frowning up at her, but there was sympathy in her eyes. The content of the little speech wasn't quite what they'd discussed. 'The police and the whole community are looking for my boy, and I want to thank them for their support. We won't rest until he's found.'

The clicking of cameras and the shouted questions from a sea of eager faces were making her dizzy. This couldn't be her. It felt like a dream, and any minute she would wake up and be watching TV with Milo. The journalists were quizzing the police now, and the sombre answers from the officers present were almost lost in the general buzz of speculation.

DI Harper appeared briefly, not meeting Holly's eyes, but adding a certain gravitas to the conference. He also appealed to the local community. Holly watched him through narrowed eyes from her seat. He certainly put on a good show for the press, telling them that all they were concerned about was finding Milo safe and well.

The questions kept coming and the flash of cameras, the sweaty heat of the hall, was making Holly feel faint. She put out a hand to steady herself on the rickety table. 'Thank you,' she whispered again, eyes hot, throat aching.

'Ignore them now, it's okay.' Karen helped her sit down again. 'You did really well. Let us handle the rest.'

Cath hugged her and they sat together on the hard plastic chairs. Holly let out a long breath. Surely when Milo's picture appeared in all the papers, whoever had him would realise they needed to give him up. Even Joey and Gareth wouldn't be able to keep him. Or . . . or it might mean they needed to kill him. The blackness and nausea overtook her and she slid from her seat into a crumpled heap on the floor.

***

By the evening, Cathryn was back sitting on her sofa, full of nervous energy. She took out a bag and spilled her manicure kit onto the coffee table, whilst she talked, thin fingers picking through the candy-coloured bottles of polish. 'Why would Jay take Milo though?'

'I honestly don't know.' Holly picked up her mug and put it down again without taking a sip. 'Actually I have one idea. I should have told you before but . . .'

'Go on.'

'The night Larissa was killed, when Jayden asked me for money, I was so mad at him for asking again, for stealing from Lydia and bringing all this shit back on us that I rang Niko and gave him Jayden's address.'

'You did what?' Cathryn was looking at her, mouth open, scarlet lips a perfect 'O' of shock.

'But Dev picked up his phone. They were round at Dev's place

247

and Niko was on his other phone doing some deal, so I gave Dev the address and told him to pass it on to Niko.'

'Fuck me. And you never told the police?'

'Of course not. Well, not until now. For years I thought it was my fault Larissa died, but when I caught up with Dev again he told me he never passed on the message. He's got no idea who tipped Niko off. It was probably one of his dealer mates or someone trying to crawl to the Balintas. But I was thinking, what if Jayden somehow found out I called Dev?'

Cathryn was breathing fast, her face white and pinched. 'He wouldn't take it out on a kid, would he? Not when he's lost one of his?'

'Maybe that's why?'

'No way. Even if he thought that you . . . He wouldn't and I really don't think Niko's involved. My money would be on the Nicholls . . . Say something, babes, you look like you've been struck by lightning.' Cathryn moved closer, putting an arm around her shoulders. 'I'm not trying to upset you. You know what I'm like, with my gob and if you think I'm wrong tell me to shut up, okay?'

'No, I don't think you're wrong, that's the problem. The police have been all over Seaview, and taken Joey and Gareth apart asking questions, and they got nothing. If it is them they've got other plans for me and Milo.' Holly jumped up, restless now, and she started collecting mugs and dirty plates for the dishwasher.

'So we go and see them, when the police are done. We can do a deal over the land they want if that's the problem. Donnie's not going to mess around with his grandkid if that's what this is all about, is he?' Cathryn pulled a bin bag out of the cupboard and started sweeping tissues and bits of paper into it.

'You make it sound really easy. I don't know, Cath, I really don't, but yeah, let's go visiting. Maybe I'll go and see Niko too.' Holly ran hot water into the sink and squirted washing-up liquid. The boiling water hurt her hands and she was glad. Milo's latest drawings from school were pinned up on a corkboard above the sink, and she focused on them, determinedly. She couldn't go to pieces – Milo needed her. The clean mugs dripped soapy bubbles from the wire rack to the floor. She blinked hard, pushing back tears yet again.

Holly's mobile rang and she wiped wet hands on her jeans, and grabbed it, listening intently to the voice at the other end.

Karen was straight to the point. 'Holly, sorry no news on Milo, but I wanted to let you know that Jayden's son has disappeared from his foster care.'

'What?' Holly couldn't process this at all.

'He seems to have gone early this morning and taken a coat and a few things he was given, so we are assuming he went of his own free will.' Karen's cool, clipped voice relayed the information with as much emotion as if she'd been letting Holly know her Tesco delivery was arriving on time. 'Obviously we've got a team out looking for him, but to reassure you, it looks like maybe he went off to find his dad, in which case we should pick him up fairly quickly.'

Holly's shoulders sagged and she shook her head at Cath. She wedged the phone between shoulder and chin and picked up a drying up cloth. 'Unless he has found Jayden, in which case they'll probably both just piss off back to where they came from.' Bitterness was breaking through, but there was still a protective flash of worry for the silent boy. How was Jayden with his son? Was he happy?

'Did you get any information from the press conference?' Holly finished drying the glass she was holding and put it back down on the draining board with exaggerated care. Her tired brain refused to process anything at all.

'No. Sorry, we are sifting through all new information and believe me, we are doing everything we possibly can.'

'What about Joey and Gareth?'

'They didn't give us any new information, and they both have alibis. We are questioning everyone concerned with the business and the family.'

'And Bailey?'

'As you've probably seen from the official statement, his neck was broken before he was hanged, but I can't comment further on that case, sorry.'

Holly finished the call, frowning. If Jayden had now taken his own child back, would he let hers go? Or was there someone else? In her mind she could see Gareth and Joey still stalking in the shadows, working towards their own end game. Gareth would think nothing of hurting children. Too late, she caught herself, but the pain washed over her as the promise from earlier echoed through her head: *'I'll kill Gareth, if I need to . . .'*

Chapter 30

Dear Mum,

I saw you last night in my dream. You were so close, I could smell your hair and you were smiling, telling me everything would be okay. I wonder if it was a memory? I hope so. It would make me happy to think I have memories of you, something that I have and Dad doesn't. He talks about you all the time, but I feel like I need a part of you for myself.

Especially now. I got out of hospital, had to go with that woman who just pissed me off, asking how I was feeling and trying to get me to talk. You would have been proud of me, because I never said a word.

You said once that before you met Dad bad things happened to you, and you never said a word, because then they could take so much, but not everything.

Now I'm back in the van. Dad's friend says we're nearly done here and by the end of next week we'll be on the move again. Back in the big white van, jolting along the motorways.

Today he's taking me to see Dad, and he says he has a surprise for me. I don't know this area, and I lost my phone in the car crash, but I can tell we're driving towards the sea. I can taste salt on my lips, see the greyness stretching into the horizon, and we're leaving the houses of Westbourne far behind.

I don't know what's going to happen next, and if I'm honest, Mum, I'm a bit scared. But I can't ever be scared, so I scowled at Dad's friend when he asked if I wanted a burger and said nothing when he ordered me a cheeseburger and extra large fries at the drive thru.

I don't know if the plan worked, if there is still more to do. My head hurts and there are guns in the van.

I love you, Mum xx

Chapter 31

Her first thought was of Milo as she rolled out of bed. Her next, stifling tears, was that she was unable to hold him, to smell his hair, put her lips to his soft forehead for a morning kiss.

The house felt empty and cold, as she took her coffee to the window. Every child walking down the road made her heart jerk. Milo was everywhere; the boy with blonde hair just turning the corner by the footpath, the children with red and blue coats skipping along beside a tall woman. Even a baby being wheeled past in a buggy reminded her of her son.

She called Dev and arranged to meet at his rented flat. Although she felt pretty much everyone was under suspicion at the moment, Dev hadn't given her any cause to doubt his story. The niggling doubts remained but she needed to do something, to be proactive, and she felt Dev would help.

There was a voicemail from Cathryn saying her family were taking a search party from the estate out towards Panfield and then back towards the coast. She had hundreds of messages on her social media accounts from well-wishers, which warmed her heart for a second, and then made her cry again. Holly made another drink and flicked on the TV, her whole body aching and her face still wet, as Milo's face appeared on the screen.

Although it was early there were a load of reporters gathering outside her house, as she banged the front door. She pushed through, feeling their eyes boring into her, trying to smile when she felt like running away.

Successfully leaving the crowd behind, she wandered along the road towards Dev's new flat in a daze of pain. Just walking the streets, taking the long way around, ignoring a few stares of recognition, her eyes searching back roads and alleys between shops; constantly searching eased the emptiness slightly. But instead of going on into Seaview, she turned left, walked over the bridge, her feet echoing on the metal walkway, too loud, too slow. It seemed to take a long time to lift each foot up and put it back down, but she couldn't stop, like some mechanical doll.

They sat in Devril's tiny flat, which overlooked the river. 'See, I made the leap.' Nothing in his manner, his words, betrayed him, but she found herself watching his face, going over each inflection of his voice, each reaction to her news. She couldn't afford to trust anyone.

'No news?' he asked.

'Nothing. The police are covering all the obvious places around our house, and the woods towards Panfield. Cathryn said a load from the estate are going out and heading towards the coast. Niko's still being questioned, and I have no idea what Tom is doing, but like I said, he has an alibi. So if Niko does have Milo, he's left him on his own.'

'Unless he has an accomplice?' suggested Devril, his light grey eyes showing nothing but interest and concern.

Holly shook her head. 'If it is Niko, he's done it because he's pissed off with me about the money, and if it's Jayden, well, I've been thinking that it's one of two things. First, I was late with the money the night Larissa and the baby were killed.'

'Come on, Holly, I don't think Jayden could blame you for that.'

'The second thing . . .' She took a deep breath and ploughed on. 'The second thing is that he might still think it was my fault

254

Niko knew where to find Jayden in the first place. I know you never passed on the message but even the police kept asking me at the time if I told Niko where he was. Lots of people must have assumed that it was me. But I still think it's Joey and Gareth who must have taken him, Dev, and that's tearing me up. They killed Bailey, what will they do to Milo?'

'You don't know it's them, and don't go paying any visits either.'

'But that's exactly what I'm going to do, if I don't have any news this morning. I'm going back down the yard to talk to them. And if I don't get any joy there, I'm going to find Niko. Somebody knows where my boy is, and if they won't talk to the police they might talk to me.' Holly's mouth was set in a stubborn line, her jaw clamping shut after she spoke, fighting tears again.

Devril sat back, glancing out at the greyness beyond the windows. 'Look, Holly, there's something else. I wasn't going to bother telling you this, because like you say it's all in the past, but now Milo is missing and Bailey's fucking dead, poor bastard . . . Well, anything that might help, you know?'

'Go on.'

'I never told you because I knew you'd be mad, but that first time Jayden vanished, he kept in touch, just the odd text, and once a phone call. He was mostly checking up on you, because he knew we were together. He said he was worried the Balintas might come after you for the money he owed. But he really fell for Larissa, and when he found out she was pregnant he wanted out of all the drugs mess.'

Holly rubbed a hand across her face. 'What? Jay didn't give a fuck about anyone except himself. So you knew where he was all along and didn't tell us?'

'No! I didn't know where he was. I asked, of course, but he never let on. It wasn't like we were in touch every day. Sometimes it would be months before I got a message.'

'But you never told me. You knew Lydia was freaking out. And

Donnie . . .' Holly turned slightly away from him. Secrets and lies again. Just like Tom.

'There's more you need to know . . . You remember when we all got arrested that one time there was a big round-up? The Nicholls' crew got hauled in over that new club in South Street and we got nicked at the same time.'

'You said it was just the new DCI cleaning up. Nobody ever actually got charged with anything, did they?' She was frowning now, trying to force her mind back.

'Right. But what I didn't tell you was that DI Harper offered some of us a deal. He said he hadn't been able to get a grass in the Balinta–Nicholls operation and he wanted an inside source. We both agreed. Me and Jay. Me, because Mason was pushing me towards the clubs, and I knew about the trafficking of underage girls between South Canfield and Westbourne, and Jayden because he was well in the drugs side of the operation. He had all the contacts. You can make a lot of money snitching to the police, and Jay had plans to get out of the Seaview too.'

'Fuck, so you were a *grass*? A snitch? You *and* Jayden?' Holly couldn't take it in. 'For how long?'

'Me, right up until Larissa's murder, and Jayden the same. Even when he disappeared with Larissa he was still feeding stuff to the police. Just who lived where, eking out his useful information so that DI Harper kept paying him.'

'Devril, why the fuck didn't you tell me any of this after Larissa was killed?'

'First up, I didn't know you still thought it was your fault about the message. Like I said, we hardly spoke after that night, did we? You cut me off totally, like you thought it was my fault. I supposed that when nothing came up with the police, or at the trial, you'd figure it out.' He sighed. 'The rest, well it was all mixed up with the police stuff. I couldn't say too much and I was fucking terrified it would come out that I'd been a grass. You know what happens to anyone who messes with the families. That's partly the reason I went abroad for so long.' He glanced away, hiding the emotion in his face. 'I spoke to Bailey's wife today. Sanita. She called me, and she was in bits but she wants to meet up.'

'Really? Why? I thought she had gone . . . What a fucking mess.' Holly drank her cold coffee, gulping it down, spilling some so it dribbled down her chin. Her brain couldn't cope with all this, and her heart was torn apart. 'Dev, I need to find Milo. Right now, I don't care about all the rest of this.'

'I know. But I want you to come with and find out why Sanita wants a meet-up. She mentioned you, and she'd seen the news about Milo.'

Holly shook out her long hair, raked it back with frustrated fingers and yanked it into a ponytail. 'Well, we need to do something, because the police have fuck-all. I'm sure Karen thinks I'm this dodgy bitch from the estate, with a failed marriage and criminal connections and . . .'

'Why would she think that?' Devril moved closer, gently tipping her face upwards with two fingers under her chin. 'It's you who thinks that, Holly, and nobody else. You're doing what we all do, getting by the only way you can. And for your information your ex is a wanker, but I think we've already covered that.' He smiled.

'Let's meet Bailey's wife then.' Holly felt emotion rising, choking her. Every couple of seconds she checked her phone. The conversation kept her distracted, but that was all. Inside she was still screaming.

'And then I'm going to visit Gareth.'

'You can't! He'll kill you,' Holly said, staring at Dev. 'He must know you're a journalist now and he knows Bailey was talking to you. You probably won't even get to talk to him. They'll just set the boys onto you, and the police will find you in a ditch somewhere or hanging from a tree.'

'Thanks for that. Give me some credit, Holly. You forget I did a lot of work for Gareth. Not so much Joey, but I was getting kids and gear across the county lines for months before Larissa's murder. He's got no idea I was a grass.'

'You hope. And you don't know what they got out of Bailey. You're an idiot, Devril Mancini.'

'Get your coat, woman, and stop nagging.' He smiled. It was a proper smile that reminded her of their old joke, but somehow her own face was frozen, her mouth too stiff to respond.

***

They drove out to Panfield, and Dev pulled over by the station car park. 'She said over by the B&Q warehouse. Look, I think I can see her . . .'

Holly peered across rows of parked cars, shoving her hands in her pockets, shivering as the icy wind caught her breath. There was a woman standing against the wall, half hidden by the recycling bins.

'Are you Dev?' She was slim and blonde, younger than Holly had expected, huddled inside a massive black Puffa jacket. Her eyes were red and she wore no make-up.

He introduced Holly and Bailey's wife nodded, a flash of sympathy crossing her face as her eyes met Holly's.

'I'm really sorry about Bailey,' Holly said softly.

Sanita glanced sharply to her left as a car started up, backing carefully out of its space. 'Yeah, he was a good man . . . He was trying to do the right thing, even though I told him not to try and be a hero. To us that's what he was . . .' She was crying again, fumbling for a tissue.

'Sanita, I hate to rush you, but why did you want to see me?' Dev was also watching the car park, eyes darting from the figures walking to and from their vehicles, to a white van that had pulled up a few yards from them, the driver ostensibly having a burger and a cigarette.

'Bailey didn't tell me what he was doing at first. About giving you information and that, but when he did, he said that he'd noticed Gareth was being a bit weird around him. Like, following him, checking up on him. It's normal to check up on the drivers, especially if they've got . . . if they've got special cargo in the back. Do you know what I mean?'

'Yeah.' Dev was nodding, clearly desperate for her to get to the point.

Holly stood with her back to the wall, constantly checking for any sign that they'd been spotted. The blue wheelie bin lid creaked in the wind, making them all jump. 'Look, Sanita, Bailey was doing the right thing, and we told the police what was happening, but he never got round to giving Dev the evidence. He was supposed to be doing it this week. Did he give you anything, or tell you anything we could use?'

Sanita dragged a packet of cigarettes from her pocket and lit up, cupping her hand against the wind, and then taking a long drag. 'The police asked me about it too, and I said I only knew what Bailey had told me, nothing else.' She pushed a strand of hair back from her face. 'But he had what he needed. We were ready to go, but that morning Gareth called wanting Bailey to deliver a load in Abbingdean. He said it was a rush job and he needed timber picked up. Bailey didn't think anything of it. He was his dad, after all . . .'

'Did he get to his destination?'

'Yeah. He called me to say he'd picked up and was going to head back, that he'd be home by sevenish. I told the police all this too. There was nothing to suggest he'd been spooked, apart from that constant worry about Gareth . . .'

'They must have killed him, driven him back to the café and then texted Dev,' Holly said.

'Thing is, if I give you the stuff you need, the Nicholls will go after me. Just now, I'm safe and I can go – me and the kids – and they won't come looking because they think I don't know anything.' Sanita paused. She was clearly terrified. 'But I heard about your kid, and I thought if Joey could kill his own nephew . . .'

Holly found herself holding her breath, willing the other woman to go on, but terrified for her if she did.

Sanita chucked her cigarette stub down and ground it out, slowly and deliberately. Her grey eyes were hard, focused, when she looked up. 'Bailey was brave, and he wanted to do this. I want to be able to tell the kids what he did, what I did, so here, I haven't got his phone – I dunno what happened to that – but he kept these printouts in a box under the bed. He never put stuff on the computer because he was afraid of someone hacking it. It's mostly screenshots, and a kind of diary of conversations and events, but I reckon even without the other evidence, it might be enough.'

'Are you sure you want to do this?' Holly had eyes on the van driver, who was now reversing slowly towards them.

Sanita shoved a handful of paperwork at Dev. 'Take it. But give me two hours from now to get away. I'm not going back to my mum's, I'm taking the kids somewhere nobody will find us.'

Dev took the crumpled papers and put them carefully in his pocket. 'Good luck.'

She nodded at both of them. 'Hope you get your kid back.'

The van turned and drove away as Sanita walked quickly down the side of the building, vanishing between the warehouses.

***

Anger was good, and it helped her to keep going, to answer her messages, to do basic tasks like cleaning her teeth, which had suddenly become exhausting. She and Dev had studied the printouts, which were interesting, and certainly mentioned some contacts and routes that Karen Marriot would be very keen to check up on. It proved Bailey had been serious about grassing up the Nicholls' crew, but Holly was worried that without his testimony or the videos, the Nicholls' solicitor would pick holes in the evidence. The police could get on and find some decent evidence to tie the brothers to Bailey's murder.

Holly found herself walking round the house, checking the window and door locks, jumping every time a car went past. Too many enemies haunted her home, and Sanita's terror had only added to her own fears. When someone hammered on the front door, she picked up Milo's cricket bat and inched towards the window to check who it was, despite the fact it was broad daylight.

'Come on, Holly, open the door!' It was Cath.

'Sorry, I forgot you were coming. Oh, did you get them done?'

Cath's arms were full of posters. Milo's smiling face, one front tooth missing, beamed up at her, and Holly ran straight to the toilet to chuck her guts up.

Cathryn followed her, holding her hair back as she retched, and then fetched a glass of water. 'Holly, you're doing great and we'll get him back. Lydia's been sorting everyone out. She's got these posters, and T-shirts done, and she's coordinating search parties to knock on doors, and everything. Honestly, she's amazing. Everyone on the Seaview is out looking now, babes, and we've got these posters all along the coast now. Tesco and McDonald's have got them up in the windows, and that big food wholesaler has printed a big fuck-off flag with the poster on and put it up near the main road. I gave some to Donnie on my way over. Bloody hell, he's changed, hasn't he? He was yelling at a journalist just like he used to in the old days. What about Tom? He can take some too, can't he?'

'Yeah he could put them up at the university. You know he hasn't been in contact since the night Milo was taken, the bastard.'

'The police interviewed him though, didn't they?' Cath frowned. 'What about him using? What happens with that?'

'Dunno. I think it has to be dealt with through social services and our solicitors. He's getting payback big time now though, especially as Beth has left him.' She couldn't help feeling a flash of grim satisfaction at the thought. 'I'll drop some in to him on my way out. I'm meeting Dev.' She decided not to mention that they were going to see Niko, and Gareth.

'Do you want me to come with you? I can ring Chrissie and get her to pick the twins up.' Chrissie, Colleen and Cayley were Cath's trio of efficient elder sisters.

'I'm okay, thanks. I feel better doing stuff, and Dev's been helping too. Lydia's coming over later. She went to see Donnie for an update.' Holly pulled a face. 'He's acting like the perfect dad, and I'm grateful, I really am, but I can't deal with anything right now except finding Milo. Anyway, I'll go out later and start handing these to the neighbours before it gets dark.' Holly smiled weakly at her. 'You are amazing too, Cath.'

Cathryn hugged her, pulling her close with her skinny arms, kissing the top of her head as though she was one of her kids. 'Hang on in there, babes, we'll find him.'

Dev called just after her best friend left. 'I'm still with the police. This is taking ages. I reckon we should go visiting tomorrow. Holly? Don't go by yourself, will you? Please . . .'

Holly thought quickly. Common sense told her that she should wait, but her primal instincts told her to go, to hit someone, to punch her way around the whole town until she found her son. She took a deep breath. 'Tomorrow is fine. I've got some posters of Milo I need to take round the shops and that. What have the police said about the stuff from Bailey?'

'Can't really talk now, but DI Harper is in charge of Bailey's murder case, too.' Dev's voice was colourless.

'Wow. Of all the . . .'

'Yeah. I'll call you when I'm done here but call me anytime if you get any news.'

Holly ended the call, put her phone in her pocket and spent a couple of minutes staring vacantly out of the window. Eventually she squared her shoulders, picked up the flyers and slammed the front door behind her. She pushed her way past the two photographers leaning against their car.

Chapter 32

The darkness made everything worse, and Milo's face was tattooed on the inside of her eyelids, his imagined pain making her jump in panic. After taking the flyers everywhere she could think of, she'd come home and Lydia had frogmarched her to bed. But rest would not come. Eventually giving up all hope of sleep, Holly went back to the sofa, creeping past the spare room where Lydia was snoring. The photos of Milo she had hung in the hallways stared down at her, and she couldn't stop herself checking her phone again and again, just in case she had missed a call. There was nothing. Her little boy had just vanished.

She must have dozed on the sofa because the sound of breaking glass sent her leaping to her feet, panicked and confused. Glass shards scattered everywhere, across her face, across the floorboards, and there was another smash.

A dark figure was swinging a baseball bat at her living room windows. She screamed and ran into the hall, slipping on glass shards, colliding with her aunt, who was fumbling for her phone.

'What's happening?' Lydia was yanking a cardigan over her pink satin nightie. 'Is someone breaking in?'

There were more smashes, and lightly further away, car alarms blaring, and yells from neighbours. Holly got through to the police on the emergency line and told them she had an intruder. Keeping the line open, she pushed her aunt towards the spare room, which looked out onto the back garden. Her heart was thumping wildly, palms sweaty. She ran across and opened the windows. 'If he tries to get us we can climb out and get through the garden to the woods,' she told Lydia, who was shaking. 'Lock the door and push that bookcase against it.'

Together they heaved some furniture against the wooden door, trying to listen for the intruder. Were those footsteps in the hallway, or was it just the noise outside? Someone was banging on the front door but Holly stayed where she was. The tinny voice on her phone was asking if she was okay, and Holly explained they were safe for the moment, ignoring the wetness on her face.

'Holly, you're hurt. You've got blood all over your cheek,' her aunt said sharply, as she snapped the light on. Her black hair was wild and her face pale without its usual thick coating of make-up. The wrinkles around her eyes and mouth were very pronounced, and her hand crept up to clutch at the folds on her cardigan.

Holly reached up and turned the light off, instead using the torch on her phone to check the garden. Her heart was thumping painfully against her ribs.

They waited in the dark, Holly considering whether to make a break for it and take her aunt to safety through the woods. But what if the intruder was in the house, in the kitchen pulling out a knife, hiding in the garden?

Clinging together they sat on the edge of Lydia's bed, shivering. They could hear distant yells from outside, and finally the welcome blare of sirens.

Holly let out a long breath of relief. She waited until she could hear that the police were actually in her house, searching and calling that it was safe, before she moved the furniture and emerged with Lydia, blinking in the light. 'I'm fine. We both are.'

Karen was followed by two uniformed officers, who were checking out the damage in her living room. The front door was wide open, fresh white scars in the wood as though it too had been bludgeoned. As she turned away from the curious stares of bystanders, Holly caught sight of her car, smashed and dented by the same baseball bat that had attacked her windows presumably. 'Jesus, the insurance company are going to do their nut on this one. Two cars in one month.'

'I'd say that was the least of your worries,' Karen told her, grimly surveying the glittering shards of glass that covered the room.

'Come in the kitchen, and I'll make some tea,' Lydia said. Her face was grey in the light and she walked slowly, shoulders hunched. Holly watched her worriedly, but she managed a smile. 'Just a bit of a shock, isn't it? After everything that's been happening.'

Steph arrived as Karen was adding three spoonfuls of sugar to her tea. 'Holly! Are you all right?'

'We're okay,' Holly said. Quickly, she told them what had happened.

'Did you notice anything about the attacker that might identify them?'

'It was dark, and they were silhouetted in the streetlights, but there wasn't enough light to make out their face. First impressions are that it was a man, average height and build, and obviously strong. Whoever it was swung that bat with enough force to break the windows.'

'Anything about the bat? Logos?' Karen asked, tapping on her iPad.

'No. I don't think so. I've never played baseball, but I could see it wasn't a rounders bat.' She tried to smile, but her mouth felt too stiff. Her heart was still beating in jerky palpitations, like a pump with a faulty valve. She coughed and took a sip of tea. Holly didn't want tea, she wanted to down a couple of bottles of wine and drink herself into oblivion, and then she wanted to wake up with a fucking awful hangover and Milo safely in his bed. As that clearly wasn't going to happen, she needed to get a grip.

A PC came in and had a quick chat with Karen, whilst she nodded and took notes. Finally she looked back at Holly and Lydia. 'We're speaking to your neighbours at the moment, but the general consensus seems to be that the intruder ran off down the road and then into the alley that leads to the woods. We'll get the dog team out and see if we get anything. It is interesting that whoever it was smashed your windows, creating a lot of noise and alerting not only anyone inside the house, but also the whole road, but then took time to smash up your car as well.'

Holly looked at her, blinking. 'So?'

'So it wasn't a well-planned attack. This was a violent, passionate and almost a spur-of-the-moment thing. The intruder wanted to inflict damage and didn't care that they would be heard. But they weren't interested in stealing anything or even hurting you by the looks of things. One of your neighbours chased them as far as the gate to the woods, and they didn't turn and retaliate, despite being armed.'

'You mean that this was just to scare us? Well, it worked,' Holly said softly. 'And how does this connect to Milo's disappearance?'

'It may not, although obviously we are considering that,' Karen said, frowning at her iPad. 'If it was Jayden, for instance . . .'

'Jayden wouldn't hurt Holly or me,' Lydia interrupted. 'And he wouldn't have taken Milo. I told you this before.'

'But how do you *know*, Lydia? He stole your money, and now he seems to have come back to cause bloody chaos. How do you know he wouldn't hurt us?' Holly was shouting at her now.

Lydia glanced down at her hands, which were clasped together, shaking slightly. Her face flushed a deep red. When she looked up her mouth was set in a hard line. 'I knew Jayden wasn't dead this time too. He's been sending me emails. About six months after the memorial, you know when he was legally declared dead, they started then. Just a couple of times a year to say he was safe, and before you ask, I don't know where he's been and he never mentioned a kid.'

Holly stared at her. 'Why didn't you tell me? Or rather why didn't you tell me when you told me the rest?'

'I couldn't . . . It just seemed wrong. We'd as good as buried him, and you had moved away, were getting on with your life.'

Karen interrupted, 'Mrs Wyatt, I need to take a statement from you, and I need to see all the emails. This could be extremely important information.' She was glaring at Lydia, who had recovered enough to scowl back.

'Fine. I'll get my tablet and show you. Don't look at me like that, Holly. You got your life sorted and when I heard from Jayden, I knew he was safe too. You didn't need to know, because you would have been upset that we were back in contact. He's still family no matter what he's done.'

'I thought he was *dead*, for fuck's sake!' Holly spat out, furious, directing her boiling emotions across to her aunt, like scalding-hot water. But it wasn't just fury at her aunt, it was pain that Jayden hadn't trusted her, hadn't thought that she might like to know he was safe . . .

The radio crackled and an officer reported to Karen that the dog team had arrived and was being deployed immediately.

Lydia returned with her tablet and began to scan through her emails, 'Look, this is all of them. There is nothing that could help, and if I thought this had anything to do with Milo I would have shown you ages ago.'

The police and Holly peered at the email conversation. The first one was dated four years ago:

Hi Lydia,

Just wanted to let you know I'm alive and safe. I'm really sorry you had to go through all that.

Jay x

Lydia's emotional response included lots of questions about

where he was, and why he had run away, but he didn't send a message back until six months later:

Hi Lydia,

I'm doing okay still. I've made a good life here. Holly looks like she's doing all right, too.

Jay x

There were only eight emails in total, and despite Lydia's long replies, and questions, Jayden's were only the briefest, non-personal updates. His last email was dated in January this year:

Hi Lydia,

It's all going well and I've made plans to come back. Hopefully I'll get to see you but if I don't, remember that I love you and everything happens for a reason. Don't worry about me, like I say, I've got plans.

Jay x

'It doesn't help at all,' Holly said, trying to read something into Jayden's words, to pick out some kind of subliminal message. She could hardly look at her aunt now. Yet another person she trusted had been keeping secrets from her, and it hurt. 'Nobody has actually seen him properly, not even Donnie. Only had texts and emails. When Dev and I thought we saw him, it could just as easily have been someone physically similar.'

'I told you, if I thought it was important I would have shown you ages ago. But it was just enough that I knew he was safe.' Lydia put a hand on Holly's and Holly moved hers away.

Karen was silent, still reading the emails. She pushed back a strand of blonde hair and glanced up at Lydia. 'We'll need to get one of our tech team to have a detailed look at these and see if we can find out where Jayden has been for the last eleven years.'

Steph nodded, and added, 'Holly is correct. There is a possibility that these emails might not be from Jayden at all.'

Lydia looked stunned. 'You mean someone impersonating him? Why would anyone do that?'

Karen answered her. 'To make you think he was still alive, to set him up to take the fall when whatever plans were being made were actually carried out. We'll get out there now, but you've got our numbers. Steph, can you get some temporary boarding arranged for those broken windows?'

Steph nodded and they departed, leaving Lydia and Holly with the uniformed officers. Holly found she couldn't even look at her aunt, and busied herself clearing up, before announcing she was going to have a shower. Lydia said nothing.

Holly scrubbed bits of glass out of her hair, letting the hot water beat down on her tense neck and shoulders. Even with her eyes closed she saw Milo's face. Who had been here tonight? Was it a warning? Her aunt's betrayal was fresh and raw. Holly just didn't see how she could have kept such a secret. Sure, Holly would have ranted at her to make sure Jayden wasn't trying to get more cash, but she would have known he was alive, not at the bottom of the sea somewhere.

Her brother must still think she betrayed him. It was the obvious answer. He didn't trust her because he blamed her.

After her shower she pulled a brush through her long hair, tied it in a knot and put on jeans and a thick jumper. Almost without thinking she picked up her phone and, alone in her bedroom, called Devril.

He answered after two rings, alert and worried. 'Holly? What's wrong? Have they found Milo?'

'No, they haven't, but someone smashed up the car and the windows of my house a few hours ago.'

'Fuck. Are you all right?'

'Yeah.'

'Who was it?'

'I don't know. I couldn't see them clearly. Could have been Jayden, could have been Niko, or a Nicholls' family member. Or you. The police will probably be round later to ask where you were last night and this morning.'

He sighed. 'Well, that's fair enough I suppose. I take it you don't think I popped over and smashed your windows?'

'No, Dev. But there's more. Lydia has been in contact with Jayden for the last few years. She has emails from him saying that he's fine and he was planning to come back at some point.'

'Holy shit! She kept that quiet, didn't she?'

'Well, so did you! I wonder who else he's kept in touch with . . . But the police suggested Jayden might not have sent them. It keeps coming up that even if he came back with his kid, nobody has actually seen him since. What if someone's framed him?'

She could almost hear him thinking, brain ticking over, reaching the same reluctant conclusion she had, that the police had. 'Pretty bad luck if he's come back here and been taken out you mean? On the other hand, how easy for a dead man to take the fall. It would be a smart move, because it's distracting us all, going round in circles with the, *is he/isn't he* still here.'

'So if it isn't Jayden then who? Tom may or may not have anything to do with Milo's disappearance, but he sure as hell wouldn't give a shit about the Balintas and Larissa's murder. He was never very interested when I told him, and if anything he was concerned that my "council estate background" might not be suitable for a lecturer's wife.'

'He actually said that? What a knob.'

'Yeah he is. Anyway, my point is that it still points towards the Nicholls. Bloody DI Harper had better get his finger out.'

'Listen, I called Gareth, and he was busy, naturally. After he'd finished chatting with the coppers, he rang and we set up a meet for this afternoon.'

'I'll be there.'

'Fine. See you at three. I reckon they won't try anything with

270

all this Bailey stuff going on, so we should be all right, but tell Donnie, won't you? As back-up . . . Do you want me to come over now?'

'No, I'm going to get cleared up and sort out some new windows for my house. Oh yeah, and a new bloody car too,' Holly said bitterly.

She ended the call and walked back into her kitchen, nerves jangling. What if Gareth was setting a trap? The washing up was still on the counter. Almost without thinking she picked up a vegetable knife. It was small and sharp, and she ran her thumb gently across the blade. A tiny drop of scarlet appeared in the white sink, spreading, blossoming and swirling slowly towards the plughole.

Chapter 33

Karen called just after 10 a.m. 'Holly, I just wanted you to know that we've arrested someone for the incident last night. Tom.'

'*What?*' She dropped the mug she was holding and it shattered into a thousand pieces, scattering across her kitchen floor. 'He came and smashed everything up? Why would he do that?'

'We don't know, but we have him in custody now. And his girlfriend, sorry his ex-girlfriend, Beth who called us. She said that he called her late last night, and they had a row. Apparently, she's left him and he was ranting on about Milo, and you, threatening her and their baby. She was scared of what he might do.'

'I see. Good for Beth,' Holly once again felt that twinge of reluctant admiration.

'Yes.'

Holly's brain was whirring. 'Are you going to ask him if he took Milo again?'

'We are. Believe me, I'm doing everything possible to get Milo back. I've got to go, Holly, but if we get any news either Steph or I will contact you.'

Holly put her phone down, nausea rising in her belly. Tom had come over here on a rampage. He had lost everything already, she supposed: the new girlfriend, maybe his job once word got out, and after a few lines of coke he probably thought it might make him feel better. If he didn't have anything to do with Milo's disappearance, he was also probably, like Holly, going crazy with worry.

Dev finally called again and simply told her he was coming over, refusing to discuss anything on the phone. Cathryn turned up at the same time, and Holly sat them both down in the kitchen. The windows were boarded up with chipboard, awaiting emergency repairs, and although she'd swept and hoovered the living room, tiny shards of glass still glinted, scattered across the bookshelves, decorating plant pots and along the top of picture frames. Not to mention an icy breeze crept between the boarding and the masonry.

'Fuck me, at least none of my exes turned up and smashed my house up,' Cathryn said eventually, as she and Dev studied each other, not entirely friendly but aware that Holly needed them both. 'Haven't seen you around in ages, Dev. You're looking good.'

He smiled at her, but it didn't reach his eyes. 'Thanks. How're the kids?'

'You know, little buggers but I love 'em. You haven't got any kids, have you?'

He shook his head.

Holly brought them both up to date on Tom's arrest and told Cathryn about Jayden's emails. Then she turned back to Dev.

'Dev, why are you here, anyway? I thought we were meeting later to go and see Gareth.' Holly glanced at Cath, waiting for the explosion.

'Fuck.' Cathryn's mouth popped open. 'Have you got a death wish? It's hell over at the yard. It's practically on lockdown and half the drivers have been sent up north to the other yard, to get them out the way.'

Dev was clearly reluctant to speak in front of Cathryn but Holly was adamant. 'Okay. So Joey called me, said he knew we were meeting up with Gareth later, but he wanted me to think on something before the meet.' Dev paused. 'He offered me twenty grand to go back and run a new operation. Wouldn't say where, but he hinted it wouldn't be in Westbourne. Despite everything going down at the moment, he was pretty confident about his offer. He said he and his brother were devastated about what happened to Bailey and he made a big thing about how his nephew was dead.'

'Like he gives a shit. Probably watched him die, the bastard,' Cath commented.

'So when we see Gareth later, I'm pretty sure he's going to ask Holly again about the Hughes business and try and haul us both in together. It's all business to them. Doesn't matter that Rohan is still in hospital, or that Bailey had to take a fall, as long as they've got the money coming in and the respect for the family,' Dev said.

'We'll just spin a story ourselves, about how I might be thinking of agreeing to the offer but only if I get Milo back, maybe?' Holly said quickly. She was still fidgeting with her phone, smoothing a thumb across the screensaver, which was Milo on the beach. Every second he was missing was tearing her apart but she was getting good at hiding it.

'Right, well I gotta go soon because I'm working later and we're short again so I'm going in early.' Cathryn pushed her chair back. 'Three people left last week, but Sara's still there. Ruby's got her now because Noah's gone too.'

'Noah quit? I thought he was great.'

'I know, but you can't tell, can you? Apparently he said he was starting to get migraines from the night shifts. Carol and Bex left too. The wages aren't enough if you gotta pay someone for night childcare, are they?'

'No. Shame though, they were all going to be good.' Holly wasn't really listening. Work was another world and thinking about it required too much effort.

Cathryn's phone rang, and she glanced quickly at the screen. 'Oh shit, it's Colleen. I hope she's okay to babysit tonight. Sorry, I gotta take this . . .' Speaking rapidly into her phone she wandered into the hallway.

'Now tell me what else happened,' Holly demanded softly of Dev. 'Because I can tell there's more.'

Dev glanced towards the hallway but Cathryn was still deep in her rather loud conversation with her sister. 'I dropped in at the transport café on my way here, and I managed to get a conversation going with one of the drivers. He works for another firm, but he knows the Nicholls. And he knew Bailey. He said Bailey mentioned Gareth once when they were talking, and he was scared of him. We know that, but this bloke also said that Gareth still has that smile. The one he has when he's up to fucking evil.'

Holly knew what Dev meant. She'd seen the flick knife switch between sanity and madness in both Gareth and Joey, and remembering made her shiver. Holly's phone rang and she clutched it tightly to her ear, trembling. 'Karen? Have you found him?'

The other two were silent and Cathryn, returning from her own call, was holding two crossed fingers on her lap, staring fiercely at Holly throughout the conversation.

Holly rang off and stared at them, licking dry lips before she could speak. 'They found . . . They found Milo's clothes on Highton Downs. A dog walker said her dog was scrabbling for rabbits on South Hill and his clothes were in a Tesco bag, shoved in a hole.' Holly dropped the phone, her eyes wide as the pain hit somewhere in her chest, and she only just made it to the toilet, heaving over the bowl until bile burned her mouth. And all the time the tears kept coming.

She heard voices but was unaware of anything else, unable move from her position, hugging the toilet bowl, the coldness pressed against her cheek.

Eventually Cathryn pulled her bodily to her feet, heaving her into the spare room and onto the bed. They lay side by side, hands entwined as they had so often on childhood sleepovers. At some point, exhausted, she must have dropped off, because when she woke, an hour later, it was to the sharp pain of loss, and a cold space where Cathryn had been.

Inching her body off the bed, Holly sat up too quickly and the room spun around. She closed her eyes and then opened them again. On the mirror scrawled in red writing in her mum's lipstick read: '*I love You Babes. We'll Find HIM.*'

All around the words Cathryn had drawn hearts and flowers and a smiley sunshine face. Blinking back tears, Holly made her way to the kitchen and found Devril and Steph sitting at the table.

Steph smiled gently at Holly. 'Your friend Cathryn is a force of nature, isn't she? She said to tell you that she's made you enough soup to feed the whole street, and she's put a casserole in the slow cooker for tonight.'

Dev was busy on his laptop and phone. 'And she's cleaned the whole house. She's like some crazy insect, and she's always been like that, even when she was a little kid.'

'What are you still doing here?' Holly slumped against the cooker, confused. The shock of the phone call was still there, making her heart batter against her ribs. She moistened her lips. 'What about Milo's clothes?'

Steph waited until Dev had made coffee and pushed a mug towards Holly. 'We need you to identify them as his, Holly. Remember, before you start imagining all kinds of horrific things that we are focusing on the positives.'

'So they buy him new clothes because . . .' In a flash Holly got it. 'Because they are taking him around somewhere where people could see him!' Hope returned, but the lingering feeling that there was also the other side, the one she couldn't think about was still there, hiding in the shadows of her mind.

'Tom has been charged and bailed for the vandalism to your house and car. We don't think, at this stage, that he has anything to do with Milo's disappearance, but we are keeping an open mind. He has admitted the criminal damage,' Steph told her. 'When you're ready, I've got the clothes here, to save you coming down the station and fighting through the press. I just need you to identify them as a formality.'

Holly stared out of the kitchen window, thinking that only a week or two ago all she had to worry about was an impending divorce and how the hell she was going to pay her mortgage. Now she couldn't care less.

Karen rang the doorbell just as Holly was mentally preparing herself for the sight of Milo's pathetic blue pyjamas. 'Holly, I'm sorry we have to ask you to do this, but as I'm sure Steph has explained, finding these clothes doesn't mean bad news.' Karen's expression was serious, her perfectly made-up face drawn and dark shadows visible under the foundation. 'Devril.'

'Nice to see you again, DC Marriot,' Dev said, but he was watching Holly.

Holly nodded. 'Let's just do it.'

Steph slid the plastic packet across the table towards her. The blue pyjamas with stars on them. She stroked them with a fingertip, as gently as if they had been her son himself. Just pyjamas, nothing else. She looked up, unable to speak, tearing running down her cheeks.

'Thanks, Holly, we'll get these down to the lab just in case we can get anything from them,' Karen said.

***

'You can go home if you want, Dev,' Holly said suddenly. 'I can manage.'

'If you're okay I was thinking that I should go and see Gareth.'

'I should go too.' She'd almost forgotten. The purpose that had driven her through the last couple of days had snapped, her energy drained. She looked dully at her ex-boyfriend. 'I should be there,' she said stubbornly.

His eyes were almost green in the light from the window, pale against his dark skin, and he was silent for a moment. Then he smiled. 'Okay but don't beat the shit out of him. We need to play by his rules, just for a bit, and see where it takes us. After that, I reckon we should drop in on my cousin Niko. Haven't seen his ugly face in a while and I'm sure he'd like to give us a cuppa.'

That almost made her smile, but her mouth felt too stiff, and she was so tired, and so cold. 'It's getting longer and longer since he was taken, Dev, and we've all heard that the longer a child is missing . . .' She couldn't finish, turning away, but he moved round gently pulling her into his arms. For a long moment she hugged him back, fiercely, holding on to his strength, his protection, and when she pulled back the fire had returned. But she wasn't sure she could keep her promise about not hitting Gareth. If he gave the slightest hint he knew where Milo was . . .

Holly's phone rang and she dived on it, listening intently. Dev was holding up two crossed fingers but Holly shook her head, her shoulders dropping in disappointment. 'Okay, thanks for letting me know, Steph.'

'Any news?'

'Not really. Tom's been released on bail, which they already told me, but after news got out that he was arrested one of his colleagues told the police that although Tom was at the meeting that night on campus, they broke for an hour to grab sandwiches and coffee. Apparently, they split off into little groups, networking in different rooms. Tom said in his original statement that he was with this bloke, Chris, I think his name is, but Chris is now saying Tom wasn't with him at all, and nobody remembers seeing him until the meeting reconvened.'

'Why the fuck didn't he mention this earlier?'

'Chris apparently covered for Tom before when he started seeing Beth, so Tom maybe assumed he would just go along with it? I don't know.'

'Bloody hell, do you think he did take Milo? That would mean we are way out with our little theories,' Dev said, watching her carefully.

'I don't know. I hate Tom but I do know if he did take Milo he would never hurt him,' she said slowly.

'You're getting quite cosy with the police, aren't you, Holly? All these calls and first-name terms. You know I said me and Jayden were informants for DI Harper? Well, he's staying well out of this investigation, isn't he? But he's picked up Bailey's case quick enough. Seems to have left you with DC Marriot. I wonder why, and I wonder how good she really is?'

Holly didn't hesitate. 'She's very good. It's been her and Steph Harlow from the start and they are putting everything into this.' She thought of the intensity of Karen's gaze as the pyjamas were passed across the table. 'I googled her and she was involved in a case three years ago with a missing child. She was working in Romford then.'

'Did she find the kid?'

'The girl was dead, but you know, I'm thinking that if she thought she failed on that case, she might be trying extra hard to find Milo.'

'Why did she fail?'

'Some sick bastard took the kid and she was dead within the first few hours . . . Oh fuck, sorry Dev.' Holly was crying again, reaching for a wad of tissues. Her eyes were sore and gritty but she scrubbed a tissue angrily across them anyway.

'It's okay, Holly.'

'No it isn't, and you know it.'

279

Chapter 34

Dev drove and Holly stared out of the window, shivering despite her coat and the warmth of the heated seats. Her eyes raked every house, every path, and shop, constantly searching, constantly choking back tears.

She might have turned her back on the Seaview, but in all the windows, Milo's posters were displayed. The bus stop was plastered with flyers, and a couple of women, staggering past with a buggy and heavy shopping bags, were wearing T-shirts with #FindMilo and his photo emblazoned across their chests. They looked hard at Holly and they waved tentatively. She waved back, tears flowing properly now.

'No fuckers had better nick my wheels either,' Dev said grimly as they pulled up outside the Nicholls place.

Holly took a deep breath, scrubbed away the tears, her hands shaking as she opened the car door. But the anger was still there, the fire she needed to get through this. She had been telling the truth when she told Dev the police were doing a good job, but some things needed to be sorted between the families. Perhaps this was what Gareth had wanted all along.

Her phone buzzed with a text from Donnie:

At home with a couple of the boys.

If you need us just shout. Don't let G fuck you around.

'Donnie checking up on you? It's like he knows whenever you set foot on the estate.'

'Yeah. Let's do this.' Holly led the way into the yard. This time the gates were pulled wide open, and they stepped quickly to one side, avoiding a vast HGV that rumbled past. The dour-looking driver gave them a thumbs-up and turned left, out towards the main road.

Gareth was waiting in the portacabin, and when they entered he nodded, and then ignored them, clicking the mouse on his computer, frowning at whatever was on screen.

After a couple of minutes Holly snapped, 'We didn't come here to play games. Get off your bloody computer and tell me what I need to do to get my boy back.'

Her fists were clenched, and her fear of the tall man turned into a white-hot flash of anger. You should never show your opponent that you were scared, never let them back you into a corner . . . But this man in front of her could be a characterisation of Death himself. The pale, soulless eyes resting on her with contempt, and his thin lips parted more in grimace than smile.

As on the beach, his gaze swept over her body, appraising. She remembered Bailey's talk of a party, and what happened to the girls, and she saw again Bailey himself, swinging from a tree. Joey was all about sex, and always had been, but his brother . . . Gareth was all about fear and pain. He got his kicks from the scent of terror, and the taste of blood. Sian had once said that Gareth was more animal than human.

Dev broke the spell. He was leaning against the wall near the door, arms crossed. 'Come on, Gareth, what do you want?'

'You asked to see me, remember.' The voice was cool, and he leant back in his chair, mirroring Dev's pose.

'Do you know where Holly's kid is?' Dev asked.

He was enjoying it, she could tell, absorbing her pain and fear, feasting on her suffering, but he shook his head, ponytail flopping. 'No. Whatever happened to him, it wasn't anything to do with us. Nicholls don't trade in small boys. Small girls, possibly, but boys . . . Nah.'

Holly pressed her hands on his desk, until they were eyeball to eyeball. 'But could you find out where Milo is?'

'Why would I want to do that? Joey told you before what we want from you, but since Dev is here I can repeat the offer. First tell me why I should give a shit about your kid when all you've done is send the filth round. My own kid is dead, and my nephew got knifed. Don't you think I've got enough troubles of my own?' But the man's face was far from grief. There was an unpleasant light behind those icy eyes and a half smirk that told another story.

'Rohan's a grown man, and that was nothing to do with me,' Holly said, ignoring his mention of Bailey.

'Maybe Donnie though? Rohan's not talking at the moment, but when he does, then we'll see.' Gareth had always spoken slowly and carefully, tasting each word before he spat it into the world. 'As for my son, well, I'm devastated, aren't I? You raise them, give them prospects, and then they try and screw you over. Kids!'

'You killed Bailey,' Dev said, scowling, his voice thickening. 'You can't blame us for coming after you for Milo's disappearance.'

He didn't bother to deny it. 'Family loyalty is all that matters. If you screw with that you take the consequences. Holly should know that already. Her mum was a perfect example of someone who forgot where their loyalties lie.' He raised a rough hand, palm outward, silencing them both. 'Focus on your own kid, Holly, and forget the past. So here's the deal . . . Say I could find your boy. I'd want payment for that, of course. Now that Dev's back, I've already asked him to come back into the business, so how about the two of you heading up a joint Hughes–Nicholls operation. You sign over that slice of pie I want, and you work for me. Normally I don't work with women, but I need a Hughes family member to smooth my path. The dealers who are loyal to your dad, will be loyal to you.'

Holly's head spun. 'Donnie will never go for it.'

'But if that was the only way to get his grandson back, and keep his girl happy, I think you could persuade him.' Gareth looked thoughtful. 'You can play up the fact it would be a partnership, soften the blow a bit.'

'And Jayden?' Dev queried, his own gaze intense as he watched the other man. 'You've forgotten Jayden's back and he might not like the idea.'

Gareth laughed. It was a cold, scornful sound. 'When I see him, I'll believe it.' His expression was one of private amusement, as though he knew far more than they did.

'You don't think he came back?' Holly asked, still turning over the words in her head. Did the Nicholls have Milo after all? It still seemed reasonable to assume they did, as Gareth seemed pretty confident he could find him. His price was nothing compared to her son's life, but she had no idea if Donnie would go for it, or if the Nicholls would hold up their end of the bargain.

The man stood up, came around the desk in three long strides, towering over Holly. She took an involuntary step back and, realising what she had done, stepped forward again, looking up into those terrible eyes.

Behind her Dev never moved, but she sensed he too was tensed to fight. For a long moment, she held eye contact, held fighting stance, and then he laughed again, and leant against the desk. 'Like I said, I'll believe it when I see it. And now you two can fuck off and think about my business proposition. You've got twenty-four hours or the deal's off.'

'What? You can't set a time limit!' Holly said.

'I can do anything I want, because I give the orders,' Gareth told her. 'Now piss off before I change my mind.'

***

Back in the car, Dev rested his hands on the steering wheel for a moment, watching Holly. 'Hell of a choice. How the fuck are we going to persuade Donnie to sell out?'

'Do you think they've got Milo?'

'Who knows, but he was practically pissing himself laughing when I mentioned Jayden, and that worries me. And what about Jayden's son?'

'Nothing. They haven't found him, so it looks like he did find his dad, and maybe they've just gone.' Holly bit back her concerns and forced a smile. 'Let's go down the road and do some more visiting.' Adrenalin was still pulsing around her body and her palms were wet with sweat.

Mason himself was staggering back into his house as they pulled up at their second destination. His black eyes peered out from a mass of wrinkles, and his grubby white vest was tucked into baggy black trousers. Recognising them, he waited until they got out.

'Mason. You all right?' Devril said easily.

'What do you want?' The old man scowled, his greasy grey hair was loose, falling in straggly clumps to his shoulders, and stubble encrusted the lower half of his face. There was a little spot of dried blood just above one eyebrow. He gave a hacking cough.

'To see Niko. I heard he's back from holiday.'

'You've got a fucking cheek. I suppose you've hooked up with her again.' He sneered at Holly.

'Mason, in case you missed it, my kid has been taken. I want to talk to Niko in case he's heard anything that might help me find him,' Holly said, scowling back. Mason was a bastard, but he'd never terrified her the way Gareth had. Just now, one left hook and he'd be flat on his back, and she was itching to give it to him.

Mason spat a mouthful of green phlegm into his bare earth flowerbed. 'Niko don't know nothing. Boy's only been out a few weeks and now they're hounding him again. Of course he didn't take your kid! I told the filth that, and I told Donnie, and now I'm telling you.'

'We know that, but he might have heard something. You lot know everything that goes on round here,' Dev said.

284

'All right for you, moving away, working for the papers and renting a posh place over the river. Yeah, I know everything you been up to, Devril Mancini, and I know Gareth offered you a job too.' The old man looked triumphant at their expressions of surprise. 'Things move on, don't they, and you'll see Niko'll get the business back up and running, and we'll be working together better than before. Maybe Donnie's past it, maybe not, but I'll go with the money, always have done.' He paused, and then waved an arm in the direction of the door. 'Go on, you might as well see him, but don't blame me if he tells you to fuck off.'

They went inside the sour-smelling house. A thin, skeletal woman was in the kitchen, painted brows furrowed in concentration. She frowned at them, opened her mouth to say something, but carried on making her spliff at the table. Her long straggly brown hair fell loose across her shoulders, and track marks scarred her bare arms.

Mason, ignoring all the usual planning regulations, had added onto his house whenever he felt like it, to accommodate his growing family. Niko had always occupied the annexe that sprawled into the back garden and was reached through a door in the downstairs bathroom.

Dev banged on the door and, not getting an answer, they walked in. The smell of weed was so strong Holly almost gagged. The shelf was lined with cannabis plants, and the music was turned up loud with some rapper yelling about death and decay.

Niko came out of his bedroom, a jack knife half hidden in his hand, expression threatening. He saw them and stopped dead. 'How the fuck did you get in?'

'Put it away, Niko, we've just come for a chat,' Dev said, amiably.

'I'm not helping you, you fucking bitch! You told the cops I took your kid and I've just spent the night down at the station. Again. Fuck off and stop causing trouble.' Niko was glaring at Holly. He looked exhausted, his dark eyes shadowed, and his shaven head and hollow cheekbones were vaguely reminiscent of a Halloween joke skull.

Holly tried to breathe shallowly, avoiding the heavy scent of the plants. 'I mean it, Niko. I didn't send the police after you and all I care about is getting Milo back. Imagine if someone took Kian! You'd do anything to get him back wouldn't you?'

The mention of his son pulled him up short, and when he spoke again his expression was softer. 'Look, I'm sorry about your kid, okay, but I don't know where he is. When I said about him being good at football, I was just talking!'

Dev pulled out a packet of cigarettes and shoved them over towards his cousin. 'So have you *heard* anything about Milo? Come on, Niko, you hear everything that goes on, and I know you've been pulling in the old crowd, trying to get the business going again . . .'

'Yeah, and Gareth is dead set on you and me coming back, but I need to bring some cash. I need that money Jayden owes me or I gotta do my own thing. I heard you saw him earlier in the week.' His glance flashed sideways at Holly.

'Whatever. Are you still trying to decide between Hughes and Nicholls?'

'Come again?'

'The money you say Jay took from you. Have you got it back yet?' Dev said. 'Because I was wondering if you were so popular because you've promised funding that you don't actually have yet.'

A flash of panic crossed Niko's face. 'Jayden's gonna pay for this when I find him . . .' He caught himself. 'Bailey's dead, isn't he? I heard he got strung up.'

'Don't change the subject. What if me and Holly were thinking of coming back properly, and what if we had funding of our own? That would be complicated, wouldn't it?' Dev said, smiling at his cousin.

'What? You wouldn't though . . . It's all fucked up at the moment. I wanna work, but I need to buy in. You know what? Gareth said nobody's seen Jayden and it's only a rumour that he's back. Roman and Alexi had a lot of enemies, but their deaths

286

have been pegged to Jayden, somehow.' Niko was edgy, cracking his knuckles in a way that made Holly want to scream.

'All I care about is getting Milo back. If you see or hear anything, then just call me or Dev. The Seaview is my place too, you know, and they are all out looking for my boy. When we find out what happened and who took him, I'm betting the police won't get to them before the people off the estate.' Holly fixed him with a gimlet eye, staring him down.

'You've got those women coppers on the case, I know.' Niko relaxed a little and lit another spliff from the butt of the old one. He moved over to the windowsill, stroking a hand over his plants. 'I got plans now I'm out. I've had eight years to think about what to do, and I've got the contacts to make the business bigger than it ever was. Screw the Nicholls, if the money doesn't come in, I've got contacts with really hot girls and we won't be staying round here. I'm moving too. The old man doesn't know yet but this place isn't right for me now. If you're serious about coming back into the business, you could go in with us. Weather's better in Spain too.' He was grinning now, relaxed and friendly as the mellow drug took hold.

Holly nodded, not caring a shit about Niko's life. 'Yeah, well, if you hear anything . . .'

Her voice shook a bit and Dev slid a hand over hers. Niko watched them, eyes narrowing against the thin blue stream of cigarette smoke.

'Niko?' Mason was yelling from the main house, shattering the moment.

'I got nothing to tell you,' Niko said flatly. 'But if I do hear, I'll call Dev. And, Dev, you let me know if you decide to come home. I mean it.'

Holly walked quickly through the filthy stench of the house, and out into the freezing but clean air. 'That was pointless. He still as thick as ever, and a bloody liar, saying one thing and then contradicting himself in the next sentence.'

287

'Niko's desperate so it was worth a shot. He hasn't got Milo though because you haven't had a ransom demand. The only reason Niko would take him would be to get money. I'm surprised he didn't think of it, actually. It would be totally his style.'

'Cathryn says he's soft on kids,' Holly told him disbelievingly.

'Yeah right.' Devril dropped her home but seemed anxious to get going. 'I can come back later if you like? I've just got some things to do.'

'Like another story on Milo?'

He met her eyes. 'Yes. But you knew that. I'm not doing anything I didn't say I would. This is where it's good to do what I do. We need the general public still looking, still caring about him and I can make them do that.'

When he put it like that she couldn't argue, and she was too exhausted to try and think, so she agreed he would come over later, and made her way into the empty house. There was a note from Lydia, who had obviously let herself in with her own key, propped against a mug on the kitchen table, saying workmen had been round and promised to come back tomorrow to fix the windows.

Holly sighed, crumpling the note and hurling at across the kitchen. Who cared? Who fucking cared about any of it? The whole house could burn down and none of it mattered without Milo.

She made herself a cup of tea, and almost in a dream began to collect things. There was a dresser shelf at the far end of the kitchen, opposite the table. She took all the crockery off the shelves, and began to replace it with Milo's things. Framed photographs, his collection of dragons, a few of his books, his old blankie from when he was a baby. More photographs – she stuck them on the wall around the shelves with Blu-Tack. In the centre she put a candle and a potted plant.

It was a shrine to her boy and she stood fiercely in front of it, trying to channel her love towards him. All those stories about mind-reading and psychics might be bollocks but she tried to send him something, eyes screwed up tight.

When she opened her eyes, she realised her phone was ringing and she ran back out to the hallway, grabbing it from her bag.

'Hallo?'

It was Karen. 'Holly?'

'Have you found him?' Maybe it had worked . . .

'No. Mason Balinta has just complained about you and Devril Mancini harassing Niko.'

'We weren't harassing him, we were having a chat. I have to do something, not just sit at home and wait for Milo's body to turn up!' Holly shouted, pacing the hallway.

'Holly! Calm down. You're doing really well. Everything we ask you to do, you do it and believe me, we aren't sitting still down here.'

'I know that. Sorry.'

'Don't give up, Holly. If you get anything else then just call me. Or call me anyway, if you need to talk.'

'You had another missing child case, didn't you? In Romford.' She couldn't help prying. It distracted her from her pain.

Silence for a while, then she answered, 'Yes, I did. We did everything we could on that case.'

'I'm not saying you didn't, I'm just saying that we've got two boys missing here and nothing's happening! Oh fuck it, I don't know anything anymore.' Holly ended the call and chucked her phone on the table.

Energy spent, she collapsed back onto the sofa, the chipboard windows mocking her, the room cold and dank. After a while she went back and sat at the kitchen table, facing the photos of her boy. It was warmer in there. She drank in his smiling face, forcing herself to focus only on him.

The builders came round as promised and the windows were repaired. Her car had been towed away earlier, and the insurance company were supposed to be dealing with the claim. Jesus, they hadn't even finished processing the last one.

She considered ringing her aunt, but after the revelation that she'd actually been in contact with Jayden there was a definite frosty atmosphere between them. It was almost as if she felt Lydia had betrayed her. Which was stupid. Her emotions were just all over the place.

As darkness closed in Holly checked the windows and doors again and again, making sure her phone was charged, half wishing Dev hadn't gone home. She paced the house, leaving all the lights on, and finally fell into an exhausted slumber on the sofa, clutching Milo's cricket bat and one of his soft toys.

***

As the light leaked through the sullen clouds, and morning approached Holly was awake and trying to scrub away her exhaustion in the shower. Two phone calls to Donnie just reached his answer phone. What was he up to? She needed to talk about this Nicholls thing. Dev had said before he left that maybe they could play it so all the families thought they were getting what they wanted, on the outside chance Milo was being held by the Nicholls. It would be a bloody miracle and if they made a mistake they'd go the same way as Bailey, but she'd do anything to get Milo back. Endangering her own life seemed trivial in comparison to any pain or suffering he might be going through.

Cath appeared with Anna and Angel just after eleven. The roar of commuter traffic on the road outside had settled to a buzz, and the feeble spring sunshine was making puddles glisten. As usual her friend had two bulging shopping bags hanging from one arm.

Holly shoved two twenties in her purse when she wasn't looking. Cath couldn't afford to shop for someone else, but she would never accept the money if she tried to give it to her outright.

The girls settled down to play with Milo's Lego, scattering a box of raisins across the carpet.

Cath sighed, kneeling to pick up the raisins. 'I saw Noah in town with Ruby today. They were at Costa, all snuggled up in a booth. Very cosy. Anyway Ruby texted me to say she thinks Noah's been accepted by the fire service. But it's in the next county so he's talking about them both moving. Oh, and Beano's left. He's gone back to Tesco's. He says they pay better.'

Holly let the gossip flow over her, grateful for the distraction. 'I'm not surprised, Beano's still got his ex-wife on his case, hasn't he?'

'Speaking of exes . . . Niko phoned last night. He wants to see Kian and he said he's got some money coming through so he's going to start paying child support.'

'Fuck.'

'That's what I said, and he said yes please.'

Holly made a childish vomiting sound, her fingers in her mouth, and Angel immediately copied her, beaming.

'Girls, you stay here. There's another box of Lego in the corner, look,' Cathryn said. 'Me and Holly are just going to sit in the kitchen with our tea.' Keeping one eye on her kids, she turned to Milo's wall. 'Nice display by the way. Is it helping?'

Holly shook her head. 'Not really. I just feel like I need a way to keep him near me . . .'

'Oh, babes, come here.'

Holly hugged her back, feeling her bony ribs, burying her head in her coarse blonde mane. It was comforting for all of ten seconds, and then the pain came roaring back. Frantically sifting through her mind, she sought a distraction. 'So Ruby is still seeing Noah then?'

'Yeah she said call her if you want to, but she understands if not.'

'I just can't . . .'

'Everyone at work sends their love and they've all been sharing on social media.'

'It is nice to know everyone's got my back but I'm so tired I can hardly get showered and dressed in the morning. Trying to act normally takes all my energy when what I really want to do is stand screaming in the street or just curl up into a ball and cry all day.'

'The police haven't called again, have they?'

'No. After the TV appeal, they always get a load of cranks phoning in claiming to know where the missing kid is, or reporting their neighbours for something, so Karen said she'd only call if anything tangible came in.'

'Holly, I need to tell you something.' Cathryn put Anna back down and she scampered happily back to her sister, who was taking all the Lego out of the basket and chucking it across the floor. 'Holly, did you ever wonder how Niko knew where to find Jayden?'

'I don't know. We've been over this, haven't we?' Holly was confused.

'It was me.'

'*What?*'

Cathryn's eyes were huge in her thin face. 'I told Niko where to find them that night. I was taking Ronnie to his eye appointment at the hospital, it was pissing down with rain and I was struggling on the bloody bus to Panfield with the kids and the shopping . . . And then I saw him. I saw Jayden when I got off at the Heath Road stop. He was walking in a crowd just ahead.'

'You saw him?'

'Yeah. I called out to him. I wasn't quite sure at first if it was him or not, but then he turned to cross the road and I was sure. I was kind of dithering. I didn't want to be late for the eye appointment, but I mean, Christ, none of us had seen him for over a year. I followed him, in the rain with the pushchair. He never saw me but I saw him go to Holborn Court and run upstairs and along the balcony. A girl opened the door to number fifty-five and she had a baby in her arms. He kissed her and stroked the baby's head and they went inside.'

'Did you not go up and find out what was going on?' Holly asked.

'No. I could see he had hooked up with someone else, had

another kid, and there was me dumped with the twins and no support. I was furious. I went to the clinic and I thought what I should do all the way home. It was obvious. I was seeing Niko, we had Kian, and Niko had been looking for Jayden ever since he pissed off. I rang him and went back to his place.' She looked straight at Holly, flicking her hair back. 'It was my fault. I told Niko where to find Jayden.'

'Shit. Cathryn, you could never have known what would happen,' Holly said. All this time her friend had carried the same guilt she had. It was a shock, but after the initial flash of horror, she just felt empty. Nothing mattered except Milo.

'I thought he might get a beating. In fact, shit I knew he would. I never thought that they'd go for the girl though . . . But that's why Niko lied about the tip-off, to protect me.'

'Was that why you broke up?'

She shrugged. 'It's hard to say, what with all the crap going on with Larissa's murder.'

Holly studied her friend's face, watching her bite her lip and start playing with her bracelets. She'd always thought at the time it was weird that Niko and Cath got together, but their short relationship had been peppered with rows. Both of them short-tempered and used to getting their own way.

'So anyway, now you know. Do you think I should tell the police? I'm scared, Holly. What if Jayden has found out it was me that grassed him up? If he arranged for Alexi and Roman to be killed, and maybe took Milo? What about the other kids?'

Holly tried to drag her mind back to the subject in hand. She'd almost dismissed her brother as a potential abductor but Cath's terror was tangible, and the room practically quivered with it. 'I think you should tell Karen, and she can decide whether it might be important. She's okay, and she won't judge you.'

'Okay. You got her number? I'll ring her when I get home.'

And, Cath, when you get home, tell your brothers, and your dad. Just in case. So you've got people looking out for you on the estate.'

'Yeah.' Cathryn was nodding, gathering up her things, prising the kids away from the Lego. 'This is fucking scary, isn't it? I guess we just hope that if Jayden's got his own kid back, he's gone away again. No reason to hang around if he managed to kill Alexi and Roman, is there? But if he *did* have Milo, he might let him go now he's got his own boy back.'

'He might,' Holly said, showing her out. If her brother wanted to torture her then this was the perfect way to do it. Where would he be, though? With a massive police search and media coverage, where the hell could he be keeping two kids?

Dev called to say he'd filed his story, and to ask whether he should come round. Holly considered. 'I dunno. It might be best if I track down Donnie on my own.'

'He always liked me.' Dev was amused.

'Yeah, all right.' She told him, then, about Cathryn's little confession.

'Fucking hell, I always wondered how he really knew. All that shit about the bit of paper through the door, which he then chucked away, was too weird to be true. Too convenient, but Cathryn, wow! I wouldn't have thought she'd have the balls to do that . . .'

'I can imagine how she felt when she saw Jayden all shacked up with this new girl and a kid too. And I can hardly judge, can I? I did the same thing. If you'd passed on that message from me Niko would have sent the boys round earlier.'

'Yeah . . . I still think Niko went over as well. I know Roman and Alexi always said they were on their own going to collect the money, but for Niko it was personal, wasn't it? Jayden had been our mate, and then he'd screwed the Balintas over.'

'The police said there was no evidence he had been in the flat,' Holly pointed out. 'But yeah, weird. You'd think he would have got a kick out of finally finding him.'

'I'll be with you in fifteen minutes, and we can head over to the Seaview.'

'Thanks, Dev.'

After locking the front door, Holly was waiting in the road as Dev pulled up. The journalists had thinned out in the last couple of days, and now mostly phoned asking for interviews. She ignored all of them.

In silence they drove up the hill, and along the coast a way, before turning back along the main road that led towards the front entrance to the Seaview.

'Anything else on Bailey?' she asked. 'Karen wouldn't comment when I asked her.'

'No. The police won't tell me anything either. Typical Nicholls job, all signed and sealed,' Dev said bitterly. 'But DI Harper's being dead quiet about the stuff we got from Bailey's wife, so I'm hoping he might just be checking it out and preparing a case. Don't forget he's wanted the Nicholls for years. It's personal.'

'Yeah, very personal. It's always good to keep things in the family,' Holly agreed sarcastically. 'Sorry, Dev, I haven't got my head around him being Jay's dad yet.'

They stopped at a queue of traffic at the bridge. The scream of sirens made Dev squeeze his vehicle onto the pavement to allow a convoy of emergency vehicles to pass through. An ambulance was on the grass verge of the other side of the road and they could make out figures in fluorescent jackets on the opposite riverbank.

Chapter 35

'What's going on?' Holly's voice rose in panic. Instinct told her it must be Milo. They must have found his body . . .

But then she saw the car.

The traffic was at a total standstill and she grabbed the door handle, even as Dev yelled at her to stay put. She ignored him and ran, gasping and panting in the cold air, dodging round vehicles until she reached the scene. It was Beth's car. A red Golf was lying partially visible in the river, the grey water swirling around it. The rear window had a yellow Battersea Dogs Home sticker, and a row of silver stars.

She had only seen the car a couple of times, most recently as it drove away from her house. At first, she was so passionately relieved it wasn't anything to do with Milo, she hardly took it in. This road was full of hazardous bends and the area coming into this end of town was a traffic black spot.

But then a kind of horror took over – Beth and the baby could be fatally injured. She had seemed so sorted and organised. So calm, that Holly had actually envied her. Envied her that she had her baby still with her and that she was escaping to make a new life. But maybe she hadn't . . . Why was she still in Westbourne?

Holly slithered down the bank to be met by a police cordon. 'Stay back please.'

'I think I know that car . . .' Holly swallowed hard. 'Is she . . . Is the driver a woman?'

The policeman gave her a hard look, like he recognised her. 'I really can't say yet. Come over here and wait.'

Holly pulled out her phone and called a furious Dev, who was still sat in his vehicle. After he had ranted at her for pissing off, she sliced through his words and told him she thought Beth had driven into the river.

'You mean on purpose, or an accident?'

Holly paused. 'I don't know, but I'm sure it's her car. Jesus. She said she was going away to stay with her parents.'

'All right, I'm not going anywhere for a while but when the traffic moves I'll leave the car in the lay-by next to McDonald's and come back for you. You all right?'

'Yeah, I'm fine. I thought it was . . . I thought it was something to do with Milo at first, Dev.'

'I know, and I'm sorry I yelled at you. I'm just worried.'

The paramedics were waiting as the woman was rescued from the car, and Holly watched from her position on the bank, shivering. The fire service had parked an appliance in the scrubby field next to the bridge, and crew were carrying an orange stretcher slowly through the reeds. Surely it must have been an accident. Beth had been so calm, so composed. She kept repeating this to herself. But Dev's words had jolted her.

She could see the paramedics working on her now, and almost held her own breath as they got a line in, moving quickly around the body. Beth's face was a blur of white, her sodden dark hair tangled across the stretcher. A while later as she was wheeled into the ambulance Holly let out a long breath of relief. She was still alive; there was still hope.

The PC came back over to take a statement and soon the traffic was moving around the cordoned-off area where the car had left the road. The metal railings were stretched and broken, and it seemed impossible that the driver could have survived such a drop. Holly wondered whether to ring Tom, but decided the police could deal with it. Tom had been very quiet since the windows had been smashed and she'd like him to stay that way. As long as he was still trying to find Milo, and the flyers were knee-deep around the university, then she'd count him as having done his bit.

She was still shivering on the bank when Dev came loping back up the road. He spoke briefly to the police in charge of the cordon and was allowed through. She smiled stiffly, her face frozen, and he took her arm, leading her gently away to a section of wall that divided the riverbank from a rough, overgrown playground. They sat side by side, not speaking, watching the activity around the river. Another police car pulled up next to the fire engine, and a tall man got out. He studied the scene, his gaze sweeping Holly and Dev, moving on, then returning to them.

'DI Harper!' Dev called. 'Long time no see.'

Holly smiled, despite the fact she didn't feel like it at all. This whole Beth thing had left a nasty taste in her mouth, and now here was a man who had been more than part of her family for so long. Jayden's dad.

DI Harper spoke briefly with another officer before making his way over to the pair on the wall. Holly swung her legs, heels kicking the graffiti-decorated brickwork, her hands plunged deep into her pockets.

'Devril and Holly. What are you doing here?' DI Harper reached them. As usual the gentle voice was deceptive. Holly got the distinct impression he was deeply pissed off to see them at all.

'That woman who went into the river was my ex-husband's girlfriend, Beth,' Holly told him. Then, before she could stop herself: 'Is there any news on my son?'

He shook his head, eyes gleaming under the shaggy brows, his gaunt frame looking as though the icy breeze off the channel would sweep him away. 'I'm sorry but I don't have anything else to add.'

'What's your take on Milo's abduction? Coz we haven't seen you around recently,' Devril said.

The other man directed his laser-beam glare in Dev's direction. 'I can't say. Obviously I am keeping in close contact with Milo's case, but then again we have to run with a great many theories at this stage.'

'Shame Jay didn't keep in touch with you when he pissed off after Larissa's murder.' Dev clearly had something on his mind.

'Why would he?'

'You and he were always pretty close. More than me and you. He always had a lot to tell you, didn't he?'

There was a shout from the river and the DI pulled his coat collar higher. 'Sorry, I need to go. I don't know what you're driving at, Mr Mancini, but I suggest you think very carefully before you drag any past history into this. Our main priority is to find Holly's child, and I would encourage you to remember that before you start chasing any ghosts.'

Holly scowled at him. 'Wait a minute! I know you're Jayden's dad, so stop pretending all this has nothing to do with you personally. How could you do that to my family? My mum died because of you, and when Jay was in trouble, when he left after Larissa died, you did fuck-all. How could you let Jay take a child away and keep it to yourself?'

He took two long strides over to them, and leant down to Holly, face finally registering emotion. 'You know nothing about any of this, so stop trying to blame me for your misfortunes. And before you say it, I'm not counting your son missing as one of those. As I said, we have thrown heaven and earth and our very limited resources into finding Milo, as we would for any missing child.'

'So tell me. I can see you're needed down there, but tell me quickly now why I shouldn't hate you even more than I ever did?' she challenged, fury sending her jumping to her feet.

He was quiet for a moment, hands in pockets, looking at the ground, and then the cool grey eyes lifted to hers. 'I was in love with your mother. I tried so hard to persuade her to leave Donnie and come away with me, somewhere where she would be safe. When she got pregnant, Donnie had been away on business, so she knew Jayden was mine. But there was just enough doubt for Donnie to think he was the father.'

'And when my mum was killed? Why did you never get anyone banged up for it? If you really loved her you would've done something more.' She was crying now, angry tears wet on her icy cheeks.

'I couldn't prove anything. That's the trouble with this job, you need to have evidence, and although I had suspicions I had no proof. It nearly killed me to know . . .' He looked at her closely. 'I don't believe Donnie killed Sian, if that's what you were thinking.'

'Who did then?' Dev asked.

'I can't say.'

'Was it the Nicholls?' Holly said suddenly. 'You don't have to say anything, just don't answer.'

George Harper straightened up, rubbing his lower back, his face twisted with frustration. 'I tried to help Jayden after Sian died.'

'Dev and Jay were your little snitches,' Holly supplied.

He winced. 'Jayden found the courage to get away, to make a home for himself with Larissa. He seemed to be doing well, and he asked me how they could make a clean break. He'd been clean since Larissa had had the kids. They needed to escape completely and by now the Nicholls were getting close to finding out where he and Larissa were. I gave them a name and a price, someone who would help with new identities. Believe me, your brother had pulled himself out of a hole and he was a good father as far as I could see, or I would never have let him take my grandson.'

It took a moment to sink in. 'You knew. You helped Jay get away after Larissa's murder? And the dealer who said he was dead?' Holly asked, incredulous.

300

The police officer shook his head, as though to clear the memories. 'You can fill in the gaps. I'm retiring next month, so none of this matters anymore.'

'I could go and give a statement, tell them all about you covering up Jay's death, sleeping with an informant. Do you think they might stop your pension or something?' Holly couldn't believe he was being so blasé about this.

'I don't care. There's a lot you don't know about me, so please don't assume, Holly. Like I said, I loved your mother, and after she was killed there was nothing left for me apart from my job.'

Holly was speechless, remembering Donnie uttering those very same words as he raised a can of lager to his lips so many years ago.

'I hope I've been able to help Jayden and my grandson, but that's all. Now I really need to go – they're waiting for me.'

'One last thing,' Dev said, jumping stiffly off the wall. 'Have you been in touch with Jay all this time? Do you know here he and his son are now?'

George Harper pursed his lips. 'I haven't been in touch with Jayden since he returned to Westbourne. I had no idea he was coming back, and he hasn't made contact. Make of that what you will, but I'll admit it worries me.' He nodded curtly at them both, and walked away, buffeted by the wind, his coat billowing around him.

'What was all that about?' Holly asked. Actually talking to DI Harper, seeing his face soften when he talked about her mother, had put a new spin on her opinion of him, but she was still angry. 'Come on, let's go and grab a coffee from that van and then get back.'

The van in the lay-by produced hot coffee and rolls and then they climbed back into Dev's car. 'Jay would never talk about him or your mum, but they definitely had a slightly weird relationship. Now I think about it, I can see all the things I missed. The way Harper would give the best work to Jay and I'd get the

301

more dangerous stuff, or they'd meet up for a "debrief", and I'd be told later on. Gotta admit, more than once I thought old Harper fancied your brother.' He laughed.

'I find it fucking odd, looking at him thinking he had an affair with my mum, that he's Jay's dad. More than weird, but part of me can see that he did love her, and I can imagine her being stubborn and saying she had to stick with Donnie, whatever, or something. If she'd gone with Harper do you think she'd have been safe?' Holly asked. A group of kids were getting off a minibus and she tracked their progress, automatically checking for Milo's face.

'Yeah, I suppose. I don't know, but he tried to get Jayden and his son away from the Seaview and that's got to count for something. I think I believe him when he says he didn't know they were coming back. After all, if he gave them the chance to get away, he'd have been pissed they were going to ruin it all.' Dev pulled out back onto the main road.

Holly sat back and sipped her coffee, closing her eyes, banishing her brother, her mum, her dad, seeing nothing but her son's face.

***

Karen came round later that evening. Holly was touched that after her lifelong experience of the police being the opposing side, she was developing something like respect for the DC, and for Steph too.

She still managed to look immaculate, but her eyes were showing the strain. 'We are continuing to follow up all the leads. There were a couple of calls that came in after the reconstruction and your TV appeal.'

'What kind of calls?' Holly's heart sped up, but she was almost holding her breath. It would just take one tiny piece of important information to break the case, and she didn't care where it came from.

'First one was from a woman who lives at Blackwell Road.'

'That road backs onto the woods,' Holly said quickly. 'Sorry, you knew that obviously.'

'It's okay. She said that she saw a red Touareg parked outside the footpath when she let her dog out at 7.30 p.m. It's not unusual and she said they get a lot of evening dog walkers over there, but in the winter they generally stick to the well-lit areas. Anyway, she saw a man get out the car and go into the woods whilst she was waiting for her dog to do its business. When she looked out the window later the car was gone. She thinks that was after dinner so around 8.30 p.m. The times fit around when you said Milo was taken, but of course she didn't see him at all.'

'Okay, so that's good, right?' Holly said hopefully.

'The second caller said she was crossing a pedestrian crossing at around 8 p.m. and she nearly got run down by a car travelling fast along Gates Hill. She was furious because he busted a red light and nearly hit her. She remembers seeing a male driver, and a child who may have been wearing pyjamas like Milo's, in the front seats.'

'Why didn't she come forward before?' Holly was frustrated.

'She went away for a couple of days and only caught up with the news when she came back.'

'I suppose there aren't any traffic cameras on Gates Hill?' Holly queried.

The other woman shook her head. 'None until you get down past McDonald's, and the bridge.'

'Which is where Beth crashed. How is she? Is the baby okay?' Holly asked.

'I spoke to DI Harper and he says she and the baby are both fine. A touch of hypothermia and a few cuts and bruises but she's okay physically. She says that she swerved to avoid a rabbit running across the road and the car skidded on some ice.' Karen's expression remained neutral but Holly picked up a hint of disbelief in her tone.

'I was almost envious of her when she left my place, you know,'

Holly said eventually. 'She had the courage to tell you about Tom, to walk away, and she still had her baby. I remembered me at nineteen and what a mess I made of my life, and she was so in control and sussed.'

'Well, accidents do happen and it was a freezing morning. We'll check out her car, of course. There may have been some technical fault, that coupled with the icy road led her to lose control.'

'I should go and see her. I know it sounds awful but I just can't. Maybe I'll send her some flowers,' Holly said.

'I'm sure she'd appreciate that.' Karen spoke absently, and was watching her carefully. 'How are you coping?'

'Badly. My kid has been missing for a week now. I know what the statistics are, and I really wanted it to be Tom, or Niko or Jayden who had him, because in my heart I didn't believe any of them would hurt him. But now I can only think of Gareth Nicholls hurting him. Nobody else is left in the frame, are they? Does that sound crazy?'

'No, not at all and obviously I can't comment on the Nicholls connection, except to say that both Joey and Gareth have alibis.'

'Of course they do. Alibis for my mum's murder, for Bailey's murder, for Milo's abduction . . . They aren't stupid!'

'We are doing everything we can, and like I said following up all these leads. If I get any news I'll call you. I know it's hard but try and leave the search to us.'

'I have to keep looking too, or I'll go crazy,' Holly said.

Karen looked at her. 'We have officers on the ground everywhere. We are doing our very best, Holly.'

'So why hasn't he been found?' Holly said, raising her voice in exasperation, the pain making her throat raw. 'And Jayden's son seems to have just walked out of that foster carer's home. I suppose you haven't found him yet either? Assuming he did leave of his own free will?'

'We think so. I can't make any assumptions, but I think it's possible Jayden picked him up, which at least means he's safe.

If it was Jayden you saw at the hospital, we can take it that he's been keeping a close eye on his son. And your friend Cath told me about the call she made on the night of Larissa's murder,' Karen said, changing the subject with an almost physical effort.

Holly frowned but allowed herself to be distracted. 'Yeah. What are you getting at? That Jayden could still have thought it was me? It never came up in the investigation or the trial, because I was fucking terrified that it would come out, and it turns out Cathryn was too, for the same reason.'

'We're pursuing every single line of inquiry I can drag up, Holly, and I mean it.'

'I know.'

Holly shut the front door, feeling the emptiness of the house, the echoes she never normally heard, the dust already collecting in Milo's toys, and the stale, unused smell in his room. She sat on his bed, hugging his soft toys, including the Disney dolphin, breathing in his scent, allowing tears to roll. 'Where are you, Milo?' she said aloud, 'Are you safe?' But all she could see in her mind's eye was her brother driving away with two boys on the back seat . . . Perhaps?

***

Next morning, she went over to Cathryn's, updating her on all the police leads. They sat on the sofa, legs curled up, mugs in hand, and Holly relaxed slightly.

Cathryn's phone buzzed with a text and she picked it up, scrolling down and smiling. 'Ruby says she's moved Noah into her flat.'

'Oh.' She couldn't raise any interest in the fledgling relationship. Nothing mattered but her son.

Cathryn was tapping out a reply, and a few minutes later her phone buzzed again, and she showed Holly a selfie of the happy couple.'

'Cute. Good for them.' Holly limbs were limp and aching, like a doll with no will of its own. She nodded lethargically. She knew she wouldn't be able to eat, but it couldn't hurt.

The lack of news was grating on her, and she wandered home, slowly, dropping into the corner shop for milk, noting the posters of Milo plastered across the window and counter. Ignoring the curious stares she scuttled out again and trudged into the wind. The pavement was still icy from the previous night and even in gloves her fingers were numb. Was Milo warm?

She kept his face in her mind all the way home and then went straight to the shelves in the kitchen. She sat in front of them for a long time, allowing her mind to run over a timeline of Milo's life. He had been two weeks early, and Tom had been on a lecture tour. The rush into hospital, the wait until he was born, eventually by emergency C-section as his heart rate dropped. The photographs in front of her showed his as a toddler, first day at school, riding his bike without stabilisers, all the usual childhood milestones that parents love. It was inconceivable that it would stop there. That she would never be able to add photographs of his first day at senior school, his first car, maybe even university.

With each day that passed she felt hope fading, and although she tried to fight the thoughts away, she couldn't help but wonder if it was better not to know, than to have a body . . .

History was repeating itself in a way she had never imagined.

Chapter 36

The wind had whipped the frost into ice sculptures the next morning, but by lunchtime the air was warmer and the clouds heavy with rain. Holly, staring at Milo's wall, forgot about lunch until her phone rang. The number wasn't familiar and she answered cautiously, fully expecting another journalist.

'Hey, Holly! It's Noah. I hope you don't mind but I got your number off Rubes.'

'Oh. No of course not . . . Are you okay?'

'Yeah great. Look this is a bit weird but . . . Rubes told me to just ring and tell you, but I think I need to see you.'

'Noah?' He sounded nervous, even a bit scared.

'So everyone knows that your son is missing and I got this call earlier . . . You know I said my dad owned a building firm?'

'Yes.'

'Well, he does a bit of gambling and that on the side, and he's got shares in a few other businesses that aren't exactly legal.' Noah took a deep breath. 'It's not something I'm proud of and I've been trying to get him to go straight for years. The thing is, he knows some dodgy people, and . . .'

'*Noah!* Do you know something about Milo?'

'I think I might, but you can't tell the police. Come and meet

307

me in the car park behind Ruby's flat, and we can talk in my van. I'm really scared, Holly, but I can't let this go when there's a kid missing. I've got a phone with all sorts of shit on it. It's got a photo of your kid.'

Jesus! Holly thought fast. Noah, of all people, to come up with something. Did she trust him? Should she risk it? 'How did you get the phone? Actually, Noah let me speak to Ruby. Is she with you?'

'Yeah, she's right here.' There was a muffled conversation as the phone was passed over.

'Holly, I think Noah might really have something, but this man who gave him the information is terrified of being caught, and Noah is really freaked out too. The phone has got loads of texts, and photos, but some are definitely of Milo. He's okay, Holly, he's alive.' Ruby's voice was quick and anxious.

'Whose phone is it?' Holly said.

More muffled conversation. 'He says it was stolen off a bloke called Joey Nicholls. Holly. Look we are *so* freaked by this, so just be really careful, and we'll meet you round the back of my flat. Seriously, this bloke told Noah he'll get us in the shit if we tell the police, and he said to only tell you, and he said he'd be watching.'

'Who is this bloke – the one who stole the phone – and why did he give it to Noah?'

'Don't know, but he just said this is what we have to do to get Milo back safe. He said he saw the pictures on Joey's phone and he saw the photos of Milo on the TV.'

'All right, I'm coming.' Holly grabbed her coat. 'I'll be there in about ten minutes.'

Her fingers hovered over her contacts as she jogged through the housing estates, heading north, but she found herself calling Dev instead of Karen.

'Hi, Holly, you all right?'

She told him, breathlessly, words tumbling over one another, giving him Ruby's address.

'Sounds like a set-up to me. I'm at home so I can be with you in five?'

'No! I mean do come, but not to meet me. Can you just follow me and then if it doesn't look right call the police? If this is a chance to get Milo back . . .'

'*Really*? Holly, just wait for me and we can go together.'

'Please, Dev, this could be my chance to get Milo back and I can't blow it.'

'Okay. Try and slow down a bit and I'll get there just before you if I run.'

'Don't let him see you, Dev!'

'Be careful, for fuck's sake, girl.' His voice was rough with worry.

***

There was no sign of Dev as she made her way round the back of the block of flats, walking past a couple of parked vans, and skirting the garages. The weather was shit. Icy rain was pelting down now, and this part of town was rundown and desolate. Every muscle in her body was tense with fear and hope.

She heard Noah calling as she got to the wire fence, and he was standing by a white van next to the derelict playground. She walked over, treading carefully, wary, but unable to see how this could be a trap. Noah was tall and muscular, but although she was out of shape, she figured she could probably take him in a fight. Her bare fingers closed in fists. 'Why have you parked over here? Does Joey have Milo? Where's Ruby?'

'She's keeping a watch from the flat. Seriously, she's going to ring the police if anything goes wrong. I'm really sorry to freak you out, Holly, but I'm really scared myself. Look, can we sit in the van so nobody can see us and I'll show you the phone?' He did look terrified. All traces of his usual charm and cheek were gone and his cheeks were pale. He slid the side door open, looking quickly around.

Wary, Holly stuck her head in, blinking at the sudden darkness. But instead the van had what looked like sleeping bags, and on the floor she could see a body, face down sprawled in the dirt, one shoe off.

Something poked hard in her side, and her whole body was cramping, muscles spasming. She couldn't move, doubling over, falling. Her insides were being ripped apart. She was paralysed, trying to breathe but she couldn't take a breath. Terror took over, and she felt arms around her, gasping as something antiseptic and minty engulfed her nose and mouth. A gag, her heavy, rag doll limbs being tied. Her brain was fogging, heart pounding the way it did when she was very drunk. Holly tried to scream but her voice came out tinny and miles away. Everything was echoing and the rushing in her ears intensified, blackness swirling around her.

Chapter 37

'Hi, Holly, join the party.' Noah was sitting on a dusty chair, opposite her, waiting, watching. But he wasn't Noah; his whole demeanour had changed. The laughter had gone from his eyes, and his body was tense. In his right hand he casually held a gun.

The blackness swirled and she raised her head. She was lying on a concrete floor. She blinked hard, taking in her surroundings. A derelict warehouse, covered in dirt and graffiti. The air was sour and dusty, but she tasted salt on her lips. Rain spattered onto her upturned face, waking her properly, 'Where's Milo?' Nausea made her drop her head back to the ground.

'He's fine. He and Ethan are having a little party of their own. You don't think I'd hurt a kid, do you?' He shook his head. 'I thought you knew me better than that.'

'Ethan?' She wriggled her numb hands, and discovered they were tied at the wrists. Her ankles were also tightly bound, and she fought down a surge of panic. How could she rescue Milo if she'd let herself get caught?

'Jayden's kid.'

This was crazy. 'How do you know about Jayden? I don't understand why you've brought me here, but if you let me and Milo go, I won't say anything until you've got away,' she said.

Dev had said he would follow her, but had he got there in time? Her body felt odd, limp and pathetic, and her brain refused to work. Of course he would have done. She would have to trust he knew where she was, had called the police, because her phone had disappeared from her pocket. 'Tell me where Milo is.'

It was a feeble ploy and of course Noah just smiled pityingly. 'It isn't just you here, Holly, I've found some other partygoers. They aren't very lively at the moment, but I think they'll warm up.'

Far above, the skeleton of the highest level could be seen, open to the elements where some storm had torn a sizable hole in the corrugated asbestos roof, exposing metal beams, one of which hung, swinging dangerously, by what looked like a cluster of wires.

There was a kind of office area on this floor, and the wooden floorboards were relatively intact. An old desk and table, sheaves of yellow paperwork and a rotting red sofa were shoved at one end. On the other side were two more mattresses, in better condition than the sofa, blankets and a scrumpled McDonald's bag.

'Here's one of them.' Noah kicked Cathryn's body out from behind a stack of mouldering packing cases, and Holly bit back a scream.

But Cath seemed to be breathing, if comatose. Her wrists and ankles were bound with the same cable ties as Holly's and she had a gag taped over her mouth.

Bewildered, heart pounding with terror, Holly watched as Noah crossed the room, lanky and confident, and pulled away a dusty curtain. She'd assumed it hid more packing cases, but instead it concealed a kind of metal cage. It was some kind of goods lift for transporting materials to the different floors. The pulleys and mechanisms of the cage were up in the damaged roof area, but the cage door was padlocked shut, suspended a few inches above the floor.

The place stank of stale urine, filth and sweat, and every so often an icy breath of wind would sweep through the place, making the roof rattle.

But Holly was staring, unable to believe she wasn't dreaming. There were no goods wedged into the cage now. Instead it contained two men, tightly bound and gagged. They were squashed together, knees against their chests, with barely three feet between them. One of the men was Niko. The other . . .

'Jayden?' Holly's voice didn't seem to belong to her. She seemed to be floating above the scene, surely dreaming. But he was there. Older, greyer if it was possible, with dried blood on his face, and dirt smeared across his bare arms, her brother sat like a trapped animal.

Noah reached carefully though the bars and ripped the gaffer tape gags away. 'Now you can talk to me, boys. Look who's joined the party!'

'What the fuck is going on?' Holly got in first. 'Jayden, what's going on? Where's Milo, and your kid?'

Noah narrowed his eyes as Niko let forth a stream of expletives, but he let him run on until the other man ran out of breath. A thin line of saliva ran down the corner of Niko's mouth, dripping onto his bare chest. His bottom half was covered in a grubby tracksuit bottoms and he looked as though he'd been hauled out of bed.

'Holly,' Jayden said. His voice was cracking with emotion. 'Holly, you need to get Ethan and . . . and Milo.'

'Did you take Milo?' His eyes met hers, pleading. For a second there was nobody else in the room, until she drew a breath and addressed Noah. 'Is this about drugs? Or do Niko and Jayden owe you money or something?'

Noah shook his head. 'You really don't get it, do you?'

'We don't, so why the fuck don't you tell us, you arsehole?' Niko said. He was struggling furiously, clearly not realising it was futile, with his bonds, whilst Jayden sat still, watching, waiting.

'Don't do this, Noah. It isn't worth it.' Jayden spoke to Noah now, but his eyes were on Holly.

'You should be pleased. You've spent years planning this

moment, telling me how you wanted to see Niko beg for his life before you put a gun to his head and pulled the trigger.

Niko's eyes bulged with fear, but this time he spluttered out a few words. 'Why do you want to kill *me*, Jay? You stole my money, so it should be the other way around!'

Jayden spoke quietly. 'Larissa.' He licked cracked lips and cleared his throat. 'This is about Larissa, all of it.'

'It was Alexi and Roman who killed her!' He turned to Noah. 'Fuck me, did you have them killed? You did, didn't you? Both of you?' Never the sharpest, Niko seemed to be slowly realising he wasn't going to get out the warehouse alive.

'You found out where Jayden was. He owed you money, sure, and he'd screwed you over, but you're a nasty little shit, and you knew exactly what your arsehole brothers would do when they found him. That was your idea of revenge. You're pathetic,' Noah said.

Holly swallowed hard. The same night she had passed the message to Dev, the one he had never passed to Niko. Thank God he hadn't. But how was she involved?

'I didn't know they were going to kill her!' Niko's voice was a whine now. 'I honestly didn't. I wanted the money and I was pissed because I'd lost a load of customers when Jay fucked off, but that's as far as it went.'

He even managed to sound genuine, and it was the same story he had told the police, had told in court. His eyes fell on Cath's body as he spoke though, and Holly couldn't help feeling a twinge of respect that he was still protecting her.

'I don't understand where you come in,' Holly said to Noah. 'What does any of this matter to you? *Did* you take Milo? Where is he?' She was trying to get her head around this and failing.

He smiled at her. 'I can't believe you haven't figured it out yet.'

Holly looked over at her brother and he shrugged, but he was staring at her. She tried to smile at him but found she couldn't. The shock was freezing her face, her limbs. Jayden was alive, sitting just across the room. Her mind was blurry, and her body still felt shaky after being hit with what must have been a Taser. Had Noah drugged her too? Cautiously, she rubbed her cold arms, feeling along the skin for needle marks. He could have done anything whilst she was out cold. 'Where's Milo?'

'You're like a broken record. Later, Holly, later.' Noah smiled round at them all and moved over to the desk. He stood like a judge and jury, raised a bottle of vodka to his lips and took a swig. Taking a party popper from his pocket, he let it off with a crack and the coloured paper blew high into the air, before falling slowly, dancing on the cold air. 'I got this tattoo a few years ago. Holly, have a look and tell me if you like it?' He walked over to her and bent down, pulling his top low to expose the bare skin.

Bewildered, she peered at his shoulder. An intertwined heart and rose, with a name across the middle: *Larissa*.

He nodded slowly. 'Larissa was *my* fiancée. *My girl.* Twelve years ago, I should have been getting married. She was perfect, beautiful, and she was mine. I loved her from the moment we first met, but you ruined our lives.'

Holly was staring at Jay, watching the confusion, the horror in his face, realising with a jolt that he had also been duped by Noah.

'It's taken me a long time to get to this point. I've had to pay money, pretend to like the bastard who stole my girl – yes Jayden, it took me a long time to track you down. That DI Harper was worth the cash, wasn't he? I wondered for a long time how the hell it was all going to work, but then I realised I was smarter than all of you. You were so desperate for revenge, you let your guard down – you are pathetic.'

'Jesus,' said Niko, his eyes bulging with fear at these latest revelations.

'Amen to that,' Noah said, moving back to his desk and picking up the bottle. 'I was engaged to Larissa, and we were in love. She was the only one with any quality, so once I got her away from her mum, who incidentally didn't give a shit and thought

315

Larissa had just moved out with her new boyfriend, I brought her down south with the other girls.' He frowned. 'She was in one of the guest houses we ran in Westbourne, but of course she never worked. Her house was one of the busiest, and Joey said she could host the parties and make herself useful.'

'Wait a minute. You *worked* for the Nicholls and trafficked those girls down from Yorkshire? That's where the other yard is, isn't it? It was *you*?' Holly couldn't fathom the switch from the Noah she knew at work, saving lives, to this monster who had stolen girls, children, to work in brothels for Gareth and Joey.

'It was easy. There are so many fucking stupid, lost little girls looking for fairy-tale endings to their shitty lives. I tell them all that I love them, that I'll look after them, marry them, whatever it takes. I give them enough time to tell any family or friends that they've got a serious boyfriend, sowing the seeds for the time they disappear, and then when they do, social services, the police do a cursory search, discover another teenage runaway and that's it.'

'What about the police? You can't tell me girls are just vanishing and they aren't looking?' Holly thought of the massive search for Milo.

'I'm not stupid. Do you have any idea how many teenagers go missing every year? How many girls run away with their boyfriends? Most of them aren't ever found,' Noah informed her smugly. 'These are kids who won't be missed.'

'She hated it! She thought you actually cared about her, and then she realised it was all a game to you,' Jayden said suddenly. 'Larissa was terrified, and she wasn't in love with you, she just did what she was told because she was afraid. She saw the other girls raped by the clients, saw the abuse they had to put up with and you told her that marrying you was the only way out.'

'Bullshit! Once we were married, we were going to move away and start out somewhere new. But she started to become distant, cool with me. I wasn't having that so I told her we'd get married sooner. I was worried she was pregnant already,' Noah spat back.

'She was the only one I was serious about, and she was perfect. Right from the day I first saw her, I knew she was the one.'

'But how could you do it? How could you work for the Nicholls?' Holly queried.

'I'm family, Holly. Noah is just a middle name. Gareth is my dad, but I stayed with my mum in Bradford, so we wouldn't have met. Shame really, I would've liked to have seen you fight, Holly. I hear you were really good. Anyway, I'm part of one, big happy family.' He was grinning now. 'I started running the girls when I was eighteen, and Gareth was dead proud.'

'Jesus . . .' Holly was lost for words. 'I never would have guessed it was you, that you're one of *them*. Fucking Nicholls. You lot are like a plague of evil. Whenever there's shit going on, one of you turns up.'

'I tracked Jayden down around three years ago. He's been in Glasgow, but maybe you already figured that out? I got him to trust me, while we waited for Niko to be released. I persuaded Jayden to let me in on his plan.'

'Jayden?' Holly stared at her brother but he just shrugged. Holly supposed she could see how clever Noah was at switching roles. After all, he'd fooled her totally, so it was little surprise Jay was convinced, too.

'I pretended that I was happy to help, that I'd lost my fiancée to drugs, my kids were in care, that I was a recovering addict with a few useful contacts. I realised that Jayden was as single-minded as I was about killing Niko, even though he was also a loser who boozed the whole time and didn't look after his kid properly. Larissa's boy deserved better. Ethan's a good kid, and he's been brought up knowing his dad was going to get revenge on the fuckers who killed his mum and his baby sister.'

'But I didn't kill her . . .' Niko said plaintively.

'So you keep saying. But you did. Oh, I know it was Alexi and Roman who did the actual killing, and they got banged up for it, didn't they? And then they both died.' Noah grinned. 'That took me a few years to accomplish, but I did it. I guess the police

317

already found out that I paid Kelly's family quite a lot of money for him to commit the murders. He had no problems doing it, he was a Nicholls cousin on Gareth's mum's side so he knew about family loyalty, and he wanted to make sure his family would be looked after once he was gone. Nice bloke, Kelly. And of course he was terminally ill, so he had nothing to lose.'

'Why not stop there? They were the ones who killed Larissa and the baby,' Holly said, trying to stop her voice from trembling.

'Then I went after Jayden because he stole my girl. Niko because he sent his animals after her, but how did Niko know where to find Jayden? Did he go looking, or find out accidentally? Or did someone tell him?' Noah took a gun from his jacket pocket and caressed the barrel, a tiny smile lighting his lips.

Holy shivered, a line of ice cracking along her spine. But Noah walked over to Cathryn and slapped her face. 'Time to wake up! Shall I pour her a drink, Holly?'

'Let her go. She's got five kids, for fuck's sake. Please don't hurt her,' Niko said. He was struggling against the bars again, banging his feet against the cage, making is sway alarmingly. A rusty cage for two guilty birds.

Cath was blinking, eyes adjusting to the light, shaking her head, and as reality hit she began to struggle in Noah's arms. 'What the fuck is this? Holly? *Noah?*'

'She can have a little drink before we chat,' Noah said, grabbing the bottle of vodka and pinning Cath to the wall he forced it down her throat. She was choking and spluttering, fists beating frantically as she tried to turn her head away.

Holly was screaming at him to stop, and Jayden was yelling too. Niko swung the cage, beating at the bars.

Finally Noah released his captive and she fell sobbing and gasping to the floor. He watched her dispassionately, waiting until she had regained her breath before he spoke again. 'Cathryn is going to tell us all how Niko knew where to find Larissa and Jayden, aren't you, Cathryn?'

She raised her head, arms braced, eyes wild. 'What the fuck is going on? Noah, what are you doing for fuck's sake? *And Jayden!*'

'Talk to us, Cathryn. It's only polite when you're at a party. Mind you, it won't be a great one for you because you seemed to have shagged most of us already.'

'Fuck off,' Cathryn said, catching sight of Holly, tied to the sofa. 'Holly? What the fuck is going on? Where's Milo?'

'Who told Niko where to find Larissa and Jayden?' Noah snapped at her.

Shock registered on her face and she opened her mouth, then closed it again, still staring at the two men in the cage. Holly couldn't blame her. She still couldn't believe her brother was sitting captive, metres from where she was tied up.

When she still didn't answer, he smiled. 'Give it up, Cathryn, Niko already told me. Oh, he didn't mean too, but he and Jayden have already been roommates for two days, so they had a nice chat about exactly what happened the night Larissa was murdered. I recorded their touching conversation, so I know . . . but it ends here. This is the farewell party, the end game, the going-away present, whatever you want to call it.'

'I didn't mean . . . I was just pissed off. I saw you by accident when I was on the way to the baby clinic. I mean, fuck's sake Jayden, you'd just vanished leaving me with your kids, and I was mad at you. So I followed you on the bus, saw Larissa holding a baby, kissing you as you went inside the flat. I was fuming. You'd gone and shacked up with someone else, you weren't paying child support – how do you think I felt?' Cathryn's voice was quiet, so quiet Holly had to strain to hear her.

'So you told Niko where to find me?' Jayden's voice was flat. 'I hoped Niko was lying when he said it was you.'

'After you left, me and Niko got together. I knew how much he hated you, and how you still owed him money. You just ditched me, after you met Larissa, but you already had two kids for fuck's sake. Just because you thought you'd found someone

319

better, you pissed off,' Cath spat at him, rage and terror evident in her thin face.

Noah was watching everyone argue, smiling slightly to himself.

Holly kept her eye on Noah's gun. If he started shooting, it was going to be a blood bath. She wriggled a little, slowly back towards the sofa, hoping the friction might fray the rope around her wrists. She could feel they were sticky with blood, but she kept easing backwards, eyes darting from the metal staircase to the goods cage. The sofa was close to the edge of the floor, and the whole level seemed to be only bordered by a set of railings. There was a long drop, maybe twenty feet to the next level, and to a load more packing cases and cardboard. It would be a risk, but if she could roll that way and fall, he might either miss her or give her up as dead. The other choice was to wait while he killed her at point-blank range. She had no doubt that was what Noah intended, and now she knew, she could see Gareth marked indelibly across his features. How had she not noticed before?

She had to hold on to the fact that he had shown affection and concern for Larissa's son. It was the only thing to believe – that he wouldn't have hurt the boys even though he had clearly abducted Milo.

Noah had another swig, and chucked the bottle onto the table, where it rolled, spilling alcohol across the filthy surface before falling to the floor and smashing. Shards of glass landed at Holly's feet and she flinched, trying to protect her face. For a second she was back in the car crash, screaming for her son, pinpricks of pain dotting her face. Noah aimed the gun at Niko, who screamed.

'So why is Holly here? Why did you take Milo?' Jayden asked desperately. 'If you're doing this for Larissa, where does Holly come in?'

'Holly found Larissa but she didn't save her life, did she?'

'I tried!'

'They played the call at the trial. You wouldn't help her, even though they told you to. That woman was telling you how to do

CPR and you said, "I froze, and I just couldn't touch her. I'm sorry." That's what *you said*, Holly. Don't worry, I'm not going to kill you. I would never kill a mother, but you needed to suffer, to understand what you might have done. You could have saved her, redeemed your family. But you're as weak and pathetic as your dad and brother. It was easy to get a job working alongside you. I have a few sets of identification and Noah Jenks doesn't have a criminal record, and he's been working for a construction firm in Dublin for the last eight years. Nice and clean.'

'Where is Milo, Noah? I'm sorry I didn't do the CPR, and I regret it, but the police said later that when they worked out the timing, she was already dead. It wouldn't have done any good!'

'Oh, stop whining. I've already explained that you need to be held accountable, for the part you played, or rather, the part you didn't play. You aren't listening! Your kid's in the van with Ethan. They're fine. They're sleeping. But you don't deserve to raise a child. Bloody women. Larissa was never like you lot. She never whined.' His face clouded with emotion and regret.

'What do you mean sleeping? What have you given them?' Holly choked on the words, struggling with her tied wrists and ankles. *'Noah, for fuck's sake!'*

'Noah, just let us go and we can work something out. How much do you want? Your cash, gear, name it and we'll get it for you.' Niko was talking fast, his face beaded with sweat.

But Noah shook his head. 'Now for the main event. God, I've looked forward to this.' He slid open a drawer in the desk and pulled out two knives. 'Niko and Jayden, you each get one of these and whoever wins the fight gets to live. That's pretty fair, isn't it?'

321

Chapter 38

Cathryn put her head down, arms around her knees, burying her face, and Holly found she was shaking so much her teeth were chattering. Surely they wouldn't do it? But what a choice to make. She found herself praying, hoping that Dev had seen Noah take her, had rung Karen, that even now the police might be on their way over . . . And what about Ruby? She didn't dare ask what had happened to her friend, not now when she knew that Noah could be as ruthless as his dad.

But Noah was talking again. 'Come on, Jayden, be a man. This is what you've always dreamt of! All those years of planning . . . Remember the buzz you got when Alexi and Roman were killed. Larissa was proud, wasn't she? Well, now she'll be even happier when she realises you're going to take out the fucker who was responsible for sending those murderers over to the flat.'

Holly tried to speak, but her mouth was dry. She caught both men's expressions of horror. Whatever her brother had intended for Niko, he clearly hadn't anticipated delivering the deathblow himself.

Noah was smiling again, moving towards the cage, when a phone rang. They all froze, before Noah pulled his mobile out of his pocket. He studied the screen and frowned briefly. 'Don't go anywhere before the party games, will you? I just need to take this . . .'

He walked to the top of the staircase, leaning against it, talking into his phone, his quick eyes missing nothing.

'We need to get out of here,' Cath hissed, writhing against her bonds. Her long blonde hair was matted and filthy, and her face was wet with blood and tears. A large bruise was spreading across her left cheek. 'Quick, Holly, we can get that broken glass from the bottle . . .'

Holly began to move, very slowly, mindful of Noah's watchful eye. The gun was back in his pocket, and he was arguing into his phone. There was a large shard of glass touching her foot. If she could slide round and get it into hands, she might be able to cut the rope.

The men, imprisoned in their cage, watched her. Niko was still rattling the bars, and at one point Noah shouted at him to shut the fuck up, cupping a hand over his ear and moving further away until he was leaning on the gantry railings.

Cath, cottoning on, began to talk, asking Jayden why he had come back, directing attention away from Holly. 'What happened the night Holly's car crashed? Was that you?'

Holly had the glass now, and she winced at the sharp pain as it cut her finger. Very carefully, she began to slide it up and down against the knots that bound her wrists. Sweat was pouring down her back, beads dropping from her forehead into her eyes, making them sting. Her face was wet and itchy, but she persevered.

'Yeah, it was me. I drove down with Noah and Ethan, and we stayed up with my mate in Panfield. Bailey saw me, didn't he? I was sure it was him with that red hair, even after all this time, so I scarpered.'

Holly tried to make her voice sound normal, freezing, as Noah's gaze swung around the floor, resting on each of his captives in turn. 'He did, and he told Dev you were back.'

'Me and Noah started checking up on all of you, and he went

after Niko one night to see how things were, while me and Ethan followed you after you took Milo to his rugby practice. I . . . I was having a few doubts about Noah. Not anything serious, but just enough for me to see that maybe bringing Ethan back to the Seaview into all this wasn't such a great idea. It was always the plan, you see, but when we got back . . .'

'You ran her off the road?' Cath said.

'I didn't mean to. Noah was with us most of the time, but I watched how Holly was with her kid, and I could see that perhaps she might be the one to have Ethan for me in case something went wrong with the plan. I know it sounds crazy, but it was a spur-of-the-moment thing. I flashed my lights, trying to get her to pull over, but then there was a van coming the other way, and something made her swerve off the road. Jesus! I slammed on the brakes and we spun off too. Ethan was next to me in the passenger seat, but the windscreen shattered as we struck something, and then he was bleeding. The airbags went off and I was trying to check if he was breathing.'

Jayden was gabbling now, his hands clenched on the bars of the cage. 'I slid down the bank to see if Holly was okay, and at first I thought she was dead, but when I found she and Milo were just unconscious it seemed like it was meant to be. I couldn't take Ethan to hospital myself, but I could leave him with Holly and ring the ambulance myself. I had a burner phone so I used that. The number was untraceable and I chucked the phone afterwards so the police would never know.'

The glass slid neatly through the last piece of rope and Holly massaged her wrists, feeling blood flow back into her hands. She had no idea what she was going to do now, but she caught Cath's eye and nodded. Her friend moved slightly until she blocked Noah's line of vision, even whilst they all pretended to be spellbound by Jayden's story. Holly found she could hardly take in what her brother was saying. On one hand, it was a relief to know what really happened that night, but on the other, they were about to

324

be killed or at least injured, and if she understood Noah rightly, he was going to take both kids with him when he left.

Stretching out a cautious hand, Holly started to saw at the ropes around her ankles. Noah was still listening to whoever was on the phone, his free hand tapping his pocket idly.

Niko was talking again, loudly and furiously. 'It was in the past, Jay. All this stuff you've brought up was in the past. I'm sorry about your girl and the baby, but like I said it wasn't me. You've screwed up my life by stealing my cash, and now that fucker over there, who *you* brought down to Westbourne, is going to kill us and abduct a couple of kids.'

'I'm sorry, Niko. I'm sorry it came to this, but you don't understand what it was like after Larissa was murdered. My baby girl was dead, and her mother, and although at first all I could think of was keeping Ethan safe and getting away, it got to me. I had nightmares, flashbacks the whole time and instead of getting better they got worse. The only way I could get through each day was by getting hammered. I knew I was barely coping, so I came up with the plan. It helped me get through day-to-day stuff, kept Larissa alive in my head, in Ethan's. I don't know if I would actually have gone through with it if I hadn't met Noah, and that's the truth.'

'And now? You see what you've done to us all? If it wasn't bad enough having Gareth in Westbourne, now his insane son has done for all of us,' Niko complained, rattling the bars again. 'Do something, Jayden, or say something. Offer him the money you've got stashed and do a deal.'

Jayden shook his head sadly. His face was grey and his expression one of abject misery. 'He doesn't want anything except his revenge. If this was Joey, or even Gareth, we could have cut a deal – they always like a bit of business – but for Noah, this isn't about money or even justice. This is about blood.'

'Don't fucking give up! What about us? Do you know what the Nicholls do to women? He might not be going to kill us but you heard what he said!' Cath said shrilly, raising her voice so that Noah looked at her.

Holly cut through the last bit of rope as Noah finished his call. She bunched her legs under her, arranging the rope around her wrists and ankles, ready for a moment when she could attack him. She was fairly confident that if he came close she would be able to tackle him before he pulled a gun. If he had a knife he might have a chance to use it, but she didn't care. She knew she would fight to the death as much as the boys were going to have to, for her son.

This was going to be it, her last fight. Without ropes or referees, without gloves or timers, she was going to fight not just for her life, but for all of them. Her muscles quivered, but she arranged her face into an expression of passive terror and let her old instincts rise.

326

Chapter 39

'Sorry about that. Just a little business with my dad.' Noah stashed his phone, walked over to the cage, and posted the knives in. He barely looked at the two women as they crouched on the floor, Cath still shielding Holly.

Instinctively, both men scrabbled for the knives, clenching the weapons in their fists, eyeing each other. But something was missing. The venom had faded, and Holly felt a surge of hope, instantly quenched as she remembered Noah's gun. Neither of the men in the cage made a move to stab the other, despite the fact they were barely two feet apart.

'Don't kill him, Jay!' Cath shouted suddenly and Noah scowled at her.

'Come on, get on with it,' he shouted in frustration. 'Jayden, this bastard is part of the plan, he's responsible for Larissa's death! This is what you've waited years to do, and I've given you the weapon. Do it!' He pulled his gun out, pointing it at the cage.

There was a sudden, swift movement, like a snake striking, and Holly cried out. It was hard to see what had happened, because Niko had reacted as soon as her brother moved but it looked as though Jayden had flicked the knife around and stabbed himself in the stomach, gritting his teeth as the bade bit deep into his belly.

'*No!*' Noah shouted. 'That's not how it's meant to work!'

But Jayden, dragging the knife from his belly, now slashed both wrists, before falling back against the cage bars, leaving Niko crouched over him, his own face registering horror.

'Cheats!' Noah yelled. 'You fucking pathetic loser, Jayden. You bottled it!'

'He's bleeding out! You need to get us out of here,' Niko was saying, panic in his voice. 'Noah for fuck's sake, get us out of here.'

'You want him dead. This makes it easier for you, doesn't it?' Noah told him, making no effort to do anything.

'We've been locked up for two days. Do you think we haven't had enough time to kill each other if we were going to?' Niko said. 'You made a big mistake doing that. We made peace. It's done now so fuck you, Nicholls.'

'You made up? How pathetic. How utterly pathetic.' Noah's scorn cut across his words and he lifted his, gun. 'Luckily Larissa can rely on me.'

'No! Please, Noah,' Holly said hoarsely. To have found and then lost her brother in a matter of hours would be the ultimate irony. Noah was walking back towards the desk, past Cath, and now he was level with her, his back was turned.

She sprang like a hunting cat, swinging her right fist, feeling it connect, propelling herself forward.

Noah must have sensed her movement because he was turning as she hit him. The gun fell to the floor with a sharp metallic click, but she hardly noticed. She was immersed in the fight, delivering a quick upper cut that made blood pour from Noah's mouth. Seconds later he hit home with a blow to the side of her head. He wasn't trained, which gave her a slight advantage, outweighed by the fact he was physically bigger and stronger.

Gasping for breath, sweat dripping into her eyes, her hair, loosened from its ponytail fell heavy and wet across her shoulders.

She went in for another shot, dancing on the balls of her feet, circling, jabbing when she could, never giving him a moment to pull the knife she felt sure he had.

He launched himself at her, grappling, trying to pin her arms, but she raised a quick knee and he released her, hands to his groin, bent double. But whilst this gave her a momentary advantage, and she rained blows down on his head, it also gave him the chance he needed to stagger over to the desk and yank a jack knife from underneath the ancient paperwork. The brittle yellow sheaves of paper flew up in the air, covered them both as he lunged forward.

Holly could hear the other captives yelling her name. It was the roar of a home crowd, and without this dirty new addition to the fight, she might have won. As it was she felt the knife slide home, pain flaring between her ribs, as they twisted and grappled, her hand closing on his wrist, pulling it away with a massive effort. Both their muscles shaking, eyes level and glazed. But as the knife jabbed again, Holly felt like her stomach and shoulder were burning, as though red-hot pokers had been stuck into her body. She was still going, but she was beaten.

Blood was running down her forearms where she tried to defend herself, making the floor slippery and treacherous. Cath was screaming now, rolling herself across the floor, trying to trip Noah. It was over. As Holly raised a hand to dash blood from her eyes, she misjudged a lunge and fell. He was on her in an instant, pinning her arms, holding the knife to her throat.

Holly could feel his hot breath on her cheek as he pulled her hair, forcing her head back, exposing her throat. Her lungs were burning, and her whole body shook with exhaustion and pain.

Noah, also gasping for breath, dragged her towards the packing cases, the knife still at her throat as he yanked a couple of cable ties from the debris and wrapped them around her wrists. Then he gave her a vicious shove that knocked her off her feet. Before she could do anything her ankles were bound again, Noah yanking the cable ties so tight they bit into her flesh.

She made no sound, peering at him through the blood. She had failed. She had lost a fight, even if it was a dirty one.

'You fucking evil bitch!' Noah told her when he could speak again. His face was swelling, both eyes showing signs of bruising, and like Holly, his clothing was torn and slick with sweat. 'My dad told me about your mum, how she was a mouthy bitch and didn't know how to do what she was told.'

Noah crouched next to her, knife poised, and she looked straight into his eyes, mouth set, chin up. No way was she going to give him thrills by pleading for her life. For others yes, but if this was Milo's legacy, she was going down as a real Hughes.

He spat suddenly and a bit of tooth bounced across the concrete floor. 'You've wasted enough time, and I need to go now, but first . . .' He took hold of her T-shirt and yanked it hard enough to tear the material, leaving her upper arm bare. Taking the knife he made two quick slashes, and Holly winced.

'Now look at it.' He put a hand to her chin, forcing her head down, so she dropped her eyes. A bloody "L" was carved into her arm, adding to the prolific wounds across her body. She was beginning to feel woozy, from exhaustion, terror and blood loss.

'So you've had your revenge, now let the kids go,' she said wearily.

'Shut up. Your kid might be okay at the moment, but I could walk out there and . . .' He made a slicing motion with the knife. The gun was back in his pocket, and he seemed to be in a hurry, glancing at his watch, frowning round at them all. 'I told you, I need to go. Let's wrap this party up.'

Holly quit talking, moving, and lay watching her brother die, feeling her own blood ebb from her body. Cath was sobbing, muffled, strangled sobs into her hands.

Noah walked over to Cath now. 'You next, you slag. I know what happened between you and Joey. Jesus, you'd shag anything that moved, wouldn't you? This might help you think twice . . .'

Cath screamed, high and terrified as Noah gripped her chin, taking his knife and slashing an "L" just as he had done to Holly.

But on Cath he sliced the letter on her cheek. Blood oozed from the wound, dripping onto her shoulder, and she froze, the horror of what he had done overriding her pain.

Unheeded, Niko continued to babble, his own knife still in his hand. He bent over Jayden's body, fumbling with his shirt. Was he trying to help? That might mean Jay was still alive, Holly mentally crossed her fingers, hope rising. It almost looked like he was pushing Niko off, but Niko had a hand on Jayden's belly, pressing down on the wound. Was he helping or was he helping him die? It was impossible to tell.

Noah, satisfied with his work on the two women, turned to the cage and raised his gun. 'Time's up. I'll put Jayden out of his misery first.'

'Dad!' A child's voice made them freeze, and footsteps clanked on the metal walkway. *'No!'*

'Ethan!' Noah snapped. 'I told you to wait in the van.'

But the child never wavered, his dark eyes taking in the two women, the two men apparently struggling in the cage, Noah presiding over the gathering. Then he raised his hand and pulled the trigger.

Holly gasped, her whole body shaking with horror. The child handled the gun with calm efficiency, as though he had done it many times before.

There was a crack and two gunshots echoed around the warehouse, deafening the captives. Blood splattered across the wall to the side of the cage and Niko slumped to the ground, his body covering Jayden's.

'Dad!' Ethan moved towards the cage now as Holly yelled at him to watch out. He spun round as Noah dived for his gun hand, trying to wrestle the weapon away.

'Noah, don't be stupid. He's a kid!' Cathryn shouted. But Noah had misjudged the boy and as his hand closed on the child's arm some sixth sense must have alerted the boy to the danger and he fired for the second time.

Noah staggered back, clutching his chest, and Ethan, with trembling hands, aimed the gun at him again. But he never fired the next shot. Even in the dim light Holly could see blood spurting from Noah's body, and he collapsed, lying still within seconds. The pool of red spread ever wider, gleaming in the light of the torches. So much blood.

The warehouse was silent, as Holly, Cath and Ethan stared at one another, paralysed with shock.

Ethan ran over to the cage, yanking at the padlock, pushing his arms through the bars to reach Jayden. His footprints, sticky with blood, left dark tracks on the floor, and the sour, sickly smell of blood and excrement filled the mouldy air.

Cathryn was vomiting, trying to get up. 'We've got to get out of here! We need to get help.'

'My dad's dead!' Ethan cried out. 'He's got no pulse and there's so much blood. He's dead!'

Holly's heart wrenched for him, for herself, but she could only think of Milo. She wriggled slowly into sitting position. 'Ethan? Ethan, I'm so sorry that your dad is dead. Please could you help me to cut these ties? There's a knife on the floor over by the sofa. Please, tell me if Milo's okay?'

The boy stood watching her. His face was white and pinched, bones outlined like a baby bird's. 'Milo's mum,' he said, and then, very slowly he walked over to the table, and picked up the knife. In his other hand he still carried the gun.

'That's right, leave the gun on the table and come over here,' Holly told the boy, carefully keeping her voice calm and even. Cath said nothing, but she could hear her friend's gasping little sobs as Ethan made his way slowly over to Holly.

There was another shout, this time from outside the building, and Holly held her breath. Ethan stopped, startled, gripping the knife, looking back at Noah's body, at the grotesque figures entwined in the cage.

'*Police!*'

'Ethan, it's okay, keeping coming to me. Is Milo okay? *Is he outside?*' Holly said urgently, as the boy slid the knife between the cable ties on her wrists. His hands were shaking, and he bit his lip with concentration, but he carried on slicing until she was free. 'Thank you. *Ethan, where is Milo?*' she said urgently.

He blinked at her, his face almost grey with shock now, and his eyes bright with tears. But this was one self-possessed kid. Either that or he was so used to violence that the deaths he had just witnessed were nothing out of the ordinary, 'My dad's dead, Holly.'

'I know, darling . . . I'm sorry.' The endearment was out before she realised. 'I know . . . It wasn't your fault, any of it. Please, Ethan, where is Milo?' The death of her brother and the revelations of betrayal were nothing compared to her son. She could see firearms officers swarming around the floor below, hear shouts as they searched.

'Yeah, he's in the van. I told him not to come in because he's got that broken leg.'

'Where's the van? Is it here?'

The boy pointed towards a set of double doors, at the other end of the floor space. It was set below a rusting sign that read 'LOADING BAY 1'.

'Go out there and the van's under the trees.' He turned away from her now and began to walk slowly towards the dead bodies, brushing past Cath as though she didn't exist.

***

Quickly, as police officers began to make their way up the metal gantries, Holly stumbled across the floor, pushing her way through the rubbish to the doors. She shoved them and to her surprise they creaked open with minimal effort, like they had been in use recently. Outside was a concrete ramp that she supposed must have been used for goods deliveries at some point. Steep steps took her down to the ground level. The flash of blue lights almost blinded her, and her wounds were agony. Holly looked around wildly, checking out the shadowed, overgrown car park, gasping through her tears. Clamping a hand to her stomach in a helpless attempt to stem the blood flow, she started forward.

Police cars and uniformed officers, some of them armed, were ringed around the main buildings, and as she staggered faster someone caught her arm, and gently pulled her to a halt.

'Holly! What's happened?' Karen was out of breath, her face red from exertion. 'Is everyone safe? Where's Milo?'

Holly tugged her arm free. 'Milo! He's in a white van somewhere in the car park.' She looked helplessly around at the huge area. 'Ethan knows where the van is. You need to bring him out! Noah's dead, and Jayden, I think . . .' She hadn't anticipated not being able to find the van, had expected it to be parked fairly close the main building.

'Okay, we've got officers sealing off the whole industrial estate, so we *will* find him. Holly you're hurt. Get the paramedics to sort you out and we'll find Milo.' Karen glanced around at the vast shadowed area. Around the buildings, powerful searchlights had been set up, bathing the scene in an eerie whiteness, rinsing the colour from everything. She signalled to a uniformed officer and quickly briefed him. The crackle of radios, the shouts and the sound of vehicles filled the industrial estate.

The white van was parked away under the overhanging trees, near to the fence that led to the railway line. More police cars were arriving towards the front of the yard and the night air was filled with the sound of shouts, sirens, and patterned with flashing blue lights.

As they surged forward, Karen swept her own powerful torch across the shadows that jostled around the edges of the searchlight. Further up, parked in amongst a huddle of rusting cars and the skeletons of several double decker buses, Holly could see the rear bumper of the van. The registration began with RH. It was the van she had seen parked behind Ruby's flats. The van that may or may not have contained a body hidden under the sacking.

Ignoring the shouts behind her, Holly was off across the concrete, and down another ramp, slipping in her haste, limping over the broken concrete towards the vehicle. Karen was shouting her name as she reached the van, panting. She ran round to the side, scrabbling for the door handle. It was locked and she went to the rear doors. Her hands were shaking, teeth chattering, as the handles refused to budge.

In desperation she picked up a broken brick and went back to the driver's door. Without hesitating she hefted the brick through the glass. The driver's window shattered and she reached in, scrabbling for the door handle, scraping her bare arm on the broken shards of glass.

'*Holly!*'

She thought it was Karen yelling, but she didn't care. Holly yanked the door open, climbing onto the seats, pushing at the bulkhead between the driver's seats and the rear, shouting his name.

Remembering from childhood her dad's customised vans, Holly's frantic fingers met a lever and she yanked it with all her strength. Thank God, as with Donnie's vans, this one had a partially collapsible bulkhead, allowing for access to the rear whilst out on the road. She scrambled over the seats to the rear of the van. He was lying on a grubby blanket, hands and feet tied, eyes closed. His plaster cast glimmered white in the dim light.

'*Milo?* Milo, can you hear me?'

His eyelids flickered as Holly tried frantically so see in the dim light, to check if he had any injuries. She leant over and pulled at the side door until it slid open on rusty runners. The harsh white light from the security floodlights poured in and Karen was running towards her.

Milo was trying to say something, and Holly bent close. His face was cold, but his breath was warm on her cheek. 'Mum? I've been waiting for so long . . . Where's Ethan?'

She pulled him gently into her arms, sitting and holding him close, feeling his soft hair, the warmth of his body. He was alive, that was all that mattered. Tears tore her body apart and she sobbed with him, clinging to her son, stroking his head over and over again.

When she looked up, the paramedics were hurrying towards her and Karen was standing at her shoulder, smiling, icy blue eyes surprisingly bright with emotion.

'Holly!' Another familiar voice broke through the clamour of the emergency services, and she turned to see Dev running across the parking area.

She was holding her son, eyes momentarily closed, when she felt a hand on her arm. She smiled as Dev leant down and kissed her, smoothing a hand over the boy's head.

'Fuck, Holly, I thought I'd lost you then, and Milo too.' His voice was shaking and he was out of breath.

'You found us.'

'I was so close behind, but not near enough to help. I saw you talking to Noah, but when he Tasered you and shoved you in the van I was too far away to get to you. So I ran after it as far as I could, then got back to my car and followed you when the van pulled away from the Buckly traffic lights. That was dead lucky he caught a red light or I'd never have caught up. I really wasn't sure what the fuck was going on, so I watched and waited for a chance to grab you, but that bloke, Noah, had a gun the whole time. He was dead careful and when I saw him carry you into the warehouse, I followed. I heard Cath's voice . . .'

'And then he finally decided to call us,' Karen said tartly, from behind him.

'Yeah, well I wanted to see if I could get her first, without any hassle,' Devril said. 'The only thing I didn't do was go back and search the van because I wasn't sure if it had an alarm on it. I figured it would be better to wait, and if Milo was in the van, at least he was safe, whereas I thought Noah might kill Holly. I had no idea what he was planning.'

336

'I imagine that Ethan slipped out when you came to meet us by the entrance gates,' Karen said soberly. 'Poor kid.'

'Mum, you're bleeding all over me.' Milo pulled away a little and his voice sounded stronger, 'You're hurt, look!'

'Only a bit,' Holly told him as she closed her eyes again and sank down onto the van step. 'I feel a bit sick now actually . . .'

Her last coherent thought was that Milo was safe, before she slid into unconsciousness, embracing the blackness.

Chapter 40

Milo sat quietly, subdued and pale, his head resting on her shoulder. He had barely been parted from her since his abduction, even insisting she went to the toilet with him, sleeping in her bed, but he was eating properly now, and had begun to talk about what happened to him. Outwardly his bruises were healing, and the cast had finally come off his leg. Steph assured Holly this was a good sign, and they were due to start weekly counselling sessions as soon as Milo had recovered physically.

'Mum, what will happen to Ethan?' He kept asking this and she had tried to shield him from it at first, explaining that the boy who had been kind to him during the long days and nights of captivity, had shared his food and water with him, and even promised to let him go, had been helping police with their inquiries.

Ethan hadn't fired the shot that killed Niko. Holly, along with Cath, had reiterated that Noah had attacked the boy, was fighting with him when Ethan's second shot went off. It could easily have been an accident, but even if it wasn't, the child wasn't to blame. The fact that he had then freed Holly, had been so concerned about Milo, were all positives, and would go in his favour.

'I don't know. We're still waiting to find out,' Holly told him. 'Do you want another sandwich?'

'I've already had three!' It was a tiny spark of the old Milo, and she laughed with him. 'Lydia's coming over later, isn't she? Do you think she'll bring ice-cream?'

'Sorry, I'm trying to feed you up, sweetie, and yes, Lydia said she'll stop off and get some chocolate chip ice-cream and fish and chips for all of us.'

Satisfied, and diverted from the topic of Ethan, he went back to watching the cartoons on TV until the doorbell made him jump. 'Muuum!'

'It's okay, love, it'll be Dev.' Holly hugged him, but he insisted on coming to the door with her.

Dev came round most days, sitting in the kitchen with his coffee and his laptop, just chatting as she and Milo pottered around. His big story on the Nicholls might have failed to materialise but he had plenty of other work coming in. Occasionally he mentioned Bailey and the fire flashed back into his face.

She opened the door now, smiling, and it seemed natural to welcome him with a kiss. It had become familiar, a ritual, and she tried not to think about the future.

'Hi, Holly. Hey, Milo! What are you watching, mate?'

'Lego Ninjago.'

'Cool. Want to play football later if the rain stops?'

'Yeah, maybe . . .' Milo went back to the sofa, and snuggled deeper into his blanket cocoon, but the smile he gave Dev was genuine and warm, and the fear had gone from his eyes.

The adults went into the kitchen, leaving the door open so that Milo could keep a wary eye on Holly. She sat where he could see her through the open door, and spoke in a low voice. 'Karen phoned earlier, and she said that Ethan wants to see me.'

'Shit. Why?' Devril opened the fridge, frowning at the contents. 'No beer.'

'I don't drink beer. He won't say why, which is the reason I need to see him,' Holly said. 'He's lost his dad, even though from what we've now heard, Jayden was struggling to take care of him, so he hasn't had a great childhood so far.'

'Okay. When are you going?'

'Tomorrow. After everything that's happened, I owe it to Jayden and Larissa as well. From what Karen has said, Jayden brought his son up with a constant reminder that their sole purpose in life was to get revenge for Larissa's murder. He took him to shooting ranges so they could both practise, and made plans to take out Alexi and Roman with the kid. Apparently, Ethan was always in trouble for skipping school, but they think now that it was Jayden training him as a little boy solider. In between times, Jay was an alcoholic. When they hooked up with Noah it got worse, because Jay probably wouldn't have ever gone through with his plans, but Noah had the brains and the contacts to do just that.'

'But George Harper said Jayden seemed so determined to look after Ethan. I wonder what went wrong.'

'He couldn't put Larissa's death behind him, according to what Karen's told me. He became so obsessed with his mission he forgot that his son was just a kid, and of course the more Ethan cut ties with his schools and the more they moved around, the more he became sucked into Jayden's obsession. It was all building up to killing the three Balintas, and after Niko was released he knew he had a shot at it, but he couldn't see how he was going to get at Alexi and Roman in prison. Jay left his laptop and phone in the van, so they pulled all his files and contacts. Sounds like it made scary reading, but in his mind, the end game was obvious.'

'Until Noah pitched up with the perfect contacts.' Dev shook his head. 'One hell of a player to pull that off.'

'Yeah. I still can't get over him being Gareth Nicholls' kid. So he was basically on the same mission as Jayden, but he had one extra person to take out. I can't believe Jay fell for it. But, shit, Noah was fucking good. *I* believed his story, and he had a good enough fake ID to go through the criminal record checks for the ambulance service. If he hadn't got obsessed with Larissa he'd still be out on the streets, rounding up schoolgirls for his dad.'

'It was a pretty extreme way to get close to you, working in the same place, but I suppose he felt it was the only way, and he certainly wasn't stupid. I'm sorry that it had to end like that. I mean, I can't really feel anything when I think about Noah and Niko dead, but Jayden – he had a chance to start again, didn't he?'

Holly sighed. 'But he didn't take it. Karen said he was set up in Glasgow with his new ID, he was working as a freelance web designer, and he had the chance to bring his kid up and have a good life but he was just eaten up with the idea of getting revenge.'

'Like Noah.'

'Right. I wish I'd known Larissa. I think she must have been pretty special. Oh, Donnie and Lydia are coming over later if you want to stay. Donnie's been talking to Mason about a business partnership. Jesus, he never gives up, but at least he's got it into his head I'm not going back.'

Dev asked the same question as Milo. 'Have they said what's going to happen to Ethan?'

'Well, I said I'd have him with me and Milo, but Lydia offered to take him on, and Donnie, and of course, DI Harper, who's retiring any minute. They all have a claim, but what would be best for the boy? He needs to get away from here, away from the Seaview, maybe even away from us all for a while, but it'll be up to social services, I suppose. I want him to be happy, if he can be. I want to see him; on top of everything else, I owe it to him for looking after Milo when they were in the van. And I heard from Tom's solicitor again today. Tom's in rehab.'

'That's good, right?'

'Yeah. Milo is going to decide for himself if he wants any contact with his dad when Tom gets clean,' Holly said firmly. Her expression changed. 'I sent flowers to Beth. She texted me her parents' address and said how glad she was Milo was found. We had a quick conversation . . . It was sort of on my mind but she swears the crash was a genuine accident and she was just tying up loose ends round here when it happened.'

'Will you keep in touch with her?'

'No. It would be too weird, but I'm glad she's okay, and the baby too . . .'

***

'Hi, Ethan.'

He looked at her, dark eyes expressionless, his jaw clenched.

'I'm really sorry about your dad.'

Still nothing.

'Milo said to say "Hi".'

That got a small smile. 'He's a good kid.' His voice was soft, but when he spoke his eyes darted around the room, like he thought he was doing the wrong thing.

'So why did you want to see me?'

'I've got something for you,' Ethan said suddenly, his words tumbling over one another. 'It's something that I drew, and I'd like Milo to have it.'

'Oh. Well, that's nice of you,' Holly said warily. She still felt protective of him, would still offer him a home in a heartbeat, but she was torn. Should they keep him in Westbourne?

Ethan looked over at the social worker in the corner and she nodded, smiling encouragingly at him. He pulled a tattered book from his pocket and slid it across the table. 'It's just some drawings I did, and I did some for Milo when we were in the van. I won't need it now.'

Holly opened the red book, gently turning the pages. There were pencil sketches, and line drawings of people, of buildings, and most frequent of all, drawings of Larissa. Jayden must have shown him photos. The poignancy made her blink back tears. The boy was very talented, and the drawings had an almost photographic quality.

'These were for Milo.' Ethan pointed to pages of dragons, and fantasy worlds. 'Is he okay?'

'Yes. He's fine. Ethan, would you like me to visit you again tomorrow?' Holly asked suddenly, impulsively.

His cheeks flushed an ugly red, and he licked his lips nervously before he answered, 'Yeah, I suppose that would be cool.'

'I will then, and I'll bring Milo too if you like?'

'I would like that, yeah.' He blinked hard and then smiled at her. A sweet, gap-toothed smile that popped out Jaden's dimples, and made Larissa's eyes glow. But the expression was all his own.

***

Donnie dropped by unexpectedly one night, alone. Holly let him in, offered tea. He still wasn't touching alcohol.

'I thought I'd see how you were,' he said, smiling, exposing yellow teeth.

'We're fine. And you know that because I spoke to you yesterday. What do you want, Donnie?' She and her dad had managed to get back to some sort of relationship, but they were never going to be hearts and flowers. That wasn't the Hughes way.

'Well, I've got money coming in now Mason and I are back dealing. We've got a nice little supply line set up . . .'

'Donnie!'

'Okay, you don't want to know. I want you to have some money. It isn't dirty money, I promise, but there's enough to buy a house – this one or another one – and set yourself up. If you do move away, then you could always set up some new contacts for me . . .'

Holly started to tell him where to go and was silenced by his rough bark of laughter. 'No strings, girl. And as for the kids, Milo and Ethan, well, they know they're always welcome no matter what happens. We're family.'

'Thanks. I'll think about it,' was all she could say.

'Do that. I'll see myself out,' Donnie told her.

***

Back at work, but part-time, Holly took things slowly. Her developing relationship with Dev, Milo's rehabilitation, and dealing with the legal stress of the divorce all took its toll. Luckily her wounds had needed stitches but not surgery. Physically, she had been lucky. Cath too, although she was still very quiet, jumping at shadows, anxious for her kids all the time, and insisting one of her sisters or Holly stay over as much as possible.

Holly'd already decided to put the house on the market. Milo had been taken from this house, and it reeked of pain and angst. They needed a fresh start. She kind of fancied a different city, but with the same job. Surely that wouldn't be too hard? Now Donnie's offer had come just at the right time, but could she take money from him, despite his promises?

The pain and shock of losing Milo and then the sheer relief of having him back safe, had taken its toll along with the other traumatic events: finding her brother and losing him again so quickly. But the real Jay had been dead since Larissa's murder. The defeated man in the warehouse had been the ghost he was reduced to. He might have stabbed himself but he was only finishing what Roman and Alexi had started. Jay had been keeping himself going for revenge and for his son, until finally, it just wasn't enough. Noah's identity, and Niko's death, remained in the background. She could see that in time she would lose the numbness, have to expose herself to the pain and process each thing that had happened, each loss.

She was also getting used to the positive things that had come from recent events too, forcing herself to be optimistic about the untangled past. It had freed her in a way, and she and Dev had found each other again. With various members of the

344

Nicholls family alluding to her mum's death, she assumed, and had discussed with Karen, the fact that either Joey or Gareth had been driving the car involved in the hit and run.

Most of all, she had her son. Her beautiful little boy.

***

Two days later she woke to the sound of Milo making dragon noises in his room. She squinted at the clock. Six-thirty.

Dev, lying next to her, opened his eyes. 'Sounds like a war going on in there. Do you think the dragons are winning?'

She smiled at him, enjoying their easy intimacy. She had a good feeling about this new/old relationship. 'No, he's fine.'

He blinked at the windows, covered in white blinds and already letting the spring sunlight through. 'We could take him down the beach this morning? Meet up with Cath, maybe?'

Holly nodded slowly, wriggling back under the duvet. 'You know, Lydia says she's going to Spain now I'm sorted. She said that even if Ethan goes to George, they'll still keep in touch. If it wasn't totally weird, I'd almost say there was something going on between those two the way she talks about him.'

Devril rolled over in bed, tangled in the sheets, one hand behind his head. He was about to answer when Milo charged into the room and flung himself between them.

'I thought you were having a lie-in.' Holly pulled her son close, inhaling his sweetness, kissing his forehead.

'Naaaah. I wanted to show Dev this book about dragons . . .' Milo shoved a large hardback book into Dev's face and he fended the boy off, laughing.

When Milo had stomped downstairs in search of food, Holly leant over towards Dev. 'So where will you go now? What will you do?'

He grinned. 'I can write stories from anywhere, so I guess I might tag along with you. If I'm invited, of course . . .'

'Well, I don't know. You are a total pain in the arse, but who else am I going to train with?'

'There is still that one story I need to tie up . . .' His expression was serious now.

'I know. You still need to take down the Nicholls,' she told him. 'And believe me, I'm right there with you on that, but that's going to be a slow burn, isn't it?'

He stood up, stretching, the sunlight flooding through the windows, highlighting the angles of his face, the glint in his eyes. 'I got a call from Sanita – you know, Bailey's wife – yesterday. She said she'd had a parcel delivered. It was from Bailey.'

'What was inside?'

Dev smiled. 'A memory stick with a whole stack of photos and videos on. And a note addressed to me. The boy done good.'

Epilogue

Dear Mum and Dad,

I hope you both got what you wanted in the end. It feels so weird not to have you around, Dad, and not to sit for hours in front of your wall, Mum.

It felt like everything stopped – time, my heart and my breathing – when I saw Dad's blood gush out across the dirty floor. I really did think that Niko had stabbed him, which is why I pulled the trigger. But he didn't, did he? Dad killed himself. I can see now that he wanted to do it for a long time, but he felt he couldn't because of me. Is that right, Dad?

But I didn't realise, and then when Dad's friend jumped for his gun, I knew he would kill all of us. I'd been listening on the stairs for a while and he had gone crazy. He said some really shit stuff about you, Mum. I did try and tell Dad he was a bit weird, but he told me I was the one who was nuts and made me sit for two hours in front of the wall.

I know Noah stole keys from Milo's mum, that he broke into her house and took Milo from his own bed. I know he gave us both drugs to keep us quiet, and you never came to rescue us, Dad. I'll try not to blame you for that.

So what now? Are you both watching me, waiting to see if I mess up or if I turn out good?

You can watch all you like, because I won't mess this up. I'll be just fine, because I've got family and I've got a plan.

I love you, Mum & Dad xx

Acknowledgements

So many people helped and supported me whilst I was writing this novel, so huge thanks to following:

The team at my wonderful publishers HQ Digital, HarperCollins, including Belinda, Dom, Gen and Abi, who are an absolute pleasure to work with.

To my lovely agent, Lina Langlee at the Kate Nash Literary Agency, and to Kate herself for her excellent advice last year!

Thank you to Brian Smith, Samantha Crowther, and Sophie Kelly for championing my early works, and to The Crazies, and The Kick Ass Girls for your literary naughtiness and genuine encouragement.

Just before I sent my first book out on submission, I visited The Author School, run by Helen Lewis and Abiola Bello, and their continued enthusiastic support and friendship has been invaluable. Thank you to my fellow authors – I have met so many wonderful writers over the years, and your advice and support is something I cherish.

Thank you also to Eric and Dee at Singularis for sharing their knowledge and experience of police work, and for reining in my imagination when I went too far!

My single mum friends, especially Sanita, and Gillian, you are a total inspiration and I am in awe of you.

Love and inspo also due to my ex-colleagues in the ambulance service, including but not limited to: Emily, Leanna, Gaye-Ann, Carol, Charlotte, Sarah, Dan, Lucy and Joe, who all kept me sane between calls.

Huge thanks to the wonderful bloggers, the readers, retailers and librarians, whose support is so vital. Thank you for buying my books, for reading, recommending and reviewing. I couldn't do it without any of you. Special mention to Jill B, who does all of the above and more!

Last but not least, I owe huge thanks to my wonderful family. My gorgeous boys, James and Ollie, who give me unfailing support and encouragement. My lovely husband, who is always happy to discuss the best ways to murder someone, and get away with it. To my parents, who are such an inspiration, and have never, ever told me to give up writing and get a proper job!

Read on for a sneak preview of D. E. White's *Remember Me*!

Chapter 1

I'd give everything to be back at the first square on the board, with all still to play for . . .

In the beginning, I was just another kid, with just another unlucky family. I used that bad luck, as I used my good looks and confidence. Nobody knew I'd already killed once. In the games I play, I have always used the charm I was born with – along with various other, less admirable, skills I have had to acquire along the way.

There are a few golden days, bottled and stored at the back of my mind, that bring a comforting glow of nostalgia when uncorked. I inhale, eyelids drooping, and allow my thoughts to drift back . . .

The grass of the school playing field was warm and smelled pleasantly of hay. It was scratchy on my bare legs and under my spread palms. I remember that day so clearly that I can summon the laughter, the scent of cut grass, the bumpy feeling of a packet of pills in my pocket. I leaned back until the sun enveloped my face in a wave of burning fire, and I enjoyed the dizziness evoked by blood-red patterns on my closed eyelids. Sprawled lazily in a semicircle facing me, a few of the other kids were idly chucking empty Coke cans at an old oak stump.

Someone was passing round an illicit cigarette, and the curling blue smoke teased my senses.

I had already discovered how to play with my pack – how to get them into a ball game, climbing trees at the far end of the field, or even a bit of joyriding when darkness fell. That day I had fewer innocent activities planned. It was the first true test of my power over my players and I relished that tingle of excitement. It buzzed through my veins like a drug hitting home. I could never have guessed how that day and night would shape my life, or how my need for revenge would become everything – a tearing, ravenous hunger I could never satisfy.

I can see us all now, as though I am soaring above the school, floating like a bird, arms outstretched. It's where I belong. The boys and the girls, so bright and alive against the scorched summer grass. The laughing, teasing group of friends and enemies, and the drifting smell of sweat and chips. Someone was singing that stupid little song we'd had since primary school:

'Three little girls, sitting up a tree,
Kissed all the boys,
But no one wants me.'

I knew exactly what was happening in my life, and some might say I could have stopped it at any time – but I didn't. I watched, and I waited. It turned out better than I could ever have imagined. That's one of the things about being a gamer – you have to know when to let fate dip a finger into your spit. It doesn't mean losing control, it just means loosening the reins for a moment.

It has always paid to be smart and, looking back, that was more important than anything. It still is. I know I'm smarter than all of them, and that will be my legacy. Before that day at school, everything in my life was just a blurred rehearsal. My heartbeat thumps deep and strong – a jungle drum to my prey. It's been a few years since I last played for real, but things have changed.

I can hear music from another room. It's a lilting, joyous sound, and it brings me back to the present. Time to play again. I pick up a phone, scroll down, type a message and hit the send button.

'*Ydych chi'n cofio fi, Ava Cole?*'

'**Do you remember me, Ava Cole?**'

Dear Reader,

Thank you so much for taking the time to read this book – we hope you enjoyed it! If you did, we'd be so appreciative if you left a review.

Here at HQ Digital we are dedicated to publishing fiction that will keep you turning the pages into the early hours. We publish a variety of genres, from heartwarming romance, to thrilling crime and sweeping historical fiction.

To find out more about our books, enter competitions and discover exclusive content, please join our community of readers by following us at:

@HQDigitalUK

facebook.com/HQDigitalUK

Are you a budding writer?
We're also looking for authors to join the HQ Digital family!
Please submit your manuscript to:

HQDigital@harpercollins.co.uk.

Hope to hear from you soon!